Club of Spades

Book 2 of The Scarecrow Trials

Tamara Brigham

he words, however, were something else, making Rhyd scowl
ath the cold sweat that sprung to the surface of his skin to be
ed away by the gentle spring breeze.
We need to talk.

THE END

(The Scarecrow will return...)

❧504❧

❧GLOSSARY❦

ottari: grandfather fucker (Icelandic)
ea: algae tea
i: androids; artificial humans made most often for the sex trade and as dancers. Sometimes used to perform other undesirable duties.
norts: very short, revealing shorts worn by dancers, often transparent
er: those who work on dehumidifying systems
he moy: my god
ko: thugs
ko-bugorra: cops and robbers (thugs and cops) child game
ger: nickname for new law enforcement due to the new breathing apparatus having a bug-like appearance. Also called bugorra or gorras
orra (bughat): nickname for new law enforcement due to the new breathing apparatus having a bug-like appearance. Also called buggers or gorras.
zers: tasers used to stun victims.
oidi: dry ice
ing: fucking
/cazzo: fuck/dick(Italian)
boludo: hey ballsack
: penis
no: watch, time-telling device, often with built-in comms
alg: cinnamon algae tea
ws: police/military force, someone not to be trusted; a snitch
ser: those who have moved outside of the city; also those who work outside but live inside
ksake: a combination of Christ and fuck sake, one of the more common swear terms.
: holodek suites used for recreation/vacations, since there is nowhere else for those in the City to go.
ker: though that usually refers to someone addicted to dekking
king: using a dek
i: those who work on heating systems

Doctet: Hebanthe Fall's Council of 10 that used to run the city in conjunction with the Founder

eblan: dumbass (Russian)

Echosys (also XCO/ekso/echo): computer; Current model is the 2 as they are frequently redesigned and built ever 5 to 10 years. There are four basic models:

w (home view screens)

d (public view screens)

p1 (personal Echos)

t2 (portable tablet echos)

All are linked to the city's Hub at the time of manufacture. Th are customizable and can be, illegally, removed from the Hut network.

fettershirt: straitjacket

filt: breathing filtration system

fotz: bitch (German)

gorra: nickname for new law enforcement due to the new breathi apparatus having a bug-like appearance. Also called bugorra buggers

grenners: grenades

Hebenon: 1) name of the drug produced by official sources, intended as population control for use by the Crows but long made available to the public after its addictive properties bec. known; 2) The nickname Hebanthe Falls gained after the rise the drug in the streets. The word Hebenon was taken from the Shakespeare play Hamlet due to the similarities in side effect experienced by its users.

Heb: the injected form of the drug Hebenon.

Hebbies: the drug Hebenon in pill form

heizer (also denki): those who work on heating systems

herpa: (from Japanese for helper) pastors, men of religious faith outside of the Church of the Founder.

hijo de puta: son of a whore (son of a bitch)

hoser: idiot (Canadian)

Hub: the central broadcasting & computer system in the city.

ICD Images: still images captured with an ICD by passersby.

ICD: Interpersonal Communication Device

incin: cremation of the deceased

injectors: air guns that fire needles laced with Hebenon

: janitor, cleaner, garbage collector

ina: sex object/boy toy

eao: one who dabbles in many trades; has their fingers in many pies

hy: handkerchief

ek: a tinker, a repairman, one who repairs things

ama: Haythem's title/slang; from kistama tama: lord of donkey balls

eada: jackass (Japanese)

s: refers to any of the lower 20 city levels. Houses most businesses and most of the population of the city.

rdita: little shit

bordo: Seaside/Seacliff; what the parah call their village

cocs: Molotov Cocktails; handmade explosives

: The Nine, the group that replaced the Doctet; potentials are selected by the whole of the city, but posts appointed by Grainger. Some were members of the original Doctet, most were not (because they were locked in the factories for so long and some died) No longer a lifetime or hereditary appointment but set for a term of five years. Can repeat service at Grainger's discretion. 1) material production; 2) distribution; 3) news/programming; 4) SCAMs and computer systems; 5) medical sciences, research, and care; 6) technical systems (including life support systems); 7) food production & distribution; 8) outside/inside relations (also monitors religious activities); 9) construction, city maintenance and upkeep (including life support systems)

urm: earwig

h: a corruption of the word pariah, used for those 'humans' who are living outside of the Hebanthe Falls in the world polluted by mankind's failings.

h (2): refers to those born on the outside, although now sometimes used to refer to those who have moved outside as well.

so: Clown (Spanish)

: phone/communication system in the Passcard

erhemp: peppermint-hemp tea

ers: air guns, firing small synthetic pellets.

poq Gai: "Go Die in the street", general-purpose swearword (Chinese)

posa: shit

prodcast: broadcast productions aired through the Echosys, rangi from news, to sports, to entertainment and educational subjec

prosser: those who have moved from the outside into the city; als those who work inside but live outside.

pushi kuratz: suck a dick (Croatian)

SCAMs: security cams used for monitoring public behavior. the are no SCAMs on the Uppers.

shed: facility out of which shaft crews work.

shoeman: maker/repairer of footwear

skolper: sewage worker. sometimes used as an insult.

Soaper: where Hebbies are made by the brako on Lev 1

source: the center of all material goods and food distribution.

spener: those who work on plumbing

streeter: those living on the streets

svodnik: pimp

swiver: someone who owns a food/beverage serving establishme or who serves food or drink; a bartender, waiter, waitress

tapper: computer hacker

Talkers: priests of the Voices of Faith established religion.

thumper: police stick used for beating prisoners to subdue them.

ticks: currency points used for the acquisition of food and suppli and services. Distributed by the Doctet on a predetermined scale.

tinger: someone who takes things, thief, vagrant living off of oth

tinging: begging

tricking: working as a prostitute

Vapors: Maemi's club/bar

verpiss dich!: piss off/fuck off (German)

vigi: vigilante

vindi/vind: venders, shops

Vivu: long live

Voices of Faith: the 'religion' supported by the Founder and Do which supports the Kemways divine right to run Hebanthe F they produce prodcasts angled toward religious faith, commu cohesiveness, and Kemway support.

wanana: debacle, clusterfuck (Hawaiian)

/ekso/echo: computer; current model is the 237 as they are
frequently redesigned and built ever 5 to 10 years
v (home view screens)
(public view screens)
1 (personal Echos)
2 (portable tablet echos)
ei: algae whiskey
: trash (Hebrew)
ed: crazy

❧510❧

ABOUT THE AUTHOR

h fantasy and sci-fi as her passions, Tamara has written multiple
els to date, including the first four books of the Kestrel Harper
a, the first installment of The Scarecrow Trials, and the stand-alone
el Suspicion's Gate. Bleed the Earth is the second book in the
od Wild Chronicles.

en not indulging in her love of words, Tamara relaxes in the
pany of her pack of Papillions, her horde of cats, and an ever-
ving collection of films.

rn more about Tamara's work at www.agdhani.com

I0576227

* 9 7 8 1 7 3 3 6 7 0 8 6 9 *

For Sally and Grant…

…who helped lay the foundation for

every word I've written since…

and for my love of Hamlet.

To die: to sleep:
No more;
and, by a sleep to say we end
the heart-ache and the thousand natural shocks
that flesh is heir to,
'tis a consummation
devoutly to be wished.

Hamlet: Act 3, Scene 1

❧ Chapter 1 ❧

The boot in his gut felt like the sour burst of Zaolei without the familiar soothing burn in his throat or the comforting after-haze left in its wake.

But it was a familiar pain, the brunt of the solid bruising force absorbed by the custom thin mesh of his attire, dense and lightweight to protect him from the punishment he endured in the wet, dark streets of Hebanthe Falls. Its construction, however, did not prevent him from being thrown by the impact into a scatter of recyclables piled against one metal-walled building. The camouflaged taggers, young and inexperienced in their chosen form of societal protest, scattered into the even darker shadows beneath dripping grated walkways, slippery metal staircases lined with drainage borings, and the dimming glow of an alglamp in need of a fresh fuel supply. The tools of their trade, the collection of spray cans both full and empty, were left behind as evidence of their passing crime. Tripping through the mass of streeters huddled under water-cloth in a world of perpetual damp, one young woman, her dark-skinned arm exposed to the moisture and bearing the bloody claw lines of a brako's metal-tipped glove, barely eluded another set of hands as she scrambled for safety.

"Fotz," swore one of the streeters in a weary, violent, Heb-thin voice before he scooted nearer a fellow user and pulled the water-cloth more tightly over their heads and shoulders. Covered thus, they looked more like a displaced boulder of gray earth then the dregs of humanity.

The streeters had no interest in the chaos. They only sought to remain dry and enjoy the fleeting sweetness of their self-destructive high. Hoping to hide. Hoping to disappear. Hoping to forget.

The Scarecrow yanked the young woman to her feet as he leaped to his and thrust her behind him, his body a shield, absorbing the blow of the brako's ill-gotten thumper that would have rendered his new charge unconscious if it had connected with her head as intended. Instead, it bounced harmlessly off his padded shoulder, one breathless moment before the Scarecrow's fist lurched upwards to strike the brako beneath his beak-masked chin.

The Crows had never been the good guys. The Crows had always been thugs. At least, they had been for all of Scarecrow's life. But until the coup, they had been the law-keepers too.

No longer.

The thunder of weighty steps reverberated through the grating, alerting him to the arrival of others before the sound of it reached the mechanical earbuds that sharpened his senses within the protective breathing hood. The impulse to swear was swallowed in favor of channeling his energy and focus into ducking beyond the grasp of another crow-beaked brako, a wiser choice that resulted in one brako barreling into another, knocking both to the grated ground.

The tagger crouched, motionless, her brush with the brako, her shock, or perhaps the disbelief of Scarecrow being there to rescue her preventing her disjointed thoughts from sending flight signals to her rooted feet. Her cohorts were long gone, not even the echo of their retreat detectable beneath the constant drip, distant electronic twang of muffled, filtered music from nearby vindis, and the ever-present rumble and roar of the Four Falls and the wild river below that filled every crevice of their world.

But the bugorra were nearer now. The brako heard them too and a few of the nearly dozen shadow figures that had swooped down on the taggers were fading into the nearest shaded alleys and unlit doorways in this barely populated, sleeping quarter of a city nestled deep in the crawling hour. The brako, while numerous, were a challenge easily met on his best night, but Scarecrow had no interest in entangling in a real-life game of brako-bugorra.

He did not feel like challenging those odds tonight. Let the brako fend for themselves. The taggers were safe. He had done what he had interfered to accomplish.

A feint to the right kept him beyond the reach of the popper's whine and allowed him to swing up onto the nearest low balcony, his foot catching one brako between the shoulder blades and thrusting him back into the midst of Hebenon's peacekeepers. He caught the tagger by her forearm, the blood there making her skin slippery and threatening his hold, and drew her up after him with enough force to surprise her and snap her survival sense into place. With his pull on her arm, she clambered clumsily onto the ledge where he crouched, the now fainter glow of the alglamp lending ominous shadows to the full-faced breathing mask he wore. The brako charged the seven bugorra who emerged through the wide chasm of the area's main thoroughfare, the fight with the Scarecrow a forgotten thing despite the three immobile figures lying in the square around them, victims of his unexpected assault.

The tagger's scramble, however, her feet sliding on the slick walkway, rang the air when the metal toe of her boot struck the steel crossbeam of the balcony rail. The sound announced their lingering presence, giving the trailing bugorra the opportunity to take a single popper shot at this unexpected quarry.

Scarecrow shoved the tagger's head down, pinning her to the grate with one hand as he threw one of the matte black biohaz-symbol shaped shurikens from the belted strap across his chest. The shot passed dangerously close to his left ear, ricocheted off the metallic surface behind him, and struck the alglamp, splintering the glass so that the nutrient-rich liquid inside dribbled out. Its light extinguished, the square was now lit only by the faintness of distant neon from nearby streets.

His razor-edged shuriken struck home, digging into the bugorra's hand so that the popper clattered to the walkway. The sharpness of the sound and the discharge of another hempplast pellet shook the air, producing a ringing in the Scarecrow's ear that he had to shake his

head to be rid of. The pellet flew wild and struck a brako in the face with enough force to shatter one of the protective eyepieces and throw the unlucky individual backward against the nearest wall.

The brako gave a cry at the impact and then lay like a discarded, broken doll, his now exposed eye a bloody mass of mutilated tissue.

Clutching his bleeding gun hand after yanking the shuriken free, the bugorra was tackled by a bellowing bull of a man with a yellowing length of cloth tied around his bicep like a badge of position or honor. As the Scarecrow was no longer a target, no longer of interest to the combatants below, he dragged the tagger up another two runs of grated stairs until they reached the rooftop of the Lev 2 structures.

If the masks of those fighting beneath were as enhanced as Scarecrow's, they might see him there…if they took the time to look. Engaged as they were, by the time they looked, however, he intended to be gone.

"Th…thank you…"

He had no time for sentiment. The brako and bugorra might have forgotten his presence and the taggers had escaped crooked justice for now, but if anyone was monitoring the SCAMs affixed on the surrounding structures, if any of them worked any longer, they would come looking for him soon enough. They always did. Best this girl be home safe and secure in her own warm bed then be out here in the streets looking for trouble in her search for equality.

"Go home," Scarecrow growled, the breathing filter and electronic modulator in his mask making his voice unrecognizable as male, female, andi or human. He squatted on the corner ledge of the buildings to watch and listen to the fight, assessing its progress, assessing his risks.

The tagger did not argue. She nodded, a gesture he did not see, and dashed away, her steps leaping the distance between rooftops and then clambering up and up and up until he could no longer hear her.

A hiss of air filtered out the humidifying effects of exertion inside his hood, keeping the tinted eyepieces clear, allowing an unobstructed view of the dwindling chaos. Buzzers were silent, the burp of poppers

had ceased, and the muffled crunch of impact from fists and feet into solid, padded bodies had ended. Two of the bugorra were down. Three more brako as well, for a total of six, the rest fled back into Hebenon's underbelly. The static burst of an ICD, while the remaining four bugorra examined each of the bodies for signs of life, would bring parameds with air-stretchers for the wounded, the dead, the dying.

He had not done that.

Death was not his calling card. Not if he could help it.

On the wall behind them, amid the moisture-eroded assortment of tagger sigs, curses, cartoons, and Voices of Faith symbols and slogans, the latest addition of crimson stood out, the fresh paint oozing from Hebenon's still-hemorrhaging wounds. The blood-red inverted biohazard symbol echoed the diskblade now abandoned in one of the few puddles collected across the silent battleground.

No longer the warning of imminent chemical hazard. To most, that symbol was now a plea for help, a call to hope.

A hazard of an entirely different sort.

It had become the mark of the Scarecrow.

❧Chapter 2❧

Eyes around the table, wary eyes silent and judging, sought the tells that would reveal who would be next among them. The Club was exclusive, its members carefully selected, the turnover specifically regulated by the internal mechanisms built into the organization at the time of its creation.

No one knew when that was. Most assumed it had always existed.

There had been others of its kind, small groups, private groups, intended to allow escape for those who suffered the daily drudgery of unwanted existence. None had lasted as long as the Spades, none had been as secretive and pervasive as the Club whose reach stretched through Hebenon like spidery steel veins, from Lev 1 at the river's froth to the highest realm of the Uppers.

It was no surprise the Club had found its way here. Those forced to endure the dank, stench of this place were, perhaps, the most desperate to escape of all.

He did not think he had it bad here. Bozhe moy, the Core had given back his life, such as it was, when he might have been abandoned to a slow, torturous death sliding into the nets where, if one was lucky, they would drown in the water of the river before being crushed by the flotsam and jetsam of debris the net collected.

It was in that saving, however, that he found himself here, staring down the other twelve men and women brought together by the pact they had made, the oaths they had sworn.

By the rank of his status, a hard fought for position that he tenaciously strove to maintain with every waking breath, and by selection of those who had come and gone before him since his initiation into the Club, he shuffled the well-worn deck of thirteen

cards and dealt a single card to each around the table. One by one, the cards lay face down beneath the work-roughened hands of the recipients until all thirteen were distributed. By the lottery of marked metal discs deposited into the filt basket hanging from a rusted hook on the wall just inside the doorway of this small, dim room, those gathered revealed their cards.

Each pulled a disc from the basket and placed it in the center of the round cracked plastic table stained by centuries of use by Core leaders and, once each month, for this secret purpose. The precious flask of potato vodka passed to the person whose number was chosen, and after a bracing swallow of the potent contents, their card was flipped face up for all to see.

Audible breaths of relief or regret followed each reveal, the only other sounds made in the room besides the clatter of metal discs, the clink of the bottle on the table or a loud swallow from its contents, or the brush of the card across the table's surface when it was turned.

The thirteen looked at one another, each nodding their acceptance of fate's verdict and then the process repeated.

Eleven times. Eleven cards.

Still, fate had not chosen. The ace remained hidden.

The final two looked at one another, one with wary apprehension, the other with unnerving blank calm. One a relative newcomer, a Club initiate of fewer than three months, a fellow with rheumy black eyes and scarred hands, the evidence of a lifetime in the salt mines of the Core. One, impeccably dressed as an aristocrat of old, a blue velvet frock coat and frills at his neck and wrists, dirty and worn though they were, lending an air of importance to one who had sat at this table for nearly two years, longer than any member who had passed through the Club before him.

It took no study of the faces around him to gauge their thoughts. Some believed the outcome pre-determined, through either cheating or the hand of fate. Others expected death to claim the lesser of men. Some craved the power and position of one they felt had held it too long…for however long the Club permitted them life. And there was

one who begged for death so that his family, such as it was in a place cut off from a life lived long ago in Hebanthe Falls, could have the best the Core could offer…if only until the next cycle ended.

A nod.

An agreement.

The black-eyed man slowly turned his card.

Held breaths in the room erupted with the barest note of surprise.

All but one rose. One by one, the members pocketed a metal disc, the only proof of their membership to exist, and circled the table towards the exit. Cards dropped into a pile where the ace lay exposed and men and women went out of the room with a hand on the seated man's shoulder or back in passing, the only acknowledgment given in honor of the pact made with death.

Soon he was alone.

He did not look at the card again. He adjusted the leather eyepatch he wore, decorated with metallic threads in an intricate pattern across its clean, unmarred surface. In his other hand, he clutched the coin, the mark he must pass on to whomever he chose to take his place when the month ahead ended with the sacrifice of his life.

Some chose a quicker end. Some chose to welcome death the night fate ordained it.

He would not be one of those.

Footsteps behind through the still open door, but he did not look at his visitor. He knew who it was by the sound of the steps on the stone-tiled floor.

"It is done then?"

The redhead nodded, his expression thoughtful.

The tousle-haired dwarf who had joined him scooped up the card from the table at the other's elbow, looked at it for a moment, and then began to collect the others into a tidy deck.

"I suppose there was no choice."

Still the seated man did not speak.

"We're doing this then?"

"Yes." This time the redhead sighed, took his engraved walking stick from where it leaned against the table nearby, and pushed to his feet. He accepted the deck of spades from the dwarf, shoved them into his frock coat, and took a limping step towards the door. "You know what to do."

"I do." He caught the taller man's hand, a gesture that prompted the redhead to look at him. "I'll let you know when it's done."

Skelter nodded once. He knew what he had to do too. The clock was ticking now. Second by second, he was running out of time.

❧Chapter 3❧

"Whiskey?"

Rhyd rolled sideways, barely avoiding falling from the narrow sofa by the foggy awareness of where he was as wakefulness displaced the alcohol haze in which he had slept. The voice registered dimly over the rhythmic hiss of the oxygen tank, and as he drew the breathing mask from his mouth and nose with one hand, he cracked his heavy lids enough to see Venn turning off the valve on the tank that was just beyond Rhyd's flailing reach.

"Venn…what are…is it…?"

Two years, or nearly so, and still there were days when Rhyd awoke to the surprise of having Venn once more in his life. Two years, and just as often, when he woke and Venn was not there, he was greeted by the fear that the rescue had all been a dream. That Venn was still gone, still Vanished, and Rhyd would never see him again.

It happened less Outside, in Marbordo, but even the assurance of the sun's warmth, the fragrant salt breeze from across the sea and the hemp fields or the sounds of domestic village life, were not enough to displace the deep-seated trauma Venn's Vanishing had instilled.

In this place, comfortable like a well-worn pair of boots, the place he mulishly clung to as home even after so many months, those waking moments of confusion were far more frequent.

"Who else?"

The dark-haired cellist, now working more as a hemp farmer like the majority of Marbordo's residents, grinned and rocked back on his heels, studying the darkening bruises across the blond man's torso before allowing his gaze to settle on the black leather longcoat hanging over the nearest kitchen chair. He did not come here often, as this dim

apartment held a conflicting mixture of memories that he did not like to evoke. There had been good times here, years of them, as he and Rhyd built a life together, a good life, a content life. Heb addiction had crept in, however, and that, and a few misspoken sentiments had brought Venn to the attention of the authorities, resulting in arrest, torture, and eventual expulsion from Hebanthe Falls.

Venn blamed no one but himself. His addiction had been on him, his words his own as well. His Vanishing led Rhyd into a mire he was unable to escape, no matter how hard Venn tried to pull him back.

It had not taken long to realize that Rhyd could not let the darkness go. That he would never let it go. Something in that darkness was too seductive for Rhyd to escape from. Frustrated and desperate to recapture what he foolishly allowed to be taken from them both, Venn continued to try.

And Rhyd continued to resist.

"You've been out again."

Rhyd grunted, glancing at the dim screen of the Echosys that he must have turned on and left running when he stumbled in some hours earlier. A rerun of a laughie played with the requisite news ticker scrolling across the bottom of the screen; he knew it was a rerun by the faces on the image, some of the many who had died in the factory plague after the dust of the Hebanthe Coup settled. Two years on and there were few new prodcasts being made.

People's priorities were on rebuilding. Repairing. Surviving. Reshaping their world from what it had been into what it was meant to be. Or what it would become at any rate.

What it was meant to be depended on who one talked to, and so far, there was little agreement on what their world should look like.

Or maybe, Rhyd thought as he staggered off the couch, shirtless and barefoot, and stumbled to the sink, putting the kitchen bar between himself and Venn, Venn had turned on the Echosys to lend some degree of normalcy to the flat they had once shared and called home. The handful of dirty cups and eating utensils that had been in the sink

were clean and set in the rack to dry, and the usual clutter of takeaway boxes was gathered into the bin for recycling.

Had Maemi come and left again while he slept?

Rhyd scowled as he filled a glass with water from the pipes and glanced at the Echosys screen again. No, this had not been Maemi's doing. It was not Maemi's day. This had been Venn.

He did not have to go into the bathroom to know that the dirty laundry had been gathered and replaced. He wondered absently, before gulping down the water and setting the cup upside down on the drying mat, if Venn had tidied the bedroom too.

The bedroom that had been unused, unslept in, since the day Venn Vanished from Rhyd's life.

He looked again at the screen. How long had he slept? Was he supposed to be working? Did he have time for a shower?

Did he want one?

"You shouldn't be out there…you don't need to be. Grainger has the Crows in hand…"

"Not Crows," Rhyd muttered. The Crows, as Hebenon's law-keeping force, had ceased to exist in the aftermath of the Coup, after the brako raided the stores and stole as much of the Crows' gear as they could, after people on the streets stripped fallen Crows of theirs as well. Now the brako had taken on the guise of Rhyd's one-time enemy, and the peacekeepers were relegated to a new style of filt-mask that gave them an insect-like appearance, thus gaining them the moniker of buggers, gorra, or bugorra…bughats.

"But you're still fighting them…"

"Someone has to. Buggers couldn't find their asses if they sat on them." Rhyd returned to the living room, a piece of cheese in hand, and began digging through the remains of clean laundry for a shirt. Typically, the room temperature was bearable. Today he felt cold.

Atmosphere controls were undoubtedly in need of service.

Venn scowled. "Why?"

"You've seen it out there. You've seen them…"

Or maybe he had not. Rhyd shoved the cheese into his mouth and pulled the clean heather-grey sweatshirt over his head. Venn spent very little time in Hebenon. Having been banished beyond the city's protective walls when it had been believed the Outside world was toxic and deadly, Venn had been afforded a longer time to adapt and adjust to the new world presented to all by Rhyd's actions and the Coup. Venn had taken to the open air, the brightness of the sun, the cleanness of life, in a way Rhyd still struggled to do. Anything Venn knew about how life was, how life had become, within Hebenon in the days since Rhyd had hunted for…and found…him, came from gossip or from the rare occasions when he ventured back to these rooms they had once shared and the tales Rhyd, Lash, Tamner and others shared.

Rhyd doubted Venn took the time to notice the conditions inside Hebanthe Falls. Clinging to the only job he knew, Rhyd's work as a bilger the only occupation he had ever trained for or performed, kept him coming back to these streets, to the tunnels and passages of filtration, drainage, and atmospheric control equipment that had been his life since the day he reached an employable age. Every minute spent in the city, Rhyd saw things. The never-ending Heb use, the chaos of the brako, the well-meant but still oppressive efforts to create 'order' by Grainger and his buggers. The constant struggle within the system to fill the power vacuum the loss of Founder Kemway had created. Why would Venn pay attention to any of that when he had no intention of living here again?

"But why you?"

Rhyd's only response was another grunt. He did not have an answer beyond the impulse, the need, to do something, to continue the fight against corruption that he had begun. He had done this, however inadvertently. He had caused it, or at least contributed to it. He had opened the chasm of leaderless lawlessness that plagued Hebenon by digging too deep into hidden crevices in his search for Venn, by pushing to free a child from the accidental fate thrust upon her.

How could Venn ever understand the burning need to set things right again? How could he not?

Maybe it was not his fight…but Rhyd believed it sure as hell should be. If not his, whose?

"Come up. Agnys is worried about you…"

"You're worried." Undoubtedly, Agnys worried; her worry was unfortunate but manageable. Venn's worry was smothering.

"Damn right. Come up, Rhyd…get some air…clear your head."

Returning to the sofa where he had slept, Rhyd fumbled to shove his feet into his still damp boots. Cazzo. He should have set them so they could air. "My head's fine. I've got things to do…"

"Things…?" Venn scowled.

"Tox is expecting me…and shift is in three."

A glance at Venn's chrono made him sigh with heavy defeat. He did not know what sort of business Rhyd might have with Tox, whether it involved the gear hung over the nearby chair or something else, but at least if Rhyd was with Tox, he was not getting himself senselessly pummeled. And a man who did not work did not get his allotment of ticks. Hebenon needed her bilgers and skolpers if she was to continue to stand in the mist of the Four Falls.

Hebenon needed men like Rhyd as much as Rhyd needed her.

"After shift then. I'll take out the recyclables; I'll keep the bed warm…"

"After," Rhyd repeated with a nod, not looking up, knowing that, as he did so, Venn would take the word as a promise that Rhyd did not know if he would be able to keep.

He knew, from Venn's hesitant steps and sagging shoulders as he took the recycle bin out the front door, that the cellist was just as grateful not to hear a promise Rhyd might not be able to keep, as Rhyd was not to make it.

❧*❧

It was not home, not the home it should be, not the home birth and marriage had entitled her to. She and her daughter had survived the

Factory Culling, as so many called it, only to emerge into a life, a world, no longer recognizable.

Oh, the walls were the much the same, the familiar corridors of white murals and recirculated air in which she had spent her entire life unchanged since the Scarecrow opened the door to anarchy inside the city in the falls. But even that air had smelled different the day she and the Culling survivors were allowed to leave their Factory prisons of more than a year. The air was now drawn in, she was told, from the Outside…an Outside not poisonous and hazardous as they had been taught but an Outside livable, breathable…open and free…unlike anything she and the rest of Hebenon's residents had ever seen.

How could they have known? Who could have foretold this miraculous change? Who could have thought such a revelation could come at such a great cost?

Neoma Kemway did not know the science of it. Did not know the truths the science council had touted since the city's conception, did not know the truths Haythem had known and hidden during his years as Founder. Science was not her forte and Doctet attendance by the Founder's wife had never been required. She had been there when duty demanded, when Haythem requested it, but beyond that, she had left the ruling of Hebenon to the man born into that position, as had been ordained by every other Founder since the beginning.

How many other Founders had known this truth?

Neoma did not know science, did not know politics. But she did understand power. She knew who had it, who did not, and who was destined to wield it in the absence of a Founder and the absence of a male heir to the Kemway bloodline.

The child Ulynda.

Her child.

The only one to survive.

"For me?" The girl smiled, unmoved by their paltry environs as she took the plain brown hempaper box with its red bow from the man now led into the room. Sometimes, as with now, Ulynda seemed apathetic about the unfortunate losses she had endured. She had

always been the most stoic and studious of the Kemway children, never prone, like her mother, to unnecessary displays of emotion or dramatics, but still, Neoma worried for the girl's frame of mind as she watched her open the gift.

The giver had little interest in Ulynda's reaction to his offering, a selection of candied fruits, costly and difficult to get. His concern, despite his efforts to hide it, was primarily for the woman who, predictably, refused to stand in greeting when he entered her home.

"Mam."

"Kal." She called the Senior Talker by name rather than title. Neoma did not believe in a need for titles, particularly titles that might put a man above her now that she was without a position in Hebenon. She watched Ulynda pop one morsel of fruit into her mouth, reach for another, and then scolded, "Don't eat them all at once."

"I won't, mother." If it had been her little brother or sister, the warning would be necessary since the youngest Kemways had not been old enough to master restraint. At ten years old, Ulynda showed more restraint and self-control than most adults Neoma knew.

She did, however, eat the second piece before putting the lid on the box as Neoma began again, "Ulynda, please…your studies."

"I know." Senior Kal's arrival in their home meant grown-up business, to which Ulynda was not privy…despite the position and status her mother often touted she had.

The last of the Kemways. The only surviving heir. It was important for her to study, to take care of body and mind, to grow up to lead…or at least grow up to marry and produce the male heir the city needed now that her father was gone.

Box tucked beneath her arm, the girl ducked into the adjoining room. The pneumatic door slid shut behind her.

"One of these days she will have to…"

Neoma cut him off with a wave of her hand and a stern expression. "She is not ready."

"Nor will she be if you do not permit…" He stopped when her mien turned icy and he smiled affably. This had become a familiar

dance between them as they worked towards a mutually beneficial relationship. Each was aware of what the other needed…and wanted…and was willing to give…and each was willing to press that need and advantage when the moment suited them. So far, however, Kal had avoided overstepping the boundaries of the woman who was, technically, by right of marriage to their absent Founder, the Head of the Voices of Faith. The Cult of the Founder could not continue to exist as anything more than a fringe sect without Neoma and her child, the Founder's child, to support them.

Kal's position and livelihood depended on his continued good relationship with her.

In her inexperience of life in the Levs, her disconnection from the lives of those the Kemways once lauded over, Neoma needed the practical knowledge and lifetime of experience Kal Driscoll provided.

He shrugged. "Of course, she may not need to…"

Neoma's gaze narrowed.

Kal continued. "He's alive."

She needed to know that too.

Neoma stared, silent, seething, seeking something in his face that supported his claim. His tone was not that of a man offering comfort and belief in the intangible. These were words spoken with a note of hinted proof she had waited a long time to hear.

"How? Where?" Almost a year spent seeking someone, anyone, who knew what had become of her husband, and yet there had been nothing, as if the man had ceased to exist the moment she and the children sought refuge in the Factory and abandoned Haythem to his fate. She had expected then that he would die, that the encroaching looters from the Levs would find their way into the Uppers, find the one, right or wrong, they blamed for the ills in their lives, and execute him like some deposed king from the annals of history or a diseased animal. She had not loved him, had not felt any great remorse for taking refuge without him, but she had not stopped to consider what her life might be like afterward. Imagining anything other than a return

to the norm, the Founder's family and the Doctet managing life inside Hebanthe Falls, had been impossible.

She had not imagined a world in which the Outside was open and the citizens of the Levs could win against the control of the Crows.

The opening of the city in the falls to the Outside had proven to be a considerable complication.

"I don't know where…yet…but I have it from a reliable source that he is…and that Grainger knows where."

It was one of the more plausible rumors to come out of the aftermath of the Coup. Captain of the Guard Oliver Grainger had seized control of the city, restored a modicum of order, and with considerable effort re-established a new police force and the Nau, a group of nine men and women selected by a citywide vote to head each important segment of business. With the members of the Doctet cut off…for their own safety at first and then by the plague that followed…within the isolated factories, something had to be done. With so many of those once a part of the Doctet lost to that Culling Plague, the Nau had remained in place once the Factory doors opened.

Though Neoma had expected to regain her position, or at least a seat among the Nau, that had not happened. Grainger remained entrenched in the seat of power where the Kemway Founders had always ruled and Neoma was left without a purpose.

Rumors rose and fell in waves, of Haythem's death at Grainger's hands, of exile to the Outside village of Marbordo, of his death at the hands of the Hebenon mob or detention and enslavement somewhere in the dank, dim Levs beneath her feet. Rumors only, never proof.

One thing that was certain: if anyone knew what had become of the Founder, Grainger was the logical choice.

His secrets, however, remained his own. Founder Kemway was a topic Grainger refused to discuss and a topic most refused to push him to talk about.

At least he had refused until now.

"I'm working on it," Kal promised, the impulse to pat her hand, the type of condescending comfort gesture he would have made with

anyone who came to him for reassurance and easing words, stifled in time to avoid the backlash he knew would come if he touched her.

No one touched Neoma Kemway without permission, not even her child…or the bearded brown-skinned man in hempleather with the popper and buzzer on his hips who entered through the front door without knocking or announcement as was required of Kal.

Neoma rose at last, her feline movement graceful as she offered the newcomer her hand.

"You will take Blayd with you…you will find this source, find where Haythem is, if he is alive, and you will let me know at once when you find him." As the newcomer kissed her pale knuckles she added, "Find him, Blayd. Whatever it takes."

"Whatever it takes, Neoma," he swore.

He noted the use of her name. Kal's inner scowl deepened but he did not show his hand. He had suspected this liaison for a long time, but until now, in this private place, he had seen no evidence of it.

Now, he wondered, saddled with the tagalong he would rather not work with, the captain of her personal security, if this might be something he could exploit.

If it was worth doing so.

"Whatever it takes, Mam," Kal likewise promised, forcing a note of intimacy into his voice he did not feel.

Neoma ignored it.

By the tension in Blayd's jawline, Kal wagered the officer had not. Good.

❧*❧

Like most vindis in the Levs, the Lanes were open around the clock, the need for social gathering places ever constant as workers trudged home at the end of each shift. In a world of perpetual dark and artificial lighting, night and day had ceased to exist when the doors of Hebanthe Falls had sealed a small portion of humanity away from the inhospitable outside world.

That had been then. Now, the Outside once again beckoned, but in the two years since the city had reopened, relatively few had ventured into it. Most were too afraid.

Instead, they came to places like the Lanes to socialize rather than isolating themselves in their homes or standing in the constant drip, drip, drip of the city's grated metal streets.

Even so, at this hour midway between shifts, the Lanes was largely empty. A group of five congregated around a center lane, whooping as the ball struck the pins or hissing and booing and swearing, or even laughing, when the ball failed to travel the path each player hoped. They were young, teens he wagered, though it had been a long time since he had been one of those.

He rarely thought about those distant days. Life had been so much different than…before the Coup…before the Opening.

Other than the pair behind the kiosk, one cleaning and inspecting equipment and the other offering food and drink to clients, there was no one to trouble the lanky fellow with the stringy blonde hair tied away from his face with a braided hemp cord. His unbuttoned hempleather vest sagged from his shoulders, revealing wilting, weathered skin that looked as if it would slide from the man's gaunt frame. Though he appeared focused on the stein of ale he had restlessly nursed since his arrival and the bowl of nuts he sporadically munched on, his gaze darted to the door every time the bell above it jangled out of tune against the ruckus the youngsters made. Mostly the ringing announced someone coming in to pick up a takeaway order, to buy a warming shot of whiskey before braving the cold outdoors again, or stepping in long enough to scan the patrons before leaving.

He knew those sorts, men looking for andis, brako looking for targets, bugorra looking for troubled they might put down in the hopes of a promotion or a few extra ticks earned for initiative taken. He had seen all of those things too many times to count.

When, finally, the familiar face he was waiting for ducked in out of the damp, he motioned to the swiver for another stein. By the time the dwarf reached the table at the farthest side of the room, where the

blonde had kept vigil, the swiver had more nuts and a second stein already in place.

The dwarf nodded his gratitude, lowered the waterproof hood of his cloak, and climbed onto the empty chair where the warming drink waited. He wrapped his hands around the cup in the vain hope that the outside would be as warming as the contents before speaking.

"Miserable night out there," he muttered after the first extended gulp burned its way into his belly. Zaolei. The good stuff, not the cheap crap many swivers served. He was glad for that.

"Always miserable out. Always night."

"True." The oddness of the other man's speech, created by his prosthetic tongue, was no longer noticed. They had known each other for a very long time.

Amidst the teens, a fight broke out, two boys shoving one another over some perceived insult, but the others in the group broke up the squabble before the swiver could intervene or the sound of it attracted passing bugorra. The dwarf turned in his chair to judge whether there would be trouble in this place that he did not need, and when he spoke again, it was with crisp, quick words.

He did not need trouble. He had enough of that in his life already.

"Joran said you…"

"Yes."

"And did he get it? Is he going to help?"

"I haven't seen him."

The dwarf frowned and muttered, "Hiro de puta," beneath his breath around the mouthful of nuts he had taken. "Joran said you'd…"

"Unless you want me to go through a third channel…"

"No…no…better you do it yourself."

"Then you gotta be patient."

"Eight days, Lash. It's been eight days. Time's wastin'."

Lash did not need the reminder. He did not know what had created the deadline, beyond secret, rarely spoken words.

Club of Spades.

If the dwarf spoke true, time was a commodity none of them had.

But it was not his fault it had taken the dwarf five of those eight days to track him down and get that message into his hands.

"I'm not his keeper. I don't have his schedule…and with the bugorra on his back…" He knew where the man in question slept, if he slept at all, and he knew where he worked. Finding him in either place was a hit or miss proposition. Joran could have gotten his schedule if Lash had asked. But Lash knew where he would be in less than an hour, if he was lucky and his intel was accurate. "Hope to catch him today," he glanced at his chrono, "…if I hurry…"

The dwarf began to speak again, a protest it appeared from his anxious, perturbed expression, but Lash cut him off. "Not my fault you took so fotzin' long to get here." He might have already been in place, waiting for the man they needed, if he was not forced to wait here longer than expected.

"Too many bloody bugorra." It was a poor, but understandable, excuse, one equaled by the one Lash had given. The bugorra…always the bugorra…hindered from storming their quarry's residence or place of business again by the man who employed them. Bugorra unable to arrest a man whose face they did not know and forbidden from scouring Hebenon in the hopes of bagging the Scarecrow.

Steering away from the bugorra made Ballard's life tricky, made everyone's lives an uneasy balancing act.

Lash did not need the trouble any more than Ballard did. He did not need to make life any more difficult for either of them.

Enoch LeRoy did not need the hassle they represented either.

"Well go then. Find him…and tell me when it's done so I can take some good news back for a change."

There were multiple questions Lash could ask, answers Enoch had yet to give him, but Lash was just the messenger this time. The go-between. If he wanted to know more, he needed to find Ballard.

Only then might the bite of those three words be pulled out of his thoughts like a stinger from his skin to be covered with the salve of knowledge…and a plan.

❧*❧

"You wanted to see me, Captain?"

Lieutenant Ilya Young was not a tall woman, and when she stood in front of the man who had once been her supervisor in Hebenon's law enforcement unit, she was reminded again of how imposing a figure Oliver Grainger was. Her stature had never been a hindrance, not with those she served beside, and not with those delinquents she brought in from the city streets. Tenacious and vicious, she was as fierce as any man, as any brako, and it was that quality that had earned her the coveted position at the head of the law force when their captain graduated to the rank of Hebenon's leader.

What exactly had happened that day to put Grainger in charge, she did not know. The Doctet had fled to the Factories, away from the rioting Lev horde, and the Founder had disappeared, and with no one to manage the city, it had seemed natural, expected even, that Grainger should fill those leadership shoes as long as necessary. The city had been in disarray and something needed to be done. The head of the Crows had been the obvious person to put that chaos in its place. He was still there, calling the shots, when there were others, the Founder's wife and the few surviving members of the original Doctet, who could surely take up the reins again now that the Factories were open.

Ilya did not understand the politics, did not approve of the Kemways' removal, but she respected the Captain, and what he had accomplished in the last two years, too much to turn her back on him.

He had taught her everything she knew about this job.

"Yes, Lieutenant; come in."

Grainger rose from the cushioned white sofa in what had once been the Founder's office, leaving the sleepy, kiss-rumpled fellow seated there, clothing slightly askew as if her arrival had interrupted at the untimeliest moment. Despite his own less than pressed appearance, Grainger showed no hint of regret, annoyance, or mortification over the interruption, nor did he speak as his companion straightened his clothes and crept from the room as silent as a shadow.

Ilya had seen him with Grainger before; everyone of import in the Uppers had. If any knew his name, they did not speak it, and if anyone questioned the not quite secret relationship, they did not do so openly.

It did not matter. So long as Grainger continued to steer Hebenon with a steady hand, his private life was no one else's concern.

"I hear you brought down Vanderwall…"

"My officers, sir, and it's his brother. He's locked. I wasn't the…"

Grainger chuckled, his gaze following the departing man through the windows of the door. "But they're your officers…and you were there. With Vito as bait, we'll…"

"I might have gotten Vanderwall if not for Scarecrow…"

The creases at the corners of his eyes twitched. "He was there?"

"With them when we arrived, yes, sir," she replied, expecting the words of acclaim to turn into words of reprimand. The Scarecrow, the root cause behind the uprising that had upended Hebenon, had been hunted since the Coup. For a few months, in the immediate aftermath, as the destruction was swept away by reconstruction efforts, there had been no trace of that particular thorn in Hebenon's side. Many had believed the vigi dead. But after the theft of the entire stash of Crow weaponry and gear, and the subsequent rise of Vanderwall's brako horde, the Scarecrow resurfaced, once more combatting the Crows though now the faces beneath those hoods had changed.

Some touted him a hero of the people.

To Ilya, a man outside the law was as much a criminal as the brako he hunted. Grainger's failure to make the vigi's capture a priority was a particularly irritating grain of sand.

Maybe she and her team had only found Vito that night because of Scarecrow. Maybe she owed him her success. But to Ilya, the vigi was as much part of the problem as the brako were. The vigi's tactics were not the solution Hebanthe Falls needed.

"He was protecting a group of taggers when the team arrived." Tagging, an equally offensive crime, and one she wanted to address now that she had Grainger's ear. "But he escaped us when the brako were engaged."

"So he kept them busy until the cavalry arrived."

Ilya took an uncomfortable side step, trying not to scowl at the chuckle in Grainger's voice, and nodded. "I suppose that is…"

"Did you find the taggers?" As far as Grainger was concerned, anyone that aided in clearing the Levs of the near-endless bounty of brako his forces could barely keep up with was worth keeping around. Public brawling was outlawed in an attempt to limit the damage the brako could do, although more and more he realized that all the law did was limit the innocents' ability to fight back. The Scarecrow was, technically, breaking those laws too, but the arrest of a handful of brako, particularly Vanderwall's baby brother, overrode any pressing need to hunt down the vigi who had aided in that capture.

"The SCAMs in that street were disabled…"

"Recently?"

"I don't know, sir," she admitted. "I'm looking into it." If they were recently disabled, it might be a tick against the brako, who were known to disable SCAMs when some big crime was about to go down. Each instance brought them a step closer, they hoped, to finding the system hacker the brako employed and the head of the brako himself.

It might also be a tick in the system against the taggers, as defacing or destroying city property was illegal too.

Ginna did not need that charge against her.

"Keep me up to date; let me know. And keep me informed of baby Vanderwall's condition; if he talks…if he has anything useful to say."

"Yes, sir."

"Oh, and Lieutenant, leave Scarecrow alone. He's not our priority. When he slips up, we will get him. Until then, Vanderwall and the brako are the focus. Once they're down, Scarecrow will crawl back into whatever crevice he came from. Is that understood?"

Ilya bristled. An order was an order. But giving Scarecrow free rein in Hebenon was no better, to her, than giving the brako the freedom to commit their host of criminal acts. Maybe Grainger, like some on the force, were content with permitting Scarecrow to do their

jobs for them, or perhaps Grainger felt it made the task of restoring order easier if he allowed the vigi to assist his efforts.

Ilya, however, could not accept that. She would bring Scarecrow to justice, whoever he was, as surely as she would strike down Vanderwall. She just had to find him first.

"Is that understood, Lieutenant?"

Clearing her throat, squaring her shoulders, she nodded without directly meeting his gaze. "It is, Captain." She would agree, but if given the opportunity, she would drag Scarecrow into this office by the hoses of his filt mask and demand that justice be done.

He had made a fool of this office for too long. It was time he was dealt with. It was time for that to end.

"Good."

She knew she was dismissed, but still she stood, wanting a private word with her superior now that she was here, a word about her sister's unlawful activities. But the words stuck in her throat, regardless of the urge to come clean of her familial infractions. She had not seen her sister since the incident. When she did, there would be hell to pay.

Grainger looked up from the Echosys screen of reports he was meant to study and approve. "Is there something else, Lieutenant?"

He had not specifically asked about Ginna. He had asked about the taggers but had not mentioned her by name. Without the SCAM footage, the odds were he did not know Ginna was involved. Banking on that lack of knowledge, deciding that, this time at least, keeping her sister safe was preferable to reporting a lawbreaker, Ilya shook her head. "No, sir. May I go?"

"Of course. Goodnight, Ilya."

"Goodnight, Captain."

She made it as far as the door.

"Say hello to your sister for me."

Hand around the latch, Ilya hesitated, breath caught and slowly released in a measured hiss before looking back at her boss. He was smiling, giving no trace of any ulterior motive in his salutations. Innocent then. That was good to know.

"I will. Goodnight."

He waved but did not look up.

When Ilya found her sister, she would be punished for the impossible position she put Ilya in. She was not going to stand for this disobedience. Enough was enough.

❦*❧

It had been a long time since he had seen Lash. Weeks at least. A month most likely. The man came Outside now and again, but mostly he stuck to the shadowed rhythm of whatever his life had been before the Coup, just as Rhyd did. Neither was the social sort, neither prone to losing themselves in the company of others. Most often, when he did see the spindly, older blonde, it was through the windows of that always dark, seemingly unoccupied flat or in the crowded collection of misfits that frequented Vapors.

When they did cross paths, it was always with a message, with details of brako activity or a bugorra raid of the sort Scarecrow felt compelled to thwart.

He assumed that was what this was, something too urgent to wait for a chance meeting, something worth the risk of open, public contact.

Rhyd's workmates pushed past through the door of the Shed, coming on shift or going off in the never-ending quest to keep Hebenon's engineered climate operating perfectly. They jostled and bumped him, few noticing, fewer apologizing for it, as Lash stepped out of the shadows and thrust something into Rhyd's palm.

Head low, mouth to Rhyd's ear, he said two words and then was gone again.

"Skelter's alive."

Rhyd's fist closed.

Alive.

The words shook and vibrated down into the pit of his stomach.

Alive.

❧CHAPTER 4❧

He had not been in this room since the Coup. There had been no reason to come here. So long as he and those he cared about were left alone, Rhyd had no issue with Grainger or the government the man was trying to organize. And Grainger had better things to do than worry about a man who was fighting to make the city better, and though sometimes the bugorra and Scarecrow crossed fists, when the innocent were being harassed or questioned or targeted for some unfair purpose, most of the time Rhyd was content to let them be.

He had not seen Grainger in person in the two years since that night, in this room, when both had come to confront the Founder. Rhyd did not know what had become of Kemway, did not care about his fate. The man and his family had been in power for too long and something had needed to change. Rhyd only wanted to protect those who needed protection. He wanted justice and stability for the residents of Hebanthe Falls.

And he wanted to be left alone.

When the Shed warden placed the summons in his hands upon his return to the Shed at the end of shift, a prickle of warning had shot up Rhyd's spine. Two years…and a summons came now. A summons…after Lash's earlier revelation.

This was surely no coincidence.

How peculiar it would look, to anyone noticing, for a bilger to be summoned into the presence of Hebenon's leader.

Wanting to know what Grainger knew, what he wanted, however, it was a request Rhyd did not feel he could refuse.

Venn's plea for him to come to Marbordo was put off a bit longer.

The room had not changed. The walls, the furnishings, were still glaringly white. There were personal touches on the desk, on the walls, artwork and mementos not there when the Founder had ruled from this place, but the room had not changed. The most startling difference was seeing the window shields retracted, providing an unobstructed view of the purple and orange of the evening sky outside and the blinding glare of the sun off the late-winter blanket of snow spread over the hemp fields all the way to the base of the distant mountains. If he turned, he could see each of the four tributaries, see the village where he imagined people were gathering for their meal. Though the thought of a meal brought the memory of mouth-watering smells with it and roused a grumbling in his belly, Rhyd pushed the hunger away to listen instead to the arrival of the larger man behind him.

He did not turn. Turning would be akin to giving Grainger power over him. Rhyd wanted no one to have power over him except Venn…and even that, he realized more every day, was a power and control issue he struggled against.

"I didn't think you'd come, my friend." Grainger joined him at the window but did not offer his hand. He did not think Ballard would accept such a gesture of familiarity.

"We're not friends."

Grainger nodded. His assessment of the man's personality, and his choice not to extend a handshake, had been an accurate one.

"No? Well…I like to consider myself to be everyone's friend." Before the Coup, he had been a solitary man, others on the force being the only regular company he kept. Since that night, he found himself surrounded by petitioners, the Nau, and a host of others who passed daily through his orbit.

He did not feel any less alone, however. Thank the gods for Joran.

"How is Zara? Still dancing?"

He had not allowed himself the luxury of returning to Vapors, to see what had become of the young woman who had captured his heart, and betrayed it, within so short a span of time. Not betrayed, not exactly, but she turned out to be something far different then what he

had expected. Those revelations, however, the events of that day, had not subverted his longing to know her better. But he had believed it wiser not to muddle his life, or hers, by having her in it while he struggled to set Hebenon on a path towards equality, stability, and freedom it had not enjoyed since the earliest days after its founding.

Though he did not look at Grainger, Rhyd's brow twitched in surprise. "You know where to find her." Despite Skelter's absence, Zara had done her best to return to the life she had known before, working with Maemi to restore Vapors to its prominence. For a man in Grainger's position, discovering that would not have been difficult…if he really wanted to know.

"Then she's dancing again. Good." He did not know if she was also tricking, but that was a detail he did not want to know. Part of him clung to a scrap of hope that she was waiting for him, even though he had done his best to move on and believed she had done the same.

The men stood silent, both watching a distant mass of movement as shepherds steered a collection of sheep and goats towards the village. The snow cover was light enough that the herds had little difficulty finding the short, scrubby grass, but by this time of the winter, they had to wander further from the village to do so.

Fortunately, a certain portion of each hemp crop harvest was stored to provide adequate nourishment for both animals and people when there was little else to eat.

"You didn't ask me here to ask about Zara."

"No…I didn't." There had been some interest in small talk, in reaching out to a man he felt he might have a small amount in common with, at least when it came to their views of what Hebenon could be, the direction the city was heading. But with the moment upon them, Grainger found he had little to say and knew that Ballard had little desire or use for unnecessary dialogue. "I asked you here because I hope we can work together."

Rhyd looked at him with the wary ghost of question on his face.

Ice broken, Grainger pulled out his desk chair and motioned to one of the empty ones on the other side before sitting, hoping Ballard would do likewise.

"We both want Vanderwall and the brako gone. We're already working to make it happen. It seems to me…it would be energy better spent if we were working on the same side instead of…"

Resisting the thought of sitting, Rhyd refused the offered chair and remained where he was. He did not even look at it. "We're already on the same side." At least, they were when it came to the brako.

"Not officially. What I'm doing is…" Grainger paused. "What you're doing is technically illegal…"

"Then arrest me."

Grainger blinked. "Arrest? Hell, without you we would probably be…" Losing the battle. But those were words he chose not to say out loud. He did not want to admit, to himself, to anyone, that he believed he needed Ballard's help. Grainger had the advantage of numbers, of equipment and SCAMs and the law. One small, unimposing man should not be the lynchpin to making a difference.

Yet Grainger could not shake the feeling that Ballard was exactly that. The crux of the entire matter.

"You've got your ear to the street in a way my people do not. I have the manpower. Working together would be a helluva lot more productive than fighting one another."

Voice quiet, even, calm, when Rhyd said, "Then keep your people out of my way and we won't have a problem," it came across with a level of menace that nothing in his posture or expression suggested. Grainger still knew very little of the other man's story, who he was, what he was; he only knew that the quest to find one Vanished man had turned him towards the dual life he now led. But Grainger had no doubt that, whether Ballard had found that man or not, walking away from the vigi life was not in his cards. It was in the man's blood now, just as this new position of power was in Grainger's.

"Not so easy when there are those who won't let go of before, won't forget…who want your head. I'm doing what I can to keep them

off you, but I've got at least one officer who won't rest until you're stopped. Down there, on the streets, I have little control over them."

There were regulations and rules and ordinances, and most of those he employed willingly upheld those things. But in the Levs, there remained a degree of wild-west law in effect, and reprimanding his officers after the fact did not necessarily prevent them from taking the law into their hands as they interpreted it…

…any more than it prevented Rhyd from doing the same.

"Only one?"

"My chief lieutenant. Not sure you've met her, but she has her sights set on you." If she had ever fought Scarecrow, she had not spoken of that obvious failure. If there was another reason she was so eager to stop him, Grainger did not know that either. "She's not going to stop hunting you…"

Not me, Rhyd thought with an internal grimace. Scarecrow. At least he had a person he could name, a warning of who to watch for. But the knowledge and warning changed nothing.

"Let her."

"I'd rather we work together, on the same side, you working with me, for me, instead of…"

"I don't work for anyone."

Scarecrow did not do what he did for payment. The thought of doing so made Rhyd feel cheap, dirty, controlled…and he wanted none of those things.

Grainger sighed as the Echosys buzzed. After a glance at the screen, an interruption announced to cut this unproductive meeting short, he stood up again.

He had not expected any other results from this initial talk. He had to start somewhere, and maybe in time, he could convince Ballard of the logic of his position, his offer. For the sake of his lieutenant, however, for Ballard, his force, their city, he felt the need to try.

Ballard understood that need. There was no point in expressing it.

"I'll do what I can," he muttered, "if you promise me you'll think about my offer. The freedom to continue as you are without being hunted. No strings…"

Rhyd grunted. There were always strings. If he accepted this odd patronage, strings would be unavoidable and they both knew it.

He accepted Grainger's escort the several paces across the room to the door as it appeared the Captain was intending to go out as well.

"If you change your mind…"

The door into the hall opened as another inside the room did likewise. Rhyd did not look to see who entered. It was not his business.

"I won't."

A hopeful note, not yet ready to admit defeat. "But if you do…"

Rhyd grunted again. "I know where to find you."

It might have been acceptance. It might have been a threat.

Grainger did not believe it was either of those things.

*

"Mierdita! You're going to get yourself killed!"

Though ten years younger, Ginna Young did not find her sister's outrage, or her position in the city's police force, to be intimidating. Ilya was more a mother, a guardian, then she was a sister, but even then, her chosen career path had kept her less engaged in Ginna's upbringing then she should have been after the loss of first one parent and then the other.

"Fourteen years and you still don't give a cazz! You don't know me!" Ginna spat, stuffing every article of clothing within her reach into the shabby hemp rucksack she had carried since her first day of school. The straps had been reattached a number of times, each marked by a change in thread color, and there were patchwork bits sewn on where holes had worn through the base fabric, but it was Ginna's favorite pack, the last thing her mother had given her before an accident in the fishery had taken her life.

"Listen to me when I talk to you!" Ilya grabbed at the bag, intending to yank it away, to force Ginna's attention from her next foolish, rebellious act. She caught one strap and pulled. One end of it ripped free and slipped from her hand to dangle like a broken wing as Ginna clutched the bag tight against her chest.

"I hate you. All you care about is law and obedience…you don't care about what's right!"

Further packing forgotten, Ginna pushed past her sister, elbowing her with enough force that, despite Ilya's intention of standing firm to block the passage, she was able to squeeze into the main room of the two-bedroom flat they shared.

Once they had slept in the same room. When depression and an out of control Heb addiction ripped their father out of their life as well, the girls found they had rooms of their own and Ilya, old enough then that they were spared the indignity of becoming fosters or being forced into a life on the streets, became the head of their family.

"You ungrateful little…" Ilya stormed after her, shoving aside the furniture the other girl darted between in an effort to stay out of her sister's reach. "After everything I've…" The door was thrown open. "You go out there again and I'll…"

It was slammed with enough force that the mechanical lock failed to catch and the door bounced open to be caught in Ilya's waiting hand. "I'm not going to protect you next time!" she shouted at the retreating girl's back as Ginna bounded down the nearest metal stairs towards the vindi district.

"Don't need your protection!" Ginna shouted, her voice retreating with her as she disappeared from sight. "I want you to listen!"

Ilya wanted to follow. Always in the past, Ginna had stormed out on arguments rather than maintain them, but always she came back after both young women had a chance to cool their tempers. This routine was not new. Ilya had shift in thirty and she was only half-dressed. Finding Ginna, dragging her home, would have to wait. By the time Ilya returned home, she expected Ginna would be sitting on the sofa as always, playing games on her Echo T2, and Ilya would try,

one more time, to talk her sister out of the activist lifestyle that was going to get her arrested…or killed.

ȣ*ȣ

"Ballard…isn't it?

The dwarf who pushed into the lift with him, grabbing the closing door with one hand, was no one Rhyd knew, and in his position as bilger, he was not exactly known or recognized by many. Other bilgers, skolpers, speners, denki, and heizers might recognize his face after a lifetime of passing each other in Hebenon's shafts, tunnels, and the Shed, but most of them would not know his name, and while there was a certain degree of familiarity with some who frequented Vapors for food, drink, and entertainment, very few of those people ever graduated beyond the level of 'recognizable face in a crowd'.

Rhyd would remember a man such as this.

His face, however, bore a hint of something familiar, even if Rhyd could not place what that was.

"Depends."

The dwarf's lips twisted into a wry expression of amusement as the lift stopped, allowed two others off and accepted three others on. The lift was crowded now, and when the dwarf did not speak again, Rhyd guessed he wanted privacy. A lift at shift change was not the best place for it.

Maybe Grainger had sent him.

Maybe it was a sign that he should have gone to Marbordo as Venn asked instead of back down into the Levs. After the meeting with Grainger, however, Rhyd wanted a strong bottle of Zaolei, something not to be had out there.

Another stop and the three got off, leaving, for the moment at least, Rhyd and the dwarf alone.

"What do you know about the Core?"

Rhyd scowled. This was not the first time he had heard the term. At one time, he had believed that, wherever it was, whatever it was, it

was where Venn had been taken. After finding Venn alive, however, Rhyd had not given the Core another thought.

"Nothing." He was not even convinced it was real. If it was part of the Levs, he surely would have located such a place by now in his time spent inside of Hebenon's system of ventilation and filtration shafts. And if it was in the Uppers…well…how could it be? A place like the rumored Core could not exist some place like the Uppers.

"You have the Spades coin?"

Rhyd's scowl deepened and he thrust his hand into his pocket where the small metal disc Lash had given him was securely protected. "What do you know about…?"

A woman and two children entered the lift when it stopped, cutting Rhyd's question short and preventing the dwarf from replying. Two more stops, two more coming on. Another three levels and Rhyd would disembark too.

Would the dwarf follow?

All of the passengers emptied from the lift at the next Lev, a popular one where Vapors and many of the vindis at this depth were housed. Slipping past the retracting door, the dwarf said, "Skelter's there," as he too stepped into the street. "Vapors. Tomorrow night."

"Wait…" But the crowd had already swallowed the small man and the door closed between them, cutting Rhyd off before he could call out again. His effort to press the buttons, to stop the lift and open the door were in vain as downward movement had already begun.

Skelter was alive. In the Core.

Where the hell was that…and what did he, or this dwarf, want from Rhyd.

He supposed, with a rising degree of annoyance, he was going to have to wait until tomorrow night after shift to learn the story, but he did know one thing without anyone saying the words.

It was not Rhyd Ballard they wanted.

It was Scarecrow.

&*&

"We don't have to listen to you, Dead Man."

Otta threw the punch that caught the loud-mouthed offender in the jaw, sending him sprawled and spread-eagled backward into the arms of his fellows. Men and women on all sides chortled and cheered and the man's friends pushed him back to his feet, egging him on to meet the fight with one of the Boss' two bodyguards head-on.

Few were interested in a fight with Otta Quell. The woman had a reputation for ferocity that few in the Core cared to test.

It was what made her Skelter's ideal companion.

Skelter's favor assured her and Colyx a fatter share of the spoils.

This was not the first flare of tempers in the Core. Colyx had seen it before, the sort of display of aggression bound to rise when criminals, miscreants, and dissidents were thrown together in a place they had little chance of escaping. Anyone sent here was a forgotten, discarded thing that ceased to exist to any outside except for those for whom they toiled, pulling long-buried salt and minerals from extended tunnels for the residents of the fall city. Slave labor was not anyone's choice, but at least it had been a purpose for living, and with no external interference save for the scheduled arrival of ore and supply carts, and the occasional new addition to their ranks, those consigned to living out their days in this dingy, gray place had set up a society of sorts of their own, ruled by whoever was strong enough to do so.

When events outside, however, had sealed the Core doors, allowing no one else in, ending the delivery of tools and supplies and no longer accepting deliveries of mined product, the people of the Core were left to their own devices. Dwindling goods, shortages of food stores, and boredom, made for heightened hostility, shortened tempers, and an inability, for some, to get along with others.

Skelter had arrived at the cusp of the change, appearing as if a ghost through solid walls, and some clung to the stubborn belief that he was responsible for bringing this growing misery and isolation.

Never mind that he had been injured, unconscious, incapacitated, for the first several weeks after his arrival.

Never mind that he had single-handedly created a system of fair supply and distribution, as well as a level of individual regulation and responsibility to the residents, the likes of which had not worked in the Core in hundreds of years.

He had resurrected order from the chaos of want and had given the majority here, those who had never had a voice amongst those of might and vicious strength, hope.

Despite a push towards self-sufficiency and self-reliance that increased their likelihood of survival, some people just needed someone to blame.

The big man ran a hand over his bald head, wiping away the layer of grime and sweat from the tattoos there, and continued to watch the altercation for a sign that it would pass from verbal to physical. So long as it remained primarily an exchange of words, Skelter would not want him to interfere. So long as it was a battle of wit and word, Skelter could handle it. Certainly better than Colyx could.

It had been bound to come to this when word got out. Unlike the population outside the Core, those living here knew of the Club. The Club was part of their daily lives, the one marked for death always obvious among a population increased only by the addition of outsiders. Colyx did not know why Skelter had made a pact with the Club almost as soon as he regained his health and mobility. Speculation was that constant pain drove him, or being cut off from the city outside had, or merely the despair of being trapped in this place. Maybe it was a combination of those things.

But Skelter said he had a plan. He always had a plan, and his plans always came to be. During the months of his unusually extended membership, with death coming for those it seemed appropriate to lose, it seemed that perhaps the redhead possessed some form of voodoo to control the outcome, their lives, their future.

His selection for damnation this time came as a dismaying shock to some, and as a timely promise to others. Without Skelter, the Core could revert to what it had been, a lawless, brutal, collection of men and women waiting for death together. Without Skelter, there was no

one person strong enough in will and heart and determination to maintain this newfound level of civility and order.

And still Skelter clung to 'the plan'.

Whatever that was.

"Do you want to get out of the Core or do you want to rot here?"

Skelter's question smothered the chortles and catcalling insults, bringing silence over the open room at the center of the passages in which they dwelt.

"No one gets out," someone sneered.

"Especially with the carts not running," challenged another.

They had heard the tales of the citywide riot that had brought Skelter here. The riot that had put most of Hebenon's security doors to the outer limbs on lockdown. For a short time, six or eight months perhaps, the carts had run again, after the worst of the disruption was quelled. Then for some reason none of them understood, the runs had ceased. Nothing else came in, nothing was taken out. Some had tried, in times past, to take advantage of the periodic window of opportunity when the carts ran to attempt an escape, but with no regular schedule as to when those in the city chose to open the tunnel, such attempts had been haphazard, ill-planned, and doomed to failure.

There had been nothing more than idle speculative talk about 'getting out' in the months since the outside coup. Resigning themselves to surviving on their own, however they could, dying of extinction at the end of it all with no one ever remembering they were here, it had become normal not to think about a future.

And without new blood coming in, there had even been talk amongst the Spades of disbanding the Club.

What point was there in any sort of population control mechanism when they were all doomed to die here?

"I've got a plan…"

"You've got twenty-three days."

"If we work together, it shouldn't take longer than that."

Work together. It was one of the Core's biggest failings. Before Skelter, the miners had been prone to infighting and conflict beneath

the leadership of hotheads. The redhead had a knack for getting people to do what he wanted much of the time, for getting things done, a knack learned as a streeter in the Levs. That knack had translated surprisingly well here.

Colyx hoped it would serve them well a little longer.

"How? There's no way out…"

"We go out through the door."

Uneasy, skeptical laughter met his suggestion. "Without an Echo, no one's opening the door…and no one's coming from outside to…"

"We open it ourselves."

Another dissenting voice. "Again with the how, cazzo?"

A chorus of murmured voices echoed the question.

"We blow it."

Colyx and Otta traded glances. Not even they had expected that.

Men and women looked at one another. There were few scientific minds among them. There were a few clever ones, a few who excelled in sneakiness and theft, but most were thugs and bullies and barely controllable brutes.

"Look," Skelter started, tapping his walking stick on the floor to refocus attention. "I've been inventorying everything we got. We can do it. We make weapons…something more than we've got. We set charges to blow the door…and charges to bring the place down behind us once we get through. They won't expect us, and there won't be a damned Core for them to send us back to. They'll have to let us out…"

"Or kill us…we die trying," muttered someone.

Otta snarled at the doubters. "Maybe…sure…but I'd rather die getting free…and hoping some of us make it…than starve and waste in this rat hole." Maybe Skelter had not told her the plan before, but what need had there been to do so? The wisdom of silence until he was sure of success, or as sure as any man could be of a plan that would depend on the cooperation of every person present, was logical. She did not hold his silence against him.

If Skelter was ready to act, to put such a plan into motion, she was ready to support him. He had her best interest at heart after all.

"So what do we do?"

"Give me time to work out the…"

"Twenty-three days, Dead Man…"

"I'll see us out of here before then," Skelter promised

"And if we're not?"

Skelter looked at his challenger levelly, raising the patch from his weak eye to give the fellow a two-eyed stare. "Then none of this is gonna matter, is it?"

ဆ*ဆ

The mountains of distant purple cast long shadows across the hemp fields as day gave way to the inevitability of night, the setting sun leaving chilled air in its wake as it stole the warmth of day. Hebenon's factories continued to churn as they had for centuries, continuing Duncan Kemway's original efforts to enable mankind's survival, allowing them to thrive, into an uncertain future in a world that had rejected them. Or that mankind had rejected. That did not matter now. The moonrise shone silver on the sparse layer of snow, magic to behold by a man who had, for his entire life, seen nothing but wet metal and artificial light. Stars were still a wonder, and though they were just becoming visible as the colors of day bled into the black of night, he found peace in them.

It was not that he disliked the Outside, the scents and sounds of Marbordo, the sea, the colors of a world reborn. He, like others, prossers they were called, came out more often now, drawn by adventure, by opportunity, by a desire to escape Hebanthe Falls' perpetual darkness. Some had come to farm, some to rebuild and rehabilitate the long-abandoned East Factory One, some to explore and seek resources the fall city did not possess. Some came to study, to learn the why of all the lies they had been told throughout their lives.

The rest continued in denial and fear of the unknown.

The rest just continued.

Some had made homes here, amongst the parah. A few of the parah had ventured inside of the metal nest for the same reasons, to work, to explore, to live. Some, like Rhyd, dabbled in both environments, drawn by the lure of the unfamiliar but unable, or unwilling, to leave what they knew behind.

Out here, there was too much space. The world was too bright and deafening in its silence. Nighttime, such as now, might have been more bearable if only the tumble of the tributaries' roar was louder.

The days' end stragglers were leaving the city through perpetually open doors now, or going into it if returning to homes or night shift jobs required it. The hope was that a day would come when the inside and outside would mingle freely, when fear and prejudice disappeared and humanity was reunited by the vision Duncan Kemway had always supported. Hebanthe Falls was never intended to be eternal. She had been built to be that way, if necessary, to be a haven for as long as mankind needed, but even the original Founder had known, according to many, that an eternity in the city of the Four Falls was not the destination of humanity.

Grainger believed it too.

After two years, however, mankind was still not ready. It would take another generation or more, Rhyd guessed, before that day came.

He would not be alive to see it.

He heard the crunch of boots in the snow and gravel on the cliff behind him, knowing who sought him without needing to turn. He should have gone straight into the village, but the lure of the starry sky and the distant sea, with the light fading behind him in the west, had been the balm his troubled head needed.

After that unexpected lift encounter, not even the half-consumed bottle of Zaolei had proven to be enough.

Arms wrapped around his waist and drew him close. In one of the rare moments of weakness he allowed, Rhyd closed his eyes and dropped his head back against the other man's shoulder. In the middle of his internal chaos, Venn was safe. Still here, safe, alive.

But somewhere down there, in an undiscovered place called the Core, so was Skelter.

Despite Venn's wishes, Rhyd knew what he had to do.

He had to find Skelter and bring him out of captivity. Skelter had helped him do the same for Venn. Skelter would do the same for him.

Rhyd could not be expected to do less for his friend.

In his clenched fist, the metal disk, an ancient coin perhaps pummeled smooth by prolonged effort and etched carefully with the spade and sword symbol which occasionally appeared painted on walls throughout the Levs, dug into the meat of his palm.

Whiskey brown eyes opened, and a turn of his head meant a meeting of gazes with the chocolate ones of the man behind him. They should be happy. Gods knew he wanted to be, as happy as Venn was, happy that Venn had come back to him. They had each other again.

It should be enough.

But Venn's protracted sigh revealed awareness and understanding of the truth. For unfathomable reasons, he was no longer enough.

He might never again be enough…and he had done this.

The lure of Rhyd's alter ego was too strong.

"What is the Core?" Rhyd thought Venn might know. Venn had more book learning. Venn was the smart one, if sometimes an impractical dreamer.

"A myth. Meant to be the home of humanity…before Hebenon. Before the end came too soon."

"Is it a myth? Is it really? What if…it's real?"

"It would have been found by now if it was real."

"Kemway knows."

"The Founder's gone."

Rhyd scowled, not willing to let the matter go. "Grainger then. Tamner said you could have been there…that Kemway knew the…"

"It doesn't exist, Whiskey. Let it go."

Someone, Grainger, or Tamner, or that dwarfish fellow, knew the truth. Maybe Lash knew. Someone had to. If the coin meant anything, Rhyd had to learn the truth. Before it was too late.

"Can't."

Venn sighed and released his embracing hold, instead threading his fingers between Rhyd's and squeezing his hand gently. "Then find it tomorrow. Agnys wants to see you. And I need you here."

Rhyd looked at their clasped hands, the once welcomed connecting gesture now feeling like a weighted anchor holding him back, dragging him under. He regretted that feeling, the thoughts of escape it ignited. Venn deserved better. Rhyd had gone through so much to have him back.

What harm would one more night cause?

He nodded, forced a smile he hoped Venn would interpret as sincere, and followed him down the cliff into Marbordo.

⁊Chapter 5⁊

Listening to his wife and infant daughter die had been the hardest thing Rafe Tamner had ever done. When the virus, whatever it was, swept through each of the isolated factory populations, Grainger had been understandably right in his decision to leave the quarantine in place. If he had done anything else, even to allow a single individual out or to allow Tamner inside in order to attempt to help, the contagion would have spread to the rest of Hebenon's population.

Besides, there were already doctors and the city's brightest minds spread between the three Factories, and each one had worked tirelessly on the problem just as Tamner had done on the outside.

His going inside would have done nothing more than expose him to whatever had devastated the population of the Uppers before the city was secure enough to welcome them out of their confinement. It would have done nothing more than allow him to hold his wife and daughter as the racking cough expelled blood and life from their lungs and ripped them out of his life.

Sometimes, he wished he had been there. But his son needed him.

At least he had been allowed the luxury of speaking with them over the Echo so that they could hear his voice, and he could hear theirs, in their final moments.

At least, by the time the plague had run its course, some new form of tuberculosis which the citizens of Hebanthe Falls had never been exposed to…but which the parah were, it was learned, immune to, and the Factories were unsealed, Tamner was allowed the blessing of reunification with his son Cori.

Approximately sixty percent of those in the Factories had died, sixty percent of Hebenon's leadership including many members of the

Doctet and their families and two of Founder Kemway's children. A vaccine was developed from the survivors' blood and the whole population of Hebenon was ordered to submit to inoculation so that the plague could claim no more lives.

Having heard about those horrific deaths, convincing people in the city to accept the vaccine was an easy thing to do. All but the most paranoid had no wish to die that terrible, blood-coughing death.

By the time the Factories opened, of course, the Nau was in place, a new government fashioned, elected, appointed from among residents throughout the city, most from the Levs, and the members of the Doctet discovered they were no longer needed in a ruling capacity. They returned to the lives they had led as designers, factory heads, inventors, scientists, historians, sports figures, engineers, entertainers and the like…but it seemed unlikely, to Tamner at least, that things would ever go back to the way they had been.

Not with the Founder out of the picture.

Not with Hebenon open to an outside world few had imagined, or believed, could exist.

Except for the familial loss he felt daily, Tamner was content in his opinion that he would have things no other way.

Events had prevented him from evacuating with the others. Events the day of the Coup had meant he was there when the door to the Outside opened. He was one of the first to see this new world, and with his scientific background in biology and medicine, he had been ideally suited to study the flora, the fauna, the people they found there. He had been ideally suited to be a member of the Nau, to head all matters of medical services and research because when the moment had come to step outside…he had.

He looked up from his survey of the green shoots poking through the late winter snow, the first heralds of spring, when the sounds of laughter drew his thoughts from the morbid musings distracting his research. Cori, for all of his interest in this new world that might, in time, lend itself to a life of scientific study in his father's footsteps, was still just a child, a ten-year-old boy who had lost so much and had,

surprisingly, found friendship with the parah child Agnys who had injected such profound changes into Hebenon's veins and opened the world to so many things that Tamner had never dreamed of.

With her help, and with the help of Venn and others who had, over the years, been banished Outside, communication and a path towards study and integration were possible. The people expelled from the city had been sent out as test subjects, with implants meant to relay data to the scientists in the city, to allow those inside to study the poisonous effects of the Outside world.

Of course, what little data they received before the implants stopped sending, data suggesting a livable atmosphere, had been denied and withheld from the populace in favor of the continuing claims that data gathering ceased due to the death of the subjects or the hostile environment that interfered with the transmissions.

Stepping outside himself had been proof of everything Tamner had come to believe…proof of everything the Founder denied…and the children chasing each other across the snowy, early morning landscape, his son, Agnys, and other parah children, as well as a few sons and daughters of those prossers brave enough to follow Tamner into this vast world, were the future Hebenon needed.

Without them, without this miracle of an unpolluted world, Hebanthe Falls was doomed to further stagnation and death within a matter of a few hundred years or less.

Tamner had seen it coming, even if no one else had.

A figure emerged from the city and stood alone, shielding his face against the glare, posture wary and uncertain. With an ever-increasing stream of crossers and prossers, as people gradually overcame their fears to pursue curiosity, seeing anyone come out, seeing that uncertainty, was an increasingly common occurrence.

It was the direct path the individual took towards Tamner that was of interest, and he got up off his knees to greet the black-clad man whose face was vaguely familiar but not one Tamner could readily place or recall. Nor did his intricately styled close-cropped hair, shaved into some manner of ancient tribal patterns over his scalp, look

at all familiar. It was the fashion of more than one security type inside of Hebenon, making his profession recognizable to anyone he met.

"Doctor Tamner."

Not an officer. He wore protective gear and weapons at his hip, a buzzer and a thumper, but there was no city insignia on his chest or shoulder. Not someone sent by Grainger then, as his appearance originally suggested.

"Where is he?"

"He?" Tamner's lips curled in bemusement. Like many in the business of law enforcement or protection Tamner found, this man's blunt, to the point question left too many details unaddressed so that there was no way of knowing exactly who he was inquiring about.

"The Founder."

Despite the planting of his feet, the tension across his shoulders that rippled down his arms into flexing fists, his darting gaze that shifted at each unfamiliar sound and the turn of his head towards each, suggested a first time viewing Marbordo's wonders, perhaps his first excursion out of Hebenon, and suggested discomfort and a potential for an unfortunate defensive reaction if the man felt threatened.

Tamner saw all of that in his cursory glance over the stranger and decided he needed to be careful. The stranger, in turn, saw a twitching at the corners of Tamner's mouth that suggested some knowledge about what he sought. Tamner knew it, regretted it, and tried immediately to school his expression to something more neutral, with a level of friendliness he did not feel.

"May I ask your name?" Perhaps initiating a small degree of intimacy would help.

The man frowned, looked as if he would not answer, but finally grunted and muttered, "Blayd," with a defiant glint in his eye, as if that name should mean something to Tamner.

How fitting. If the name was intended to mean anything beyond the suggestion of violence and strength, Tamner made no effort to guess it. "Well, Blayd, I don't know what you…"

"You know where he is."

Tamner shook his head. "I'm afraid I don't. I don't know if he…"

"Not what I've been told…"

Like many in Hebanthe Falls, Tamner knew the rumors. Every few months, someone came looking for answers, came seeking the Founder who had disappeared from the public's eye the night of the Coup, and had not been seen or heard from since. But few had come seeking the man out here.

And few knew that Tamner was one of a small fraction of those aware of the truth.

He was sworn to silence, and as this truth was one that could have devastating repercussions, it was a secret he gladly kept.

"Whoever you've been speaking to, whoever sent you…"

This time Blayd's growl was more of a snarl and the involuntary act of reaching for his buzzer made Tamner take a step back.

He had little fighting ability and there was no one near enough to be of help. Against a man like Blayd, he was sure to lose.

"She has every right to see her husband."

Neoma.

Tamner was surprised it had taken the woman this long to seek the truth. He knew there had been little love between husband and wife, but after the evacuation, Neoma, unlike so many others, was left without a purpose. No duty to tend, no function to perform, no job to see to. Only a daughter to console and raise.

Maybe it had taken her this long to come looking for Haythem because it had taken her this long to piece together some sort of existence for herself and her child.

Or maybe it had taken her this long to realize she had few options, and the husband she bore little fondness for was her best prospect for a life. Alive or dead, Neoma could use her husband's status to survive.

"If," Tamner stressed the word, "he's alive, if he's anywhere, you'll have to ask the Captain. If anyone knows it would have to be him." He was not claiming ignorance, but he was also not admitting anything. He was only pointing direction. He was also not casting

doubt on Grainger. If anyone knew the truth, Grainger had to be that man. Everyone in the city knew it. And Grainger would never talk.

The choice to reveal the Founder's fate, his whereabouts, was entirely in Grainger's hands. The choice to give any of that evidence to Neoma, to allow or disallow her access to the truth, was not in Tamner's control.

He trusted Grainger to do the right thing…whatever that was.

Releasing a hissing breath through clenched teeth, Blayd nodded. It was the answer he had expected, that both Kal and Neoma expected. Since the Senior Talker's source had pointed to Tamner, it was with Tamner Blayd began. And with Tamner, he had found his first hint that whatever there was to know, the doctor knew it. In a different setting, he could have persuaded the doctor to talk.

Here in this uncomfortable, unfamiliar place where he had no desire to be, Blayd had learned enough.

And when he stalked towards the city door, with a pace just short of running, Tamner wondered if he needed to talk to the Captain himself. Blayd might get to him first, request a meeting before him, but he was not as likely as Tamner to gain a swift audience.

"Cori…stay with Agnys. Do as you're told."

"Yes, Father."

With Agnys, Cori was safe. Out here, Tamner felt his son was safer than he could ever be within the nesting walls of Hebanthe Falls.

⧜*⧟

"Thanks for letting me crash out here." Ginna swept her hair from her face and scooted sideways on the lumpy sofa so Xiaodan had room to sit. He handed her a steaming cup of cinnalg tea before doing so, shrugging as he kicked a shoe sideways to avoid stepping on it.

"Not my place," the young man said, shrugging again with a glance around the crowded flat at the others on cots and mats or on the bare floor wrapped in blankets to stay warm. Whatever this place had been, whoever had once called it home, it was now a streeters' squat,

used by the young men and women she knew from past tag parties, protests and rallies. They came here at Xiaodan's invitation-only, were only permitted to take refuge here if he allowed it, but never, in the months Ginna had known him, had she seen him turn anyone away.

She had come here many times, but this was the first time she would sleep here, the first time she felt certain she could not go home.

She smiled after a sip of the soothing tea. "More yours than anyone else's." At one time, abandoned flats had been carefully monitored, registered to families, and streeters were chased out if they were found to be squatting in unauthorized shelters. Since the Coup, however, there were more empty flats than before, as the deaths and arrests during those long, violent days had thinned Hebenon's already struggling population. Those in charge now had better things to do than monitor the too numerous empty buildings, and with the streeters no longer huddled in doorways, under overpasses, in tunnels, or congregated in diners and rec facilities and other businesses, the crime and disruptions they had once caused were minimal.

The side effect to squatting was that each of these huddles of humanity allowed for the spread of messages of discontent, those who felt Captain Grainger was not going far enough in his reform efforts, who thought that more work was needed to contain the brako who had risen up to challenge the bugorra in the absence of any legitimate authority. Some thought the Founder should be reinstated. Some thought the city should be closed and everyone should move into the Outside. Radical, fringe ideologies sprang up in the conclaves of outcasts. Some thrived, some did not, but they were impossible to weed out entirely.

"Only because I found it. Needed somewhere to go after…" When he did not continue, Ginna nodded sympathetically. "I woulda brought breakfast, but I'm low on ticks and couldn't risk Maemi catching me in the cooler." Going up into his grandmother's flat had not been an option either, nor was borrowing food from Tox's station as the woman had been in for the evening. Vapors' stores had been the only option, but with so many coming and going from the kitchen, sneaking

anything out without notice, without the theft coming quickly to Maemi's attention, was not a risk Xiaodan wanted to take.

He had barely seen the women since the Coup. They were on the same side now, facing a common enemy of injustice, but after what he had done to Tox, what he believed he had done to her and to the city, returning home felt like a closed-door option.

And so he had come here, building a family with streeters and dislocated young people without families to support them, building what he had begun to call Scarecrow's Spinks, after the tiny birds kept as pets now, once said to have eaten the chaff left in the fields, when there had been fields to plow.

The disenfranchised sought to take in any morsel of freedom the Scarecrow could give them, picking at the chaff in his wake and willingly working for his favor and support.

Xiaodan had not started the movement, but he had become, when the riot began to settle in the city after the worst of the violence leeched away, one of its most outspoken supporters.

A disruption in the street, clattering and shouting, drew Xiaodan and Ginna to the window, to tentatively draw back the heavy, soiled blackout curtain that provided the squatters privacy. As the sounds woke the others in the flat, they crowded behind the pair or else clustered around the other window to see what was happening, if it was an altercation they should be involved in or if they should, instead, flee for some more secure and secretive location.

But the skirmish was taking place a half Lev below them. A cluster of Talkers, proponents and supporters of the ancient Voices of Faith and Cult of the Founder, had gathered, their shorn heads glistening wet beneath the glow of flickering multi-colored neon from the display of the nearest vindis. They threw small items, discarded popper pellets, rotting food, pebbles that occasionally found their way into the city from the Four Falls, animal bones and other things, at the three bugorra who passed on their daily rounds. Bugorra had a routine, always traveling in groups of three or more, always making their passes through their assigned Levs at more or less the same time every day.

This allowed for such ambushes, for protestors and dissidents to lay in way for the time of their passing and for criminals to wait for an hour when it was unlikely any bugorra would be about.

It could not be helped. The time it took to traverse from one side of a Lev to another, to move to the next on their route and circle it as well, meant that an estimating timetable was unavoidable.

Without more bugorra on the force, there was no means of dividing the patrols differently. Only an altercation such as this, or disrupting act of a felonious nature, or the need to come to someone's aid, could cause their route and timetable to vary.

Today, the Talkers had counted on their paths crossing.

"Take down the payaso!" some shouted.

"Banish the imposter," cried others.

"Poq Gai," roared the less religious in the crowd.

"The Founder is our hope!" added other voices, while similar slogans and slurs followed the assaulting debris to bounce harmlessly off of the protective armored clothing the bugorra wore.

Whether the words were similarly harmless was impossible to judge behind the bug-faced filts over the peacekeepers' faces. They were trained not to engage with such a crowd, unless there was an imminent threat to life or property, and so the trio did their best to ignore their detractors. Only one of the three barked, "Verpiss dich!" at a particularly antagonistic Talker, pushing him roughly aside when the Talker stepped directly into his path and attempted to yank the mask from the gorra's face.

By then, seeing who the opponents were, the Spinks had poured onto the grate for an unobstructed view of the ruckus. They were not afraid of the Talkers, and so long as they did not directly engage the gorra, they had nothing to fear from them either. When the Talkers attempted to draw the buggers into a fight, the Spinks began to toss their own collected debris assault on the Talkers. Takeaway boxes, hemplastic bottles, partially food and anything else they were able to get their hands on. Distracted by the barrage, trying to protect their

heads as they scattered, the Talkers dispersed and the bugorra continued on their way with only a glance at the Spinks.

To them, the children were just streeters.

To them, the cries of "Vivu Scarecrow!" were the idle cries of kids who could not understand the truth about the man they supported.

Xiaodan and Ginna grinned at one another as their friends cheered the break-up of violence. The bugorra had no idea.

❧*❧

"Che, boludo!" swore Tamner, dropping the scalpel, narrowly missing the sharp blade embedding in the thin surface of his lab shoe. "You shouldn't sneak up on people like that."

"You should pay more attention to your surroundings." The whooshing of the pneumatic door should have announced his arrival, but whatever the doctor had been intent on had clearly absorbed his attention. Not thinking about whether his shoes were clean enough, or if they might somehow contaminate whatever Tamner was doing, Rhyd crossed the room and stopped beside the table where a large fish of a type he was unfamiliar with lay cut open as the other man studied the creature's insides.

He did not ask what Tamner was looking for. It was none of his concern…and he doubted he would understand any explanation given.

"It's been awhile." He had seen the blonde from a distance in Marbordo several times, but he could not recall the last time they had crossed paths within the city or exchanged words.

Or rather, he had not seen Ballard in Hebenon, since the Coup.

"I need information."

Tamner retrieved the fallen scalpel and waited, assuming it was Scarecrow who needed information rather than Ballard himself. Unless someone was ill, or dying, he could not think of any information he could have that the bilger would want.

"Where's the Core?"

Releasing a breath he had not realized he was holding, he let the sound of the scalpel's clatter on the examination tray fill the void.

"I told you I don't…"

"Tell me what you do know."

"I've already told you." That had been two years ago, however, when Rhyd was swallowed in the maw of desperation, trying to find a man who had been ripped out of his life. Later, of course, Tamner had discovered that the man in question had been one of his test subjects sent Outside, but as they had never taken the names of those sent out, only assigned them case numbers corresponding to the data recording implants each received, there had been no way to give the information Ballard had wanted then. Either about Venn, or the Core.

"Tell me again."

Tamner pulled over his stool and sat, unfastening the top button of his shirt in order to rub one hand around his neck. Ballard was a much less imposing figure from the vantage point of the stool, and taking a seat felt like a form of surrender he hoped would offset any annoyance Ballard felt.

"In those days, when people were taken, where they were sent depended on a lot of things. I don't know who had the final say; I'd guess it was Founder Kemway, maybe the entire Doctet. Maybe they were judged by their usefulness. They could be sent to the Factories to work; they could be sent here for tests if their health was bad. They might be sent Outside…as you know…" He frowned and raked his hand through his short hair. He had thought this would be easier. "Some…repeat offenders, violent prisoners or those someone wanted to go away might be sent into the Core, to the mines."

"What type of mines?"

"Salt mostly…some minerals and ores…I don't know. It wasn't my department. Someone in production perhaps…or the Founder would certainly know…"

"He isn't exactly available for comment."

Head bobbing once, Tamner agreed. "No…he isn't."

Rhyd knew the internal layout of Hebanthe Falls better than most, having spent years in the tunnels and filt passages on every Lev and, more recently, the Uppers, as work teams were consolidated and the load distributed amongst those who remained alive and were capable of work after the Coup. Core suggested center, but there was nothing at the heart of Hebenon that would lend itself to the detention of many prisoners, nothing that would allow any sort of mining. And there were no tunnels or shafts drilled down into the riverbed.

In the earthen walls on the edges of the city then…but he had never, to his remembrance, come across a place that would allow for the mining of goods or the depositing of criminal manpower…or the guards and overseeing personnel required for such an undertaking.

If such a place existed, the access had to be in the Uppers and had to function on its own air, water, and waste systems. Or maybe not, and Rhyd had simply never known what he was looking at when the answers stared back at him from some familiar shaft.

He was going to have to pay more attention.

"You don't know the histories?"

The look Rhyd gave him, perplexed, intent, interested, put Tamner at ease. They were old stories, from the time of the Founding, myths now to most in Hebenon, just as Duncan Kemway was a myth to all but the most Faithful and those in the Uppers who shared that ancient lineage. To any family in the Levs, not raised under the sway of the Voices of Faith, such stories might never have been told. Even many in the Uppers doubted the reality of a place like the Core, and those who had very limited interaction with it, receiving the salt and the ores, consigning prisoners to the mines, must have been sworn to silence for Tamner had never met anyone who could tell him where the Core was…if the mines were real.

Nor had he ever asked.

What had been the need?

"Before the Founding, the Core was built. Supposed to be…what Hebanthe Falls became…but something went wrong…and it was never used." Even Tamner's knowledge of the Core myths and history

was limited, as he had never had much interest in the topic. He was no historian. He was a scientist.

"But there's a link…a passage…some way to get to it?"

"Obviously." Tamner looked thoughtful for a moment. "Judging by production…I'd guess one of the East Factories." Now that he thought about it, maybe he knew more than expected.

"Why East?" East was where the hemp entered the city, where, as far as Rhyd knew, it was processed and turned into the commodities Hebenon needed to function as a society.

"I don't know. Salt is processed there, so I assume…"

Never assume anything, Rafe, his mother had always told him. That was what science was for. Test and verify.

Until now, there had been no reason to verify data about the Core.

"Who would know?"

"Grainger. He may be the only one…if anyone knows now, it would have to be him." There were others, factory heads and production leaders who might, but to Tamner's knowledge they did not know the 'where' of their commodities, only that they asked for them and they appeared. Who did the work to get salt and ores into their hands was, to Tamner's mind, not their concern.

Rhyd did not relish another face to face with the man who, he was sure, would again try to manipulate him into accepting the offered partnership in exchange for the information Rhyd required.

If any of what the dwarf hinted at was true, Rhyd would find that offer too tempting, for the sake of finding Skelter at least, and he had no wish to be tied to the bugorra. Not even, he admitted, for Skelter.

There had to be another way.

"Perhaps I can find out for you."

It was not that Tamner felt he owed Ballard any debt. Rhyd could have killed him, but he had not. He had needed Tamner's guidance and protection that day, or thought he did. If anything, Ballard owed him for saving Venn's life from that single popper round that had been meant for Scarecrow. In exchange, however, Ballard had opened a new world, leading those from Hebanthe Falls into the Outside where,

from all appearances, they should have been for hundreds of years already. As far as Tamner was concerned, he felt they were even on the owing scale, any debts already settled many times over.

But he did not do things on a favor basis usually. Whatever Ballard wanted in the Core, Tamner judged it to be important simply because the blonde had risked coming here for information. And the scientist in Tamner was now curious about what was in there that Ballard wanted…and just where the Core really was.

"Do it. If I don't get back to you soon, get what you find to Lash."

Tamner shuffled awkwardly on the stool but nodded in agreement. Lash had been their go-between for other exchanges over the last two years, delivering oddities from the Outside that Rhyd thought Tamner might be interested in, refills for oxygen tanks when Rhyd's usual source was unavailable, medical supplies or treatments for the villagers when some bureaucratic snag prevented them from getting what they needed quickly enough. At one time, years ago, when both men had been younger, they had traveled in some of the same scientific circles but Tamner had not known Lash well. Then Lash had gotten on the bad side of the Founder, had his tongue taken and was banished to the Levs. Better than death, perhaps, better than banishment to the Core or the then believed deadly Outside world, but it was banishment all the same and Tamner had felt certain he had seen the last of the man.

He had no idea what Lash's life had been like since that day, and though they interacted sporadically now, brought together by Scarecrow, it was not enough for Tamner to say he knew the man any better than he had.

But Ballard trusted Lash, as much as he trusted anyone. And he was one of the few associates shared between them that Tamner had any contact information for. Venn was the other, but he judged by the blonde's expression and demeanor that this matter was not something he wanted Venn involved in.

"I will," he promised.

Accepting that answer, Rhyd paused when he reached the door as it opened to say, "Don't waste time. This is important."

There were no audible footsteps. The door hissed closed.

Tamner wondered if Ballard was expecting an answer today…and how in the name of fate he was supposed to make anything happen that quickly.

He had already had one audience with Grainger this morning. The Captain was unlikely to welcome a second.

❧*❧

Grainger's breath misted on the glass, attesting to the difference in temperature between the corridor where he stood and the barely lit room beyond. Bright lights agitated the fragile-looking man inside, when he was coherent enough to notice it, and so the lighting was kept as low as it could be without leaving him in complete darkness. Medical wisdom held that keeping the man's room cooler than average was better for his abnormally high metabolic rate; the Heb overdose Grainger had injected him with had not killed him, but it had significantly affected his mental acuity and his bodily functions. He either ate voraciously for days or not at all. He sweated like a man in the throes of great physical exertion with very little movement.

And he either ranted and rambled incoherently for hours or he sat stupefied in a corner of the unfurnished, padded room, drooling, glassy-eyed, and limp as overcooked algnoodles.

Grainger hated to see him like this, a reminder of what he had done, how they had gotten here, with this glass between them, how Hebenon had fallen from the heights of human accomplishment, as far as any of them knew, to daily rioting, supply shortages, a demolished population, and fear of the unknown that had opened to them.

He had not wanted this, but he did not regret his decisions. The city would heal, mankind would adapt, the unknown would become the accepted normal, and humanity would survive as they had done when a decaying Earth gave birth to the founding of Hebanthe Falls.

He only regretted the state Haythem Kemway was in now.

Heb addiction could be reversed.

But an overdose, if not treated in time, could kill a man. Or leave him so severely affected that his life became no life at all.

In those minutes after the injection, with violence spreading throughout Hebenon in Scarecrow's wake, there had been no one available to offer medical treatment. They had all evacuated into the Factories to avoid potential slaughter.

Rioters had never invaded the Uppers. Some had made it as far as the trading doors but the rest had never come further than Lev 20.

The news of the livable Outside had washed backward against the tide, stopping the flow of the masses in its tracks. With nowhere else to go, with fear of that Outside halting their progress, the bedlam eventually subsided.

Hebanthe Falls survived.

Grainger had assumed, amidst all of that, Haythem would die.

Not that killing him had been his intention.

Stubborn komeada that he was, however, the Founder tenaciously clung to life so that Grainger had been forced to lock him away, out of the public eye, instead of leaving his fate for all to see.

"Ever wish you'd died?" he muttered to the man beyond the glass who swayed side to side, arms wrapped against his body by the fettershirt, a necessity in his more manic and violent moments to prevent him from hurting himself or someone else. He was coming down from that phase now, and soon the staff would clean him, feed him, change him into unsoiled clothes.

There was never any telling how long this depressive phase would last. Such periods of near motionless silence typically lasted longer than the violent ones, but there was no predictability to it.

If he was ever going to allow Neoma Kemway to see her husband, this was as good a time as any.

Allowing such a visit, however, was likely to open a host of problems Grainger was not prepared to manage. The public knowledge of the Founder being alive, when many believed he was

dead, was but one of them. There would be questions about how he had ended up in this condition, perhaps the request for an inquiry that Grainger could not grant, which would, in turn, lead to further protests from the adherents to the Cult of the Founder.

Claiming ignorance, denying Neoma's request that had come to him third hand through her bodyguard, through Tamner, and finally to Grainger, now that she had broken her months of silence in the wake of her return from quarantine, would have much the same results.

Six of one, half dozen of the other.

Killing the man, putting him out of his misery, was another option. It would, perhaps, be the kindest thing. It would be in Grainger's best interest, certainly, if it left no trace of the Founder to be discovered.

But he could not do it. Not without provocation. Not in cold blood.

No matter how sick the daily ritual of visiting the man made him.

"Not today," he muttered aloud, hand to the window, leaving his palm print in the evaporative mist formed by his breath on the glass. "Get some sleep, Haythem. You're going to need it."

In order to make this decision with a clear head, so did he.

❧*❧

Setting aside the meeting at Vapors in favor of a covert search at the outer edges of the lowest floors of the Uppers and the topmost of the Levs where he knew the city met the stone walls of earth on the eastern and western edges had not been his best decision. After leaving Tamner, it had made sense that a passage into an underground bunker would be nearest the surface levels, so that seemed the wisest place for Rhyd to begin looking for an entrance into the yet unproven Core.

It might take him days to search every Lev, unless he used a portion of the numerous free days he had accumulated from work over the years, but he knew they were days Skelter might not have. He could not wait a few more hours to meet with the dwarf.

He had to start now.

His search was delayed long enough to don his alter ego.

Besides, the dwarf had not told him a time to meet. If it was important enough to him, Rhyd figured he would wait.

Rhyd's hunt was important too.

Nothing was found to lend itself to a passage out of the city into any underground bunker, no corridor or tracks or lift that might allow for extracted ores to be moved or to allow people to pass into, or out of, such a place.

Lower then. Or else in the Factories, as Tamner suggested.

Getting into the Factories would be more difficult than anything Rhyd had ever attempted, but he might not have any other choice.

A beep in his earpiece, a warning that the oxygen level in his assist tank was running low, cut his hunt short, as did the realization that he had been on the prowl longer than intended and that the dwarf might not wait for him indefinitely. As the tank had been full when he suited up, it meant a leak in the system that he was going to need to repair tonight if he wanted to go out again tomorrow.

That, in turn, would mean missed sleep before his shift, which certainly would not be the first time he had pulled an all-nighter, or else a delay in his extracurricular activities tomorrow. Unless he gave the tank and gear to Tox to fix. She was his best option; having helped design and build his equipment, he wagered it would take her less time to find and repair a leak then it would take Rhyd to do it himself.

Do that, he mused as he began his descent through the tunnel system. Go to Tox and he would be on hand to meet with that dwarf.

There was still time for that, he hoped. He was not used to doing these things on someone else's schedule.

Tox's kesfek stall, still her home, still her livelihood, even after the hell the Crows and Kemway had put her through, was but a few doors away from Vapors. Rhyd was not surprised she had gone back to that life; most of Hebenon's residents had done so after the Coup. Fear, disbelief, and distrust of the bugorra under Grainger's command had kept them here where the world was familiar, and if not safe, it was at least a familiar sort of danger compared to what was Outside.

Tox was stronger than she looked. Rhyd had always known that. Exposed to the Outside by her efforts to help Rhyd that night, she began to conduct business in Marbordo as well, to be near her half-brother Venn now that he had returned to them, but her heart, her life was still in Hebenon. She, like so many others, was not yet ready to turn her back on the past and embrace the changes, but she was eager to benefit from exchanging inside products for outside ones.

Besides, being a kesfek was the life she knew and her being here, doing what she did, meant support for Scarecrow. Having her and Maemi and Zara to keep an eye on Rhyd when he insisted on returning to Hebenon night after night was the only reason Venn had not forbidden Rhyd's double life.

Rhyd did not, however, expect Venn's support to last much longer. The signs of cracking grew deeper every day.

With Zara's help, extra security units and protective traps were installed in Tox's backroom flat, her hidden workroom, her stall, after the raid the Crows had sanctioned against her, when Xiaodan had been less world-wise, to alert her to unwelcome visitors. Grainger, as an apology for the tortures the Founder had inflicted, the damages done to her shop and home, made certain that no one would trouble her again. She had been cleared of all suspicion about being the Scarecrow, about being connected to him, and because Grainger alone knew the truth, taking her and Rhyd off the watch list, along with a host of other names so as not to single out Rhyd's identity, meant that certain locations…Tox's home and work, Vapors, and Rhyd's flat, were off-limits to the bugorra.

That did not mean, Rhyd knew, as he emerged from the shaft onto the vindi level where Vapors was, that they were safe. Someone was bound to investigate every name on that cleared list, to connect the dots between Grainger's orders and the Scarecrow. Rhyd never assumed he was safe.

Which was why, as he closed the shaft grate behind him, he knew he was not alone, forms in the shadows, long-beaked figures clustered beneath the stutter of a red neon shoeman's sign. His enhanced

mechanical hearing detected them there before he emerged, but as there were many vindis here, people seeking nessies was to be expected. Even their equally mechanical breathing was not an accurate identifier of their nature, as there were others, like Rhyd who required breathing assistance in the perpetually damp environment in which they lived. They could be bugorra on patrol.

Or they could be, as he discovered from the hidden place where he hesitated long enough to investigate the situation, brako.

Nine in total, with another three individuals inside the shoeman's vindi. The raised voices suggested a shakedown, a demand for protection payment or favors owed from someone who had not paid up as expected. No trace of bugorra nearby, no stray shoppers to be hurt if it came to a fight, only the brako and the other vindi operators assigned to this dead-end passage of this particular level.

Nine or ten brako was a suitable risk. Twelve was a stretch, but doable. Something crashed, someone shouted, and Scarecrow reacted.

The dwarf would have to wait a little longer.

They did not know he was there. Crows masks were designed for protection, for breathing assistance, but had fewer of the enhancements Scarecrow's mask and hood had built into it. The brako had no need for such things, relying as they did on brute bullying, intimidation, and the weaponry stolen from Hebenon's law enforcers. The well-aimed throw of one of his two thumpers struck one of the bird-faced brako in the head, ricocheted left, and caught a second across the throat. The first fell, unconscious, the second dropped gasping for air, as the thumper returned to Scarecrow's hand. In those few seconds of surprise, as they turned to meet the unexpected assault, Scarecrow sprang from the darkness to knock a mask off a third, and with a low kick put another onto his back on the wet metal grating. The act took neither the third or fourth out of the fight but it did delay their entry into it long enough for Scarecrow to swing around an iron pole and plant a boot into the chest of the fifth, propelling the fellow against the nearest wall with enough force to stun him.

Three out of commission. With the breather low on oxygen, this was a fight Scarecrow could not endure for long. That knowledge, however, did not keep him from trying. But two who were inside the vindi emerged into the street, one unmasked, short and scruffy with bloody fists that suggested he had been the source of the violence inside. The other was an imposing figure, wearing the filt mask of a fellow bilger…or else equipped with a stolen or traded filt unit. Around his bicep, a yellow cloth was tied, the same as it had been around the arm of the man who had been killed, or at least blinded, during the Scarecrow's last fight.

Not at Scarecrow's hand, but as the other armed lifted and pointed directly at the lone vigi who dared to take on so many, he growled in a low, garbled, angry voice, "You're mine," that told Scarecrow he was being held responsible for that incident.

He had heard the prodcast reports, highly edited and censored though they were. The injured man was believed to be the brother of the brako boss.

It meant one thing.

Vanderwall.

He knew the name. Almost everyone in the Levs did. A name to be feared, a name that had risen to prominence after the Coup, as the brako fought for control of Hebenon. But Zara's hacks of the city data stores revealed no one by that name, no one with even a variant of that name, and as the man had others do most of his work for him, no one had yet put a face to the moniker. No one had, to Scarecrow's knowledge, faced the brako boss in the city's streets…until now.

The other six individuals drew back to the street edges. There was no stealth, no slow stalking steps or menacing actions. Only three long strides to close the gap between them, and then the brako swung his big fisted arm. Scarecrow saw it coming. He ducked the blow, but the larger man, anticipating that, caught him with the other fist with a blow that threw Scarecrow sideways against the handrail of the nearest stairs. The composition of his suit absorbed the majority of the impact and he barely managed to scramble to his feet away from the following

blow that would have struck him in the head. From the dent Vanderwall's fist left in the railing, Scarecrow knew the hit would have rendered him unconscious, and in turn dead.

Such strength was not normal. A weighter or wrestler then, as well as a bilger. Maybe one of those who hauled nets from the river on Lev 1 to clean them of caught fish, debris, and the occasional corpse of man or beast. Such a job might also lend itself to a filt mask.

A man who favored his left hand. A man who, when Scarecrow delivered several rabbit punches to the man's stomach and then lower back as he danced around him, moved with an uneven gate, a leg injury perhaps or one leg slightly shorter than the other. A man who fought hard but sounded just as winded as Scarecrow felt without his oxygen.

Also breathing impaired then…or else a man not accustomed to exertion and combat despite his size and strength.

The screech of a bugorra wailer announced the approaching law-keepers and Scarecrow assumed one of the vindi owners had called in the altercation. The distraction was enough to draw Scarecrow's focus for the few seconds it took Vanderwall to grab hold of the breather hose and yank hard enough to dislodge it from the mask. The force of the dislodging again threw Scarecrow off-balance, through the open service window of the shoeman's vindi, against the work table with its scraps of sewing materials, fabrics, and needles. The collection scattered in every direction.

"I'm sorry…so sorry," the shoeman begged, a sprite of a man bloody from the beating the brako had given who was, it seemed as he tried to help Scarecrow to his feet, grateful for his savior's arrival.

On the passage outside, the brako began to scatter as the bugorra came closer. Scarecrow's gaze met Vanderwall's through the vindi window, both pairs of eyes hidden behind the tinted eyepieces of their masked hoods. Again Vanderwall pointed at him.

A threat. A promise.

"Through here…come. Come." The shoeman knew the bugorra wanted the Scarecrow as much as they wanted the brako, knew they did not respect or approve of a man who often did their job better than

they did. He pulled Scarecrow through a curtain of plastic beads that clattered as they scurried, as the buggers now pursued the fleeing brako into the alleys and up, or down, to the Levs above and below.

One stayed to call a pick up for the unconscious brako left behind.

A few more arrests. A distraction that let Scarecrow escape to safety through a back door to an unlit Lev passage snaking between living flats of sleeping families. Scarecrow limped towards home, wheezing, gasping.

The dwarf would have to wait.

❧CHAPTER 6❧

Before the world ended, when mankind was scrambling for solutions to avoid the poisoned world they had created, before war had decimated the continents and left people with fewer options for survival, six sites were chosen worldwide, six sites where water with the adequate requirements flowed in sufficient force to serve humanities purpose. Duncan Kemway and the Kemway Conglomerate carefully designed each fall city to house the maximum number of people each water source could sustain, knowing as they did so that the very act of saving so many would inevitably condemn millions of others to a long, agonizing death in a world barely fit for survival.

Some tried their luck off-world. Colonies on the moon, on Mars, and long-distance colonization crafts had gone into the sky and never returned. Most did not have the resources, money, skill, or luck to be included in those journeys. What became of them, no one knew. In the decades since, with no word sent back, it was assumed they had died.

Or that tales of that exodus were as much myths as many others.

Meanwhile, as the fall cities were designed and built, underground bunkers were constructed near to each, bunkers intended to house the scientists, the researchers, the leaders required for this new phase of mankind's existence. The cities would house everyone else, with the uppermost levels providing the hubs of education, entertainment, medical facilities, and peacekeeping units.

The bunkers, completed first, were staffed, up and running, connected to the fall cities through multiple passages. Once the cities were built, and those chosen to live in them were brought inside, the doors to the outside world were sealed.

Humanity was cut off from what had once been.

For a time, there had been communication, with those outside, with the other fall cities scattered across the globe. But as the decades past, little by little those forms of communication failed as equipment broke down and the contaminated world devoured civilization.

As far as anyone living in Hebanthe Falls knew, they were alone.

The world inside the city in the Four Falls, and the bunker called the Core, began to change.

Earthquakes and accidents blocked all but one passage between them, and the Core, the backup built in case the city failed, began to experience a host of technical difficulties of its own. The collapse of passages meant the breaking and malfunctions of water lines and air and waste filtration units. Those residing in the Core moved into the Uppers, forcing some of those living there to relocate below. The move had not been a bitter one. Those people in the Core were needed if the city was to continue, and so the change was gladly accepted as one of necessity. It led to a redesign and repurposing of units meant for the public into lodging, meant that housing in the topmost Levs had to be converted into the sports complex and entertainment facilities that were displaced. People shifted, life adjusted.

When the collapse of another passage left only the Factory corridor open, it was decided to abandon the Core.

For decades the Core remained empty, abandoned except by those who mined the surrounding earth for salt and other minerals and metal ores it contained. But as history was wont to do, times changed. The flow of workers from the Levs through the Uppers to the mines and factories became an irritant to those living in the Uppers, and an eyesore to those privileged enough to live in those pristine white halls, away from the perpetual damp and dark of the Levs. Another way was discussed and debated, until at last a solution was agreed upon.

Prisoners and criminals, the undesirables and the troublemakers, would be sent to the factories, housed there, to serve as a perpetual workforce. Factory workers at least had privileges, better food, better living conditions, the possibility of returning to homes and families on retirement or after a predetermined number of years of service. Soon,

those factory employees became self-perpetuating and, for the most part, it was unnecessary to sentence many others there.

The worst infractors, however, were sent into the Core, into the mines. Once there, there was no getting out.

Most in the Uppers eventually stopped asking questions about where the offenders went, or who produced the goods from the Factories and ancient mines. Things just were. The Core was overlooked, grew into a myth as forgotten places tended to do, and only the Founder and two others were ever permitted to know the Passcodes required to open the door into the Core.

The Founder. The Head of Production. And the acting Captain of law enforcement.

Those inside became as invisible as the place itself.

Now, however, thought Skelter as he continued to take stock of the precious stores they had on hand with which he might be able to fashion weapons and explosives, that was about to change. He refused to remain trapped here until the Spades claimed his last heartbeat. He had a life outside these walls that he was determined to reclaim.

But it was not going to be an easy thing to accomplish.

He still was not quite sure how he had gotten here. He remembered the injector, the sting of the dart beneath his eye, the pelting of popper pellets. He remembered falling, and the impact against several metal railings as he fell. And he remembered the water.

He had been certain he would die. Nearly all those who fell into the river were dragged into the nets by the fierce current, pummeled to death by debris or drowned. Unable to swim due to the fractures and breaks sustained in his fall, surviving had been an unlikely option.

And yet fate had other plans for Ivan Furrell, the ever-resourceful kaheao and svodnik known to most as Skelter.

His battered body had been fished up through the long, narrow well shaft that had once supplied water to the Core, fished out by Arturo Colyx and nursed to health by his adopted daughter Otta Quell and the dwarf Enoch. Skelter was the only man ever to have entered

the Core that way, the only one living in the Core now who had not been sentenced here by the whim of the Founder.

And after a lengthy recovery that left him with a metal pipe as a walking stick and the patch that protected the eye which was never quite right after that injection of Heb into his bloodstream, Skelter had set about doing within the Core what he had done in Hebanthe Falls.

Learn everything, know everyone's business, manage supplies, distribute goods, obtain that which was difficult to obtain…

…always at a price.

Enoch had proven invaluable in that regard, for the dwarf had a secret that not one other person, other than Skelter, and now Otta and Colyx, knew.

With Colyx and Otta as his self-proclaimed bodyguards, it had not taken Skelter long to establish some degree of order in the Core. And he had used the Club of Spades to do it.

But there were those who preferred a return to chaos, and his time in the Club had finally run its course. It had been a gamble that he could run that gauntlet long enough to find his way out. Now he had a plan, but if he could not get what he needed from outside, if he could not get Scarecrow's help, he was going to have to do it all himself.

Or else run out of time and be forced to end his life as the rules of the Club demanded. He refused to take the coward's way out and have someone else do the deed for him.

If he was going to die, it was going to be at his own hand…or in the effort to be free of this dreary place.

If what Enoch said was true, they might not have the advantage of numbers and strength in the Core, but they had enough brutes to fight their way through the officers now called bugorra if they had to. At least some of them were likely to survive. Most imprisoned here were cocky enough, brave enough, or stupid enough, to willingly take that chance. Forgotten as they were, left to starve and die now that it seemed no one on the outside would send anything more in, beyond what Enoch could smuggle during his covert excursions, the people of the Core were angry enough to take any risk necessary. If they used

the element of surprise in their favor, they would only have a gaggle of factory workers to contend with. Some of them might die, but better that then to succumb to the slow ravages of disease and starvation.

Skelter, however, would not be at the forefront of that fight. He had another plan, another option, that might only work if Enoch could reach Ballard and bring the Scarecrow into play. But Enoch's late-night, empty-handed return without Ballard's promise was a grim reminder that there might not be another choice. Going out the front door might be Skelter's only play.

But he still had alternatives up his sleeves, other cards to throw down, others he could reach out to in the city in the Four Falls. He did not want to risk any of them, because he did not want anyone hurt. Only Ballard had what it might take to survive this fight.

If it came to it, Zara just might be his best chance. Enoch would try again, and if he could not impress on Rhyd the direness of the situation, Zara it would be.

But Skelter could not be certain she would forgive him for taking so long to let her know he was alive.

❧Chapter 7❧

It was the sting of antiseptic that brought Rhyd to conscious awareness of the hiss of oxygen and the faint tumble of running water in the kitchen sink. He did not remember the details of making it home after the fight, but what images his foggy brain did dredge up did not include removing the protective gear that was nowhere within visual range when his eyes cracked open to the pale light of the ever-glowing alglamp near the front door. Zara knelt on the floor between his knees, swabbing the bloody, darkening of a bruised abrasion across the front of his shoulder, her expression pensive. A sideways glance revealed Tox in the kitchen. Rhyd could not see what she was doing, but the gurgle of water pushing through tubing suggested she was testing his filt to find the leak in the oxygen system where Vanderwall had pulled the hose free.

Hopefully, she would find the other leak as well. He did not need to point out the mechanical failure. He trusted she would find it.

"You don't remember calling her, do you?" asked Zara as she pressed a bandage into place. The other injuries Rhyd could see had already been cleaned and treated, and those internal ones he could feel were not the sort that Zara, or anyone other than a doctor, could mend.

"No." He shifted, straightened, and rose with a groan when Zara slid away, his muscles complaining about the abuse he subjected them to. "Is it…?"

"You've been out for a few hours, but there's time before shift," replied Tox from the kitchen. Her tone suggested that going on shift would be inadvisable, but she did not say so. "What the cazz did you do to this thing for crucksake?"

"Vanderwall."

Tox emerged from the kitchen, eyes wide with disbelief. "You've seen him?"

Rhyd nudged past, took the bottle of Zaolei from the cabinet, and took a long drink without a glass. "Not his face…but yeah."

"I'd heard on the prod that the buggers nearly caught him last night. You were there?"

Another swallow, a nod of his head, and then a swipe of the back of his hand over his lips before the bottle was sealed and returned to the shelf. "Wasn't intentional."

"No one sees Vanderwall intentionally." Even Tox, with her variety of clients, had yet to make the man, as far as she knew, nor had anyone she had ever met. If they had, they weren't talking.

"Think he's a bilger…or something close…or a netter from Lev 1. He had a bilger filt…and his size…his strength…"

"Makes sense." Those from Lev 1 tended to be a surly, standoffish lot, a keep to themselves crew who barely mingled with anyone else. It was an ideal place for the brako to thrive.

"Could you I.D. his voice?"

"Too filtered…but maybe." With the right software, and Zara's access to the sometimes spotty Echo Archives that had not been lost with the damaged equipment during the Coup, they might be able to track the brako boss by voice, but even limiting the search to recordings of bilgers, heizers, and other shaft workers or the residents of Lev 1 would take an excruciatingly long time. Right now, Rhyd had more important things to do.

"Gives me a place to start," Zara began, gathering the scattered medical supplies from Rhyd's kit while he rummaged through the icebox for anything worth eating. His stomach wanted something more substantial than whiskey, so he settled on his staple of cheese and boiled eggs.

"Gonna take this with me," said Tox as she tucked the mask and gear into her duffle. "Need my things to patch it up. Need it tonight?"

Though he shrugged, not having given thought to what might come after his shift, Rhyd answered, "I've got others." After the Coup

and confiscation of the gear found in Tox's workshop, it had reinforced the importance of having additional equipment stashed throughout the Levs in places no one else knew about. If he decided he needed it, he could retrieve one of the backups.

"You need to come by Vapors…someone you need to meet."

Brow cocked, Rhyd asked, "You know the dwarf, Zar?" It had to be the dwarf…and it would not surprise him if she knew him. Skelter had been a true kaheao, a man with business hands in all sorts of endeavors, with contacts both legal and not, throughout Hebenon. Zara, in turn, by her association with him and her career as a dancer in Vapors, had known many people too, and often assisted Skelter with things like forged passcards, computer records, hacking jobs and the building of electronic and computerized devices.

Tox and Maemi likewise knew a variety of the city's residents. It was Rhyd, his work as a bilger keeping him in the shafts, who was isolated from the public.

He had become more isolated when Venn had Vanished, and to be honest, he preferred it that way.

"Enoch waited as long as he could."

Rhyd scowled. He could tell when Zara was being evasive, when she knew something she did not want to tell him, or knew something she thought it best he heard from someone else's mouth. She did not like to be the bearer of bad news, and so he wagered that it was bad news this Enoch wanted to share.

Had he told her Skelter was alive? Did she know?

Or was it too late? Had Rhyd waited too long?

"Did he tell you what he wants?" He wondered if he was supposed to be the one to tell her.

She shook her head as she followed Tox out the front door. "Just that he was expecting you. But that's not…just come to Vapors after shift. They'll be there."

"They?"

"Just be there, Rhyd," Zara said over her shoulder. "If Enoch says it's important, it is."

To Rhyd, that did not sound particularly compelling or reassuring. But if Zara wanted this meeting as much as the dwarf did, Rhyd knew he had to be there.

He could not fail Skelter the way he had failed Venn.

❧*❧

"Don't even think they tried," snorted Ginna, kicking over the recycle box and scattering its contents and the water accumulated at the bottom across the side alley between the vindis of this short, dead-end run. She made no effort to keep her voice low, but another girl with pink-dyed dreads clamped her hand over Ginna's mouth in response to the harsh stares of the other four in their group.

No one, not the vindi operators, not the shoeman repairing the neon sign damaged in the previous night's fight, not the patrolling bugorra who passed on the platform, paid the streeters any heed.

Streeters were too commonplace to be chased away.

There was nowhere else for them to go.

This was the place. They all knew it from the prodcasts viewable on Echos throughout the Levs, inside businesses or on the external walls so passersby never missed important bits of news. The Founder had installed the first public Echos so long ago for propaganda purposes that they were now as much a part of Hebenon's landscape as was the constant roar of the Four Falls.

This was the place the bugorra had let the brako boss get away.

"They don't want him caught," whispered another. "Better to keep us 'fraid and 'pendent on 'em for protection."

"Scarecrow's the only one who'll stop him."

Heads bobbed in agreement with Xiaodan's statement.

"Then we need to pick up the pace, find where the brako meet, where he is, let Scarecrow know," growled Ginna, her voice quieter as she pushed the hushing hand from her mouth.

"We need to recruit. Isn't enough of us to cover all the Levs."

"And we need to let the bugorra know we're on to them…"

"So we tag."

"Where?"

"Everywhere." Typically, they tagged in groups, safety in numbers, but there was too much city to cover, too many places to leave their marks where the SCAMs could see and report their work to Grainger and the bugorra who were not, in the Spinks' eyes, doing enough to protect the people. "Get the word out; we meet this evening at the Lizard Lounge for assignments…to share supplies…and we'll pick a time and go out in twos and threes…hit everywhere on this Lev." Of late, this Lev seemed to be the brako's focus of attention, so it made sense to Xiaodan to draw the bugorra's attention here.

And it made sense to put the Lev-wide call to the Scarecrow as well. He would see their call and would answer it. Somehow he would stop the brako boss and end their oppression.

It was just going to take time…and help from the Spinks.

Even Scarecrow could not do this alone.

❧*❧

"You got everything?"

It was not so uncommon a place to meet, as deks were a popular means of entertainment, and though often enjoyed alone, it was normal for friends and family to participate in a group dek experience as well. The three-dimensional holographic experience projected into specifically designed pod rooms was the nearest anyone in Hebanthe Falls had come to experiences like sunshine, a walk in the forest or park, a day at the beach, a glimpse at a starlit sky or climbing a mountain peak, for centuries. Auditory and olfactory stimuli were included, at extra cost, the sounds of birds and animals, ocean waves, the wind in the trees…or as close as anyone could get to imagining what those things must sound and smell like, all experiences lacking within the stagnant, claustrophobic world of Hebenon.

How real it was, most did not know; without real-world experience to compare it too, but it was infinitely better than the neon-lit wet gloom in which they spent their lives.

Enoch had yet to venture out amongst the parah to judge the likeness, the reality, of the dek experience to the actual thing. He had not even made it to the Uppers to view the Outside through the alumaglass windows. Curiosity had thus far not compelled him. The dek was as close as he would come, a preferable experience when he wanted to shed the seediness of the Levs.

Though the Hub recorded data about the most often used programs and those used the longest in an effort to create programs the public wanted, they did not, they claimed, store the identities of the users, allowing a degree of anonymity to an individual's private interests.

Enoch was not that naïve. He knew there were those who used dekking as a substitution for the old world pursuits of hunting, auto racing, flying and the like, and more than a few of those people programmed in humans as their prey. Safer than actual murder, but Enoch personally knew of one case where the murder of three elderly men was directly traced back to a dekker…who frequently used such a program for practice, or as a substitute for the real thing. Enoch doubted the killer would have been caught without a dekking record.

As he was unwilling to be tracked in such a way, he resorted to visiting with passcards swiped from people in the streets, in clubs, or shopping at vindis, cards he then disposed of where someone else could later find it and return it to its owner minus the ticks it required for a dek session.

Today, however, they were here under the passcard of the man he was meeting in this garden park bench setting. Long-necked white birds floated like angels across the glassy surface of their iris-encircled pool, clouds against a royal blue, rippling sky.

He was glad Jaron had picked this program. He needed peaceful today. And though he expected the younger man to have been here ahead of him, he had sat in this tranquil place for a full fifteen minutes before Joran's arrival.

Another five minutes and the session would expire.

Enoch did not have a passcard on him to request more time. He did not know if Jaron would or not.

"Not all of it," the other man sighed, the stilted, digital voice filtered through the implant at the hollow of his throat, words spoken without lips or mouth moving. He handed the canvas pack slung over his shoulder to the seated man and dropped onto the bench beside him.

"Jaron…"

"I know. I know. But he's getting suspicious…not of me but of the missing nessies. And some of it…" He shook his head, dark curls swinging as he did so. "Not exactly easy to get…or transport…you know. I can't just walk in here with a case of Zaolei and a tooler. I'll have both at the drop…but some's going to take more time."

Enoch grunted and for a few moments they watched the silent birds in their watery ballet. The three-minute warning buzzer on the timer went off, flashing a crimson tint over the dek image, lending a bloody hue to the birds that made Enoch frown.

"You'll come tonight though? You'll be there? Seven?"

"I don't know. I don't know if I can get away."

"You have to be there. You two meeting is the only way to make this work."

Enoch's insistence made Jaron's brow furrow. "Make what work?" he asked as they got to their feet and he assisted Enoch with adjusting the heavy pack on his back. He had put as much of what Enoch had requested into it as he could, not an easy burden for most due to its bulk and weight.

Enoch barely seemed to notice.

The one-minute buzzer to the countdown began and the dwarf still had not answered his question. "Enoch…"

"Just be there. Vapors. Seven."

The bench they had been seated on vanished, as did the foliage, the blue sky, the swans on the pond. The door of the dek pod opened.

"Who do you want me to meet?" And why.

There was no response as they passed into the waiting room and then onto the walkway in the cold outdoors. A fire burned in a metal waste container on the opposite walkway and the heavy aroma of oregano and garlic belched with the steam from the nearby Italian eatery. The smells made Enoch's belly growl, but there was no time to enjoy such pleasures.

Skelter was expecting him, and he had to be fast about the delivery if he was to make it to Vapors on time.

"Thought you trust me."

"It's not that…you know it's not."

It was the man Jaron was in close proximity too that Enoch did not trust, the man once in the Founder's pocket. Anything connected to that family was suspect, and though he knew why Jaron was there, he worried about the corrupting influence of that sort of power.

He knew firsthand how it could destroy a life.

He pulled his coat collar around his neck and looked up and down the path. No one was near. The screen on the nearby SCAM was black, the power light flashing orange as the unit rested in dormant mode.

They were safe enough.

Still, he lowered his head so that there was no chance the SCAM might be able to run a facial recognition algorithm or might be able to read his words from the movement of his mouth.

"Scarecrow," he admitted, choosing to trust Jaron with this as he trusted him with so much else. "I want you to meet Scarecrow."

He hurried away, leaving Jaron with his hands in his pockets, staring after him, hoping he had not just made the biggest mistake in his life. Some risks were worth taking. He hoped this was one of them.

If not, he might soon be dead.

❧*❧

"So everything in Marbordo is good?"

Tamner nodded, still uncomfortable in his role as liaison between Grainger and the Nau and the parah in the village. Though others were

gradually venturing out of the city to form lives, or at least connections, outside of Hebenon, mostly those with an interest in agriculture and animal husbandry or the sciences, none thus far had a suitably easy relationship with the parah. There was Venn, of course, and others sent out as test subjects over the years, but most of those seventeen individuals were warier and reluctant to interact with the city's leadership then the parah themselves were. And there was Ballard, but Tamner was not the only one to know that the bilger would never fit into such a role. He was no ambassador or bureaucrat.

He lived a double life, maybe a triple one as he struggled between existence in Marbordo, his life as a bilger inside, and the one behind the vigi's mask. Adding diplomat was a layer Ballard could never adequately maintain.

Tamner spent as much time inside as out, as a doctor and acquaintance of Venn's and Ballard's, and even a friend of sorts of the child Agnys, whom he had protected as best he could and helped to free. That enabled him to establish trust with the parah that most from the city did not have. Whether he was the best, most qualified choice for ambassador, he was the person chosen by both the parah and Grainger to speak between them.

"Like I said, no problems. Soon as the ground thaws a little more, spring planting will begin. Everyone's healthy, villagers, prossers and crossers…and we've seen no rise of new health issues." After the plague in the Factories that had killed so many, it had become imperative to test everything, water, air, food, building materials and decorative ones, to do their best to see that necessary inoculations were available and utilized for both populations. Isolation from the world had lowered the resistance to some ailments and raised it for others inside the city, and outside, the worldly exposure and lack of it to generations of vaccines and the genetic shifts of a population crammed into a dark, wet, urban environment had done the same. Unfamiliar ailments cropped up all the time, but for the last few weeks, there had been nothing new or unexpected on Tamner's radar.

Except for Rhyd's inquiries about the Core.

"Good. That's good."

The council table was empty, the last of the Nau having shuffled out minutes ago after Grainger asked Tamner to stay behind. His question about Marbordo had been a redundant one, as Tamner had made his statistical report to the Nau as was established custom for each of the nine. Provide an update about the areas of city welfare and business they headed, discuss problems they faced, make requests or recommendations and work out any issues that needed correcting.

Thus far, other than the shortage of salt and minerals and ores created by the closure of the mines, the biggest problems in Hebanthe Falls came from the decreased population and the largely unchecked disruptions caused by the brako. No matter how many arrests were made, the brako continued to crop up and until Vanderwall was contained, it was unlikely that would change.

Grainger was doing his utmost to stem that anarchy, but without the help of reluctant Nau members whom he believed had some notion of the man's identity and where he could be found, or without recruiting the Scarecrow to the cause, apprehending the brako boss was going to be a slow, uncertain process. But it would happen.

Grainger was confident of it.

"That's not why you asked me to stay."

"Do you think we can stabilize Haythem…long enough for…"

"Neoma's reached out to you too." Grainger studied Tamner with a puzzled expression. "One of her people grilled me on where they could find him…wanted to know if he's alive, if she could see him. I didn't tell them anything, referred them to you…"

An annoyed grunt accompanied Grainger's settling against the back of his chair and folding his arms over his chest. He appreciated a man following directions when he had instructed that no one who knew the truth was to reveal the Founder's fate or whereabouts. Part of him, however, wished that someone else was responsible for the decision placed before him.

"Whatever they think they know…if I continue to deny that he's alive, or continue to disallow her to see him, she'll use it against me. I've never been a very good liar."

Only at the end had he hidden anything from Kemway, and he suspected the only reason Kemway had not noticed was because he had been preoccupied with capturing Scarecrow, finding the parah child, and hiding the truth about the Outside from the public. From what Grainger knew of Neoma, she was more cunning than her husband. If he saw her face to face, Grainger doubted he would be unable to satisfactorily hide the truth from her.

"And if she sees him as he is…in a stupor or rage…she'll use that too." It was what Tamner would do if he was in a position to need it.

"Can we explain his condition without referring to Heb?"

"Head injury…psychosis due to the events that cost him his position, family and the city. Either might be enough to explain this. By now there's no trace in his body…no indication he was injected."

An astute doctor might question either diagnosis, might make note of all the typical markers of a Heb overdose, but no amount of tests could prove that to be the cause. A head scan might rule out brain trauma, but after two years, an overdose diagnosis would be a guess.

No diagnosis would prove it was not, either. Suspicion would taint Haythem's condition in whatever direction someone wanted to skew it, even to Kemway being kept drugged to produce his state and keep him under control.

"Maybe before you allow her to see him…if you intend to do so, you make a public admission of his condition. Chop the head off the snake before it grows…"

"And lend credence to the Voices who have proclaimed he's alive all along." Grainger's sigh, drawn-out and painful sounding, was cut off by his sudden straightening in his chair, his eyes on the conference room door where Tamner caught movement out of the corner of his eye. He did not see who it had been, but by Grainger's abrupt rise from his seat, Tamner could guess.

"Jaron…wait."

His guess proved accurate.

The curly-haired younger man reappeared, his expression slightly sheepish or perhaps cornered, a little like a child caught sneaking home when they should not have been out. It was a look Tamner had seen on Cori more than once when the boy insisted on sneaking Outside to spend time with Agnys and the other parah children instead of doing his schoolwork.

"Ollie…hey…I didn't want to interrupt…"

"You're not. We're finished…aren't we, Doctor?"

Since remaining at the end of the Nau meeting had not been his idea, Tamner was happy to be free of this room. He had given the Captain the only input he had regarding the Founder. If the man needed more information before making his decision, Tamner was sure he would seek it later.

"Yes, we are." He pushed back from the table with a leisurely stretch, not wanting to appear in a hurry or reveal any more of his discomfort with the previous conversation than Grainger was already aware of. "I've got some tests to finish. Good day, Jaron."

"Good day, Doctor." Jaron stepped aside to allow Tamner to pass but watched him go rather than look at Grainger. He had already formulated his excuse for being in the Levs, should the question arise, and even though it was true to a degree, dekking and making vindi purchases…and Grainger never dug too deeply into his personal business, there was always a chance he would not be believed.

"It's good to see you." Stopping behind Jaron, his hands on the smaller man's waist, Grainger pressed his nose and mouth to the top of his head and breathed the familiar, comforting scent.

Such a relationship was still new to him, as he had not been in any relationship longer than a few weeks before the Coup…and he had, before meeting Zara, never considered himself open to a relationship with another man. It had never been a matter of repulsion; such things were commonplace and accepted throughout Hebenon as long as those who could do so contributed to a steady population. Such an attraction

had simply never come up for Grainger…until he met Zara…and more recently Jaron Rei.

He allowed no thought to any notion of permanence or a future with Jaron. Nor had he ever asked Jaron what his desires were. Grainger lived in the moment, with the secret, barely acknowledged assumption that the other man would always be in his life now that he had entered it.

Jaron chuckled, the sound peculiar due to the electronic filtering, but it was no different than any other time Grainger heard it. There was no reason to question it.

Kemway had robbed Jaron of his true voice. Grainger felt some deep-seated desire to give him something in exchange. He had offered the smaller man a return to the labs where he had once worked, but Jaron refused, preferring instead to continue his job as a data archivist in the Levs rather than return to the world that had spurned him or take up a life of kept leisure in the suite of rooms that had once belonged to the Kemways. While Grainger felt that such work was beneath a man of Jaron's intelligence, it was honest work and it kept Jaron immersed in the world he had been part of for more than ten years.

That immersion, that position, was the primary reason he never asked where Jaron went when he left him Duty was duty, friends were friends, and they both had theirs.

"It's only been three hours…and you've been busy."

"I have been…but I'm not anymore. Come up with me…have a drink."

"I should get back."

"So soon?"

Grainger scowled and drew back, turning Jaron to see his face. It was not suspicion in his eyes, but it was something just as disturbing in its desperation. The man had something on his mind, and while a drink typically led to other things, had become a code word for the only intimacy the Captain allowed himself, it might also be an opportunity to glean morsels of information.

Most often they were morsels Jaron kept to himself, stored for the edge they might later provide. It was such morsels that had brought him here, kept him here, when he might have done things very differently with his life.

"Let me call off…"

"No…no, I don't want that…"

"Ollie." Jaron squeezed the other man's forearms tenderly. "It's okay. It's not like I make a habit of calling off. They owe me." Other than the weeks spent in recovery and seeking employment after his exile and the procedure that had robbed him of his voice, and the weeks spent healing from the speech implant surgery, he could count the number of shift days he had missed in all those years on two hands.

If something was weighty enough to prompt Oliver to request the favor, it might be worth it for Jaron to learn what the matter was.

Besides, he was not scheduled for a shift tonight. The matter he would have to call off from was significantly more important. He would either reschedule for the next night or else steal away later when Grainger slept, taking whatever secrets Grainger shared with him.

He would not know which until the time came to decide.

"Give me twenty and I'll be there."

"Twenty," Grainger agreed, expecting that brilliant mind to help him out of the dilemma he found himself in over Haythem Kemway. Jaron did not yet know the Founder lived, but if anyone could help Oliver decide what he should do, he believed it would be Jaron.

"We're going to need better explosives if we're going to do this."

Back against the wall on the makeshift double cot he had fashioned, one leg stretched out against it with Otta between his legs, leaning against his chest, he combed his fingers through her short shaggy pink and purple hair. He liked that she changed it so often, and he liked that she approved of this sort of attention. Usually, she did not welcome anyone touching her, not even accidentally. But keeping

his hands busy helped Skelter to think, and kept him from restlessly pacing their room as he talked. His eyepatch hung loosely about his neck, revealing that, though his eye was discolored now, a pale blue where it had once been green, his eyesight was mostly unaffected by the Heb dart that had tarnished it.

Weaker…slower…but he could still see.

In the privacy of the room he shared with Otta and Colyx, there was no need for the show of the patch and the stick.

Most of the sleeping rooms were doorless cubicles with a hemp curtain over the passage to afford the occupants a bit of privacy. There were others, however, with solid doors, rooms often fought over and highly prized when they were won. Colyx had won this room long before Skelter arrived in this place, had claimed it as his for all of Otta's life, and no one had ever been able to take it away from him.

While Skelter had been here, no one had tried.

On the cot between his legs, Otta sorted the items emptied from Enoch's pack while the dwarf and Colyx played their second hand of poke for the evening. Skelter could not tell who was winning, but it never mattered. The only stakes they played for were rolled hemp smokies, of which Enoch seemed to gather an endless supply any time he went out of the Core.

They were valuable bits of currency here. Skelter often wondered if the inmates had any idea what they would lose when both he, and Enoch, were no longer here.

Colyx was not as prone to sharing or distribution as Skelter was.

"And where do you suggest I get that?"

"Jaron…"

"Can get a lot of things, but that's pushing the limit. And blowing the passage is gonna be noticeable. Everyone in here is gonna hear…"

"Not if it's done right…at the right time…something we can set…blow when we're through…"

"Through?" Colyx's brow furrowed as he glanced suspiciously at Skelter. "The door?"

Skelter shook his head. "No…that's for them."

"None of you are going out the way I go; you won't fit," Enoch reminded him. The collapse of the last Core passageway had left a narrow gap through the stone just barely big enough for someone of Enoch's stature to wiggle through. Otta had discovered the opening as a girl, behind the metal cabinet that blocked it most of the time, and had used it to hide from the man who had raised her when she wanted to get out of some chore or punishment. Over time, it had been cleared of debris, widening it, and though she was strong-willed, headstrong, and brave, she had never dared to crawl through to the outside until she was too big to fit through the passage.

Enoch, however, having found the tunnel from the outside, having used it as a place to hide from the Crows and as a shelter from the damp when there was nowhere else to go, had been more than willing to make the trip back and forth from the moment he realized there was a world beyond Hebenon's reach, from the moment Otta's hand had met his through the then partially collapsed stone passage.

"We try to widen it, we're gonna bring down the whole thing," Colyx added.

"I'm working on that." When Otta craned her neck to look at him, Skelter pouted with more disappointment than he felt. "What? Don't you trust me? This is the sort of thing I do."

Enoch grunted, "I don't think you've ever attempted anything quite like this. And I don't know that we can get what you need…in time. Do you even know what you…?"

"Ballard will know. He can do this."

Truth was, Skelter had an idea, but he did not have the expertise to pull it off. Not the way Ballard and Jaron did. Between the two men, Skelter was sure he could succeed. He did not want to jinx his efforts by speaking of it too soon, however. Not even to Otta.

Fortunately, he believed she trusted him…even if the skepticism on her face hinted otherwise.

❧*❧

Rhyd slid the upended glass across the slick bar top, signaling to Maemi that he had drunk enough for the evening. He was sufficiently inebriated to blunt the edges of frustration and annoyance, but not so drunk that he would be unable to make it back to his flat.

He should go topside. He should go home…to Venn.

But Venn did not like to see him this way, did not like to see the reminder of the pit Rhyd was unable to claw out of.

And when the dwarf failed to show, after practically demanding Rhyd be here tonight, when Zara was unable to provide an explanation or excuse about where the dwarf might be…stood up the way he had stood up the dwarf the night before…Rhyd figured there was nothing else to do for it but drink.

He had debated suiting, debated hunting, in case the brako or the bugorra had gotten to the dwarf first, whoever he was, but between Zara's cajoling and Maemi's willingness to supply him with cheese curlers and Zaolei, Rhyd had been persuaded to wait.

There would be no hunting, no fighting, tonight.

A night for his body to heal.

Venn ought to be pleased with that, even if he did not approve of the drinking that deterred Rhyd from it.

"Going home," he slurred.

"Marbordo?" asked Maemi?

Rhyd narrowed his gaze but did not reply.

❧Chapter 8❧

Sunrise on his skin. That's what he remembered clearest in that brief moment on the cusp between sleep and wakefulness. Sunshine…and the low, sweet buzz of cello strings. The pleasant pull of those notes made him turn where he lay, body seeking the source of those long-missed sounds. But turning made his right arm flop to one side and smack painfully against the couch table at the same instant another memory, the eruption of boots kicking open the flat door, brought him instantly awake, instantly upright, to a room that spun on the tail of the alcohol vapors burning off in his blood.

By now, he scowled, rubbing the back of his neck with his non-throbbing hand, he thought that dream should be gone. Venn was safe, no longer Vanished, restored to life and the making of music with the newly re-forming orchestra he was drawing together from the musicians still living in Hebenon.

He was missing in Rhyd's life, however, for the common ground they once shared seemed an increasingly distant memory, slippery and impossible to grasp.

Rhyd did not want to let go, stubbornly persisted on clinging to the notion that everything was going to be right again, although he knew damn well that nothing had been right since before Venn had Vanished. Not even getting Venn back was enough to change that.

Hoping to drowned out the loud mutterings inside his skull and the forced labor of his breathing, he growled, "Echo on," pushed to his feet, and trudged into the bathroom.

Another day. No shift to keep him busy though. He wondered, as he let the hot water burn against his skin as if to burn the Zaolei from his pores, what he was going to do with himself.

Go topside. Find Venn. Help till the little plot of earth where Venn was attempting to nurture seeds cultivated in Hebanthe Falls to see if they would grow in Marbordo's soil. Listen to Venn talk about plants, listen to him hone his skill with the restored cello. Read with Agnys and the village children who were being taught the magic of words on paper that none of them had seen in centuries.

Find the dwarf.

Find the Core.

Those things seemed more pressing, more interesting, more urgent, better uses of his time than going Outside. He did not know how long Skelter had, and enough time had been wasted with missed opportunity. Skelter needed him.

Afterward…after there would be time for Venn and Agnys and the stagnant nature of a life without a purpose.

It came down to purpose. Inside Hebenon, Rhyd had purpose. He was a damn fine bilger. He gave the Scarecrow life, gave the city hope. Outside the shafts, outside the city, he had none of those things. He was nobody, an accessory to Venn's life, a shade without a function.

He did not belong out there.

Daily allotment of bathing water used, the steaming stream ceased and he depressed the nob to the off position, disappointed that the shower had not silenced the noise inside his skull.

Only action was likely to do that. He knew that. So many years of crawling through Hebenon, ear to the streets, had proven that pushing his focus out of himself, into the city, was the best way to avoid thinking. That, or drowning the racket in Zaolei.

Towel around his waist, he rummaged through the collection of clean laundry on one of the dining chairs for something to wear. Easy enough. Black trousers. Black shirt. Black underlings. Well-worn bilger boots and the hempleather longcoat that kept him dry when beyond the walls of the flat. Many in Hebanthe Falls opted for garish brightness, like the glow of neon vindi signs, that helped them not blend into the world's perpetual gloom. Not Rhyd. Blending, disappearing, invisibility, were the necessities of his life.

The less he was noticed, the better he felt. As long as he had purpose.

The name Kemway on the Echosys burrowed into his brain and he glanced at the screen, muttering "Echo, turn up," to the voice reader that would obey his command.

Not Kemway on the prodcast, however, or rather there was a still image inserted into the live feed Grainger was presenting. Rhyd glanced at his chrono. Early for a prodcast. Something was up.

"He was badly injured during the Coup," Grainger was saying to whatever question Soleia was asking. She and her husband Kenneth were the only members of the Ximenez dynasty to survive the plague, and both had returned immediately to restoring the prodcast systems after the breach and damage the Hub sustained during the rioting. Heavily pregnant now, the couple still young enough to have children, they appeared to Rhyd as if they had moved on from the tumult, as though nothing in Hebenon had changed. Her image on the screen made Rhyd frown but there were many in the city who appreciated having that one bit of old and familiar to cling to in a world built on upheaval's shoulders.

"He has been under constant medical supervision; the doctors and their staff have been working tirelessly to restore him to his former capacity and health. He has his good days and bad days…"

"Will he ever resume the duties of Founder, as many hope?"

Many? Rhyd grunted. Perhaps many…but that many was the minority. A return to the old ways, as Soleia suggested, was asking for the Levs to rise all over again. With the brako behind them…for certainly the brako had no desire to give up the power they were attempting to consolidate throughout the Levs…the Founder and whatever backers he might have would never stand a chance.

Grainger shook his head, his expression pristinely sad as would be expected of a man in his position. "Impossible to say. The doctors are hopeful, but will he ever be able to lead…I don't dare speculate…."

"Perhaps the doctors can give us his prognosis?" The woman sounded like she was prepared to push to get those answers.

"They have better things to do than entertain your questions," Grainger chuckled in the hopes of sounding both lighthearted and concerned for the Founder's welfare and care.

"But perhaps…"

"Perhaps." Throwing that crumb of hope to the woman would distract her from further pushing, for now.

"Will we be able to see him? Speak to him? Why have you waited until now to reveal this? The citizens of Hebanthe Falls will…"

"I wanted to be certain he would live. Surely you understand that," the Captain chastised her. "I'll not make him a public spectacle until he is himself again." The Founder had loved being in front of his captive audience, a proud man who would have found being paraded before the world as a drooling, silent fool, or else a violent, manic beast, to be horrifically embarrassing.

Soleia gave her best professional smile. "You must admit this is fantastic news, Captain. Hebanthe Falls has clung to the belief he is alive, but this news, after so long, is hardly proof that it is as you say."

"I'm not letting cams in," Grainger adamantly reasserted. "I'm not parading an ill man for your ratings. Only one person will be permitted to see him…and that person is not you."

The Captain stood, signaling the end of the interview. Being professional and restrained enough not to make a scene on the prodcast and wanting to encourage a good media relationship with the Captain, Soleia smiled and offered her hand as the prodcast switched to what must have been the much earlier announcement the Captain had made.

Founder Kemway was alive.

Why now?

Rhyd had believed it, though without proof. Grainger might be a lot of things, but a cold-hearted killer he was not. At least Rhyd had not judged him to be so during those brief mid-coup encounters. Like many men, he wanted power, wanted control, and he was probably the best man for the task of restructuring Hebenon's government and putting the city back together. What had become of Kemway after that three-way encounter, however, was a mystery Rhyd had thought very

little about. There had to be some unrealized need for making this announcement to a city who had half thought the Founder to be dead and half suspected, or hoped, that he lived.

It took no stretch of thought to guess who Grainger was intent on giving access to the Founder, who his prodcast was meant to reach.

Neoma Kemway.

It would not be Rhyd, although the impulse to find the man, break into his hiding place and force from him everything he knew about the Core was a powerful one. If he could not, however, Neoma might be his chance. She might even hold some of the answers Rhyd needed, for while she had not shared all of her husband's secrets, she had to know some of them.

Finding her, however, was not going to be simple.

Finding her was going to require Zara's help.

Finding her might fill the majority of his day, while he waited for an opportunity to connect with the dwarf. Perfect excuses to avoid going out Marbordo.

❧*❧

Elbows on his knees as he sat on the side of the bed, chin on his balled fists, he pondered the benefits of going back to sleep or starting his day. He knew it was too early without looking at any chrono, knowing the hour by the parade of pre-dawn brain-dimming sales pitches, rehashed news from the week before, Voices of Faith soundbites, segments of dredged up propaganda and laughies found in what remained of the prod-archive after the Coup.

He had not been surprised to wake alone, was not surprised that the Echo opposite the bed was on. Oliver turned it on first thing in the morning to catch up on any events that may have occurred during the night of which he should be aware.

The Captain's face, when it appeared on the screen, framed by the pre-dawn western skyline of the outside world through his office windows, did not surprise Jaron either. For good or ill, Oliver had

already made his decision before settling into conversation with Jaron as they relaxed in a post-intimacy glow. Maybe he had wanted Jaron to agree with him. Maybe he had wanted Jaron to change his mind. Jaron had done neither, only provided a sounding board for pros and cons of each path from the perspective of a man who lived and worked amongst the people of the Levs and had a better understanding of how they thought, how they might react to the revelation that Founder Kemway was alive.

Jaron rubbed his face. Eighteen months, minus a few weeks, and Grainger had hidden that knowledge even from him. He had known there was some secret weighing on the man's shoulders, a secret he refused to discuss, and he knew it had not been distrust that kept the Captain silent. It was the size of the secret and the difficulty of knowing just what to do with it that had meant keeping the knowledge to himself for so long.

Now the world knew.

Or they would once they awoke and watched the early morning reports over breakfast as they prepared to go about their day.

Jaron wondered if he should report to work for what promised to be a very busy shift.

He wondered what Enoch would say. And Lash.

He wondered what impact this would have on Enoch's plans.

He wondered if any in the Core would care, if they heard the news.

He wondered if this revelation would bring the Scarecrow back to the Uppers.

His stomach nervously flip-flopped and he raised his head at the distant sound of a door sliding open and then closing again.

No footsteps.

Like most in Hebenon, what he knew about Scarecrow was rumor. He had seen the tags, the logo and slogans left on the sides of buildings, on the undersides of walkways, anywhere it could be planted for Hebenon's savior to see. He had seen grainy, shadowy SCAM images caught at odd hours when they were least expected. And no one, to Jaron's knowledge, knew Scarecrow's identity. No one

except apparently Enoch, maybe Lash…who seemed to know much of what there was to know within the city…and perhaps Skelter who seemed to know everything about everything. There was some connection between those men, and Jaron was curious to learn what it was. So long as he could avoid further punishment for sedition.

His father had been unfortunate enough to be sent to the Core for his dissidence; Jaron had gotten off with banishment and the surgical alterations to his larynx that left him unable to speak of the things he knew. It had seemed a stupid punishment even then, for a man could still write, but those in power had believed that the trauma of such punishments would render a person unwilling to reveal whatever had instigated the punishment to begin with.

Since the next step would have been banishment to the Core, or to the Outside, most of the time, that gamble was accurate.

Jaron had lost his father to the Core. He had little hope the man could be alive now, but Enoch's plea to aid those inside, aid Skelter in particular, was one Jaron could not ignore.

Skelter had been instrumental in getting his voice back. Jaron owed him. If there was a small chance his father lived, Jaron owed him too.

Though Scarecrow had not done anything to directly influence Jaron's life, beyond instigating the Coup which had affected everyone, Jaron knew he would not be here now, with a free pass into the Uppers, with the opportunity of an outside world and the marvels which Jaron had been unable to imagine. He had not yet steeled his nerves enough to go out, but every day he got a little closer.

When that day came, he wanted to thank Scarecrow in person.

Unable to get away last night to meet, unable to reach Enoch to beg out of the engagement, he worried that his chance to meet the man behind the vigi mask was lost. But he had today, a day without disruptions he was sure, for Oliver would have his hands full juggling the firestorm he had created by announcing that Kemway lived.

He likely would not even notice Jaron was gone.

⊱*⊰

"Lieutenant, how delightful to see you. What can I do for you?"

Ilya grimaced at Senior Talker Kal's smile, the sort of smile that looked artificial and glued into place instead of sincere, the one he wore in his weekly Voices of Faith prodcasts, the sort of smile rehearsed before a mirror in the hopes of luring and lulling a gullible flock in to tick donations or some more fanatical expression of piety.

The sort of smile that, in Ilya's view, never carried into his eyes.

"I'm looking for Ginna. Have you seen her?"

Kal gestured at the over-cushioned chair across from him but voiced no surprise or regret when she refused to take it. "She hasn't sought refuge here in a long time. Have you checked with the herpas?"

The thought elicited a skin-crawling sensation that made Ilya shudder. While she had no use for religion, no need to believe in some unseen power to guide or protect her and no logical reason to believe the Kemways were the eternal saviors of humanity, Ilya knew there had been a time, after the loss of their father seven years ago, in the days when Ilya's energy was consumed with joining the ranks of the Crows, when Ginna had been left to her own devices, seeking answers to the why of being orphaned, seeking the why of the illness that had consumed their father after a work-related accident and the churning river below had stolen their mother previously.

Every day Ilya had berated Ginna to let the past go, to stop seeking answers where there were none, to focus on education so that she could make something of herself. And every day since, Ginna pulled further away, seeking answers from the array of religions infesting Hebenon, seeking it in Hebbies, seeking it in whiskey and criminal activities that Ilya was sure would be the death of her baby sister.

Death…or permanent incarceration.

The Talkers had been the first stop in Ginna's spiral away from Ilya's guidance. It was still the first place Ilya looked when Ginna was missing longer than overnight, in the hopes that the spiral would eventually bring the girl to her older sister's wiser way of thinking.

The thought of Ginna slumming with some seedy herpa, no matter how well-intentioned such people tried to be, was only marginally less upsetting than imagining Ginna tinging.

"You'll keep your eyes open for her?" Their parents had been strict adherents to the Voices of Faith, ardent supporters of Senior Talker Kal. Ilya thought Kal owed Ginna that much.

"You know I will. Would be a shame for anything to happen to her out there." He tilted his head in the direction of the world outside of his office. "May I ask a favor in return?"

Though Ilya bristled, she nodded. Favors for Talkers typically involved police protection for public talks and rallies. The Kemways had kept the precedent of support in those ways for so long it was now expected on both sides, regardless of the need for it or the officers' desire to provide.

Today, however, after the morning's prodcast revelation, the explosive news that had rocked Ilya's world and the lives of everyone who heard it, she imagined Senior Kal wanted inside information about Founder Kemway.

Kal swiveled his chair, reached for a bottle of red wine, and poured himself a glass before looking at her again. He held out the bottle in offering but Ilya shook her head. "I want to see him."

She was right.

"I don't have access…"

"Of course you do, Lieutenant. You are the Captain's primary…"

"I did not even know he was alive…like everyone else," she growled. She was more annoyed with her superior's failure to provide her with the news prior to the prodcast then she was with the Senior Talker. "I don't know where he is being held or…"

"You can find out."

She defiantly shook her head, her features stern and thin-lipped. "No one is permitted to see him…he is not…"

"Not even his wife and daughter?"

"That, you will have to take up with the Captain."

"Ilya." Kal's needle-blast tone relaxed into a note of defeat. "I am only doing as the Voices expect. They want evidence."

"I thought you people work on faith."

"Touché…but this is different and you know it. Ask him…for me. For Neoma. Let us work together on this, on cutting down the Scarecrow before he finds the Founder first." Seeing that he had struck an emotional nerve with that offer, he continued in his Talker-gentle voice. "This news is going to propel him to increased action. Hearing he failed…he's going to want to finish what he started."

Despite her own beliefs, she said, "There's no evidence that Scarecrow had any hand in…"

"Don't be naïve. Why else go to the trouble of instigating a coup if not to do away with the Founder?"

She could not argue with a question she often asked herself. No one knew the details of what Scarecrow wanted, only that he had been hunted that day, pursued until the throngs in the Levs lashed out in his defense. A few had sworn to have encountered him that day in the Uppers, releasing medical test subjects, looking for something, but no one knew what. Why else would a man like that, the bane of the Crows, be in the Uppers if he was not looking for the Founder?

How else had the Founder disappeared? How else had he been incapacitated by the time Grainger found him…as the Captain claimed in his prodcast?

It made sense, fit in neatly with the puzzled that pushed Ilya every day to stop the man's vigilante tactics, but she was not going to admit any of her questions to the Senior.

Not if doing so might find its way to the Captain, who had told her to set aside the hunt for Scarecrow in favor of finding Vanderwall.

Kal continued after emptying his glass. "I have resources. People. But not the permission or ability to stop him on my own. Together though, together we can do great things. Stopping that madman will mean that people like the brako will not feel the need to rebel."

Though she doubted that, Ilya decided to compromise with his suggestion. If she was lucky, there might even be congregation members who could lead her to Vanderwall.

"You…your people…give me everything you know about his movements, his sightings. Who he is, if anyone knows. And you give me the same on Vanderwall…and I'll see what I can do to get you in to see the Founder. No promises," she added with a warning. "Captain has the final say…" And there was no guarantee she could sway him.

She was not about to risk her position on the force to connect Senior Talker Kal with the Founder. Risking it to stop the Scarecrow and Vanderwall, however, was something else.

❧CHAPTER 9❧

"The man I wanted to see."

With rumor upon rumor about this masked individual swirling through Hebenon, the tales of his connection to the Coup, to her husband's disappearance or death, Neoma had expected him to hunt her down the moment she and Ulynda emerged from the factory. If ridding Hebenon of the Kemways was his intention, removing wife and daughter was certainly part of his agenda. After so many months, however, with no attempts made against her life, with the Scarecrow's continued activity now focused on the brako, she had begun to think his motives had no connection to her husband, her family, at all.

Perhaps it had been all about opening the world to the Outside. Perhaps something else she had yet to discover.

With the half-expected but still unsettling news this morning, brought to her by her frenetic daughter who had seen the prodcast before Neoma, Blayd, or anyone else in their circle of acquaintances, it came as little surprise that he would seek her out, hunt her down.

He came for her because Haythem was still alive.

His silhouette squatted on the midpoint of the stairway in front of her, on the path she needed to take to return to her daughter. After a heated discussion with Kal over how to get to Haythem, how to free him from whatever hellish captivity he endured, a discussion about whether such an act was in the best interest of Hebenon and the Kemway family, Neoma was disinclined to friendly discourse. Senior Talker Kal wanted the Founder released, into his wife's care or into his, it mattered not. Neoma, more pragmatic and feeling little emotional connection to the man she had married for familial and political reasons when they had both been very young, wanted far less.

She wanted only to see with her own eyes that it was true. After that, she did not care what Haythem's future held.

Blayd pushed in front of her, buzzer aimed at the vigi's head.

"Blayd…please." She clasped his shoulder with a gloved hand firmly enough to draw his attention if her voice failed to do so, firmly enough to convey her desire whether he heard the order or not. She was not in the mood for discourse, but she would hear Scarecrow out. Better that than a bugorra-drawing confrontation. "Let him speak."

If he wanted her dead, she would be dead. She wagered he wanted something else.

Haythem most likely.

"What do you know about the Core?"

The question caught her off guard and for a moment she stared at him, adjusting her coat collar against the damp and cold as a means of covering the delay her surprise created.

"There's nothing in the Core worth…"

"Not even the mines?"

She had not denied the Core's existence. That told him enough. Few in the Levs knew where the main supply of salt came from, how the earth's salt was processed into the variety of types the city needed to survive, beyond the briners located on Lev 1 with the fisheries, waste processing, and water purification units. Without this knowledge, the shortage was difficult to comprehend, contributing to the ongoing riots and unrest.

It was rare to find anyone in the Levs who knew about mines. Neoma's estimation of Scarecrow's intelligence rose.

She met his question with a dismissive wave as she lowered her hood so he could see her face. "There's other means of production…"

It was the typical flippant sort of remark with which those in the Uppers often met the concerns of the people in the Levs, either out of their own ignorance or else a sense of superiority and entitlement.

Behind the mask, Scarecrow frowned.

"He has entrance codes…he knows where the doors are…"

Neoma laughed airily. "And you think I know those things? That he shared such things with me? Why would I need such tedious information? Why would he entrust…"

Scarecrow growled, cutting her off, but he said nothing, only continued to stare at her, trying to decide if she was being honest or evasive. Tamner had told him few had access to the Core. There was little reason for Neoma to know…except that he could perceive in her the desire for power, and that natural inclination indicated a likeliness for seeking out information of importance.

Controlling the mines was important.

"I might be able to get them…if you can get me in to see him."

Her voice was a purr, and the seductive step she took towards him brought a possessive, protective growl from the man at her side. His fingers around the buzzer's grip twitched and flexed as he drew closer to her. Her alluring expression, directed at Scarecrow, a man she could surely manipulate as any man could be with the right lures…did not change, but Blayd abruptly stopped and his scowling face grew redder with outrage and something Scarecrow recognized.

Jealousy.

Tension rippled through his crouched body, starting at his fisted hands, spreading up his arms, into his shoulders, until it finally accumulated at the base of his skull. He had no doubts about his ability to take on Blayd, but he did not trust what she would do.

With Venn's abduction, any trust he might have had in the Kemways had evaporated long ago.

"The Voices want him too, of course. You know they do. If they get to him first, it's only a matter of time until he's passed off to the brako. We might not love each other, Haythem and I, but he is still my husband…and Ulynda's father. And neither of us…you or I…want the brako to have any more influence than they already have."

Having never seen evidence of collusion between the Talkers and the brako, Rhyd doubted her claim. But for either side, the brako or the Talkers, having the Founder in their camp meant power.

Neither faction was the sort of stabilizing powerbase Hebenon needed to survive.

"I've got supporters. And I'm not my husband." A slight movement of Scarecrow's head suggested he was about to speak but she continued. "I've no claim of my own…but our daughter…I must think of Ulynda…her future. She's the heir. If Haythem is unable to…it makes her the Founder…and I will do everything to protect her, see that her future is secure. Help us…help her…and I'll get you what you need from Haythem."

It was a promise she could not make, not if Kemway's health was as precarious as Grainger alluded to in the prodcast. Scarecrow was not naïve enough to believe that a minor child could sort Hebenon's multitude of problems. No, Neoma would become the one pulling those reins of power, and everything about the woman screamed with the desire to return to the old ways, when the Uppers were separate, when those living there controlled, production, knowledge, resources, and law…and everything else.

He did not want to be a partner to that any more than he desired to work jointly with Grainger and his buggers.

"Hebenon is beyond that. We're not going back."

Never again would Hebenon be a city divided. Not that way. Not if Scarecrow had anything to say about it.

Until that moment, he had not had a concrete goal for his activities beyond suppressing the brako, defending those unable to defend themselves…and finding Skelter.

They were not the words Neoma hoped to hear, and her hardened expression said more than her words could. She was disappointed, aggravated, but not surprised. Her chin tipped up, her cold blue eyes narrowed, and she drew the hood of her coat back up over her head.

"Do not get in my way," she said icily. "Ulynda will have what is hers. Not you, nor anyone else, can prevent it."

Confident he would not attack her, not here in the relative open, not anywhere if she did not lift a hand against him, she stalked away, willing to take a longer route home rather than force him to move. It

was not worth having Blayd force passage. Not when she was in near enough proximity to be hurt in a fight between two deadly opponents.

With Blayd directly behind her, however, his senses tuned to the possibility of an attack from the rear, she felt safe.

"I want him gone," she hissed. "I don't care how…just gone."

Blayd glanced back, contemplating the possibility of getting off an unexpected shot, to see that Scarecrow was no longer there.

❧*❧

Twenty-six Spinks gathered in the safe house they called the Lizard Lounge to distribute and share the supplies scavenged from homes, places of employment, and vindi displays. They split into pairs, allowing them to stake out thirteen of Hebenon's twenty-three levels. The top three, designated the Uppers out of a lifetime of habit, were too risky to infiltrate, too well lit to allow for the mission the Spinks had planned for the night. The bottom three Levs, teeming with brako, were only targeted for tagging when the Spinks could travel as a larger team. It would leave some Levs untagged, but the pairs agreed that, should any team successfully cover their assigned Lev with supplies, and time, left over, they were to claim one of those and signal to the others which Lev they were taking.

By night's end, they would gather again, measure their success, and any Levs not covered, or not adequately covered due to unforeseen interruptions, would be scheduled for tagging at a later date.

Not the following night, however. The buggers would expect that.

The Spinks were smart enough to avoid that sort of trouble.

Ginna and Xiaodan moved together, the pair most familiar with this particular Lev as both had familial homes here. It meant a risk of being spotted by family, but they knew their families' routines. They knew the best paths, the best buildings, the best places to take refuge should the bugorra set chase.

In crimson, in yellow, in algae-reflective green or white, the Scarecrow's call-sign, the inverted bio-hazard emblem confiscated by

some unknown tagger in the early days of Scarecrow's rise, the emblem resembling the shurikens sometimes used when his targets were beyond the reach of his fists, was left everywhere deemed important, everywhere he might see it. On vindi walls, in public toilets. On vinyl vindi signage of those places deemed unfriendly to the peoples' cause. On awnings and overhangs and at the end of alleys where grated drainage shafts leaked water and worse. On recycle crates and delivery wagons. On the fur of a bulky white dog tasked with pulling one of those carts.

Effort was made to cover over brako markers and Voices of Faith emblems. Scrawled pleas for the return of the Founder were made unreadable.

And when the gorra finally gave chase, summoned by some irate resident or vindi owner, the pair split, scattering into the shadows, the evening's work done well enough. The message was there, all around them, for Scarecrow to read.

Come to us. Give us hope. Give us security. Help us. Set us free.

No Talker, no brako, was going to give them that. More and more, as the hours rolled into barely changing days, it appeared that the bugorra could not give it either.

For Hebenon's lost, their hopes were pinned entirely on one man.

❧*❧

Lieutenant Young knew without a doubt who the reported taggers had been. One of them, at least. The description could have been any one of the dozens of streeters now calling themselves Spinks, mostly kids, teens, and young displaced barely adults who, while adorned in the typical mishmash of discarded, scavenged clothing the streeters typically wore. All had begun to wear bandas to cover their faces save their eyes, black bandas with the same symbol painted on as that which they had adopted for their tags.

What did they see in that anarchist, for crucksake?

He was not going to save them. He was going to get them killed.

The Coup was proof of that.

No. It was not a personal description of the taggers that tipped this one's identity. It was the painted yellow plea, the words 'Help us,' that gave this one away.

Even when tagging, her looped H was a tell.

Ilya wondered if it had been left intentionally, left in open rebellion against everything her older sister stood for and believed.

If she was caught, Ilya was going to have no choice but to bring Ginna in. She could not continue to look the other way indefinitely. Ginna had to learn the truth about life, had to give up the fantasy that no one, not her, not the Spinks, not the Scarecrow, was above the law.

"Hosers."

On this busy pass, people bumping by to businesses or to and from their shifts, Ilya had paid little attention to those moving around her, those who, seeing a uniformed bugger, even without her hood, would be prone to stay away, having no wish to risk arrest for the pettiest of reasons or for no reason at all. There was a time the Crows were known for that sort of thing, when that was considered the mark of their trade. But under Grainger's direction, the law enforcers were no longer prone to unnecessary arrests, no longer the scavenging beaked Crows picking at Hebenon's scabbed, raw, underbelly.

After generations of ingrained distrust, however, it would take more than two years to prove they were no longer like that.

Having a curious passerby stop beside her was to be expected in spite of that. There was always someone willing to take the risk in the hopes of a morsel of news or gossip they might be able to sell or trade for a drink, a favor, a scrap of food.

This particular face, however, was not one she expected.

"Blayd."

"Been awhile," he said, studying the taggers' handiwork instead of the woman next to him.

"Ten years."

"So long?" While Hebenon was not a large city, a little over twenty-four square miles in total, there were enough Levs and

residential clusters, enough vindi quarters and lifestyles, that it was impossible to know everyone. Once Ilya had chosen the path of law enforcement, it had taken her out of the small circle of childhood friends created on her home Lev. She had not seen or heard about Blayd since. Ten years was a long time, and though he had changed, his beard lending maturity to his features and the patterns adorning his scalp telling her what he had been up to since they had last seen one another, she still recognized his face.

She had thought about marrying him once, though he had not asked. Maybe that was why she remembered him so well.

"You made it to Crow…uh…gorra now, I see."

"Chief Lieutenant." She was proud of her success. She believed she had a right to be. Such an achievement for anyone in the Levs was hardly commonplace. They rarely rose above the level of beat patrol.

"Really?" That made her the top of the pecking order, below only Grainger by his reckoning, and made her exactly the person he needed. "Congratulations. Your ma must be…"

"She's gone," Ilya replied without intonation in her voice. "Fisher accident." She did not like to discuss her parents, with Ginna or with others. Grainger knew her background, it was on file in her entry records when she had applied for the force, and perhaps some of her fellow officers did too. But even with Ginna, it was always an illness that had ultimately taken their father after their mother's accident. Ilya had never been able to tell her little sister the truth.

"I'm sorry. She was…I liked her." How many times had Ilya's mother welcomed the youngsters in Ilya's circle into her home after morning's classes? How many times had she fed them? Watched them when their parents needed it, patched up skinned knees and hands, helped with their schoolwork? She had worked part-time in the fisheries, but still, she had been there for them all, an easy woman for the children to like. "I'm sorry."

He sounded sincere. Ilya believed his sympathies. But she could not allow them to soak into her soul. She was better than that. Stronger. So she shrugged and resumed staring at the tagged wall rather than

study him to see if his sentiments were rooted in the eyes she had always liked so much.

"He'll never give them what they want," he said when the silence proved she would not verbally acknowledge his sympathy.

She could have said, 'I know,' because she was certain of that assessment too. Instead, she asked, "Why not?" interested in hearing the opinions of someone not in law enforcement.

For a moment Blayd was silent, pondering his answer or else deciding if he should speak. Finally, the words came out, but they were not the words Ilya expected to hear.

"Because I am going to kill him."

Now she did look at him, one brow raised, silently prompting him to say more.

Though it might be considered self-implication, Blayd believed he could trust her. Ten years was a long time, but a shared history, many childhood hours together, lent itself to trust he felt with few others.

The same trust his employer was gradually eroding as he realized more and more that she was not what he wanted to believe her to be.

But a promise was a promise. He would prove his worth, his adoration, and she would reward him for it. He chose to believe that, though he was less certain what form that reward would take.

At the root of the promise was his belief that Scarecrow was not what Hebenon's future needed.

"It needs to be done. Hebenon will not heal as long as he's out there causing trouble. Taking care of him…it's my duty."

Ilya nodded. "Mine too." She did not know how such a duty had come upon Blayd, what he did for a living that required such a duty. He was equipped as though someone's protector or perhaps as a security agent for one of the tradesmen who moved goods around Hebenon and the patterns shorn into his hair indicated his occupation, but she had no idea who that might be or why the Scarecrow was of interest to them.

"I didn't think the bugorra were allowed to…"

"Kill? Not if we don't have to." Hebenon's population was too sparse, too fragile for that, making the need for attempted reintegration of all but the most violent criminals a necessity.

"So how will you…?"

"Whatever it takes."

Blayd shuffled his feet, a gesture of contained energy rather than nervousness. Something about the tag agitated Ilya, he could tell, but without probing into her personal life, a right he did not feel he had after so many years spent apart, he could not know why. But there was something else he could do.

"We work together. I've got resources. He won't stand a chance." Neoma would be pleased to have the buggers on her side, even if it was a tenuous link made through the Chief Lieutenant rather than through Grainger. It would, he hoped, be enough.

It might serve to undermine the man who had usurped the Founder's rightful place.

"When I find him…I will tell you. We stay out of each other's way in this…or we do it together if we can."

Lips drawn into a tight line, she considered the pros and cons of Blayd's suggestion. Whoever his employer was, she did not think it was Senior Talker Kal and the Voices. His family had been the most unreligious people she had known, and until they lost touch, his refusal to believe in any sort of divinity had mirrored Ilya's. Maybe his employer had connections and resources. Maybe his duty, the need to stop the Scarecrow, was not connected to anyone else but was something more personal.

Working with one man versus working within the corrupted nature of the Voices was a preferable compromise.

And if Blayd did kill Scarecrow, was willing to shoulder the possible punishment for that act, it would protect Ilya's position on the force. She wanted Scarecrow gone, but she was not -set on doing the deed herself. With Blayd's help, she would never have to dirty her hands and could still see the end results accomplished.

"How do I reach you?"

"Here…" He pressed a number sequence into his chrono and held it against hers, syncing the numbers so they could message each other privately when they wished. It was shady tech, something the Founder and Doctet had discouraged, but it had its uses. It saved either of them needing to rely on a meeting place too easily compromised and would keep her employers, and his, from knowing about their alliance until the time arose to reveal it.

"It's good to see you, Ilya," he murmured as he shoved his hands into his coat pockets. "Take care of yourself.

"You too." This unanticipated meeting might be the key to everything, Blayd the tool that might allow her to get what she wanted, even if it meant sacrificing him and a lifetime's friendship to Grainger.

The uncomfortable knot in her stomach was an unexpected consequence she was going to have to ignore. Blayd was no innocent. Blayd intended to kill a man. Whatever he got after that, he deserved, regardless of how it might benefit her.

❧Chapter 10❧

"What you're doing isn't safe…"

"Neither is what she's doing!" Xiaodan shoved his finger in Tox's direction but his gaze burned at his aunt, daring her to tell him she was wrong. The elderly woman who had once served as cook in this place, the woman who had raised him when his parents' deaths, had suffered through the Coup and been forced to give up her position to a younger fellow, an acquaintance of Maemi's who chopped vegetables at the far end of the counter and ignored the argument between the other three.

Ignoring was not the same as not hearing, however, and unwilling to risk exposing the secrets they harbored, Maemi grabbed her nephew by the back of the neck and dragged him into the stairwell that led to the living level she had re-secured after the Coup violence subsided.

Vapors was much loved by its patrons. No one had been willing to challenge Maemi's rights to it, so far, not even the brako. There had been damage repair, a dance stage to rebuild, chairs and more to replace, but like so much else in Hebanthe Falls, it now showed few visible scars of the troubles.

"What Tox is doing is necessary…"

Exasperated, Xiaodan snorted, "I know! I didn't know then…but I do now." He hated the reminders of the guilt he still carried over his contribution to the Coup, to Tox's arrest, which was why he rarely returned to Vapors' orbit anymore. After the previous night's activities, however, the safe house turned out to be less safe than hoped, staked out by poorly hidden buggers, so he had taken shelter with his grandmother while Maemi worked.

His bedridden grandmother would keep his secret.

His hopes of being gone before anyone noticed him, however, had been defeated when he descended the stairs as Tox was going up with a delivery of nessies for the woman.

How was Xiaodan supposed to know she would do that?

"I have to do something! He can't defeat the buggers or the…"

"He's not going after the bugorra," started Tox.

"How is tagging going to help?" Maemi challenged at the same time. "There are better ways…"

"Don't you think we know that?"

Maemi squinted, trying to read what the boy was not saying. "What does that mean? What are you doing?"

"Supporting…"

"How?"

"What does it matter? All got to do our part. You said so yourself. You do what you can. Tox does what she can. So do I."

He broke free of the woman's grasp and stomped down the stairs to disappear in the swirl beyond the bar's backdoor, where the cooking steam blew into great white clouds of fragrant mist. Tox hurried after him, hoping to catch him, hoping to convince him to come back to work for the day, resume his apprenticeship, continue learning the trade that allowed her to do what she did for Scarecrow.

If anything happened to her, as had almost happened before, someone needed to be there to pick up where she left off. Helping her was a better, safer way to help Scarecrow's efforts, and it would rein him back in off the streets where he was going to get himself killed if he was not more careful.

By the time she cleared the vapor, Xiaodan was no longer in sight.

She had no idea where she should go to look for him.

❧*❧

"I've had no part in any of that, I assure you. Why would I? What would it gain me…or Ulynda?"

The woman was draped over the cushioned chair as if she owned this office, having seated herself behind his desk before he arrived as if she belonged there. He had found her behind that desk in the past when he had come into this room in search of the Founder, and suspected she daydreamed of serving in her husband's place.

Before Haythem's disappearance, that had been impossible.

With the future of Hebanthe Falls in flux, with so many vying for control, the chances to attain it were higher than they had ever been.

"I'm no fool, Neoma. We've had eyes on Kal…"

"Kal! Exactly! He wants my support, of course; he wants Ulynda to take her father's place."

"And you do not?"

Red-faced as if the notion was repugnant and offensive, Neoma set down the drink she had poured before his arrival. "Ulynda's a child. She isn't ready to serve as Founder, and without the Doctet…"

"But there is the Nau…and there is you."

Grainger was not entirely opposed to the child taking her place as the city's figurehead, a symbolic figure of leadership, so long as the Nau, the people, retained the true fist of power. It would let him get down to the dirty, hands-on business of creating order in Hebenon.

So long as there were cunning people like Neoma Kemway or Senior Talker Kal to pull the girl's strings and steer a return to the old ways, letting the child anywhere near a seat of power was a bad idea.

"I wouldn't do that to my girl. She has an opportunity to have a normal childhood; she is not ready for any of this. In time, perhaps…"

In time…when you have a strong enough support base, Grainger thought with a grunt.

Neoma continued, "Kal has the clout, if he can work around…"

"Just as you do."

"I have my hands full with my daughter…and trying to build some sort of life for her after…" Her voice trailed off and she ran her fingers across the desk as if smoothing down absent paper or wiping away dust from the highly polished surface. "Which is why I want to see him. For Ulynda. She saw your statement and has been inconsolable.

Her brother and sister lost…she thought him dead…and now he's not? You can see how this confusion could be upsetting for a child, surely?"

Grainger scowled. While he had chosen the path with the full acknowledgment that Neoma would get the news and come to him, he had given no thought to how the Founder's child might take the news.

"If I could see him, let her know he's okay, that it is true he's alive, perhaps she will stop asking questions and be able to sleep at night." She paused for a breath and added, "I'm his wife. I deserve this."

"You don't care about Haythem." Grainger knew that from a career-worth of time spent watching the Founder's interactions with his family. That Ulynda might care about Haythem, Grainger could believe. Neoma caring was ridiculous.

"Of course I care. Do I love him? No; I've never hidden that. Do I care about him? Of course I do."

They stared at each other.

She cared, yes. Cared if he was alive or dead, for the effect either would have on her plans.

Oliver came around the desk and stood next to the chair to loom over her, hands behind his back, feet set, his commanding posture forcing her to look up at his impressive height. "It can't be today; business, you understand." She did not need to know the nature of the business. It had been the privilege of the Founder to use business as a tool of avoidance for generations, whether genuine business or not. He had made plans for his day and he was not going to bend them for Neoma's wishes, just to satisfy her. "Tomorrow; I will schedule a time and let you know when. In return, you will keep the Talkers off my back. You will convince Kal to stand down, to call off his followers."

Having access to the Hub, sending a private message to anyone in Hebanthe Falls was an easy thing, even though it bordered on an invasion of privacy and he rarely used it. How close it was to invasion could be seen in Neoma's expression as she slid the chair back to rise, refusing to give him the power of that off-setting contact.

"See that you do, Captain."

The authoritative note of command in her voice, in her tone, in her words, something she had been prone to in the time when she had her husband's position and might to back her, made him growl. She had not agreed to his terms.

As if realizing she had overstepped her boundaries, or else satisfied to have had that effect, Neoma smiled. "I'll talk to Kal. He'll listen. I look forward to hearing from you, to seeing Haythem again."

"You and you alone," he grunted. "If I permit this…it will be no one but you."

She nodded once, having no intention of allowing Ulynda near her father, regardless of his condition, and unwilling to bring Senior Kal with her. She strode from the room with graceful sashaying steps meant to seduce and smooth ruffled nerves.

For Grainger, it did neither.

❧*❧

Wondering how many times he would have to make this passage, worming his way through rock bored out centuries before, Enoch was grateful once again that he was not claustrophobic. Each trip between Hebenon and the Core required wriggling and writhing on his belly, pulled along by calloused hands and well-padded elbows, pushed forward by the toes of his too-scuffed boots, through a space barely big enough for his head, shoulders, and hips to pass through.

Skelter, thin as he was, might be able to do the same, just barely, but Enoch knew Otta and Colyx never would. Nor would the majority of the Core's population. If Skelter did not intend them to exit through the front door with the others, how did he propose to achieve it?

What did the redhead have in mind?

As he crawled, he mused over what ideas Skelter was pondering that would make it possible for them to escape their prison. There were fissures in the stone here, where moisture dripped, groundwater, river seepage and the spray of the falls accumulating to find its way into this little tunnel. There was a variety of ways to widen the passage, some

taking longer than others, but all would require a disposal method for rock and debris…and would require time Skelter did not have.

Explosives would draw unwanted attention from the rest of the Core's population that Skelter did not want either.

The final few feet were covered, the external sheet of metal siding pushed aside when Enoch believed himself to be alone, and then he slithered free to brush the mud and water from his clothes.

It helped disguise him, helped him continue his long-standing ruse as a streeter, kept the authorities from looking at him too closely, even though his stature brought more than its share of attention.

Look left. Look right. Look above. Look below.

No one.

Good.

It was time to find Jaron.

Skelter, he asked himself again as he reached the nearest staircase and began to climb. What in the cruck are you planning?

❧*❧

He did not know where Grainger was going, nor did he care. Having been unsuccessful getting information from Neoma, and not yet having gone to Zara for assistance, his intent had been to force more details about the Core from the Captain. Grainger had known Kemway was alive. Kemway held the key to the Core. Grainger knew more than he was telling.

Scarecrow was certain of it.

He knew the way through the ducts and vents from the Levs to Grainger's office at the top of the city, having taken the time since the Coup to learn those details, those passages, in case he ever needed to go there again. His efforts today brought him to the office as Grainger was leaving, and though the passcard tracker Zara had devised for him, with the Captain's ID programmed into it, he was able to follow the man to the nearest solid-sided lift, grasp the cables that lowered the

unit to ride the moving line until it stopped, and then slither through the nearest adjacent shaft to see where Grainger was headed.

Where it was, was too close to Rhyd's home, to close to Tox's vindi, for comfort.

What neither expected, however, with this lift lacking alumaglass sides that would have provided a view of each Lev he passed through, was for Grainger to emerge from the lift into an awaiting ragtag ambush of men and women…and at least six Talkers that Scarecrow could see from his bird's eye position.

With no time to draw a weapon, surprised by the crowd who began to pelt him with sharp objects and rotten food, Grainger backed into the lift, growling in frustration and annoyance. Something weighty struck his forehead, stinging as it hit, drawing a rush of blood that dripped into his eye. Grainger kicked the closest individual back, creating an opening between himself and his assailants.

Using the walls and narrow door of the lift as protection, he pulled the injector from its holster, deciding not to risk an extended fight by using a popper that would drive the crowd back but not lessen their number, or the thumper that would require hand-to-hand engagement.

Before he used it, however, before the first shot was fired into the shoving, shouting mob, a smaller body dropped into the open space Grainger had just made, his unexpected appearance enough to drive the crowd back a few steps.

"Where's the Core?" Scarecrow hissed over his shoulder. "Tell me how to get inside."

"Traitor!" shouted one of the Talkers. "He did this to us!"

Some in the crowd took up the chant and surged forward while others, idolizing the Scarecrow who fought on the side of the masses, remained apart, confused and uncertain.

Scarecrow did not want to fight so many innocents, understanding they were egged on by the Talkers. Whatever the accusations, these were not bugorra, not brako. These were unsettled citizens whipped into a frenzy by those with garish words…and by the news that their Founder was alive and held somewhere secret by the man in the lift.

The Captain, trying to reach beyond Scarecrow to swing at the crowd with the thumper, did not reply to the question.

He knew Scarecrow was not going to fight these people unless he was forced to. They were not his enemies. As acting leader of Hebenon, however, and head of law enforcement, Grainger had no such constraints.

He had already sent the backup call on his ICD. Within minutes, whatever buggers were in range on this Lev, above it and below it, would come to his aid.

So too, they learned too late, would a handful of brako, their beaked faces emerging from the shadows, shoving through the crowd with little interest in the mob or the Talkers.

They only wanted the men in the lift.

A whine. A snap. A pop. A cry of surprise as the force of the pneumatic bolt sinking into his shoulder flung Grainger with enough force to stun him when he hit the back wall of the lift. Scarecrow flung himself into the crowd to meet the brako head-on after slamming the flat of his hand against the lift buttons.

The door closed and the lift began to ascend, leaving Scarecrow on the platform surrounded by the Talker-whipped mob and the newly-arrived brako.

He could escape them. Fighting the brako would be satisfying, but there was too much possibility for the innocent to be harmed and he did not want that. Forward was not an option. Left or right onto either half Lev came with the included risk of being struck by one of those bolts. His body armor would protect him from the sort of injury Grainger had sustained, but a hit could knock him off balance and a fall into their midst might leave him vulnerable.

As long as he kept his footing, kept his head, he could survive.

The wheezing of buzzers and the surprised squawks of one person after another announced the arrival of the summoned bugorra and the mob, Talker-supported or not, was not interested in the risk of arrest. The Voices had not yet convinced their followers to risk life and freedom in a quest to free the captive Founder.

They began to disperse, the crowd thinning as they scrambled up the left and right stairs, cutting the Scarecrow from those paths of escape. Many of the brako, finding a new opponent better equipped than the lone man who had previously been their target, though less formidable, turned their attention to the outnumbering force. Two pursued the cluster of Talkers who made the mistake of lingering on the fringes too long while the last, an average height fellow with impressively broad shoulders and thick arms, charged the Scarecrow.

There was a bounty for the vigi, both with the bugorra and with Vanderwall. Any who survived the fight would share the credit for his capture equally if they succeeded in bringing him in…dead or alive.

He charged.

Scarecrow caught him across the throat with his outstretched arm, causing the surprised man to drop, gasping. Squatting, fist balled to deliver a blow that would render the brako unconscious, a sound, a voice, something, brought his head up.

Through the array of flying fists and thumpers, he made eye contact with her.

Lieutenant Young.

He did not know her, had never met her. But he had memorized her face from Archive footage and Hub records, in case he came across her in the streets. She was not wearing the gorra mask as those around her were, nor the rest of the on-duty gear, and that lack of protection kept her out of the thick of this fight.

Seeing Scarecrow, however, was an opportunity she was not going to pass up.

Her arm came up, injector in hand.

Scarecrow grabbed the lapels of the brako's heavy coat as the man, still struggling to breathe, attempted to scramble to his feet. Rolling backward, pulling the brako with him, brought the fellow up as a shield. The injector dart hit the brako in the back; it stuck briefly in the thick fabric of his coat and then clattered to the grated walkway to roll away and slip between the metal rungs.

The spasm of the brako's body announced the influx of some of the injector's Heb into his system and his weight, bearing down on the Scarecrow, continued the rolling momentum until both disappeared over the lip of the lift shaft.

Ilya ran to the place Scarecrow had been and looked over the edge. It was too dark to see the bottom of the shaft, too far of a fall for any normal man to survive…but if the lift that had gone up was to return to the bottom, anyone, anything, down there would be crushed. If either Scarecrow or the brako survived the fall, they would never survive the weight of the lift.

But she wanted the bodies, damn it. She wanted proof.

"Barkley…Torvel…Lev 1 shaft A. Now!" she cried to two of the officers who had chased off the Talkers. She would prefer to go down herself, see the bodies, bring Scarecrow in for all of Hebenon to see, as proof that he was not the savior they hoped for. But the brako violence was her leadership priority and so she joined her officers in putting the skirmish down.

Scarecrow would have to wait.

One body hit the bottom of the shaft with a snapping crunch and lay twisted and still.

The other clung to a metal crossbar in the darkness, breathing hard, waiting for the danger above him to pass.

❧Chapter 11❧

He did not know who had pulled him from the lift or how he had come to be in his own bed, but when Grainger opened his eyes, he was alone, with a pulling sting above his left eye that indicated sutures or a plast. When he attempted to lift his right arm to touch it, to determine which had been applied, he discovered that his arm was numb from the shoulder down, some injected agent having incapacitated his limb to allow for unimpeded medical care. A glance down revealed a wide square of gauze held in place by medical tape, with blood seeping through to the surface.

Such bolt weapons were scarce in the city, the risk they posed to filt lines and systems, as well as their deadly nature, considered too dangerous for the average person to possess. Only a handful of his elites were allowed them, deadly shooters used to take out threats while hidden in Hebenon's shadows.

The majority of buggers were not allowed access. The majority were not trained to use them.

As with the Crow body armor and masks, however, and every other weapon in the law enforcement arsenal, piercers had been stolen by the brako as well after the Coup. It was not a surprise to find one in use, or to have it used against him.

It was, however, a surprise that this was the first time, to Grainger's knowledge, that the brako had used one.

"Jaron?"

The lights were dim but not off, the way he preferred when he slept, his dislike of darkness a remnant of a childhood never talked about. Not many knew he turned the lights to this level when he slept, and so he presumed Jaron was here, or had been here when he arrived.

Jaron did not reply to the call.

Grainger frowned, closed his eyes, and tried to massage feeling into his shoulder with his other hand. Perhaps Jaron had gone for nessies. Perhaps he had escorted the attending doctor to the door or had gone for one if he had provided this care himself and wanted a doctor's reassurance that his patient was well.

"Jaron?" he tried again, aware that his voice was slurred from the anesthesia in his blood. Medic-injected or Heb on the bolt, he wondered groggily.

Thump. Thump. Footsteps.

"Jaron, thank gods…"

"It is me, Captain."

Grainger did not need to open his eyes to recognize Tamner's voice. But he did, hoping his ears were wrong. He was sore, nauseous, and wanted Jaron there. He wanted Jaron to take this discomfort away.

There was only Tamner.

"Where is…?"

The doctor pressed his hand to Grainger's forehead, avoiding the plast that had sealed the head wound closed. He nodded with a satisfied expression. "He has not been here since I arrived. You should rest. Let the meds do their work."

On shift then. The rest of Tamner's words were lost behind the drug haze and the drowsiness that crept back into his head.

"Want him…here…" he muttered.

If Tamner made a promise, said anything, the words were unheard.

❧*❧

"If you cannot learn to control your followers, I shall," Neoma spat, her face inches from Kal's, unafraid, undaunted.

How easy it would be to kiss her, the Senior thought with a smug, barely hidden smirk. One kiss. One kiss could change everything.

He believed that as surely as he believed in breathing.

But not now.

This was not the time or the place.

A kiss might cost him with that short serrated blade pressed against the tender belly flesh below his ribs.

The look was not so well hidden that Neoma did not see it, however, and the blade pushed and twisted enough to snag the fabric of his shirt and nick his skin. Kal sucked in a squeak of air but did not pull away or otherwise show that he was frightened by her gesture.

There would be blood there later. A little at least. So long as a little bit was all there was, he was okay with a flick of pain.

"You want to do this here…now…where Ulynda will…?"

"Leave Ulynda out of this." She could barely stomach her daughter's name on the Talker's lips, but his words were enough to remind her that blood shed here, in their home, would be impossible to hide from the child who was in bed in the next room. As satisfying as puncturing his flesh would be, allowing the man to bleed out as she watched, Neoma had never actively taken anyone's life.

If it could not be Scarecrow, this smug, self-righteous man who thought to use and manipulate her would do.

At least he had the nerve to bring this news himself.

"I didn't plan this. By the time I learned of it, by the time I was informed, the clash was over."

"I thought they answer to you." Her knife lowered and she drew back, his arrogance clashing with hers in a way that made her dizzy.

"They do…but I don't control them." Only the set of his shoulders relaxed as she moved away, the only evidence there was of the concern he had felt for his safety.

Not deep concern, but it was there.

"Matters of doctrine…matters of morality and teaching, but the day to day of life…I don't direct them. Not that way."

"You better start if you want me to have any chance of getting Haythem away from Grainger."

The corners of Kal's mouth drooped. "You are planning to…"

"I'm meeting with him tomorrow…and he will take me to Haythem…provided your people haven't hurt him too much. You

want him out…where people can see hm. I want him out…for Ulynda. That's not going to happen if I cannot prove to the Captain that the Voices will stand down their harassment of the gorra…"

He considered arguing that dealing with the Scarecrow was more important, in the short term, then a delay such assaults might have on gaining the Founder's freedom. But as he had already indicated that the vigi had intervened to protect Grainger, it was a futile argument.

He would have to consider how to word such revelations more carefully in the future.

He had not been aware of her success with Grainger, an agreement to see for themselves that Haythem was alive and that the prodcast had not been some sort of manipulative hoax.

It was good news.

"I will go with…"

"I go alone or not at all. The Captain's stipulations." And a wise move, limiting access to the Founder. Too many visitors at once would be difficult to control. Allowing a single person through was exactly what Neoma would have done, if their positions were reversed.

She did not believe Grainger would be so brazen as to arrest and imprison her too.

"The others will not be pleased…"

"Make them pleased. Make them understand. Use your famous Voice, Kal. That's what you're paid for. We play the Captain's game. We do what we have to, to get Haythem back, and with his supporters behind us, behind Ulynda, we unseat Grainger and reestablish order. But," she warned, seeing Kal about to protest again, "it will only work if you trust me…if they trust me…and they stay out of my way."

Thoughtfully, Kal tapped his fingers on his thigh before nodding in agreement. He knew Neoma had a plan. Such women always did. But he also knew that, if it came down to a confrontation between them, he had the strength of numbers to force her aside, to force her to back down to his demands. He could help her get Ulynda into the Founder's seat of power…or he could take Haythem from her, if it was deemed a wiser path.

Whatever her plan was, she would not succeed without him. Whatever the end result was for whoever would fill Hebenon's position of power, it would be Kal and the Voices who put them there.

Nothing Neoma could do would stop him.

❧*❧

"You look like zevel," said the woman behind the bar as she plopped the glass of Zaolei in front of the man who had just taken a place at the end of the counter. It was his usual seat, a place almost reserved for him as there seemed to be an unspoken agreement amongst Vapors' patrons to leave the stool vacant for his arrival. Or else Maemi's sixth sense knew when he was coming and she chased anyone seated there off to clear it for him. Rhyd only knew that, every time he arrived, the seat was empty.

He did not have to fight anyone for it or seek somewhere else where he would feel uncomfortable and out of place.

The Scarecrow's gear was stored in Tox's workshop for safe-keeping, the body armor, mask, and gloves, so that there was little visible evidence of the recent altercation that had occurred some seventy-five yards from Vapors' door. His boots were wet and scuffed, but that was normal within Hebenon's damp boundaries. His knuckles were red from the force of punches thrown, but there was no blood, and the abrasions, cuts and other injuries his body had taken had been absorbed by the armor.

None of those things erased the weariness or strain from his face and eyes, however, and his hair was tousled, damp with sweat, as if he had forgotten to smooth it down when he shed his alter ego.

The look he gave Maemi in response to her lighthearted ribbing suggested he was not aware of that failure.

She did not ask if he wanted anything; he looked too tired, too distracted for a meal, but as she knew he regularly ate little and would need a good dose of protein to counteract the whiskey, she tapped the kitchen serving counter, caught the cook's eye, and gestured.

The cook nodded and readied the usual order without question.

At the midway seat of the bar, a man Rhyd had seen dozens of times before, an older mustached man with the word excelsior emblazoned in deep blue across the back of his dusty denim jacket above a bullseye symbol of red and white with a star at its center. Rhyd had never seen that symbol on any vindi, had never come across any indicator of what it stood for, but the elderly man wore that same jacket every time he was in Vapors, without fail. Though a friendly fellow, he kept mostly to himself or chatted up the pretty young men and women who sat near him. But tonight, he drank alone, looking older than usual and weary with his life.

He lifted his glass towards Rhyd and said, "Vivu," speaking to Rhyd for the first time ever.

Blanching at the word, having seen and heard it often directed at Scarecrow, and wondering if this fellow somehow knew who he was, Rhyd lifted his glass with a nod, hoping it was not seen as some sort of acknowledgment of who, or what, he was. Returning the toast was the polite thing to do. It seemed for some reason to be important to acknowledge the fellow tonight…as if he might never have the opportunity to do so again.

Behind him, at the song change that began with the downing of his first shot of the night, Zara Peru took to the rebuilt stage of brightly lit pressure plates that flashed with each step she took. Even without Skelter, Zara was Vapors' most popular draw, and Maemi had seen to it that she was protected and well-managed when she insisted on returning to her former vocation. There was no need for her to do so, except that she enjoyed dancing, enjoyed the attention of the crowd. She had given up the sex work, sometimes worked the bar, but mostly she continued working with Echos and electronics…and danced.

Rhyd was glad to see it. Glad she had given up that other life. As much as he liked Skelter, Rhyd had always believed that Zara could do better, was meant for better things.

He had never told either of his friends that, however. What she chose to do with her life was up to her. Whatever agreement she and

Skelter had shared, it had been none of Rhyd's business so long as Skelter treated her well.

He always had.

She saw him at the bar as she began to sway, her pale skin bare except for the metallic high cut b-shorts and though she smiled to acknowledge him, she was too savvy to direct all of her attention to a single patron, especially at the start of her set. Rhyd nodded back and then turned when the clatter of a plate at his elbow announced the arrival of the cheese curlers he had not ordered.

He almost protested, was tempted to reject the offer, but the rumble in his stomach was an acknowledgment that he could not let the food go to waste. He nodded and accepted what he was given.

"Ask you something?"

"Depends?" he muttered defensively around the morsel of fried cheese he had popped into his mouth.

"Xiaodan. You know he's one of your Spinks, don't you?"

"One of my...?" He looked at her with a puzzled, narrow-eyed expression. He knew the term, knew the younger streeters who fancied Scarecrow to be a hero, a savior, had adopted that name for themselves, but he did not consider them in any way to be his.

"You've seen it. The tags." She knew he had, even if he did not speak of it. They were impossible to miss. "He's out looking for you."

"Not me..."

"You know what I mean, Whiskey," she scolded before stepping away, bar rag over her plastic-covered shoulder, to fill the drink requests of others at the far end of the bar near the door. Rhyd glanced at them but made no notice of anything particular as he continued to eat. Just a trio of off-shift workmen, cleaners from the looks of the dirt permanently ground into the crevices of their hands, all three moving with the slight jerkiness that indicated recent Heb use.

Not the Heb he was used to. Not the sort meant to enhance one's view of their bleak, dark world. This was the new Heb, a stronger sort that resulted in a bright, blinding flash of high, the sort that had come into the streets when the Upper source stopped producing after the

Coup. Its use was more insidious, the effects immediately noticeable, the addiction rate faster, and more complete, then it had ever been.

Not for the first time, Rhyd considered tracking the production source and putting an end to it.

Perhaps he would. After he found Skelter and brought him home.

Maemi returned with the bottle of Zaolei and refilled Rhyd's shot.

"I haven't asked anyone to…"

"They want what you do. Make things better. They want to help."

"I don't need help." He knew that was not entirely true, as he relied on the information and resources provided by others. But the last thing he desired was to put anyone in harm's way for helping him.

Tox, Maemi, Zara, Venn…Skelter. They had all suffered for their involvement with Scarecrow.

"Then talk to him. For me. Give him something else, some other way to make a difference, before the buggers drag him in for tagging and he gets slapped with punishment he can't escape from."

Fines. Detention. Expulsion. Sent to the Factories. To the Core. Death.

Which punishment Grainger might mete out for tagging was anyone's guess…though death hardly seemed likely.

"I'll talk to him." Nothing Rhyd could say or do would change Xiaodan's mind, but a little gentle nudging might steer him from harm.

He felt compelled to try.

Another blast of cold air blowing across the bar announced further customers. Across the rim of his glass, as he swallowed the familiar comforting burn, his eyes locked with crystal blue ones over the heads of those seated between them.

Blue like the sky. Blue like ice. Blue like the irises Rhyd's mother had grown in her flower boxes. Blue that sucked the air out of his lungs and held the whiskey burn in the center of his chest. The fellow's hair was dark, blacker than Venn's, shorter, a curly-mopped mass, and there were stubble traces along his jaw, his chin, above the nervous twitching of his lips that attempted not to shyly smile when he was aware of being stared at.

Younger…but not too young.

Similar height. Similar build.

The illuminated disk at his throat matched the one at his temple, a direct link, Rhyd knew, to the speech center of the brain. He had seen that tech only twice before, on people incapable of speech without it.

He wondered what had happened, a birth defect or accident or…

The stranger was moving towards him, pulled along by the hand of a much shorter man, whom a quick glance revealed to be the dwarf Rhyd had met in the lift. Behind them…Lash.

Close to hyperventilating, oxygen cut off by the Zaolei that refused to go down through his nervously constricted esophagus, Rhyd shifted on his stool and waited.

Was this the man the dwarf wanted him to meet? Those Zara had wanted him to meet?

Out of the corner of his eye, he caught what he thought was a nod from the woman on the stage but it was likely no more than part of the dance. He opened his mouth to speak after a painful swallow, noting that the curly-haired man's eyes had grown rounder with astonishment as they approached. Enoch beat Rhyd to words.

"Somewhere we can talk?"

Maemi tossed a passcard onto the bar next to Rhyd's hand. "Upstairs."

Rhyd nodded, closed his fist around the card, and led the way through Vapors' back door.

The half-eaten plate of cheese curlers was forgotten, erased by the stranger's blue eyes and the intrigue of whatever the three men wanted to discuss.

The beep of medical machines keeping Maemi's bedbound mother-in-law alive was audible from the main room, but when neither Lash nor Rhyd bothered to search the flat for security breaches, taking seats instead at a kitchen table littered with med bottles and two empty water cups, Enoch decided the location was safe enough. Had to be.

"Enoch LeRoy…you both know Lash," the dwarf started, hoping he sounded less nervous than he felt. He was not a shy man, but this

organizing role was a new one for him. "This is Jaron Rei." He gestured again and finished, "Rhyd Ballard."

Jaron only nodded, in awe that this unassuming man, little different in height and build to his own, could be the one so many clamored for or feared. No one needed to tell him who Ballard was. Enoch had said they were to meet with the Scarecrow.

Jaron knew Lash was not him.

"What's this about?" asked Rhyd, edginess translating into a testy growl he did not intend. "The Core? Skelter? He's alive? He okay?"

"You know Skelter?" The digitized voice, prefaced by the tiny sound which activated the speech unit and kept private thoughts silent, asked the question without Jaron opening his mouth as the younger man's eyes blinked nervously. There were many uncomfortable with such tech enhancements, preferring muteness or hand communication instead that very few knew.

He was relieved when Rhyd, though staring at him briefly with unsettling curiosity, replied. "For years," without showing a distaste for the unconventional disability or means of communication.

"Odd that you two never met," said the dwarf.

Rhyd shrugged. "He kept his associates to himself. Safer for everyone." And Rhyd was a man who kept to himself too, more so after Venn had Vanished.

Enoch nodded. "Skelter's alive, okay when I saw him last, but he's running out of time."

"Because of this?"

The metal disc Rhyd had carried since receiving it days before was taken from his pocket and placed, etched side up, in the center of the table. Jaron reached for it but stopped short of touching it.

"Thought the Spades were…"

Lash grunted, cutting Jaron off. "Very real," as he scratched absently at his arm.

"More so inside," said Enoch. "Population control, you know."

It made sense to Rhyd. No matter what materials or supplies went into a closed environment, there would only be so much to go around,

particularly with new mouths to feed being added all the time. Every time the Founder, the Doctet, or the Crows condemned another to that place, supplies would grow a little scarcer. It made sense that the Club had found its way in via any of those sentenced there, and would become a tool those in charge inside could use.

What did not make sense to Rhyd was how Skelter had gotten in there when he had been presumed dead, or why he had become involved with the suicide club to begin with.

Maybe he had no choice. Perhaps everyone in the Core was an automatic member.

"He has a plan…but needs outside help. Needs both of you."

Enoch looked back and forth between Rhyd and Jaron and the two looked at one another, thinking much the same thing.

What could they possibly do to help?

"Been looking for the entrance," started Rhyd, "but Kemway isn't exactly available for comment, and Grainger's stonewalling me…"

Jaron sighed and lowered his gaze. He understood then. That was where he came in. Getting information from Oliver. He had been doing that for Lash for months, had been aiding Enoch with medical supplies, tools, and other easily transportable items to help those in the Core who needed helping after the final exchange was made and the mines were sealed off from Hebanthe Falls.

"Factory East. That's all I know. I've seen it from inside but never from up there."

Elbows on the table, Rhyd asked, "You escaped the Core?"

Enoch shook his head. "Not escaped; found my way in. There's a narrow pass on Lev 2…probably drainage once. Not big enough for most people…kids maybe but…without blowing the rock…"

"And doing that," Lash muttered, "risks the stability of Hebenon."

"Might kill everyone in the Core…and if it didn't it would take too long to clear it to be practical. Not to mention alert the gorra…and it'll shake up Factory East. Skelt's not got that much time."

Jaron raked his hand through his curls, a gesture that attracted more stares from the whiskey-eyed man across from him. "We can't risk all those lives…there's families in the Factories…"

"We know," Enoch assured him. "But it might be a risk we have to take. There's families in the Core too, such as they are, who are gonna die of disease…or starve to death when supplies run out."

"And we need the salt." From a purely economic standpoint, Lash was correct. The mines could not stay sealed indefinitely, and if Grainger was waiting for the stability of Hebenon before opening them again, it might be a lifetime or more before the reopening came.

Skelter, and everyone else inside, would be dead by then.

Criminals or not, no one deserved the sort of slow, lingering, agonizing death they had been consigned to.

Given the Founder's previous record, Rhyd thought with a scowl, how many in there actually deserved to be?

"What's he need from us?"

Enoch sighed. "Not exactly sure." He slid a folded, sealed bit of paper across the table to Rhyd, hoping he could make sense out of what was written there. "Tools, welding gear, chain, explosives."

"I thought we weren't going to…" grunted Lash.

"It's only the start of a plan," Enoch shrugged. "He hasn't said more. I think…" He covered Rhyd's hand on the table with his own, "that's why he needs you. Jaron can get access to equipment and information, schematics…but Skelt needs you to complete a plan."

Rhyd pulled his hand away and leaned back in his chair. It made sense. Skelter had always been the one able to get things for other people. Maybe Jaron had always been part of that acquisitions loop. But Skelter was not a tactician, and inside, his resources were limited.

"Welding gear…I can get that. Tools…but I need specifics. Need to know what he's blowing to figure the best explosives. The rest…I don't have easy access to…"

"Jaron can help with that."

Jaron took the paper from Rhyd, their fingers brushing in the exchange. Their gazes held until Rhyd growled and stood up, fetching

a bottle of liquor from the kitchen cupboard and bringing it back to the table in order to put distance between them as Jaron read Skelter's brief request.

"This is dangerous…"

"If we don't try, Skelt…all those others…are going to die. His number's up. Sixteen days…and if he doesn't have it by then, its either take his own life or someone in there will do it for him. Posa…every moment of every day there's a chance someone will call him on it."

"He might not have sixteen days," Lash finished for the dwarf.

The crunch, the restraint of that pressure, prompted Rhyd to a long drink from the bottle. The liquor would either knock him out or clear his head. When he set the bottle heavily on the table, he stared long and hard at Jaron, surprised, at that moment, that he was able to do so with a relatively clear mind.

The plan was forming.

"Get what you can. Get it to me, through Lash, through Enoch, through Maemi if you have to." He did not want to involve her, but it was obvious they knew her. With shipments coming into Vapors all the time, a few additional crates or boxes would not seem unusual unless someone poked around where they should not. "I have places to…" He had no idea who the younger man was, what connection he had to Grainger, what access he had to the items and materials on Skelter's list. But if Skelter trusted him, trusted Enoch, if Lash trusted them both, then the best thing for Rhyd to do was try to do the same.

"Gonna need time," Rhyd continued, "need to see that tunnel. Need to know where the Factory door is…how Skelter got in. Need to think. And you," he growled at Enoch, "need to keep him alive."

Being kaheao, Skelter could get anything, get others to do things for him, get anybody whatever they wanted and needed. As always, he needed others for their connections, for what they could provide so that he in return could provide for others…or at least himself. And he needed Scarecrow for his physical strength, his ability to plan, his willingness to fight.

However this went down, whatever they chose to do, there was going to be a fight. It was going to get messy. Lives would be lost. It was up to Scarecrow to formulate a solution that would limit the mess and the casualties. It was what Scarecrow did.

"How long?"

"I can't get any this overnight," replied Jaron, taking some of the pressure off of Rhyd to perform an immediate miracle. "I have to track good stores…and theft is going to get flagged in the system. If we're not careful, Oliver is going to get suspicious.

The use of the Captain's first name brought an uncomfortable flash across Rhyd's face, a steeling of his expression where moments before there had been something much different. The man disappeared behind the upended bottle again.

"Tell Skelter I'm on it. Ask him if freezes will work," Rhyd grunted after lowering the bottle and wiping his mouth on the back of his hand. "Tell him to stay alive. Tell him to let me know what he's thinking…and I'll let him know what I can do."

He offered his ICD reluctantly to the dwarf. They were going to have to trust each other, needed some way to communicate and signal each other from wherever they were on the Levs.

And he was going to need whatever information on the others that Zara could find for him. He needed some idea of who he was dealing with. They obviously knew who he was. He needed to know the same before deeper commitments were made.

If they were going to succeed he wanted transparency and honesty.

Especially from Jaron Rei

☙Chapter 12❧

He did not ask where Jaron had been the night before. Thanks to whatever meds Tamner had given him, Grainger slept so soundly that he slept through a number of appointments already this morning and had no idea of anyone's' comings or goings out of his room. The recorded message on his PCD was an apology from Jaron for missing him, hoping that he had slept well, a promise that he would see him at the end of shift for dinner.

Jaron had been here then. He did not check the logs to see when, did not check his shift records. There was no reason, no need.

He trusted Jaron, despite the nagging little voice in his center that was beginning to hint that he needed to formalize their bond somehow.

But did he dare?

Sorting through the reports left for him, however, called for a meeting with his Lieutenant he did not want to have. That summons was sent before he received one of his own, and now he stood with Doctor Tamner at the tinted window, watching the raving man behind the glass throw himself against another wall with a screeching wail that, while muffled by the sound-absorbent material of his chamber, was still felt by those watching him. There were medics standing near the door opposite the window, on the outside where Grainger could not see them, waiting for the word to sedate the violent man before he harmed himself.

Before the visitation Grainger had intended to allow today.

"Will he be alright if we let him be?" he asked Tamner, voice low as if to mask it from others.

There was no one else nearby.

"As long as he doesn't break an arm or a leg, yes," the doctor assured him, wondering what Grainger was thinking. Sometimes he ordered the Founder to be sedated, but only when this manic phase had gone on for so long that he feared dehydration or worse would set in. This episode had begun during the night, and though Kemway, restrained by the fettershirt, howled and threw himself about, clawing at walls, floor, the window where they now viewed him, he had thus far done nothing more than bruise or soil himself.

The phase would pass. Perhaps within minutes. Perhaps within a few more hours.

If he was sedated, it was going to take a day or more for him to begin to function normally. Or as normal as the man could be now.

"Then we let him be…monitor him. If you think it necessary to…"

"Captain," Tamner protested. "I have tests…I have…you said she was…I don't have time for…"

Grainger's PCD beeped in his pocket, alerting him that his next scheduled meeting was at hand. "He's the Founder," he muttered wearily. "Make time."

Haythem might not control Hebenon any longer, but Grainger still reserved some respect for the status their patient had held.

The name and bloodline, however, were not enough to make him the leader Hebanthe Falls needed.

In his office, Lieutenant Ilya stood at attention at his desk, in uniform without her breathing mask, wearing the cold, neutral expression of an officer expecting a reprimand or other bad news. Grainger did not yet know if that was on the agenda, but he did have questions she needed to answer.

"Did you find him?"

The corners of her eyes twitched. Her lips parted. He believed she would ask who he meant, but instead, without shaking her head or looking at him, she continued to stare through the window at the mid-morning landscape and reply, "No, sir. Only the brako's body was in the lift shaft. It appears…"

There was no appearing about it.

Scarecrow had eluded her.

"Tell me what happened." Grainger only knew how the start of the altercation had played out. From the written reports of officers and the SCAM footage viewed earlier, he knew some of the other details. Every lift had a SCAM directed at it, a way of monitoring movement between the Levs, a remnant of the days when the Founders had been paranoid enough about their hold on power to want to be sure that none from the Levs accessed the Uppers who should not.

The Lieutenant had been out of the SCAM's field of vision much of the time.

Grainger had seen the Scarecrow pull the brako up as a shield, saw the brako struggle and then his whole body reacted at the impact of the injector that struck him. He had watched the Scarecrow roll backward, with the brako curled over him, and then both disappeared over the precipice of the lift platform.

The Lieutenant had appeared then, looking into the darkness, as the clash continued behind her.

"I shot…" There was no need to deny it. Weapons were checked in at the end of each shift, examined, the number of spent and available rounds tallied to make certain there would be no unexpected shortages of munitions, and no unauthorized use of force.

Production and use of most materials had to be carefully monitored. Hebenon had to keep strict control over everything they possessed if they were to survive.

"The round hit the brako; he was found at the bottom of the shaft."

"And Scarecrow?"

"I don't know, sir. He fell but…we…I…lost him after that."

"And this after I told you to…"

"Sir, it was my…our…best chance to…"

"He saved my life!"

There had been no need for it. Once more, Scarecrow could have killed him, just as he could have twice on the day of the Coup. Dazed, incapacitated, Grainger would have died before the gorra arrived, at the hands of the crowd, the Talkers, the brako, if not for Scarecrow.

If he was willing to spare the Captain's life, fight at his side, there was still a chance he could be persuaded to join Grainger's team and work together to better the city.

He could not do that, however, if he was dead.

Ilya lowered her gaze from the window view to the desk in front of her. "Yes, sir. He did." And she had tried to kill him for it.

It was not an attempt she regretted, however. Her only regret was her failure…and what that said about her loyalties to her Captain.

Grainger snorted and dropped into his desk chair, favoring his injured arm as he did so as if to remind her of the injuries he had sustained in that fight, a reminder of the debt he owed Scarecrow.

Her gaze moved left, away, and returned to the window.

He pressed a key on the Echosys and tapped the screen with one finger. "You report about the tagging…these…Spinks you call them."

Her shoulders tensed. "They consider themselves his…little birds? He's going to get them…"

"Have you seen him with them? Does he command this little army of street birds?"

"Not that I have seen. But they are breaking the law for him…"

"By tagging…"

"And in other ways…I'm sure of it." Just because she had not yet caught any Spink in the act of a crime, just because none of the streeters arrested for Heb addiction, theft, or public brawling had claimed to be a Spink, did not mean such things were not being done on the Scarecrow's behalf.

"Your sister s one of these Spinks?"

Ilya sucked in a surprised gulp of air. Her reports on the recent tagging surge in the Levs had left Ginna's name out in the hopes the younger woman would be protected. But she had not seen all reports made by other officers from other investigations, had not viewed all available SCAM footage, and did not know how deeply her sister was involved in Spink activity.

She had only seen that single, incriminating tag.

That was enough to condemn Ginna, however.

"I want you to bring her in…"

It was punishment for her insubordination in trying to kill Scarecrow as much as it was an arrest warrant. Uncomfortable, wanting to protect both herself and Ginna, she replied, "I do not know where she is, sir. I've not seen her in several days."

"That's unfortunate." He did not explain, leaving ramifications of this knowledge to Ilya's imagination, and continued, "I will not be able to protect her if she is caught breaking the law, but if she is arrested, I will do what I can for her."

If, Ilya heard, she agreed to the terms of such an arrangement. If she desisted in her efforts to take down Scarecrow.

"Sir, I…"

There was shouting beyond his office door, a recognizable voice that Grainger reluctantly knew he would have to face before the owner burst through the barely open retracting doors.

"You promised!"

"Neoma. This is Lieutenant Young." Voice calm and pleasant, he attempted to disrupt her outrage by pointing out that there was another in the room to witness it.

Neoma did not seem to care.

"They won't let me see him! You gave your word that I would…"

"I did no such thing. I said I would let you know when it was a good time…and we agreed," he added pointedly, "that you would keep the Voices from interfering with my…"

"I had nothing to do with that! That was them…not me!"

"And supporting you…your daughter…is what they do. We had an agreement, Neoma…an understanding…and you did not uphold it." As much as he regretted Ilya being here to hear this, Neoma's intrusion gave him no choice. "The Founder is not well enough for visitors today…that is why you may not see him. When he is better…if you keep your word…I will send for you. That," he emphasized, "is what I promised to do. Now, if you do not get out of my office, I will make certain you are not permitted to see him at all."

She charged him and stopped when there was less than an inch between them. To Ilya, it looked as though the woman would strike.

"You have no right! I am…"

"Mam Kemway, please," Ilya began.

"You are nobody," Grainger spat. "If Hebenon is to have a Founder, it will be Ulynda. Not you. You are only her mother. You are not a Kemway by blood. You, like the rest of us, are nobody."

Her hand lifted, the threatened strike impending, but Ilya caught her wrist and held it. Neoma hissed, growled at the lowly officer who dared touch her, and then yanked her arm free before stalking out of the office without a word of agreement or challenge.

It was not clear, in her exit, what her intentions were.

"Watch her. I want to know everyone she talks to, everyone she sees, everywhere she goes. Hebenon has had enough violence. I will not allow her, or anyone else, to ruin what we are trying to build."

Ilya nodded, snapping to attention, wondering if that statement included Scarecrow as she slipped back into the professionalism her position and duty demanded.

The discussion of Spinks, taggers, Ginna and the Scarecrow were tabled for now, except for the slamming of Grainger's palm against the intercom button and one final barked command.

"I want Mr. Weyer in my office. Now!"

Ilya wondered who Mr. Weyer was.

❧*❧

He had been unable to sleep after that meeting, the possibilities of Skelter being alive, how he might get his friend free, warring with the pressing urgency of Jaron Rei and why that man would not get out of his head. The need to know who he was, the need to know more, lent fuel to Rhyd's restless night, had brought him to Zara's door at the end of her shift, in search of any details she could hack out of the Hub.

It had not surprised him when she gave the location of his place of employment and nothing more without even accessing the Hub.

Zara, like Skelter, had contacts and clients to protect. Confidentiality was key in their business, even when it was all in the cause of bringing Skelter back into Hebenon's bosom. She knew both men well enough to know where both worked. She also knew that Rhyd would seek that information eventually, and seek more on his own without her.

And it was obvious now that she had been told Skelter was alive.

The place explained Jaron's access to resources Skelter had wanted, or needed, in the past. Archivists kept track of everything in the city, production, sales, marriages, births, deaths. They recorded daily criminal activity, changes in residences, vacancies, arrests the needs for repairs throughout Hebenon, prodcast viewing data, Voices of Faith attendance, shift logs and more. Any data that passed across the Hub and might prove useful to tally and record. Most of that data had once fed to the Uppers, to the Hub, so the Doctet could monitor the lives they depended on in the Levs, but it was also those archivists who fed data to the Sheds so that men like Rhyd knew of needed repairs before that need created a crisis. Without the Sheds, without the archivists, Hebenon might have fallen long ago.

It was also the archivists who recorded history as it happened, free of the filters the Founder imposed on the news fed to the general populace. How much was hidden, buried, only the archivists knew. Those that recorded the most sensitive data were strictly watched and controlled, more so when the Founder had ruled, so as not to allow sensitive, questionable data into the hands of the wrong people.

Rhyd wondered, as he watched the door to the crowded, multi-leveled, multi-stationed building, what Jaron's knowledge entailed.

Jaron was on shift. It was the one bit of data he had coerced out of Zara that she had needed to access the Hub for. By Rhyd's calculation, that shift would end soon, and so he waited in the shadows, hiding so as not to appear to be loitering, uncharacteristically nervous in a way that he had not been since…

No. He shook his head to erase those memories, refusing to compare this feeling, this moment, with the treasures of his past. This was not that. This was something else.

He could not allow it to be that.

When the doors opened, however, the Archive's hour of downtime beginning as one shift ended and the next prepared to begin, he watched each face that came into the street for the one he wanted with uncharacteristic anticipation.

Not familiar, he reminded himself. The only reason it seemed familiar was because it refused to get out of his head.

When his target appeared, there was a fleeting hesitation, Rhyd's feet reluctant to move under the assault of the nervous tumbling in his stomach. But if he was to be of use to Skelter, he had to do this.

Or so he told himself when he reached from the shadows to take hold of the dark-haired man's arm.

He regretted the moment of panic on the other man's face, the moment of fear he instilled there, but when Jaron saw him, those weightier emotions were shed like water off of an oily surface.

"We need to talk."

Jaron nodded and followed.

No one around them reacted to the exchange.

They descended the nearest flight of stairs and paused, Rhyd not having considered where they could talk in private. No, not private, he immediately reminded himself. He did not want to be alone with Jaron. That was a sort of danger he was not prepared to face.

"I know a place."

Interpreting the hesitancy for what it was, Jaron cocked his head. Rhyd followed. They pushed through the between shift crush of people to a door with a blue four-point star in a circle glowing upon it.

A dek.

It had been a long time since Rhyd had dekked. Not since before Venn's Vanishing, when they had saved enough ticks to share an hour-long experience. Five minutes, ten minutes, twenty minutes was the norm, the limits of what most could afford, and the most common periods allowed in order to maximize the number of system users and provide the most uses of the dek pods in a day. Longer periods, up to two hours, were possible, but each increment was more and more

expensive. That sunny hilltop picnic he and Venn had shared had been an anniversary treat both had looked forward to.

With the outside world open now, Venn had no use for deks, and Rhyd had been unable to enter one after Venn's disappearance.

After finding him again, he had never given dekking a thought.

Jaron ran his passcard through the reader on one of the six dek pod doors, punched in a numbered sequence, and then ushered Rhyd inside. Once the door closed behind them, a familiar electric hum reverberated through the air and the room came alive. Not with a hillside or an ocean view. Not a forest or a field or a park.

Instead, Rhyd found himself on a city street with small tables and matching iron-wrought chairs placed in front of a café window with a tall, pointed tower in the distance.

"Paris…1930…or so I'm told." Jaron sat at one of the tables, smiling as he motioned for Rhyd to sit opposite as pedestrians, couples, women with children, men in dated business suits, strolled the boulevard, disappearing in and out of shop doors. It smelled, to Rhyd, like spring, like baked bread, like sweet spice and air recently washed by rain that left the pavement wet and sparkling beneath the midday sun.

"My father used to bring us to this…" Jaron gestured around them, "as a treat when our studies went well. My mother thought it an excessive indulgence, but it pushed us to excel, my sister and I. He wanted us to remember our history." His smile turned sheepish and he shrugged. "Whatever that is. He said our family came from France, when there was a France, when there was a world out there to…"

The more Jaron talked, the less noticeable that pre-speech sound became in his voice. It must have taken the younger man some time to learn to use that vocal command, to avoid broadcasting thoughts and sharing only what words he wished to share.

"Have you been out? Have you seen it?" Rhyd found it easier to stare at the distant tower then to look at Jaron. He did not know his own family's history. Perhaps he could have Jaron investigate it, trace it back to the first of his family to step inside Hebenon's walls.

But what did the past matter now?

A fat man with slick black hair and a pencil-thin moustache, wearing a pristine white apron over his equally white clothes, emerged from the café and offered something hot from a steaming kettle. From the corner of his eyes, he saw Jaron shake his head no.

Rhyd did likewise.

"Not yet. Seems a bit much, just the idea of it…being out there."

"You should Worth seeing, even if you come back here." Someday, Rhyd imagined all of Hebenon's population would have moved out of the city's protective shell and the 'nest' as the parah called it, would gradually fall in to ruin.

Not in his lifetime, however.

"You'll have to show me."

Surprised by the words, by what sounded like an invitation that Rhyd did not know how to address, he glanced at Jaron who was looking at his empty hands on the table and not at Rhyd. With a mixture of relief and regret, Rhyd returned his gaze to the tower.

Had he expected Jaron to be staring at him?

When Rhyd did not speak, Jaron continued "I've seen you before, with Oliver."

"Grainger?"

It was the only man Rhyd knew with that name.

"Few days ago…he was warning you about Lieutenant Young. He wanted…wants you…to support him."

Defensively, Rhyd muttered, "I'm not siding with anyone but…"

"Hebenon needs a leader. The Founder, his wife and daughter, Senior-Talker Kal, Oliver…or you." His gaze came up to meet Rhyd's now and he nervously licked his lips. Hearing the protest before it began, he continued, "Oliver's not a bad man."

"You say it because you're futzing him."

There was something in Rhyd's tone that made Jaron's face grow hot and red, something in the way Rhyd looked away as soon as the words were uttered, that made Jaron rush on with his words.

"He's willing to lead. Of those who are willing to tackle the job of rebuilding, he may be the only one without an agenda…"

Swallowing back the surge of emotion that prompted that outburst, the one that followed when Jaron did not deny what he could have, thus proving Rhyd's suspicions correct, he muttered, "Everyone has an agenda. Everyone. Especially those in power."

"Even you?"

Rhyd's fist closed around the cloth napkin nearest to him, randomly wondering how long Jaron had booked the dek for.

"Even me."

His agenda, until that moment, had consisted of securing the safety of the people of Hebanthe Falls, freeing Skelter from the prison he was in, and finding peace in his relationship with Venn. Not necessarily in that order of importance.

Jaron compromised the last item on his agenda, and Rhyd was abruptly angry about it.

When the blue-eyed man did not press for details or confessions, Rhyd swallowed several gulps of air and willed himself to be calm.

Whatever he was experiencing, feeling, it was not Jaron's fault.

If they were to rescue Skelter, they had to work together. Rhyd needed to get hold of himself.

"Can you get freezes?"

Jaron shrugged. "I can locate enough of them for whatever you have in mind, but I'm not a thief. And I can't do both at once…"

"I can get them out…"

"You'll be caught…and when they go missing…"

"You alter the archives."

Lips pursed, Jaron stared at the blonde. Of course he would have to do that. It was not the way Skelter had done business; in the past there had always been a trace. But trading in explosives would raise as many flags as the theft of them would. The only way to move any quantity of them outside of a legitimate sale or transaction was to doctor the records.

Jaron was not sure he could stomach doing it, but Skelter, and Rhyd, expect him to try.

"How do I know I can trust you to…"

"How do I know you're not going to report all this back to Grainger to blackmail me into cooperating with his designs?"

"I would never do that!" Offended by the thought of such a betrayal, Jaron looked as if he was about to leave Rhyd on the Paris street where they sat.

Voice dropping low, Rhyd huffed, "You know who I am…you know what I do." Jaron had not said it, but why else would Grainger try to coerce a nobody bilger into supporting him? If Jaron had heard enough of that exchange, he knew.

And after the previous night's meeting around Maemi's table, who Rhyd was had to be obvious.

"If you want me to trust you, you're going to have to earn it."

"How?"

Though Jaron did not open his mouth, though there was no tension in his throat to create a squeak in his tone, it was still registered through the implant that read his thoughts, his emotions, and translated them into spoken word when he wished it to.

"You're going to help me get freezes…and you're going to get me a layout of Factory East…the whole thing… maps, schematics, data, anything you can find about the Factory and the Core. And if Grainger knows the Passcode for that door…you're going to get that too."

It was a lot to ask. Some of that data, factory schematics for example, Zara could get. But an archivist could access any history there was about both locations, so long as the data had not been compromised or lost during the Hub crash at the time of the Coup. Rhyd would need both to device the best plan available to them. And an archivist would have an easier time manipulating stock and production data to cover the theft of the items he and Skelter wanted.

"You tell Enoch where…cover my ass when I go in…and I'll get what we need."

If anything went wrong, if his efforts were compromised, Rhyd would make damn sure Jaron paid for his betrayal.

No matter how difficult that retribution would be to carry out.

The dek timer light flashed red. Time was up.

"I'll do it," Jaron promised, rising when Rhyd did so. "Enoch will let you know." Refusing to reach out to Rhyd at his home, his place of work, when he could easily access that information, was one way to gain a measure of trust, but that did not mean he did not already know those things.

"Give me a day or two." He would not be back on shift until tomorrow, and digging into the records unnoticed would be tricky. But no one would question his right to that access. He could do this.

The only one who might ask questions would be Oliver…when Jaron began asking questions of his own. Getting information from the Captain was going to be a lot more difficult to accomplish.

❧Chapter 13❧

Venn had never been in this room, in the Founder's office. To his knowledge, very few people from the Levs had. There were fables told to children at bedtime, of the opulence of the Uppers, of grandiose rooms where the Founder took care of all of Hebanthe Falls, where the daily decisions were made to benefit all that remained of mankind. Riches of all sorts, an abundance of food and drink in a world adorned with simulated daylight and an artificial sun and moon, things that had never existed in the Levs.

But the room he stood in was stark, white, barren save for a few works of art on the walls and the retracted shields above and around him that afforded a view of Outside that could only be gotten here…or beyond the city in the world itself.

If this was the view the Founders had witnessed for centuries, how could they have continued to proclaim a parah world poisoned and unlivable? If the Founders had known, why had humanity been allowed to stagnate, trapped in the dark, in the wet?

Was this the revelation for the people that Rhyd had fought so hard to share?

Was Venn wrong to prevent him from his efforts to give the rest of humanity the beauty, warmth, the future now possible to them?

But why Rhyd?

He swallowed his frustrated groan as the door opened behind him.

"Mr. Weyer. Thank you for coming."

"My pleasure," I think. "Thank you for inviting me. But really…what is this about?"

Grainger had been there at the time of his arrest; Venn would never forget that face, that voice. But he had been an addict, had made

some unfortunate comments against the Founder that he could not now recall, and had been lawfully arrested because of it. Whether the law was right or wrong, policy was policy. Grainger had been doing his job and Venn did not hate him for it.

Perhaps if he told Rhyd the truth beyond the obvious error of his addiction, Rhyd would not feel the need to continue seeking recompense for that arrest.

"How is the orchestra coming?"

Venn smiled, relieved. After banishment, he had fought hard to beat addiction and remain free of it. Being outside in a world of fresh air and manual labor in the soil had made those things easier to accomplish then they had been inside Hebenon, and he had been worried, when summoned, that perhaps he would be accused of some other crime…or that the one that had been the original impetus for his arrest had returned to haunt him.

Not that the Founder was around to care. Why then, he wondered, would the Captain?

Questions about his orchestra, however, made relieving sense. "We will be ready for the first performance."

"Good. I'm hoping you'll do me the honor…when you're ready. Jaron will appreciate it, I know."

Assuming that Jaron was the man's wife or partner, sibling friend, or child, Venn nodded enthusiastically, "Of course I will."

"Good," he repeated. "In the meantime, there is another matter I hope you can assist me with…because I don't think there is anyone else who can."

"Another matter?"

"Rhyd Ballard." Grainger watched the shadow fall over Venn's face and wondered if he had miscalculated. "He went to a lot of trouble to find you…to learn your fate…to rescue you from what he assumed was a state of horror. If anyone can reach him…"

Venn shook his head. He was aware, through small details the child Agnys let slip now and then, that Grainger knew the truth of Rhyd's dual life. Rhyd had not tried to hide it from Venn as he did

from everyone else, but nor did he talk freely about the devouring darkness that had driven him. "If you want me to talk him out of…what he does…I've tried. I've failed."

"So you don't know why he…?"

"Wish I did. He's got everything now. He's going to get himself killed if he keeps it up."

So perhaps Venn had not been the cause behind Scarecrow's continued mission. Without the need to free Venn any longer, there had to be something else driving him. Grainger had ideas, including the rise of the brako, but he did not think Ballard was going to sit down with him over tea and outline his agenda, his plan, his hopes.

"On the contrary, Mr. Weyer, I don't want you to talk him out of it. If he's going to persist in…well…I would rather he work with me than against me."

"With?"

"If we're working on the same side…" Not fighting. He avoided using language that he felt would be counterproductive with Weyer, "I can protect him, at least from my people. If we're trying to accomplish the same things, we can help each other…and I can stop worrying about my people putting a popper in the back of his head."

The threat of death from the bugorra, something Venn had not considered and did not want to think about, made him frown. "I don't think he'll…"

"You want him to stop being a vigi. I want him to work with me rather than against me. If we compromise, if he continues under the auspices of the bugorra…"

Grainger could see that Venn understood the advantages and that he was even willing to entertain the idea of Ballard as gorra instead of the hidden vigi lifestyle he currently lived.

"Think about it, Mr. Weyer. Talk to him. We want what is best, for him, for Hebanthe Falls…and he is not going to find it by fighting all of us."

That much they could agree on.

❧*☙

Blayd did not recognize the imposing man sharing a bar seat and drink with Senior Talker Kal. It could have been anyone. Talkers were not forbidden to drink alcohol and their outreach brought them in contact with all sorts, streeters, addicts, thugs and workers alike. Sharing a drink with someone Blayd did not recognize meant nothing.

But the stranger did not need any identifying mark for Blayd to bet his ticks on one thing.

That man was brako.

He could not get closer without being noticed. This bar, one of the seedier sorts that littered Levs 1 and 2, was sparsely populated at this crawling hour, far enough between crawls that the previous shift drinkers had migrated home for a meal and a sleep before repeating the cycle of drudgery. There were enough here though, that Blayd's seat in the dimly lit corner nearest the toilet room was partially blocked from the view of the pair he watched.

He should be hunting Scarecrow. But his belief that the vigi had his roots here in Hebenon's bowels, just as the brako did, had brought him to Lev 2, and seeing Kal skulking into this bar to join the other man was too good of an opportunity to miss. Scarecrow could wait a little longer.

He did not trust the Senior Talker, and nor, he believed, should Neoma. One whiff of the man's connection to the brako would be all it took to soil his reputation, to erase his favor with Neoma.

Removing that one obstacle to her success, to her heart, would be almost as good as removing the Scarecrow.

❧*☙

"What the cazz is that?"

The scratching sound behind the metal cabinet, the signal always used when Enoch was returning, was loud enough that everyone in the room, including the three grime-covered men clustered in the doorway of the sleeping room Skelter shared with Otta and Colyx, could hear

it. The speaker, the tallest of the three who held Skelter by the throat, a knife in his other hand, making demands for supplies Skelter did not have, was distracted enough that he did not see Skelter's fist coming from his blind side.

"Rats."

The blow, though not containing the power that the miner's fist would, was enough to rock the man off balance, enough to make him drop Skelter, who in turn missed the swing of the knife aimed at his exposed armpit.

The shiv wielder's stumble pushed the man to his right off balance and back into the corridor. The crash of the second man into the metal panel outside was accompanied by Otta's war cry when she shrieked and launched an attack on the only man remaining upright.

They had dared to attack Skelter. It was the only impetus needed.

The sounds of the brawl brought others running, including Colyx, who threw people aside left and right as he charged to the aid of his friend and the woman he had raised as a daughter.

Inside the tunnel, Enoch scrambled back, beyond the range of any light source the curious might use to look inside…if they got past Otta's fists, feet, and knives.

The riot spread back along the corridor into the central room of the Core, the tension born from rationing the dwindling food supply and the increase in agitation from a delayed escape attempt that Skelter promised to provide and had not yet delivered turning into an unrelenting free-for-all.

Skelter's backers outweighed the others in numbers, but the opposition had enough frustration and anger to make them a formidable matching force.

Otta, however, would not relent. One of the three was down, clutching his throat, unable to breathe with his windpipe crushed beneath his hands. The second, his shiv lost as it protruded from Otta's thigh, fell beneath the impact of Skelter's black iron pipe walking stick, disoriented as blood trickled from his ear where the blow had landed. The third man, back on his feet, tried to scramble over his

fallen cohorts while Otta yanked the shiv free, and though she threw it with dangerous precision so that it imbedded in the eye socket of another, it left an opening so that another woman who appeared in the doorway was able to throw a knife of her own in Skelter's direction.

That second knife nicked Otta's attacker's scalp as he planted one sole-worn boot in Otta's belly and sent her flying into the cabinet which blocked the tunnel from view.

Enoch flinched and scooted back further.

With Otta out of his way, the third fellow took two stomping steps, yanked Skelter up by one arm hard enough to dislocate it, and swung his other big fist into the redhead's side, fracturing ribs and leaving him gasping on the floor. He intended to finish what he started, but Colyx was suddenly behind him and with a blow to the base of his skull, caused the man to crumple to the floor.

"Anyone else?" Colyx roared at those accumulating around the doorway. When no one moved, he knelt at Skelter's side, seeing that Otta was already struggling to sit up, and after adjusting Skelter's position so that his breathing came easier, Colyx grabbed the dropped walking stick and waved it at those at the door.

"Anyone?"

The only movement at the door was people moving away.

❧*❧

There had never been an admonition against using the Echo in Oliver's office. One terminal was like another, and as every individual in Hebanthe Falls possessed their own identification number, save for some of the streeters who had fallen through society's cracks, there was little danger of someone accessing sensitive information without the know-how to hack their way into the Hub's coding.

As an archivist, Jaron had different privileges than the average person, and thanks to tips from Zara over the years, he knew how to worm his way into digital files where other, more secretive, information might be stored.

He also knew, after so much time with Oliver, how to access the Captain's log-in information. While he did not want the man to suffer negative consequences from what he intended to do, it was entirely within the Captain's rights to monitor production and supply stores throughout the city. No one would think twice about him accessing that material.

Indeed, there was no one to monitor him doing so.

Jaron set up the algorithm to find all facilities, all stores and manufacturers, of the freezes Rhyd was looking for. He would study the data gathered later, in private. Oliver was in a meeting when Jaron arrived, so he presumed he would have ample opportunity to begin the hunt for the information Rhyd requested.

It was the only way, he believed, to get the blonde out of his head.

All it really did, however, was push the man to the fringes of his thoughts, since everything he was doing, as he began researching the Core…historical records, mining records, inmate records, to hopefully find a Passcode…was at Rhyd's insistence.

The fascination, he told himself, was only because he now knew the face behind the mythological Scarecrow.

It had nothing to do with those whiskey eyes or the scarred hands that suggested a life of hard work and violence. It had nothing to do with the fact that Ballard had taken it on himself to make a difference in Hebenon…for everyone…when Jaron had only dreamed of doing so since the day he had been stripped of his voice.

Fear and shame had subverted his own resolve to help. Oliver Grainger had begun to reverse some of that negative impact at last.

Now, in the course of two short meetings with Rhyd, making a difference was all Jaron could think about.

He did not have Ballard's training. He had no stomach for violence, not enough courage for conflict or public protest. But this, finding information that would help Ballard and men like him to succeed at what they did…this Jaron could do. Maybe it would lead to other ways he could be of service.

Oliver, however, was going to hate it.

The light in the room came up as the man in that final moment of thought entered the office and Jaron's hand's faltered on the keypad. Swallowing his nervousness, he looked up from the screen as the bigger man said, "Didn't know you were here. Thought you'd be asleep already."

Jaron glanced at his chrono as he turned off the Echo program he was running, hoping the action looked absent and innocent enough. "Was waiting for you. Didn't realize it was so late."

"Working?" Oliver looked distracted too, distant and troubled. He also sounded edgy and Jaron wondered why.

"Sort of. Something came up on shift today…I'm trying to find supporting data…"

"About what?" Grainger did not make Jaron move from his chair but rather took one of those on the opposite side of the desk with casual ease and agitated weariness.

"The mines…salt production from the Core…"

"You've been talking to Ballard," Grainger growled.

"Who?"

For a moment, Grainger stared, prepared to snap or snarl, but able to resist the impulse. He did not want to frighten Jaron, did not want to give him any excuse that might prompt him to leave. There was a twitch at the corner of Jaron's eye that might suggest complicity, or fear, and he waited to see what the younger man would give him.

Such things as the productivity of the mines would be recorded in the Archives. It would not take much deduction for a bright, curious individual to equate the mines with the mythical Core. Most people never thought about those things, and thus the Core remained something only existing in the legends of the city's history. If some archivist had made note of some peculiarity in the data somewhere, or a businessman pushed for answers about the ongoing salt shortage, questions were bound to be asked, questions that might inevitably find their way to the city's acting leader. Once, the need for such information would have been for the Doctet and Founder to sort out, their questions to answer, their secrets to hide.

Now they did not exist to ask.

Grainger did not want to provide answers he did not have. Tonight he wanted to forget about the day he had struggled through and forget about the ache in his head and shoulder that Jaron knew nothing about.

He had surely noticed the plast, even if he had not yet asked about it. Maybe he had been there before Tamner's morning arrival. Maybe he already knew.

Such data-seeking did not mean that Jaron was part of whatever Ballard was up to. How could he be? The two men had no reason to know each other, no reason to have met.

Besides that twitch, however, Jaron's puzzled, nearly blank expression suggested Ballard was a stranger to him, an unfamiliar name, and Grainger wrote the anomaly off as eye-strain and fatigue and fear at the way he had just snapped at the smaller man.

"Never mind."

Jaron shrugged, accepted that the matter was dropped and was secretly glad for it. Whatever the cause of Oliver's foul, suspicious mood, he was not going to get answers from the man tonight.

"What's that?" He pointed to his own forehead, in the region where Oliver's plast was still in place.

"Voices." Jaron noting the injury made Oliver feel better.

"That ruckus the other day?" Jaron frowned. He had not been there, nor here to learn about it. He had only seen the prodcasts and had not been here when Oliver needed him.

Maybe that was the emotion underlying Oliver's current mood.

"How about a drink?"

He let his voice trail off into a familiar note that brought a spark into Grainger's eyes. If he could get Oliver into a better frame of mind, perhaps they could talk about the Core.

It would at least get Rhyd off of his mind.

❧*❧

"Xiaodan."

The young man, his sprayer raised to refresh a faded tag on the side wall of a vindi abandoned after the Coup, jumped, the blast of neon yellow going wide and splattering haphazardly on the wall.

"Now look what you made me do!" he exclaimed as he turned to face the unexpected person beside him. Having never come face to face with, or even seeing, the hero he summoned with his tags, he had no reason to recognize the mechanical voice. But he did recognize the mask. It was enough to cut his tirade short, but instead of fawn and grovel as some might do, stutter and stammer out of fear that his illegal activities might warrant punishment or rebuke from the vigi, he lowered the sprayer and shoved his free hand into his coat pocket.

"How the cazz do you know who I am?"

"You are directing the Spinks." Scarecrow's words were more of an information-seeking statement than one of conviction, but it had the desired effect.

"Maybe."

Scarecrow examined the remnant of previous tags with what Xiaodan imagined was interest, but might have been indifference. It was impossible to tell through the mask.

"You should be more careful. People are worried about you."

"People? You mean Tox." He believed Tox knew Scarecrow's identity, or that she at least interacted with him as Scarecrow, but she would not tell him anything. As irritating as not knowing was, he knew how difficult that secret would be for him to keep, should he learn it, so he did his best to be content with not knowing.

"She's helping. I…we…gotta do something…"

Scarecrow grunted. "There are better ways. Safer ways."

"Oh yeah? Like what?"

"You're a bright young man. Persuasive. Talk to people…"

"No one listens. I'm too young, they say. What do I know, I'm just a streeter…"

"Then stop being a streeter. Go home…and never stop talking. Keep talking until they hear you. People will listen if you speak up

often enough. Hand out fly-cards with your message. Record prods. Stand in the streets…"

"They don't listen," he repeated.

"You and the others…say it over and over until they do. And if you want to do something, start with making Hebenon better. Not this." He gestured to the too-tagged wall. "Pick up the zevel. Paint so Hebenon is beautiful. Fill empty flower boxes. You're good with your hands…you're a kaheao. Fix things, windows, signs, stairs, doors, leaking roofs. Anything that needs it. Clean out abandoned places. When you see someone doing something wrong, hurting someone, report it. Discreetly."

"That's just…"

"It is as important as anything I do," Scarecrow assured him. "We don't all need to fight. We can't expect the Nau, the captain, the gorra, to do it for us. We have to do for ourselves. And when they," he pointed towards the busy, well-lit street beyond them, "see that you're serious about making Hebenon better, they'll listen."

Xiaodan stared at the sprayer in his hand, his expression dark and scowling. "Maybe," he growled, not sounding convinced by words he had not imagined Scarecrow would say. If anything, he had expected there would be a rallying cry given to fight the system.

But in the after-Coup turmoil, there was no system. There was only anarchy.

Maybe Scarecrow was right. Maybe fighting the non-existent system was the best thing. Maybe working towards establishing a new one was a better use of the Spinks time and talents, while Scarecrow fought to uproot the brako.

Maybe together they really could change things.

"I'll talk to the others," he finally agreed. When he lifted his head, expecting words of praise or inspiration, Scarecrow was already gone.

❧*❧

"Should have been here to help."

Colyx threw Enoch a look that suggested he had doubts about anything the dwarf could have contributed to the fight his arrival had prompted. On Colyx's bed, Otta curled around herself, like a child with a stomach ache, her glassy-eyed expression worrying them both. It was not quite as worrisome, however, as the still unconscious, unmoving Skelter on his own bed. Enoch was doing his best to make the redhead comfortable as Colyx righted the scattered, broken furniture while keeping his ears open to the sounds outside the room.

Skelter's supporters had won this round and were confining the instigators while tending to the wounded. The tension was briefly released, but each passing day would continue to dredge it up until it spilled over again, or Skelter carried out, and succeeded, with his plan.

If he did not succeed, if he died before it could be attempted, Colyx did not want to remain in the Core to witness the degeneration into madness their lives would become.

There was too much of that before Skelter. Enough was enough.

Construing the big man's look as an accusation, Enoch grumbled, "How was I supposed to know? I can't see through walls…"

"You find him? Will he help?" Colyx cut off the protests with questions Skelter would ask, if he was conscious.

"He's on it…they all are."

"When will we…?"

"That's gonna be up to him." Enoch glanced again at Skelter.

"We attack the door, easy enough…"

Both looked at the speaker in the doorway who was returning with a bowl of steaming water, cloths draped over her shoulder, and a makeshift medkit tucked between her arm and her torso. The ratty-haired woman who was likely very pretty beneath the filth and decay, was one of Skelter's more ardent supporters. She had helped break up the riot despite the doubts for their future she clearly held.

Now she crossed the room to stand over Otta, squeezing the injured woman's hand and smoothing her hair as Enoch challenged, "That would be…"

"You're not even one of us," she continued matter-of-factly, without any trace of malice or disdain in her voice. "You don't belong here…didn't come to be here…like the rest of us."

"Neither did he," Colyx pointed out with a glance at Skelter.

Enoch shrugged, not arguing the point. It was true; he had not been condemned to this life like so many others. He was no hardened criminal sent into the mines to waste and rot away. He could leave and not return if he wanted. "If you want out of here, you need me…he needs me…and you need him. He has the plans…" he tapped the side of his head, "and I get what he needs. Even if blowing the door is the plan…without me, without him…"

Her look of skepticism was no surprise. Few in the Core gave Enoch much thought. Many attributed not seeing him around constantly to his stature making him unnoticeable. Most knew Skelter provided a steady, if somewhat haphazard, stream of hard to come by commodities. They assumed he had discovered a hidden vault somewhere in the Core, a vault built when the Core was built, and that he was parceling out the goods as a means of controlling the Core's population. Those who wanted that stash, who wanted the power-wielding it would provide, were keen to beat the information out of Skelter. But until today, Otta and Colyx had kept that from happening.

That the dwarf had a way in and out, that he was the key, a link to that stash, almost no one knew. And those who did know did not entirely trust the little traitor as they called him.

If he could come and go as he pleased, why couldn't they?

"You need to tell them," Otta whispered. "They need to know."

"Know what?" Enoch asked.

There was a loud static pop and the room, the Core, went dark.

Her voice in the blackness. "We're running out of time.

The dwarf sighed. "Believe me…they know."

But maybe they needed a push. Or maybe there was something more on the outside he could do to help.

He looked back and forth in the darkness between people he could not see, imagining each one nodding.

There was little use in waiting for Skelter to open his eyes. When he awoke, it would be good if Enoch had news. The power was out as Enoch had suggested, in an effort to settle the Core's residents in brief darkness, though the dwarf did not know how it was accomplished. With Colyx's help, until Skelter woke up, Enoch would proceed with his own plans.

If Skelter did not awaken, someone had to do something., carry on without him.

Later, when the way was clear and the Core was still again, its people settled into sleep because there was little else to do when the power was down, Enoch would find the Scarecrow.

❧Chapter 14❧

Leaning back against the headboard, one hand behind his head, Blayd watched Neoma at the vanity mirror, working through her morning routine of moisturizers and cosmetics that she, in his opinion, did not need to be a stunning, majestic creature. The paints gave a degree of youth to her face, but it was not her youth he admired.

It was her lust for power, and what he could gain from it in turn.

She had been in a frenzied state when he found her yesterday, irate and, he thought, uncertain about what the future held for her daughter but mostly for herself. Despite her claims, Blayd had few illusions about what her intentions were…even if she never spoke of them. He was willing to do anything to help her achieve those goals, if she would reward him in kind. But he was beginning to have doubts about her relationship with Senior Talker Kal.

And about his own with Ilya.

No, he corrected his thinking. Ilya was a shadow from his past, a distant dream, and while they might be able to help one another to get what they wanted, Scarecrow out of the way and the brako under control, Ilya could not give him what he wanted most.

Only the woman at the mirror, the corners of her mouth drooping into a tighter frown, possessed enough power, or had the potential of enough power albeit unattained, to give him that.

"Come back to bed," he murmured, holding out a hand.

She was no cuddler. Acts of affection were not in her repertoire, even with her child. She used her bed, wielded her body, as a weapon, a tool for getting what she wanted…and occasionally for the physical release of emotions she could expel no other way. When he was with

her here, however, he never felt as though he was being used, as if there was any power being wielded over or against him.

She shared her bed with him because she wanted him…as much as he wanted her.

It was not love, but he dared hope she needed him.

"Do you trust him?"

"Him?"

"Kal?"

"No." That was an easy question. He was a Talker. Blayd never trusted anyone who put a religious agenda ahead of anything else.

"Why?"

"Talker. Senior Talker." She scowled at his reflection and he shrugged, sliding to the edge of the bed to put his feet on the floor. The room was small enough that he could reach and touch her, but he did not. From the glint in her eyes, he thought she would strike him if he tried.

"He's got his own agenda. Talkers want to control Hebenon…talk us all into submission to…"

"They're Voices. They support Haythem." Her tone was pointed, probing, not a desperate plea, not begging for support. She wanted his thoughts, his interpretation of the state of things around them, and she expected him to provide it without sweetening the sentiments.

"They support the Founder when the Founder supports them. Parasites leeching off the system. If they can't have him, they'll take Ulynda…as a figurehead to prop up their rules."

"Ulynda's not…"

Now he did touch her, both hands on her shoulders to turn her on the swiveling stool so that they faced each other. "You know damn well they're not going to accept you there, no matter what Kal promises. You're not a Kemway by blood and you can't be manipulated. Not the way she can be; not the way…"

Not the way the ailing Founder could be, if they could get their hands on him.

Neoma nodded. It was what she saw in Kal too.

"But he's not controlling them, the others, the way he should be."

"Without Haythem," she agreed, "he has nothing but words."

"Without the Founder, or the Founder's daughter," Blayd reminded her. "If he can't have one, he is going to do everything he can to get the other." Including, he left unsaid, removing Neoma from play to get to the girl. That was a very real concern for both her and Blayd, and he was glad she saw it. "He's making alliances everywhere, and that's never a good thing…but he'll never get close to you. I'll kill him before that happens…just like I will Scarecrow."

Neoma ran her fingers over his lips, down his chin to the hollow of his throat before pressing her palm over his hammering heart without breaking away from his gaze.

He swallowed hard past the shortness of breath created by her touch, having lost himself in those moments to the blue of her eyes. "He's not going to get to you, or her. I won't let him. I'll kill him first."

The frown on her lips turned slowly upwards and she slid from the stool to straddle his hips. There was time before the day began. Time to cement a course of action before undertaking any other.

"I know you will, Blayd," she purred before kissing him.

She was counting on it.

❧*❧

Skelter's eyes fluttered opened to darkness, unfamiliar darkness, total and startling unlike any he remembered. It did not frighten him, very little did, but it did puzzle him and cause him to doubt whether he was actually awake or was dreaming of waking.

Feeling movement beside him, however, real movement of warm flesh, the curves and limbs familiar in their shape and pressure, convinced him he was neither dreaming nor asleep.

"Otta?"

"Mmm?"

Pleased that she was awake with him, he stroked her tinted hair and kissed the top of her head against his shoulder.

"The lights?"

They were dimmed from their usual pale illumination when the Core residents slept, conserving what power they had, but he could not hear the generators' hum in the distance and that concerned him.

No generators meant no power. To anything. If they were out of fuel or the generators had failed, life was going to become unbearable in short order.

"They're working on it."

He grunted. Who they were, and what was wrong, would be something he would worry about when his body hurt a little less. Those aches brought back memories of the fight and those memories, combined with the underlying strain in Otta's voice made him frown.

"Are you…?" he began.

"Enoch's gone for Scarecrow. He's going to bring him…to talk. He's rigging a line…for communication."

That had not been what he intended to ask, but it was good to know. What sort of line Enoch could rig would wait for discovery when there was power enough to see by…and to run it.

Hopefully, it was not a line that relied on the generator's power.

"You okay? They didn't hurt you, did they?"

Hurt was a relative term. Otta was tougher, more resilient, than almost anyone Skelter knew here in the Core. He was pretty sure only Colyx outmatched her. But she had gone down hard before he had, and he worried, even though he could not feel any damage as he stroked his hand over her in the dark. Nor did she flinch or groan in pain, suggesting she was either alright, or a damn good actress.

For many minutes the room was quiet, the absence of Colyx's snoring suggesting he was not in the room, possibly off overseeing whatever matter had resulted in total Core darkness. The gradual steadying of Otta's breathing meant she had fallen asleep and was not going to answer his question.

She might not have even heard it.

He closed his eyes, intending to sleep as well, to wait for light, for waking, for another chance to inquire about her wellbeing.

There was a gulp, an intake of air beside him, followed by her heavily weighted words.

"I might have lost our baby."

Though his arm tightened around her, drawing her closer in mutual comfort, he spoke not a word.

What could he say to that?

He had not even known she was with child.

❧*❦

"I don't know if this will work."

"So many concoctions, mixtures of chemicals and herbs and tinctures, had been tried in an effort to stabilize Kemway's manic episodes that Tamner was beginning to feel like a witch doctor creating potions. Gradually, with each new effort, they had come a little closer to finding something that calmed the rages, subdued the unstable man without having to resort to tranquilizers to knock him out. But the doctor worried about the effects so many injections, so many chemicals, would have on the man's overall health.

Not that it could be much worse than it was, but the possibility that one of his attempts would kill, or permanently incapacitate the man who had no say in his treatment was an ever-growing risk.

Some of his rat test subjects had died.

But none of them were infected with the host of Heb-induced symptoms the Founder possessed. And rats were not people.

The man in his fettershirt snarled past the gag in his mouth and tried to break free of the arms attempting to keep him still. Eyes wild as if he feared the injector in Tamner's hand, he tried to kick the doctor away, but his legs were bound and the effort meant he had neither foot on the ground for leverage and was now controlled entirely by the strength of the medics holding him. His attempt pitched them to the padded floor where they struggled to wrestle him face down to the mat. With two men pinning him, his continued struggles grew less

effective. Tamner was able to press the injector against Kemway's neck, releasing him to whatever effects this latest mixture would have.

As happened after every injection, Kemway's body went rigid.

The assistants and Tamner stepped clear but remained close enough to monitor his initial condition and reaction to the medication.

His body relaxed. Tamner rolled his limp form over and ran a medscan over his body to get a readout of his condition. Heartrate normal. Blood pressure normal. Breathing steady. His eyes were clear as they had been in the days before the Coup.

He was not a drooling, blubbering, mess of a man, not a wild thing out of control, but nor was he normal. He was just…there.

At least he was not hurting himself.

"Even if it works," Tamner said to the man beyond the glass window who would only hear him over his ICD, "there's no telling for how long. He could relapse at any moment."

"Then we get her up here. Now."

"That may not be wise, Captain…"

Grainger did not want to hear it. He wanted Neoma out of his way. He wanted her to stop pestering him and his staff for approval to see her husband, for proof he was alive. Better she saw him like this, and perhaps saw him slip into one of his other states, then for her to continue as she was. "Stay with him, Doctor. I'm sending for her."

If something went wrong, then the woman could blame Tamner.

Tamner, knowing it was his neck, his career on the line, now had every incentive to keep the Founder alive.

At least long enough for his wife to see him.

☘*☙

It was easy to convince the younger Spinks to launch into a 'clean up Hebenon' campaign. They were often excluded from the tagging efforts of their elders, and the claim that the 'order' had come directly from Scarecrow sparked enthusiastic gusto. With recycle bins and waste boxes in hand, they began in the streets nearest their crash,

picking up anything discarded in walkways and alleys and window boxes and hauling it to the nearest chutes for disposal and repurposing.

The vindi owners, peering from their stands and shops to see what the gaggle of streeters was doing, nodded their heads approvingly and offered snacks and drinks to the children in exchange for their efforts.

No having to steal a meal.

No being yelled at and chased away for loitering.

Xiaodan realized as the morning progressed that perhaps Scarecrow was on to something. The streets looked nicer, the younger Spinks were being fed and felt useful, and when asked what they were doing or why, they could claim to be helping the Scarecrow.

Not everyone, however, appreciated the message, even if they approved of the cleanup efforts. Conditioned by a lifetime, by generations, of experience, when the bugorra appeared on the Lev where the streeters were working, the Spinks scattered into the shadows, not willing to trust that their innocence would be believed just because they were working for the city's future rather than sapping it with unsavory, unbeneficial skulking about.

Xiaodan, however, determined to make a difference, determined to put Scarecrow's faith to the test and take a stand for the cause of a better Hebenon, stayed where he was, zevel bin in hand half full, his hands dirty and wet from the work but no more so than anyone else's would be.

"You. What are you doing?"

"What's it look like?" he replied to the woman with the lieutenant insignia on her lapel, trying to sound as undefensive as he could. He knew Ginna's sister was a lieutenant but did not know if there was more than one, and without being able to see the speaker's face or hands, he could not tell if this woman would be on his side or not. "Picking up zevel."

"You're the Yin boy, aren't you?"

The tone of the question made him tense; though his eyes scanned the nearest routes of possible escape, he did not move. He had done nothing wrong. They had no reason to bother him.

"I'm not doing anything…"

"Bring him."

The hands of two gorra closed around his arms in spite of his efforts to duck away. They could have asked him to come along and he might have done so, but the order, and the force with which they held him and propelled him away from the hidden watching eyes of the Spinks struck Xiaodan as being too much like an arrest.

Maybe for his previous tagging.

Maybe for no reason at all.

"Tell him," he shouted over his shoulder to those who could not be seen. "Tell him they've taken me!"

Scarecrow had been wrong, but he was not giving up on the man.

He had done nothing wrong. He just had to make the bughats see it.

⊱*⊰

Archivists did it all the time. Swipe their passcard for entry into the Hub. Log in, access the day's data, sort, catalog, compare, categorize. Look for anomalies, question the sources if a discrepancy looked dubious or ping the system if it appeared to be a technical or typographical error.

Nothing Jaron did looked out of place. Nothing he did appeared different to any who might have looked his way, nothing was different than any other day spent at this terminal. Every set of eyes on this floor was similarly engaged in data watching so none could spare the time to make note of what anyone else was doing at any given time.

It was a routine they all knew by heart.

Many archivists did not last more than three to five years before burning out, numbed by the parade of numbers, letters, figures, sound recordings, SCAM footage, and ICD images.

Jaron had been here so long that he was like a permanent fixture, part of the furniture, part of the building, a given that none questioned.

He was trusted. No one ever asked what he was doing.

It did not erase his fast heart rate and pulse today, however, as he copied the data sent by the algorithm he had programmed the night before…in Oliver's office. It did not quell the nausea in his belly.

But no one came, no one questioned, and when the download was complete, he shoved the passcard into his pocket. The Archive system would record the blip, the change in his physical condition that was monitored at all times in an effort to keep the archivists functioning at peak performance levels. Alert them of a need for a break if necessary. He could blame the nervous state on the tall cup of spiced algtea sitting to one side of his station, something he did not normally have, a caffeinated cover that would certainly contribute to an abnormal state of alertness and energy.

The SCAMs and the monitoring units would make their report to whatever station registered that data, someone would look at it without the need for flagging suspicious behavior, and that access would be archived too.

Only later, when off shift, in the privacy of his room with the untethered Echo Zara had supplied him with…likely at Rhyd's insistence…would he peruse the data he had accumulated and determine what, if anything, they could use.

❧*❧

"Please be careful."

Tamner might as well be talking to the door, or to the Founder, for all the heed Neoma gave when he allowed her inside. She had stood at the separating glass window for ten silent minutes before demanding to be allowed into the room with the man whose blank stare indicated he had no idea he was being watched.

As if he did not care.

Convinced that seeing him face to face would change things, or that it would at least prove that the man she saw was not a mannequin, a falsity placed to give her unverified hope, she insisted on entering the room despite Grainger's wishes to the contrary and Tamner's

better judgment. He quickly relented, accepting that she required more compelling proof that her husband lived.

"He won't hurt me."

"He won't know you." Maybe she believed her own words, but she moved no closer to the man seated against the side wall, legs outstretched before him, hands at rest in his lap, head erect rather than lolling to the side as he stared at the opposite walls. The fettershirt had been removed for Neoma's benefit, and Tamner hoped he would not regret that order too. "When his mood shifts, it happens fast, so be careful."

"He looks harmless."

Tamner nodded with a sigh. "Yes. For now."

"Leave me with him."

"That is not a good idea. If he…"

"He's my husband. I haven't seen him in two years. He doesn't move. I'll stay away. I just want to be alone with him. A few minutes."

Tamner glanced at the window where he knew Grainger to be though he could not see him through the mirrored panel. His better judgment told him to stay for her protection rather than to intrude on any words she might want to say to Haythem. But there were three taps on the glass, instruction enough, and again he sighed. "I will be on the other side of this door. Stay at least eight feet away from him…and do not say anything that might upset him. He may not look like he hears us, but I believe he does. Agitation is not good for him. Shout if you need me. You've got ten minutes."

He was not willing to give her more. He would rather have given her fewer, or none at all. They were already approaching the limits of how long past injections had lasted. He held up his arm and tapped his chrono, a signal Grainger would see and hopefully understand, and then stepped out of the small room.

Neoma knelt in front of the seated man she barely recognized after so much time apart. He was thinner, whether from his condition or a failure of her memory she was unsure. He was familiar, but not the

same, and any attraction she may have once felt seemed to have evaporated with the loss of familiarity.

It had gone the way of any affection felt early in their marriage.

But he was Founder still, her husband, the father of her children, though only one of those remained, and she knew she was being watched from the other side of that glass panel. She had to put in some believable effort now that she was here, to convince them even if she could not convince Haythem or herself.

"How are you. It's good to see you. I'm sorry it has been so long."

Did he have any concept of the passage of time? Was he aware that she had not seen him in over two years? Did he remember the Coup, the last time they saw one another when she had manipulated him to stay behind while she and the children evacuated? Would things be different now if he had come with them?

Would the world have gone back to the way it was before?

"The children are doing well...you should see them. They're getting so big." She might not feel any affectionate attachment to him, but she did not think it fair to mention that two of their children, his heir and his favorite, had both perished. He probably did not know. He might never know. His ignorance was a blessing in disguise.

Voice lowering as she gambled that those outside would not be able to hear, she continued, "I'll make this right, Haythem. You had your faults...but you gave up everything for Hebanthe Falls...for nothing...but I won't let it end like this. You doubted me...but you won't. You'll see. I will do what you could not...and the city will be better. We're outside now...do you know that? There's a world out there...vast and new...with all of its resources waiting for us. I have not seen it except through the dome, but I will. The children will too. As soon as the city is in hand, you will see it too."

She forced an audible sigh, hoping she sounded appropriately mournful to the spies outside of the room. Before speaking again, she lowered her voice to a whisper, wanting no one to hear her next words.

"I can't have you in the way. I can't risk you coming back to us. That can't happen, you understand. I have to make the effort...but

you'll never leave here. Not alive, not for long at least. I can't let that happen. You'll be a martyr, you'll be what this city needs, you just won't be here to see it. You understand; I know you do."

As she spoke, leaning forward to look into his vacant eyes, his body began to tremble. Doubting that he heard her or comprehended her words, believing him to be locked inside of his head the way Grainger claimed, Neoma guessed that Haythem was on the verge of slipping into what Tamner called a 'manic phase'. She refused to show fear or panic, refused to show intimidation, but as she rose to her feet, she never took her eyes off of the man she intended to never see again.

She had done her duty, seen him once. Once was enough.

"Goodbye, Haythem. I will give the children your love."

There was no need for Ulynda to see what her father had become. Best for the girl if her memories of her father stayed as they were.

Outside of the room, the lock buzzed, clicked, and Tamner and two of his staff pushed into the room, prepared to subdue their patient should they need to while the doctor escorted the woman out. The further she got from the man on the floor who had yet to shift positions, the more violently he shook, his fists balling on his lap.

She reached the doorway, was about to pass through it with Tamner's hand on the small of her back, when Haythem lurched to his feet as though he had been jettisoned from a popper, crying, "NO!" as the medics caught him by the arms.

Tamner looked back before the door closed. The medics had the man in hand and would wrestle him back into the fettershirt before he hurt himself or someone else.

Both the doctor, where he escorted Neoma, and Grainger on the other side of the room in a different corridor at the observation window, wondered what was said or done to elicit that reaction.

Or if the Founder, in his fugue, had recognized that one link with his life and simply had not wanted her to leave.

As he continued to howl within the padded walls of his captivity, doctor, captain, and wife doubted they would ever know.

But they did know it was the first word he had spoken in two years.

❧Chapter 15❧

They had kept him in a small cubicle of a room for hours. He did not know how many as there was no Echosys on the empty, unadorned walls, only the blinking red eye of the SCAM that recorded every moment of his waiting. He did not have a chrono as his had been lost in the streets, and he had never been a very good judge of the passage of time. But he counted the steps of people passing the room, counted the number of times a gorra stuck his head in to assess their captive's condition or be certain he was still there, and then left again.

Where could he go, with the gorra outside the door? Did they expect him to open the passlocked door with the palm of his hand?

Eventually, a pale-faced fellow entered and spread a series of SCAM images across the scratched and dented table in front of him. He asked Xiaodan to identify the faces in the images, but he refused. Some he knew, some he did not, but he was determined not to crow on anyone.

Especially not Ginna.

His interrogator left him, the images still on the table, and Xiaodan, believing that whoever was behind the SCAMs would note any he lingered over, any one he picked up, leaned back in the chair and closed his eyes.

Let them hold him. If they had accusations to make, proof of anything, they would probably have used it already.

Anxiously wondering when Scarecrow might come to his rescue, he dozed in that awkward, bent-necked position long enough that, when the sound of the door opening and closing lurched him awake, it was to an ache at the base of his skull that he rubbed to ease as he looked at the woman who had come in.

Lieutenant Young.

"Did you rest well?"

Xiaodan scowled. "How long have I been here? What am I being charged with?"

"No one said you were…"

"You can't hold me in a locked room if I'm not being charged. That's the rule."

It was a rule, however, that everyone in the Levs knew the Crows had circumvented more times than were countable. The bugorra taking people was less noticeable, seemed to happen less often, but everyone believed that the practice of taking people for the hell of it was still in effect. Nothing had changed.

Xiaodan being brought and held here was proof of that.

"Who said it was locked?" She sat across from him and leaned forward with her elbows on the table. "I brought you here because I'm looking for my sister." They stared silently at each other for several moments, she awaiting a response, he awaiting a question, a hint of who exactly she was looking for and why she thought he would know.

He knew who she wanted. Who she was. But he did not know what she knew about him and refused to offer gratuitous information.

"Ginna," the Lieutenant sighed, drawing the younger woman's image from the desktop lineup, "has been missing for several days. She isn't with her friends…with the Talkers…and if she's streeting, I want to know. I want her safe. The way you look after those kids, lead them…I'd say if anyone knows who's out there, if anyone has seen her and knows where she is, it would be you."

Flattery. The corners of Xiaodan's mouth twitched but he said nothing. He doubted, from the way Ilya said 'friends', that she even knew who Ginna's friends were. She had likely lost track of who Ginna was, what her views and feelings were, who she spent time with and what she did, a long time ago.

"Not my job to keep track of everyone out there."

"But you do. You manage all those kids…"

"She don't look like no kid to me." He indicated the image beneath Ilya's hand. "And I don't control nothing. Sometimes we work together…"

"Like cleaning up the Levs?" she prompted.

"We were promised payment."

"By who?"

Xiaodan did not reply.

"What sort of payment?"

Still, he was silent.

Ilya, frustrated, was not surprised by the streeter's stonewalling. She leaned back as well, folded her arms over her chest, and observed him for a moment. Streeters were notorious for three things. Heb use, which this youngster was obviously clean of, turning each other in as an act of self-preservation, which he seemed unwilling to do, and keeping everything they knew to themselves and protecting one another at all cost. It was typically Heb users who were guilty of the second, and thus not trusted by true streeters, thus Ilya knew she was not going to easily get information out of this one. In the past, her predecessors might have tried to beat the information out of him, or threatened him with banishment or involuntary enrollment in one or another medical experimentation program.

Grainger would not allow those tactics anymore, and Ilya was not in favor of them either. If she tried, and Ginna learned she had abused her friend, she would never come home. But there were other, better ways to get what she needed.

"You can tell me what I want to know…or I can let you go. If I do that, you realize I'll be watching everyone you know, your aunt, your grandmother, your…"

"Watch us all you want," he snorted. "We haven't done anything." While he was marginally concerned that the gorra watching Tox might somehow be a threat to Scarecrow, and that it would be Xiaodan's fault if anything happened to Tox again…or to Scarecrow…he steadfastly believed that both of those people were too smart to be seen together in public and would not be caught again.

"You're free to go then…and tell your kids to stay off the streets."

"They were cleaning up," he protested, standing when she stood.

"They were trespassing, loitering…"

"Ain't no trespassing on the streets…and we weren't in anyone's buildings." Not yet, at any rate, and he was not about to stop the kids from following Scarecrow's wishes now that they had them. "Don't see no buggers out there making Hebenon decent. You're all too busy rounding up kids just trying to make a positive difference."

There was a pang in Ilya's chest when she realized just how often Ginna said words so similar to those. He knew Ginna alright. And he was probably the influence behind her unruly, disobedient, disruptive behavior. He was probably the primary tagger as well.

But without proof of that, she could not hold him.

"And you will," she continued, opening the door to let him out of the room, ignoring his outburst as meaningless protest, "tell Ginna to come home…that I'm looking for her."

He had been warned. If he refused to heed the warning, it would not be her fault.

When he did not reply to her final admonition, she knew he was not likely to pass her plea along to her sister either.

It did not matter. She and the gorra would follow him now…and he would lead her straight to Ginna.

⤳*⤶

It was never easy to be anonymous after your face was displayed across Echos throughout the city, when the entire population knew your name, your business, your history.

Or thought they knew.

But in a place steeped in shadows and damp, when long coats and hoods, hats, and gloves, were a standard accessory for every man, woman, and child, it helped raise the possibility of anonymity, so long as one's attire did not speak of wealth…the brako…or the bugorra.

It was the drab, dirty brown hooded cloak that allowed Neoma to disguise all but her stately stature as she descended the staircase, fingers gripping tightly to the rail in the hopes that she would not slip and fall. She hated this dampness, hated the cold, and wondered, as she scanned the cloaked shadows passing too and froe along the grated walkway, how these people could bear it, how they could survive in this nightmarish gloom that she had grown to despise in the short time living here. The Lev 20 flat she had been assigned to, an outcast of the Uppers now, was above the worst of the cold and moisture, sparing her this much of the time, but the need for food and nessies meant trips below, except when she could convince Blayd or someone else to go for her. But today he was preoccupied with the pursuit of Senior Talker Kal as she had asked.

And this was something she had to do alone.

She had to come here, to Lev 2. This was a meeting she could have nowhere else.

"Didn't think you'd come."

The shadow behind her, as she stepped off the stairs and turned left onto the walkway, cut off the glow of the alglamp on the corner of the nearest building, casting his bulk into a featureless black mass that stood a head taller than Neoma and was more than twice her breadth.

It was no wonder people were afraid of him.

"Not here." While not afraid of him, she was not eager to be alone with him either. But there were conversations best not heard by others and neither could risk being seen together, being recognized. Some partnerships were better kept private.

His head tilted towards the doorway of a nearby building, from which rolled the stale stench of death and blood and offal, of small creatures packed too tightly together for their short lives because there was no room in Hebanthe Falls to raise animals properly.

The efforts to be humane were often lost when it came to the matter of survival.

She followed, holding her breath so as not to gag on the stench.

"Breathe through your mouth. It's easier."

Easier. She tried and promptly closed her lips again as the taste of the foul air settled on her tongue and clogged her efforts to swallow and breathe. Eyes narrowed, thinking there had to be a better place to talk, she forced her hissed, "You haven't done as I…"

No one inside, none of the workers she could see, paid them any heed. She felt secure enough to speak here, isolated from eavesdroppers, but the smell was quickly making her ill.

"Hijo de puta is hard to pin down," he snorted, his tone heavy with insult and contempt. "If it was easy, your joguina would have done it already. Or the buggers would have."

Neoma's eyes narrowed more and her chin tilted so that the hood of her cloak slid far enough back for her blue eyes to catch the refracted glint of the interior lighting. "They're too busy looking for you."

He shrugged. "It's what we agreed on."

An agreement born of necessity, but one it was time to change. "He's in my way; they both are," she huffed, finding the effort to speak increasingly difficult when she was trying to avoid breathing the putrid vapor. "And the Senior is stepping beyond his means…"

"You want me to take on the Talkers too? That'll be extra."

"Not all of them…just him." Undoubtedly, another Talker would step in to fill the void the Senior left behind, but no other Talker in the city held as much sway as Senior Kal. No one else would be as much of a threat to her plans as he was.

And testing this man's loyalty, after the covert meeting between the brako and Senior that Blayd had stumbled upon, was imperative. If the man before her balked at the task, she would know where his loyalties lay.

No one else had the nerve to try.

"I'm good for it, you know I am…"

"Not yet, you aren't." But she would be, if she could step into the power vacancy the Founder's absence had created. Grainger was trying, but it was not the same. The Captain did not have the stones to do what needed to be done.

Her partner showed no reluctance to perform the task she asked of him, only the sort of cautious thoughtfulness she expected to see in a man plotting someone's death. "What about your husband? Is he…?"

She wiped her gloved hand across her nose, revolted that the smell seemed to be settling into the fabric as well, and grunted, "He's no threat. I will deal with him." She had endured enough of this place. As much as she despised them, the cold and damp outside were better than this. Intending to exit the building, she turned and elbowed the swinging door open.

She did not know how yet, as getting past Grainger's security and med staff would not be easy, but she was confident there had to be at least one member of that staff, one cook, one jani, she could bribe or manipulate to her cause.

He caught her arm, fingers long enough, hand wide enough, that they encircled her bicep like a vice.

"You better. If he…once they find out…"

Though unarmed and no physical match for her opponent, the scathing look she gave prompted him to let go. He did not move, did not step back, but there appeared to be a sudden distance between them filled by the straightening of her shoulders before she adjusted her hood to cover her face. "He won't. They won't."

The days of evacuation in the factory had given her ample time and opportunity for planning. Certain contingencies had to be adjusted upon the deaths of two of her children, the changes in Hebenon during those long weeks, and the exposure of Hebanthe Falls to the Outside, but Neoma had been thorough. She had been very meticulous in her planning and design.

As long as those hurdles were cleared from her path, she had nothing to lose. And if she could pit those obstacles against each other, set them to doing for her what she could not do herself, all the better.

❧*❧

With the gradual warming of the air came the plowing of thawing fields in preparation for the planting to begin once the changes announced the end of winter. It was a routine Venn knew well, having participated in it for enough years that it felt comfortable and exciting to await the budding of new plants.

It felt like home.

Believing Rhyd was out of his life, with the city closed to him and Rhyd trapped inside, Venn had done his best to build a new existence here, to move on, to start again. It had been a struggle, through addiction withdrawals, through the loss of his cello and Rhyd, through the communication barriers and the variances in culture, but he had settled into it and eventually grew to embrace the differences.

He straightened, one hand against his back until it popped, the other shielding his eyes from the setting of the sun over the mountains. He should see to a meal, see to the evening fire, but he was so close to having this plot plowed that he hated leaving it unfinished.

Thirty minutes. If he pushed, he could finish before the sky grew too dark to see, and if he was lucky, he would push through the front door of home and find Rhyd had already started a fire.

But he could see the door to the small home from where he stood; no light burned through the single window and the door was closed. Dark. Deserted.

No, Rhyd would not be there. Not tonight.

Perhaps never again.

How many nights had it been? Venn had not counted. He had wandered the paths of familiar vindis, through haunts they had shared, and spent hours in the rooms they once called home. As the movement of time in the perpetually dark Levs was different, night and day marked only by sleep cycles and artificial lighting, it was possible Rhyd had been on-shift these many nights, unable to return. If that was true, however, Venn should have found the blonde sprawled on the bed or the sofa at least once, breathing mask in place, forgetting to shut off the Echo, forgetting to pull up a blanket, forgetting to put away the remnants of his meal…or forgetting to eat altogether.

But the flat had been empty, with no sign of Rhyd being there. No dirty dishes or rumpled bedding. No damp towels or clothes discarded on the floor. No pillow on the sofa or blanket flung over the back.

Only the oxygen tanks that seemed to move about the flat on their own each time Venn entered indicated that anyone had been there.

Perhaps Maemi moved them when she came to restock the nessies that Rhyd often did not think about. Perhaps she had cleaned and put away used dishes, taken laundry for washing, made the bed or sofa so that Rhyd did not have to think about those things.

Or maybe, Venn thought with a scowl, Rhyd was in trouble somewhere. Maybe he needed Venn's help.

But he was not Rhyd. Venn did not have the inner fortitude to embark on the dangerous life Rhyd had undertaken after Venn's arrest. If Rhyd was in danger, there was only one thing Venn could do.

He had delivered his concerns about Rhyd's welfare to Grainger, along with the disappointing news that he had thus far been unable to deliver the Captain's offer of compromise. The matter was in the hands of the bugorra. If Rhyd was in trouble, it was up to Grainger to get him out of it.

Or he would have to get out of it himself.

Or die trying.

Venn wiped his eyes with a trembling hand as he again lay aside the plow and looked at Hebenon's metal shell. He would go one more time to the flat, see if he could find evidence of Rhyd's double life, of any life…and he would plead with the man to come back to him if he found him, to share his life as he once had.

Venn despaired, however, that those days were behind them.

Curse the day he had picked up that first hit of Heb.

Curse the day addiction had rooted and ripped their home apart.

Huddled beneath a lesser-used set of stairs between Levs, behind recycle bins and a wagon of zevel waiting for a jani pickup, stairs used mainly by the Talkers who called this complex of flats and meeting rooms home, Scarecrow shuffled deeper into the shadows and

adjusted his coat against the chill. The manhunt underway for him by both gorra and the militant arm of the Talkers since that lift skirmish had kept him on the move for so many hours he had lost track of time. Up and down between Levs, zig-zagging through shafts and alleys, streets and rooftops, making it difficult to continue a hunt of his own.

He could have retired after that meeting with Jaron, gone to the flat and avoided those tracking him. Venn would be looking for him too. Perhaps others as well. Yet everything about that brief meeting with Jaron had set Rhyd on edge, driving him to the streets. It had not taken long to notice the increased bugorra and Talker activity, to hear the murmurs that suggested he was more wanted than before. His fall into the shaft had prompted questions as to whether he was alive or dead…and everyone, it seemed, hoped to be the ones to find him.

Curious about the Talker's motives, unclear whether it was because he had made an effort to protect the Captain or something more, he fell into a cat and mouse game with them until the third replacement oxygen tank he had picked up along the way began to bleed dry. His decision to pack in his efforts, to cease his hunt for Talkers, for brako, for any hint on how Skelter had come to be inside the Core, if not through the Factory East mine entrance…had brought him to this hidden alcove. A large group of gorra, heavily armed and bullying everyone they passed, forced him into what he had expected to be temporary hiding, only to have their passing followed quickly by the onset of a Talker pilgrimage into the Voices' headquarters.

This place, on the Talkers' doorstep, proved to be sufficient shelter as no one, Talker or bugger, looked here as they marched or shuffled past.

If Rhyd had been the hunter, not the prey, such an alcove would have been checked at once.

Maybe they thought hiding so close to the Talkers' nest was a risk Scarecrow would never take. Or else the gorra had been en route to somewhere else and the Talkers too intent on the purpose of their gathering to give hunting him further thought.

Where he was afforded a full view of the steady stream of Talkers, arriving alone or in small groups, rounding the corner of the building and gathering inside, behind the wall Scarecrow crouched against. There was too much extraneous noise from nearby flats and vindis for him to hear what was happening inside, even with the enhancements to his hood.

Only a mention of 'Kemway' by a pair of stragglers gave him any clues. It made sense that the Talkers, those whose business it was to tout the tenants of the Voices of Faith to the people, would need to convene to discuss the news that the Founder lived, to decide what this meant to them and to the city. He doubted so many gathered could be good, however, expected some nefarious scheme about to be hatched by an organization he had never trusted, but at least this gathering meant the Talkers were no longer searching for him.

He would take his chances with outwitting the gorra.

Electronic chortles from the run of laughies playing on the Voices' external Echo at the far end of the complex announced the hour, for such programs ran at scheduled times each day, announced the jarring realization that he was expected to be on shift in sixty.

But from where he was, still adorned as the gorra and brako's worst enemy, there was little hope of getting to the shed on time unless he hurried. It might be best to call in for a rare day off and perhaps take these unexpected hours to either catch up on missed sleep or seek the Core entrance without the mask to hide behind. How quickly he could get home would depend on how fast he could move through Hebenon's arteries.

A lull in foot traffic, now that the Talkers were sequestered behind closed headquarter doors, allowed Scarecrow to slip from the shadows, up the stairwell and across a grated juncture between half-Lev structures into the nearest shaft entrance. That path allowed an unimpeded flight to the filt chute that opened into his flat, where he was safe enough to remove the mask that hid his face from the world.

He should have been alone. As he dropped into the room, pulling the mask free, it robbed him of the auditory enhancements and thus he

did not hear the breathing of the man who sat at his dining table nursing a glass of whiskey.

The tang of alcohol in the air was the first thing Rhyd noticed.

Impulse prompted him to throw a shuriken as he spun around, but the underlying knowledge that the intruder could be Venn or Maemi meant that the bladed metal disk struck the bottle instead of flesh, knocking it away from the intruder's lips but not out of his hand.

The blade ricocheted to one side and imbedded in the sofa.

Enoch stared, more shocked and surprised than he let on, and let out a long slow breath when he realized how close he had come to death…or at least serious injury.

"Do you greet all your guests like that?" he quipped, hiding his unsettledness behind sarcasm and the burn of Zaolei.

"Guests don't break into my home." Rhyd dropped his mask, stripped out of his coat, and snatched the bottle from the dwarf's hand in a few quick motions. If it had been Maemi or Tox, or even Zara, they had access, hard-won from him from long months of gained trust. Any one of them could have been here just as easily as the dwarf.

Perhaps one of them had let him in.

Shrugging, pulling his elbows from the table and resting against the back of the chair, Enoch replied, "Was either that or loiter at your door in full view of the buggers…and from the looks of things out there, that sort of attention would not have been good for either of us."

"They want you too?"

It would not be a surprise. Although the survival of children in Hebenon was of the utmost importance to ensure the continuation of humanity, those with certain types of defects were most often culled from the population at a very early age killed or kept from future breeding. Whether Enoch was a criminal or not, the flaws in his genetics could be enough for those in power to desire his detention.

Or at least, it had been enough when the Founder and Doctet were in power. Rhyd did not know Grainger's views of such things.

"You could say that." His tone, the shifting away of his eyes to look around the room he had most likely already examined were

evasive enough to be his answer. Whatever his crimes might be, why he might be hunted by the gorra, Rhyd did not need to know.

Neither said more as Rhyd peeled out of layer after layer of damp clothing down to his shorts. The body armor provided protection from damage, but his pale skin was littered with bruises gained in his last several fights, the display reminding Enoch of the images he had seen of old-world jaguars…darker in the center, yellowish on the edges. Most men would not be able to endure such physical abuse without Heb or some other agent to dull their senses.

Though there was the Zaolei, from most of the stories Enoch had heard, Ballard was not most men. There was a reason Skelter trusted him, wanted him for this job.

"Take it this isn't social." Rhyd was untroubled by the dwarf watching him undress. Even unarmed, he was a match for many, and as far as he could see, Enoch carried no weapon that could harm him.

"Shower; you smell like a skolper. It'll keep a few more minutes."

Rhyd grunted, delayed long enough to call into the Shed for a sick day, as he suspected Enoch's visit was going to do more than make him late for his shift, and trudged to the bathroom.

By the time he returned, the bottle of Zaolei was empty and a second bottle, unopened, sat on the table in its place. He assumed the other had been set out to recycle, although he had not heard the door. Maybe it had been left in the kitchen, out of his sight. Towel around his waist, skin damp and hair still dripping, he took the seat opposite Enoch, opened the bottle, and offered it. Enoch shook his head.

"Had enough for one evening."

Rhyd doubted that. Enoch had emptied an entire bottle in one sitting, however long that sitting had been, and he showed no hint of intoxication.

"What's this about?"

"Skelt's in a bad way."

The raised bottle was set down as Rhyd leaned forward, contents still untouched.

"He'll live," the dwarf continued. "He's a tough bastard. But there's going to be more attempts if he doesn't pull this off quickly."

Rhyd did not know much about the fabled Club of Spades, but he had heard that once your card was drawn, there was no way out. You either found your end, or someone found it for you.

"I can't get you in, but you two need to talk."

"How?"

"With this?" He held up a tiny interface plug, something Rhyd had often seen sprinkled about in the flotsam of electronics Zara frequently had scattered across the tables in her flat. "You've got a PCD link in that thing, I assume?" He gestured at the discarded hood.

"I do." He had never interfaced with a system in a way that required a direct link, but Tox included the tech in case it was needed.

Tox included a lot of things that way.

"I've got a line run, I can show you, but it'll be tricky to get there."

"Where?"

"Lev 2 East."

The fringes of brako holdings. Thus far, Rhyd had not pushed his hunts there, content to handle the brako bleed-over into higher levels in the hopes of luring Vanderwall to him. It was not fear that kept him from that place, only a wisdom that taking on the full force of the brako on their home turf would be suicide, even if he took Vanderwall down with him.

Rhyd was a lot of things. Suicidal was not one of them. Not since Venn had come back to him. Not anymore.

"I can get us there," Enoch continued, addressing the matter of unspoken concern. "Where I get in and out. Might be best if you're you…and not him…" Again he gestured at the mask. "But we'll need it unless you have another idea, another device."

"I don't." Not knowing where he would be led, what they might encounter along the way, he would feel better with the protection of Scarecrow on hand. But a bilger could travel the Levs unhindered, and he trusted that wherever Enoch led, the dwarf had traveled the path dozens of times before, always safe, always unhindered.

"Give me ten."
Sleep forgotten, the whiskey too, he wanted to talk to Skelter.
And Enoch was offering it without reservation.
Rhyd wondered why he had not been given this chance before.

❧Chapter 16❧

How Enoch came and went from the Core was revealed with the exposure of the minimal tunnel, litter more than a drainage channel, burrowed through rock, hidden behind layers of long-unused metal floor grates leaning against Hebenon's earthen eastern wall. The grating might have been replacement panels, kept here until needed or for later repurposing, or made and never used, forgotten like so many other things. Water seeped from porous stone over the entire exposed surface, meaning that no one considered that the excess here might come from some other more substantial opening. With the number of panels leaning here, it would take multiple men to move them away. No one had deemed the water, in a world of constant damp, to be worth looking into. If the tunnel had been there at the time the first grate was placed, no one had bothered to investigate.

Such oddities from the world before were to be found throughout Hebenon. What was one more? As small as the opening was, no thought would have been given to the possibility of a man passing through it, or to it leading anywhere important.

The grates were covered with a tarp to minimize moisture damage, a largely failing effort that had likely provided shelter for more than one streeter since the day it had been hung there.

Enoch moving in and out of that makeshift shelter had probably never raised any brows or drawn unusual attention.

A bilger inspecting the wall for seepage would not do so either.

Their passage down the stairs to Lev 2 had been unimpeded. No one lifted their heads to take notice of the bilger and the dwarf, none made eye contact or muttered greetings or insults when elbows were bumped or bodies jostled past. It was the way of things in Hebenon,

where civility had grown nearly extinct in too many circles. Better not to be noticed then to draw attention to oneself with unsolicited words.

Especially in the city's lowest Levs.

Rhyd took the opportunity as they made their way down to discreetly examine faces, hoping to identify out-of-uniform brako, perhaps notice someone with the size and build of Vanderwall. Dressed in varying shades of drab, in coats and capes that kept out the prevalent moisture, hunched and slumped for additional protection and the conservation of body warmth, most people looked so much alike that Rhyd was unable to tell them apart. He decided that focusing on the path so that he could find his way back here was a better use of his attention, and when Enoch lifted the canvas flap to usher him beneath the tented grates, he was thankful he had shifted focus.

He might not have suspected this place otherwise.

The passage in the mountainside was big enough for the dwarf to fit through with little room to spare, though it was likely not an easy path even for him. A claustrophobic individual would find it impossible to endure. If it was bored out another six or eight inches in diameter, Rhyd might be able to squeeze through, but that was debatable and not worth consideration as there was no time to expand the entire tunnel. The light of the electric torch Rhyd drew from his coat pocket pierced no more than a dozen or so feet to where the tunnel curved up and slightly to the left. From what Rhyd could see, the path grew no wider there.

"How far?" He set the bilger's tooler on the ground by his knee as Enoch fumbled with his gloves and grabbed hold of the black-coated line dangling out of the shaft. Hands flat on the stone, Rhyd used the sensors in his gloves to measure the earth's density, how easy it would be to blow, to clear, to make that passage easier to traverse.

He did not think the possibility likely, but he wanted to be sure.

Enoch shrugged. "Never measured. Far enough. Couple hundred feet I'd say. I've cleared the debris…in all the times through." He offered the PCD plug to Rhyd.

He had not tested it. He had no idea if the line was good, if the plug was good, if it would interface with Rhyd's gear, but it was the only chance they had for communication. If it worked, it would mean a more direct dialogue then relying on Enoch to travel back and forth with messages and the hope of finding each other when they needed to pass information along.

As it was, if something happened to Enoch, it meant the line of communication was broken. It had to work.

From his tooler, hidden beneath bilger equipment where it would not have attracted attention if some bugger had stopped them and demanded a look inside, Rhyd withdrew the familiar mask and offered it to Enoch, expecting him to connect the line to the port. Instead, the dwarf pulled the mask over his head, his grin disappearing beneath it moments before he snapped the plug into place and began to speak.

"Skelt? You there?" He ignored the marginally threatening look Rhyd gave him. "Got someone who wants to talk to you."

Inside the room at the other end of the line, the lights flickered and sputtered, popping and hissing as the units struggled to maintain a steady glow at the end of the less than adequate power generator. Power had been restored lighting in the public areas of the Core, but to the private rooms, where the residents did little more than sleep, the flow was reduced, barely sufficient to allow heating, intentionally funneling some of that power to the ICD that crackled to life at Skelter's bedside.

There was power enough, but it was being stored now, rationed for use when their escape attempt came, or so Colyx had said to their fellow Core residents to explain the reason for the reduction. And there was always a shortage of parts, of bulbs and alglamps and gas for lanterns, things they were often forced to conserve or do without for a time. No one argued the necessity of it as it had happened before and would, inevitably, happen again until they were free or they were left in the cold to die. In truth, the unused lighting was meant to keep the population contained to a small area, allowing for a redirect to the ICD

line, allowing communication through it, without anyone noticing or overhearing.

Skelter cracked one eye open, not surprised that Otta was not with him, that he was alone in the room. After her revelation, she had left his side sometime later, while he slept, and when he awoke, still stiff and sore but feeling well enough to sit and eat, he found rations left, lukewarm but passably edible. He had slept again, his mind and body determined to recover from the assault before the deadline on his life came to an end.

He was not going to sleep the last of his life away while there were plans to be made.

It was as easy to let his mind work behind closed lids as it was to rise, to pace, to scribble ideas and calculations on scraps of hard to come by paper.

The unexpected static burst made him scramble to sit, to snatch up the ICD headset Enoch had procured for him.

Anyone passing his room might hear him talking, but as his room was at the end of the corridor, and he was prone to thinking out loud, he doubted anyone would come here or be overly suspicious.

"Eeney…that you?"

Enoch scowled behind the good, glad Rhyd had not heard the question. No one called him that except Skelter, and he was determined to keep it that way.

"Hold on." He yanked off the hood, handed it back to Rhyd, and scooted to the canvas flap opening to ensure an uninterrupted conversation.

"Gave us a damn scare."

"Whiskey." Skelter's relieved breath hissed long in Rhyd's ear. "You don't know how good it is to hear your voice."

"Bout as good as it is to hear yours." It could have been an impersonator, an imposter, and Rhyd had been prepared for such. But the hood's enhancements and his familiarity with Skelter after years of acquaintance supported that this was, indeed, the man he hoped it would be. "Hear you're looking for help."

"You get what I asked for?"

"Workin' on it. Trying to locate some freezes. Best explosives for what you've got in mind. Gonna take a bit. Whatever you've got cookin', it's not like blowin' a filt line."

"I know…but I don't have much of that, I'm afraid."

"How long?"

"Thirteen days…give or take their patience."

Rhyd frowned. "Don't think blowing this pass is a good idea." Even if he could get freezes tonight, could get them in place before morning to blow the tunnel, clearing it would take longer than Skelter had. And that did not include taking time to inspect Hebenon's support beams that sank deep into the earth on all sides, in order to minimize the damage to the city.

Freezes in the wrong place could threaten the integrity of Hebanthe Falls. Rhyd did not want to be responsible for something like that.

"Not a lot of choices. Workin' on the front door…but that's gonna be a wanana if there ever was one, if it works…with everyone else wanting to go out the way they came in."

"You didn't."

"Get in that way? Hell no." Skelter's head jerked up at the sound of an argument and something breaking in the corridor. "Gotta go; hook me up with Zar, will ya? She oughta be able to run us a better ICD."

"I will." His response, however, was made into dead air as the connection broke. For several moments he listened, straining to hear anything in the tunnel, through the hood's enhancements, that would tell him what was happening deep behind the rock. There was nothing but the faint whoosh of air that proved beyond any doubt that this tunnel went somewhere.

"Show this to Zar…get whatever she needs to rig a secure line."

"I don't…"

"Can't get back and forth here every time we need a line. If we're gonna do this," whatever this turned out to be, "we need better communication."

Rhyd pushed the flap aside and began to exit their cover.

"Where are you going?"

Rhyd did not reply. He was going to figure out how the cazz Skelter got in there while Enoch attended to equally important matters.

Maybe Enoch knew. But Rhyd saw no reason to waste time in both of them risking passage through the only other place Rhyd could think of to look.

Lev 1.

❮*❯

The destination of the eight Talkers did not matter to the shadow that followed, nor to the scatter of Spinks when the two groups crossed paths. What mattered to the Spinks was the support the Talkers offered the deposed Founder, the support they gave to an obsolete system that oppressed the Levs in favor of an aristocracy class who once resided in the Uppers and hoped to do so again, who supported segregation and compliance to an idea of a world that no longer needed to exist. Outside was open, the world expanding, and though few streeters had taken the risk of finding their way into it, they had no desire to go back to the way things had been either.

The world demanded change. Change forward to something new, not backward to what had been for generations.

When the Talkers appeared at the end of the walkway, many of the Spinks gathered around Xiaodan and Ginna on an empty stairwell to plan their next endeavor, scattered into the shadows. Their movement was noted but ignored by the authoritative adults who assumed the streeters had merely gone into hiding to avoid recrimination for loitering. There was no plan, no projected course of action, but when Ginna directed her cry of "Afatottari!" at the man in the middle of the Talkers' ranks, those Spinks who had not fled

followed her lead, hurling debris, rocks, and insults at those deemed to be part of the old system they had grown to despise.

A command caused the Talkers to close ranks around Kal, but they took no other action at first. Such displays, while not common, were not unheard of either, and though insulting, they were not deadly. There was no cause for retaliatory violence. But today, perhaps emboldened by the rotting vegetable matter that stuck to the Senior Talker's face, eliciting laughter from the Spinks, those who had fled reemerged from the shadows, drawing together into a mass of young people that cut off the route the Talkers were traveling.

"Move."

The Spinks, indistinguishable from one another due to the generic drab protective clothing they wore and the bandas over their faces, only laughed or continued their chant and bombardment.

"Hey, komeada! We don't want you here!"

It was not the most insulting words Kal had ever heard directed at him. Usually he endured far worse. But today, having little patience and a pressing desire to get where he was going, he snapped, "Move them!" just as the Talkers pulled more tightly together and one of the Spinks drew back an arm to throw something else.

She had a straight shot at the Senior's head with a chunk of metal debris that could be deadly if it struck just right. One of the Senior's underlings recognized the danger as the arm came up. When he grabbed for the girl's arm, catching it, yanking it down, and twisting so that Ginna was forced to her knees, Xiaodan leaped forward, swung his fist with enough power to catch the Talker in the temple and drop him to the walkway.

Spinks charged, whooping like wild beasts, heedless of the thumper someone wielded that caught Xiaodan on the side of the neck. He went down as well, his body sprawled atop Ginna's now forgotten form beneath the eruption of violence.

At the rear of the skirmish, emerging from the dark where he had dogged the Senior's path through the Levs for the past few hours, Blayd too saw the chaos as his opportunity to act, his opportunity to

remove the threat Neoma perceived in the man who would use and manipulate her husband for his own gain. When Kal withdrew to the rear of his entourage, allowing the others to fight the unruly band of streeters, Blayd snuck up behind him, long knife in hand.

One thrust. One between the ribs. They were far enough from any source of medical assistance that the Senior would bleed out, would drown in his own blood, before aid arrived.

What Blayd did not foresee was the arm that came from his left, wrapped around his neck, and dragged him away from his target. A pair of brako, one big enough in bulk and height to be the rumored boss Vanderwall, emerged from a nearby vindi, turning Kal to face it. Making a split moment decision, the Senior drew a buzzer from inside his coat and took aim at the brako with a chokehold on Neoma's man.

It would be most expedient to let the bodyguard die. He was a thorn in Kal's side and an inconvenience, and his place in Neoma's bed prevented Kal from moving closer to the Founder's wife.

But allowing the brako to kill the fellow would call his loyalties into question, and Kal was too wise for that. Besides, sparing Blayd's life, saving it, might gain favor, both from Blayd and Neoma.

So he took aim at the brako holding Blayd. The second brako, masked as the first, was a towering mass of a man that Kal did not notice until it was too late, when the fellow's gloved fist lashed out sideways. The blow caught Kal in the chest as the buzzer ignited and flung him into the midst of the Talker and Spink tussle. The injured brako released his hold on Blayd and fell back through the doorway they had just come out of.

An unexpected reverberation ran through the grated metal beneath Kal as he fought for the breath stolen by that blow. He did not know the blonde who entered the fight, some stranger whose first punch sent the big brako staggering into a glass vindi window. His attention turned to the Talkers assaulting the children and one Talker after another was tossed aside, knocked down or disabled.

Rhyd's intended search for the way Skelter had gotten into the Core had been cut short by the unexpected bedlam. Verbal altercations

between Talkers and streeters, between Talkers and anyone at all, were common enough not to warrant concern or attention. But Xiaodan's voice in the middle of it was. Rhyd arrived a half-Lev above the chaos just as Xiaodan jumped to protect another, as he went down beneath the violent clash that followed in his wake.

Rhyd was not dressed for this fight. He could don the hood, but there was no time. The blow Xiaodan had taken could not have been a good one. If the young man had any hope for survival, Rhyd was all he had. He had to get the boy out of there. Fast.

He knew few of these people. He recognized Senior Kal and he knew from the band on the big brako's arm that he had once again crossed paths with Vanderwall. The fellow who thought to take aim at the Senior was a familiar face too. But none of them would know him. His was a common face. There was no reason they should.

But they might know him by his fighting skill.

It was a risk he felt worth taking for Xiaodan's sake.

He reached for the nearest object and threw it at the SCAM on the corner of the closest building. Electric sparks snapped and popped as the unit went dead and he jumped into the fray.

As the fight ensued, a buzzer burned against Rhyd's side, but the coat he wore protected him. The sting of electricity was enough, however, to twist his body sideways so that his head knocked against a walkway railing. Someone snatched at him but he rolled away, causing the other to stumble with enough momentum to fall against the same rail, and then over it towards the Lev below with a scream that ended abruptly with a faint crunch and shouts from beneath them.

Talker or brako?

From the dogpile of Spinks and Talkers, Ginna emerged, bruised, her hands raw, but otherwise unscathed from the beating she had taken. Her banda had been pulled down, revealing her bloody lip and nose. A blond stranger, some passerby with obvious dexterity and some degree of fight training, had cleared a swath through the Talkers, pushing them away so that she was able to get to her feet next to Xiaodan's unmoving figure.

"Get him out of here!" barked the blonde, his words barely audible over the thunder of boots on wet metal and a cry of "Ginna!" from one of the four bugorra now arriving from the path to the right. A Talker swung his thumper at the girl, only to be met with a cracking blow across his forearm from the stranger that was enough to fracture bone.

Ilya watched what she was certain would be the death of her sister…and the subsequent act that ended that blow and drove the Talkers back several more steps. Some turned their attention to apprehending the last brako menace behind them, though they were ill-equipped or trained for it. Only protecting the Senior, while the bugorra closed in, made sense.

The thumper clattered on the grate. Ginna took the opportunity given to struggle with Xiaodan's weight, intending to drag him out of harm's way. Two other Spinks, not as tall as Ginna but taller than most of the others, scurried to help her, and with the arrival of the buggers, a whistled signal was given and the Spinks began to retreat.

"I want him alive!" shouted Kal shrilly, trying to mask his voice, scrambling towards a hasty retreat from the arriving bugorra. It was unclear if he was speaking of the imposing brako or the stranger. He did not know who the blonde man was, whose side he was fighting on, a do-gooder out to help the children perhaps, nothing more. But a man of that ability could be useful if he could be swayed. Kal could utilize an ally of such skill.

A man like that might be a match for the Scarecrow.

Stopping the brako would gain him favor with Captain Grainger. Both choices had their benefits.

How could he have known when this began that one of those streeters was the Lieutenant's sister? There had not been the time or opportunity to recognize her. He did not want any blowback if the girl had been injured during this fight. Best he not be found here. Best he left matters to the rest of his entourage.

But he would not leave without that final command.

Rhyd's target, however, as he protected his fractured arm and dodged several sets of hands attempting to catch him, was the brako

boss that no sane man, no normal man, would go up against unarmed and unprotected. In the autopilot of combat, however, honed by years behind the Scarecrow's hood, the lines between his identities blurred. There was only the objective.

Stop Vanderwall.

Ginna and the Spinks, those not lying injured on the path, had retreated into the safety of the shadows.

The Senior and his likewise uninjured Talkers, had done the same, leaving their fallen behind.

Head down like a battering ram, Rhyd caught the unsuspecting brako in the lower back with enough force to knock him off his feet. One of the Talkers, following the order given by the retreating Senior, grabbed Rhyd's arm to yank him back, to detain him before the mountainous brako killed him. Rhyd shouted in pain as his shoulder was wrenched from its socket and Vanderwall's fist caught both Rhyd, and then the Talker, across the sides of their heads.

The opposing forces of punch and pull silenced Rhyd as he fell…and rolled over the edge of the walkway, his head striking the railing pole as he did so.

Ilya, her team spread thin with the efforts of attending the casualties, the injured, from what had been one of the worst anti-Talker clashes she had seen, saw him fall out of the corner of her eye as she scanned the dark crevices in the direction her sister had gone.

Eyes peeped out behind vindi blinds, from windows and doorways, watching the fight but refusing, afraid, to get involved. On the relatively protected position of the half-Lev platform above them, Enoch saw Rhyd fall.

&Chapter 17&

"Make no mistake," Neoma's voice, tense and suitably emotive to convey her belief in the words she uttered, "the Talkers, the Voices, are no longer the friends of the people!"

Her face, typically serene and dispassionate, regal and aloof, bore traces of bruises and her eyes were red-rimmed as if she had been weeping. On the bed behind her, a bed typical of many in the medical facilities scattered throughout Hebenon that it would take effort to determine which one she was in, a young man, dark-skinned and showing a similar level of abuse to his bearded face, wore a brace around his neck and had a tube down his throat. The monitors around him beeped and whirred a steady stream of reports while he seemed to sleep away his pain.

From the place Neoma stood, blocking a clear full-bodied image of him, it was impossible to tell if he was breathing on his own or not. If he was breathing at all.

"This attack on my employee, on myself, is only their first. The Founder…and her father…will be next. Have no doubts, good people of Hebanthe Falls; the Voices are not for us. They are against us. Me, you, all of us. They must be stopped. You have seen the footage. You know the truth! We cannot trust the bugorra to do this for us. They have lied to us for too long. We must unite. We must do this together!"

Grainger growled and muted the prodcast, his hand slamming down on another button as he shouted, "Someone shut that down!"

Anyone with the know-how could hack the prods, it seemed. Too often, since the Coup, it had been done, typically by pranksters and perverts, the Igraci spreading their doomsday propaganda, and others equally willing to stir dissidence.

Just as Neoma was doing now. Never had she tried before. Never had a hack been so inflammatory.

"She's going to get people killed!"

They thought the Coup was bad. Another call to arms, another uprising against the bugorra and the Voices in a city already weakened and depleted of people and resources, was going to be a disaster.

"She has no grounds," started Tamner, knowing grounds meant little in the face of public opinion. The Captain of the bugorra had hidden the truth of Founder Kemway being alive and now the Talkers seemed to have committed treason by attacking the Founder's wife. "She wasn't even there..."

He and the too-quiet Joran had been with Grainger when the file came in, had seen the SCAM footage collected when Grainger did, as it was protocol for the Captain, and previously the Founder, to review such images before it was released to the public, particularly when there were participants, criminals, or unreported victims to be sought and brought in. Though outnumbered, the bugorra had quashed the skirmish, largely because their arrival prompted the participants to flee, but there had been enough left behind, bleeding, unconscious, to warrant investigation.

The three watched the streeter children clash with the Talkers, watched one man come up behind the Senior, watched a pair of brako intervene, watched the unexpected arrival of a stranger before the SCAM unit was knocked offline.

What had happened after could only be pieced together by unreliable witness reports.

Joran had noted an exchange of looks between Tamner and Oliver at that moment the stranger interceded but he kept his face blank, his realization to himself.

So both already knew the truth.

Other SCAMs in the vicinity had provided additional snippets from the fight, but the stranger was not seen again.

Not once was Neoma visible in that footage.

That did not mean she had not been there, off-camera, out of sight. The injuries she presented to the world appeared to support her claim. Grainger had not yet been able to interview Lieutenant Young, as there was a report that her sister had been involved, and one of her sister's friends had been badly injured. The Captain was waiting on her assessment of the situation, but none of the others he had spoken to had seen the Founder's wife. Grainger guessed he was not alone in thinking her injuries to be nothing more than well-applied makeup.

On the Echo, the muted woman continued mouthing words.

"Let me talk to Soleia." Joran had fostered a good relationship with the Ximenezes since their return into Hebenon's life. He might be able to ask the right questions about what they were seeing. His experience with the Archives and theirs with the prodcast system meant that between them, they might be able to shut down this rogue prodcast, remove the block it had created on regular programming, and stop it from happening again.

At least for a short time.

Offering to do so would get him out of this room to reach out to the one person he knew could do that…and who he hoped would have some word on Rhyd. The fear in his belly was the most bitter thing he could remember feeling since the day he was robbed of his voice.

Rhyd had to be alive. Not just for Skelter…but for Joran as well.

"Do it…and increase his security," Grainger snapped, expecting without specifying that Tamner would know the second order was for him…and would know what the order meant. His hand slapped the ICD button again and he added, "I don't care where she is…get me Lieutenant Young."

Family be damned. He was going to get ahead of this before things went from bad to worse.

❧*❧

Pain and bright lights had alternated for a few short minutes, perhaps one created by the other, and then darkness devoured him

again. Rhyd remembered being pulled from the ledge on which he had fallen, rough hands showing little gentleness as if they expected a man in such condition to be dead already. He remembered a swing that got him free of bruising hands, freedom that ended in a splash of icy, churning water that sucked the breath from his lungs as surely as the current sucked him hard against the metal netting that strained debris from the river's flow beneath the city's bottommost Lev. He remembered a period of relentless pummeling as he fought for air, fought to keep his head above the river's assault. As strong as he was, however, he was injured and no match for the river, no match for the discards of life that dropped here to press against him, pinning him.

He remembered briefly believing he was going to die, that the waters of the Four Falls were going to succeed in doing what no man in the city had yet managed to do.

Darkness came again. Metal hooks and more hands. An influx of air that came without the splashes of water and filth, a moment where a halo of light shown around a distorted, inhuman face.

Then nothing.

❧*❦

Only the knowledge that Ginna would live enabled Ilya to succumb to the demand Captain Grainger made. Ginna and the other streeters had not made it very far into hiding with their burden before the gorra caught up to them, and their treatment by Ilya's squad, as suspected troublemakers and criminals, was only marginally less brutal than the fight with the Talkers had been…and only because they were children. They had been hauled into custody, the limp young man taken away for identification and treatment, and Ginna was booked and processed before Ilya was able to get to her.

The delay caused by sorting out the chaos, following protocol, bringing in Talkers, trying to pursue Vanderwall and the unidentified bystander who had tried to help the kids and paid the price for it, meant that Ginna was now forever marked in the Archives as a dissident.

Nothing Ilya could do would protect her anymore.

Thank the powers that stranger, whoever he was, had saved Ginna's life.

A life the Talkers, the Voices of Faith, had tried to snuff out. A life the legal wheels of the city would make miserable from now on if Grainger chose to do so.

Ilya wondered, as she buzzed for admittance into the Captain's office, if she might be able to sway him into clearing Ginna's name.

"Captain," she began as she stepped through the opening the retracting door provided. Her voice was steady, as calm as she could manage, but her hasty perusal of the man's face told her she was not likely to find any favor with him right now.

"Was she there?"

"Who, sir?"

"Neoma! Was she there?"

Blinking, perplexed by the questions when she had thought this interrogation would revolve around her sister, Ilya pondered what she remembered from hours before. She had not yet seen the prodcasts, but she had seen a significant portion of that commotion, Senior Kal, Vanderwall, Blayd, Ginna…but she could not recall anyone who matched the tall Mam's description.

"I did not see her."

"Not disguised? Not lingering nearby? Not…?" He gestured to the woman's mottled face on the silent Echosys screen.

Ilya scowled before letting her gaze move to the man with the neck brace on the bed behind the speaking woman.

"Unless she was dressed as a Talker, or hiding by the time I arrived…no, I did not see her nor anyone likely to have been her."

Grainger snorted and drummed his fingers on his desk. Her report matched those of the other officers so he knew she was not lying about what she had witnessed.

If anyone was lying, it was Neoma.

"She thinks she's going to make that child…" He snorted again. "You're late."

"I'm sorry, sir. I had to make sure Ginna's…"

"Your duty is to your post, Lieutenant. To this city…to me."

He caught himself as he said those final words, realizing as soon as they were uttered how much like Kemway he sounded, how often the Founder had put duty, his own wishes, before the lives of those beneath him. When Ilya bristled in response to the reprimand, he was tempted to withdraw it, but the words had been said and he could not take them back nor undo their effect.

"I'm sorry, sir," she muttered tersely. "It won't happen again."

The strained note at the edge of her voice said otherwise, however, and Grainger chose not to call it out. "Next time, make your report, then see to your sister." It would have taken only a few minutes to dictate her account of what had transpired, something that could have been done in the lift between Levs. He was not asking her to ignore familial obligations…only to be sure that all of her obligations were met in a timely fashion. In a situation as volatile as this one had become, Hebenon could not afford a delay in shared information.

"I'll make my report at once."

Assuming she was dismissed, she backed towards the door, allowing ample opportunity for him to stop her if he wished. He did not, nor did he inquire about her sister or any other detail.

She chose not to press him. In his current mood, he was not likely to act in her, or Ginna's favor.

But maybe if she could gain a few moments alone with Blayd, she could bring back something Grainger could use.

Perhaps that would be enough to win Ginna's freedom and expunge her record.

༄*༄

Maemi's efforts to console the old woman's wailing was made ineffectual by her own stream of tears while Tox pressed the medical staff in hushed tones for information about the young man laid out on the metal slab behind them. He was covered now, the thin protective

sheeting forming a ghostly silhouette where his handsome face should be. The cause of death was obvious, the bruising across the side of his twisted neck announcing a blow with some object solid enough to crush his windpipe, snap bone, sever his spine. It had been mercifully quick, the medi said.

Where was the mercy in that, the old woman demanded? Where was mercy in a young man's death?

The medi had little details about what had occurred to land him here, however, what or who had killed him. Some sort of altercation between Talkers and streeters, broken up by the buggers. That was all the medi knew. It took no stretch of thought for the three women, distraught in their own ways, to guess that Xiaodan had been amongst the impulsive streeters. But who had been the instigators of the confrontation, whether the Talkers had struck first or the streeters had, the medi did not know. As there were no bugorra on hand to explain what had happened, and the only news broadcasting over the Echos was the Founder's wife blaming the Voices of Faith for the violence, showing the same snippet of fight over and over, giving no hint of how it began or who was to blame, it was easy to believe what she said.

The Talkers were guilty.

Knowing her apprentice as she did, however, it was also easy for Tox to believe the young man had stepped into the fray, maybe had ignited it, without serious thought to the consequences.

The events of the Coup had taught him a lot about the world, but he had not been mature enough, wise enough, to temper his actions.

If Rhyd had talked to Xiaodan, as he had promised, his efforts, it appeared, had failed.

There was little left to do except sign the body over for disposal.

Until they could talk to Rhyd, however, it was a step both Maemi and Tox were reluctant to take.

They did not know he had been there. But they believed he should be with them now. They believed he was a piece of a puzzle whose picture they could not yet envision.

❧*❧

The dim alcove in the tea vindi seemed a questionable place to meet, but it was the place Zara requested and Jaron chose not to argue. Unable to reach Enoch, unable to reach Rhyd, Jaron took the risk of approaching the dancer on his own. He knew her through Skelter, through Lash, through Enoch, but he did not know her well.

He also knew she had a history, however brief, however involved, with Oliver. He had never probed, never asked, but he knew that history was there.

Through Skelter, he knew that, if anyone could shut down Neoma's repeating prodcast, it was Zara. She would do it for Jaron, he believed, because he asked. She would do it for Hebenon because it was for the best. And she would do it for Grainger…for the sake of whatever the Captain was to her.

She tapped furiously at the Echo keys as Jaron sipped hot tea and kept a casual eye on the doorway to their right.

The Echosys above the bar continued to play Neoma's plea. Some patrons were gathered at the counter to watch, to listen, as did many in the streets throughout the city. Many more, however, did no more than glance at the screen before going about their day.

Most had seen the message enough already.

Neoma was not the Founder. She was part of a shared history that many were eager to leave behind, even if they were not yet ready to step out of the city into the light of the fresh-aired world.

Jaron hoped that meant that whatever the woman intended with that impassioned appeal, it would fail to take root and grow into the threat Grainger feared it would become.

"Are you almost…?"

"Hush now."

He scowled at her scolding tone but stopped talking as requested.

Five more minutes. Ten. A second cup of tea while Zara's first cup grew cold. Men and women moved in and out of the vindi, including a couple of laser-eyed buggers wary about congregated

groups of people in the aftermath of that recent clash. The gorra looked about, but upon noticing a gaggle of tingers shuffling past, they chose to return to their patrol, to break up the group of tingers and send them each on their way.

The strain, the prospect of another violent outbreak, was high. The order had been given. Grainger was not taking chances.

Disappointed groans at the bar announced Zara's success as she picked up the cup of tea and leaned back on her stool. Neoma's face was abruptly replaced by the more mundane fair of a repeated bowling prodcast from the day before.

"Ought to keep them out for now," Zara said, setting aside the metal, man-shaped infuser to casually sip more tea in the hopes of distracting anyone's notice as she casually closed her Echo with one hand several moments after the broadcasting change took place.

"Will they be able to…?"

"In time, maybe. They're good; I'll grant them that. But I'm better. Any attempts to get around my coding is going to set off an alert, so I'll cut them off when that happens." How soon such an effort might come would depend on their determination. Perhaps that one repeated prodcast was all there was.

It might have already done what it was intended to do.

"Have you heard from him? Rhyd?"

Zara met his gaze over the rim of her cup as she finished the tea, questioning his inquiry.

"He was there…in the fight. I saw him on the SCAM…"

"Scarecrow?" She knew about the fight between the streeters and the Talkers; anyone catching Neoma's message or the previous news prodcast knew, and by the time that cast had aired, the gossip about the altercation was already spreading. She had learned about Xiaodan's involvement when Maemi was summoned to the Lev 2 medical facility. Then had come Jaron's request to meet, and she had not been there to learn what had happened to Xiaodan, had learned nothing more about the small riot. She had not viewed Neoma's prod herself only overheard the woman's voice as she worked.

"No. Not…as Rhyd." His nervous voice trailed off. "He was there, at the start, before the buggers. I've tried to reach him, but I can't."

"Maybe he's on shift or…"

"Tried there…and no one answered his door." It was possible the man had gone to bed, injured and exhausted after that fight, but Jaron had a troubling suspicion that something was not right. "No word from Enoch either…or Lash."

The dwarf being out of touch was normal, as communication did not pass easily into the Core. And if Lash was Outside in the parah village, he would be difficult to reach.

Maybe that was where Rhyd had gone. It was a possibility Jaron had not considered until now.

Zara set her cup down with deliberate, pondering slowness. "You going back up…to Oliver?"

It was the first time Jaron had heard her say his name. "Now that the prod's down…he'll be looking for me." Assuming that Jaron and the Ximenezes would be the cause of success, Grainger would want to know it was gone, and if it would be the end of the matter.

She nodded and he thought briefly she would give some message to pass on, or make some request to keep her name out of this matter. Instead, she stood up and said, "I'll check on Rhyd. Let you know."

"Thank you." He decided to linger longer, keeping up some innocent appearance that might keep others from questioning their actions, their motives. Waiting for her to leave seemed a good idea, less suspicious. Oliver would not notice a few minutes' delay.

⮞*⮜

"Don't start." Ginna did not look up, did not turn from the small window through which she watched the ever-present moisture drip from the eaves to the grated path, where it flowed to the lowest point and fell again, seeking to rejoin the river that had originally birthed it. Hunched forward, curled into herself with her arms wrapped around her knees, she was in obvious physical discomfort but that pain, Ilya

suspected, was inconsequential compared to the emotional pain Ginna was wrestling with.

She had sat in that same posture for days after each of their parents died, a little girl lost, having no one with whom to share her grief.

Ilya had tried, but her efforts to push Ginna back towards a normal routine, to carry on and be strong as if that would make her feel better, had been ineffectual. The pain of abandonment had been buried, never healed, and now, abandoned for the third time, Ginna was bombarded with that grief all over again.

Ilya did not know how to help.

The tirade that had tumbled through her head, the scolding admonitions she had intended, dried on her tongue.

"He was your friend? That…boy?" She almost said streeter, but without knowing more about him, Ilya decided such an epitaph was better held in reserve.

The silence promised no reply, only the repetitious drip of water and the buzz of the neon kitchen light, the only illumination currently brightening the flat. Ilya waited, struggling to be patient, just to be there if her sister wanted to talk, until Ginna began do draw in the breath mist on the glass an increasingly common, familiar symbol that made Ilya bristle to see it.

A plea for help, for retribution, for the Scarecrow.

"He understood me."

Ilya sighed. "I want to understand, Gin. I do…"

"You have to listen to understand…and you never do. You only judge…never want to hear…" Ilya's ICD buzzed as Ginna finished the symbol and her hand dropped to the sill. "You've always got something more important."

Though about to protest that nothing was more important to her than Ginna, about to curse the timing of Grainger's second summons of the day, she swallowed what would have been pointless words with a groan. She had a duty to the city. She could not just brush that aside.

But there had to be an exception.

"I need to take care of this…we're trying to find the person responsible for…"

"Senior Kal is responsible," Ginna muttered bitterly.

"Wait here, Ginna. Right here. We'll talk as soon as I'm back. I will get to the bottom of this. Whoever killed him…your friend…they will pay for this. And whoever saved your life will…"

"Xiaodan did that," she whispered with a grunt, without moving. Ilya accepted that as acquiescence to her instructions to stay put, grabbed her coat, and scurried out the door, not wanting to keep the Captain waiting again.

It was difficult to tell if Ginna's blank stare was watching her go or not.

❧Chapter 18❧

He had seen Ballard fall and hoped to be the one to find him, hoped to discover him alive, if a little worse for wear, and get him safely home before the brako, the buggers, or any of the Talkers got to him. But the lifts were too slow and his legs would only carry him down the staircases so fast. Half-Lev down, scramble. Another down, another scramble. Until he reached the mists of Lev 1, where there should have been two men, alive or dead.

But there was only one.

The brako who had fallen first, being dragged away by bugorra patrol who were nearby when he fell.

That meant the river.

Enoch's heart sank.

He followed the flow, skirting those who worked and lived here, sliding through alleys and between fisheries and grow houses and hosts of other facilities that provided the array of food Hebenon needed to survive. He knew where the nets were, the tightly woven lattices stretched across the churning water from one side of Hebenon to the other. There were three, moving away from the Falls in succession, there to strain debris from the flow, to scavenge logs or other usable material from the water and to retrieve anything, anyone, fallen into it from the Levs. If Ballard had fallen into the water and survived the pounding surge over the submerged rocks, then he would be carried to this net, the last in the series before the water made its final race towards the distant sea.

That it was the last net meant possible survival, as most of the Falls' waste and about a third of what was lost from the city would

have been caught in the first net, and at least a third of those cast-offs would be caught in the second.

Rhyd might not be pummeled by debris, but he might still drown.

By the time Enoch reached a vantage point from where he could spy on the net's crossing, fisherfolk had pulled Rhyd from the water with great metal hooks and clawing hands. There was excited, unintelligible chatter as they searched for signs of life, conversation Enoch could not hear over the bellow of the river.

Soon enough, they lifted Rhyd to carry him away, barely making it ten yards along paths they knew better than Enoch before others intercepted them. Plain looking individuals, dressed no differently than the first group, but after heated words and an exchange of blows, the newcomers took the days unexpected catch and turned in a different direction.

Enoch tried to follow, but he could not keep up, could not risk stepping into the open where his efforts might be noticed, and soon enough, he lost them.

Lost Rhyd.

To the brako, he was sure, for who else would resort to bullying tactics to take what they wanted from others? Who else had Rhyd wronged by causing the death of one man and assaulting a fellow who stood out from the rest by virtue of size and the banda on his arm?

Vanderwall?

Enoch did not know, but on the off chance he could learn anything, could overhear something that would point him in Ballard's direction, he decided to make Lev 1 his home. For now.

There was no point in going to Skelter with his news yet. No point in giving up too soon. Ballard was still on Lev 1. Enoch believed it.

Now he had to prove it…and do whatever he could to free him.

Before all they were left with was his corpse.

⪼*⪻

He was sure his eyes were open, although he was equally certain they were swollen to the point of uselessness from the repeated battering his face had taken. Already bruised, beaten, and mauled by debris in the river and the biting pressure of the net against his body as the racing water thundered against him, he could not fathom what his keepers hoped to gain through further abuse. The hammering in his skull drowned out external noises, as if his ears were stuffed and wrapped with insulating materials of the sort men of his ilk used to wrap the city's ducts, used to protect the living places from the ever-present roar of the Four Falls.

If those who held him asked questions and expected answers, he did not hear them. Maybe that was why they beat him…because he failed to respond.

Now he was alone. No light or sound, only the beating of his blood through his veins and the crashing between his ears.

If they thought to drive him mad with this silence, they would be sorely disappointed.

He was used to silence. Over the last few years, silence and solitude and darkness had been his constant, best companions.

Even pain was a familiar bedfellow.

Rhyd felt right at home. But he did not feel right.

❧*❦

It was the second time the young woman came to the medi-facility to see Blayd, the second time Neoma turned her away. His coma was a convenient excuse, but sooner or later he would awaken and she could not stay with him forever.

Ulynda needed her too.

Neoma did not know who the woman was, but she recognized her face, and recognition was enough to spark flames of worry. Not jealousy; Neoma refused to be jealous of anyone Blayd chose to spend his time with. But he had sworn to be there for her, sworn his fealty, his loyalty, and anyone encroaching on that was suspect.

She should set someone to watch the other woman, but with her best man unmoving in a medical bed, her best man now a suspect himself, she did not feel she had anyone to spare.

Anyone else she could trust.

That was a situation she was going to have to rectify.

When the bulky man with scarred hands came next, alone, removing his skull cap to reveal the recognizable sparse hair and features, he stopped at the end of the corridor and waited, exchanging no more with her than what appeared to others in the corridor than a casual glance between strangers.

She took another look at Blayd through the dividing window, wanting to be here for him but vehemently refusing to be in there, frowned, and then drew her coat around her neck as she stalked down the hall. Past several similar windows and rooms with other ailing and injured patients, past the mountain-like man who had come in, past the check-in desk where the chrono beeped to announce the passage of time as she went out the front door.

Visitors and families had to check in, had to be approved.

It was the only reason she believed that, even if she was not here to protect Blayd from that prying, persistent young thing, she would not be able to get to him.

The platform in front of the medi-facility was wider than in front of most other establishments, the need for constant foot traffic, for the rushing in of patients, for a place for visitors to gather when there was more than the inside waiting room or corridors would allow, demanding that accommodation. Against the rail opposite the double doors, as far to the left as the platform would allow, she pulled out a hemp leaf smokey from its silver tin and stared at the display of lights and foot traffic below.

Drab, dismal, a life of constant darkness and drudgery.

"You get used to it when it's all you know," said the man stopping beside her, lighter in hand, the offer made to light her smokey as though he had heard her unspoken criticism of the Levs. Without

looking, she held the smokey for him to light and then took a long drag from it as the lighter clicked closed.

He had replaced his cap, but it made no difference. She knew who he was.

"He's not talking." That his captive seemed unable to hear the questions put to him was an adequate reason for that, but he did not say so. "We're trying something else.

Something else amounted to giving the swelling in the man's head time to subside so that he could hear. He did not mention that either.

"You can't kill him. We need him alive."

She felt her companion's frown and fleetingly wondered what efforts they had taken to get the hapless fellow to talk. Hapless, for being in the wrong place at the wrong time, but he had prevented both Kal and the brako from killing Blayd.

She had already come down hard on the man beside her for that error, but there were too many pieces pitted against one another, and friendly-fire mistakes were bound to happen. She should not be surprised when those pieces ran afoul of another with cross purposes.

She needed Senior Kal out of the way, yes. But she also needed him in place a little while longer. And she needed someone other than the brako to remove him when that time came.

Assuming his silence to be a query, she said, "Anyone willing to jump into a fight like that…with obvious skill…we can use."

"We need a way to turn him." Finding a man's weakness was the door to compliance, but they had not yet succeeded in breaking through to him. But they would.

Snubbing out the partially burned smokey on the metal handrail after a single drag, she said, "Then find a way. I want him on our side."

She needed a man like that. Before the Senior got to him first.

❧*❧

A different blindness now, hot and white, searing through the slits of his swollen lids, jarring him to consciousness as if out of dreamless

sleep. He did not think he had been asleep, however. In the devouring silence, it was difficult to tell. A familiar buzz of lighting, a sound he felt sizzle over his skin as much as he heard it with his still stuffy ears, replaced the previous quiet.

But with every prickle and ripple of electricity over his exposed arms, he wished for the return of silence. The hum was maddening.

He was alone in the narrow room, its walls of polished metal a dull gray behind the brightness of the overhead lamp, the rivets in the plating and the latch on the door suggesting a facility used for storage of cold goods or carbidi ice. There was none of that here now, and the expected churning of coolant through the walls was absent. Though the ambient air temperature was cool, it was no colder than any other room would be in Hebanthe Falls without a heating system to warm it.

As empty as the room was, it had not been used in some time.

He was suspended by his arms in the room's center, directly beneath the light source, but the effort to tip his head to see it brought a searing pain in the back of his neck that suggested how long he had been suspended here with his head lolling forward. Beneath him, his toes barely touched the ground. There was no good way to get leverage in the hopes of yanking free from what felt like scratchy hemp ropes binding his wrists, and his one attempt to do so, to snap the rope, to pull whatever held him out of the wall, to free himself, ended in the excruciating reminder of his shoulder's dislocation…just before the pain of it sucked him from the light into blackness again.

৯*৶

Worry proved a deterrent to concentration as Jaron struggled through his shift's work, his efforts to catalog and collate and identify his assigned morsels of data constantly undercut by the snatches of remembered SCAM images that proved how fierce Rhyd Ballard could be, whether hidden behind his alter ego's face or not.

Jaron had heard the stories, had scoured the Archives for every snippet of SCAM footage that proved the skill and strengths of the

mythical figure that until recently he had little interest in. Now he knew and understood, knew the face behind the mask, knew on a deeper level, though they had barely spoken, the man behind the mask, and it was only that knowledge that enabled him to cling to hope that wherever Rhyd was, whatever the reason for his silence, he was alive and, Jaron hoped, unharmed.

A man with his skills, his strengths, his instincts could not have been snuffed out in the act of helping children.

Jaron struggled to cling to that hope, though each minute ticking past without word ate at his belief like time-termites. Not that Rhyd would reach out to him; beyond their joint mission to free Skelter from the Core they were nothing to one another. There was no reason Rhyd should let him know he was safe.

But surely he would let someone know. As important as he was to the mission, surely Enoch or Lash or Zara would hear from him, and would let Jaron know what was next, how he was to proceed. He had located and cataloged every cache of freezes in the city. He had calculated where it would be easiest to take what they needed, where it was least likely to be missed, where it would be simplest to doctor the Archives to cover the theft.

Theft.

He had never thought himself a thief. But unless someone gave him different directives, unless Rhyd failed to turn up, he just might become one.

Oh, what his father, mother, and sister would have thought of him.

His eating break, one typically spent in the archivists' communal room, was cut short by a familiar face at the public desk. A man less familiar from personal experience than from his numerous appearances on the SCAMs, when the Voices of Faith had worked diligently with Founder Kemway to retain a constant influence on Hebenon's population through propcasts, sermonizing speeches, and repeated messages of unity and prosperity that never quite rang true for the majority of Lev residents. Senior Kal wore a more familiar face than Neoma Kemway. For him, there would never be anonymity.

It was not unusual for people to come to the Archives seeking information. Tallies of population numbers, productivity, criminal activity. Statistics of all sorts or old SCAM footage of historical events. Families hoping for some lost fact, an image or life detail of someone lost, someone whose life they intended to remember, to celebrate, to venerate. Someone hoping to delete themselves from Hebenon's records in the hopes of ceasing to exist.

Jaron had seen all manner of requests come through the Archives. Senior Kal was not the first Talker to seek information, nor was this the first time the Senior had been here. But the itch between Jaron's eyes as their gazes met when he passed the main desk, an itch that did not subside as the Senior's focus returned to the request form he was completing, prompted Jaron to grab his meal from the cold storage and return to his cubical to eat.

It was not the first time he had worked through his eating period. Many people did, out of boredom or with the hopes of gaining kudos, a promotion, or a few extra ticks for increased productivity and diligence. Some used the opportunity to research data of their own.

No one questioned his being there. No one questioned his early log in to the Archive system. Especially during the last few shifts when he had done both often enough.

No one at the nearest terminals cared enough to make note of which Archive requests he fulfilled, even though such requests were typically not within his jurisdiction. The request had not yet been processed, as new incoming requests were often screened for potential criminal activity or in order to defend what meager privacy rights Hebenon's residents had.

A request for the identity of some random individual on the street, a request such as this one, was most often denied unless it was made by a member of law enforcement. Even such a claim as this, of wanting to thank someone for saving their life, was most often denied, for who was to say that thanks was truly what the requester intended.

But a request from the Senior Talker, a man respected as an icon even as the popularity of the Voices of Faith continued to wane,

seemed harmless. The brako had tried to kill him. Anyone watching the recent prodcasts knew it. They also knew that an unidentified man seen by many, thanks to Neoma's SCAM footage hack, had saved his life. What man would not want to identify such a savior?

There was a beep. A flicker of the screen as the system updated.

The request was approved.

Despite Jaron's expertise and effort to block Rhyd's identity, by the time his eating break was over, the screen refreshed several more times…and the man's identity was revealed.

Not only his identity, but other details of his life. His occupation. His partner's name.

Thankfully, not his personal address, for that data was reserved for law enforcement and medical personnel. But his occupation made him easy enough to find.

Thanks to the great care Rhyd had taken thus far, there was not a shred of evidence linking him to his off-shift activities.

Scarecrow was safe.

But for how long, now that a man of Senior Kal's clout had his hooks into the first scraps of personal information?

Throughout the remainder of his shift, as time dragged and the tedium and nervousness refused to end, Jaron wrestled with what he knew…and who to share it with. Oliver seemed the first logical choice, but Jaron quickly ruled him out. Oliver might know Rhyd's other identity, but he did not know that Jaron knew it. He would ask questions Jaron could not answer. As there had been no illegality to the information request, nor the filling of it by the senior archivist on duty when the request was made, there was little reason to suspect anything sinister.

Little reason except for Jaron's sixth sense. A sense that told him Rhyd was in danger. Or would be when he showed his face again.

Lash then. Lash and Enoch. If there was a problem, they would know what to do.

If that problem created difficulties for their plans, it was better they know now…before Skelter ran out of time.

❧*❧

The thud, the crack. The heavy weight of a thumper on his calves, his thighs, his biceps and shoulders, his sides just below his ribs. Blows that fell with practiced precision to inflict maximum pain without incapacitating, life-stealing damage. Hot snaps of the rod against the soles of his feet that he last recalled being encased in boots.

And always the same questions.

Who are you?

What is your name?

He imagined it was what they had been asking before, when he had been unable to hear them, but the answer remained the same.

Silence.

Tongue swollen with thirst, throat raw with an agony left by the too-distant consumption of alcohol, Rhyd did not speak, gave no more than the involuntary sounds of pain that accompanied the strikes. Who he was, was not important. Not to them. Not to anyone…except Venn and a handful of others who needed his other self more than they needed him.

And if someone suspected his duality, having a name to put to the Scarecrow's hidden face was the last thing he would give them.

Right after any leverage that having a name might give them over him.

He would rather die.

‣Chapter 19‣

"Mister Weyer, is it?"

The evening's rehearsal complete, Venn had just closed the latches of the cello case when footsteps approached from his right. It had been a good rehearsal, despite his frustrated distraction, and as was often the case, visitors stopped to watch, to listen, friends, neighbors, loved ones, those interested in joining the gradually growing collection of musicians or those interested in retaining them to play at some private event or gathering. Faces came and went from the room and Venn paid them little heed.

If he had picked out this particular face in the crowd, he would have been better prepared to face her.

"Mam Founder." He bowed with a congenial smile that came easily in public and social situations. It was part of his charm, had helped the advancement of his career and was winning him a gradually growing base of admirers. He had seen her before, at his only First Chair performance prior to Vanishing, but he had never spoken to her, had never been near enough to shake her hand.

"Please." Her tone, her smile, were dismissively disarming while remaining slightly aloof, making him relax into the conversation she sought. "It is nice to hear such music again; it has been too long."

"It has been." He did not think she remembered him; too much had happened in the long months between that fateful performance and now. In those days he had been no one special. Banished to the Outside, he had become even more of a no one, but he was working diligently to change that in the hopes of making Rhyd proud. With her notice, he realized he might be on the verge of it at last.

"Ten days until our debut; you must attend."

Neoma smiled again, making a mental note of the date, and nodded. "I shall not miss it. Please; may we have a private word?"

No one was nearby save for a handful of orchestra members chatting near the door and the conductor and another member sifting through Echo pages of musical notation as if searching for something specific. The polite thing to do was acquiesce to the request, and so he took up the cello case and walked with her into the empty corridor outside of the rehearsal hall.

They were in the Uppers here. No endless drizzle, no constant chill or eye-straining gloom. She could not remain long, as she knew her welcome was tenuous and he looked to have somewhere he was expecting to be, so she cleared her throat and got to the point.

"I've seen the footage; it took some effort to track you down, but you're the only chance I have of finding Mr. Ballard. I'm hoping together we can help him."

"Rhyd? Help him?" He failed to hide the panic in his eyes and voice, and his grip on the case handle tightened. "What has he done?'

"Done?" She tucked her hand around his arm as they walked slowly along the warm, white corridor. "Saved my friend's life, of course, and Senior Kal's as well…"

"He did?" Outside there were no Echos, no SCAMs, and Hebenon's gossip was slow to filter there. Venn had heard some talk among the other musicians before rehearsal of a ruckus in the Levs, of an attempt on the Senior and a group of Talkers by the brako and streeters, but there had been no mention of Scarecrow…and the chance that someone had connected Scarecrow to Rhyd was chilling.

Neoma continued. "I'm afraid for his safety, Mr. Weyer, and I'm hoping he is with you. If the brako have him…"

She ignored the growing horror on his face as they neared the lift that would take Venn back to the East tunnel, to the Outside. Agnys waited by the door with a smile. She was not his child, but she expressed a deep fondness for him, and particularly for Rhyd, and she often waited here or at the outer door for them to return. Seeing her there was a comforting thing.

Noticing the way Neoma looked at the unfamiliar child in parah clothing, the first parah she was aware of seeing, was not.

She grimaced but continued speaking as though they were still alone. The parah were animals after all. Crossers might live out there, among them, and some might have come inside to work, but that did not mean they were civilized enough to understand her.

"I'd like to find him, to bring him home if he is being held…or simply to thank him if he's safe and well. It's not often a passerby risks their life for anyone in Hebenon; selfishness is far too rare a thing. I would like to personally thank him for what he did. Is he well? He looked to have taken quite a hit when he fell…"

"He…" Venn's face paled and he cleared his throat. A passerby's interference meant Rhyd and not Scarecrow, but that knowledge did not offer the relief Venn hoped for. "He's tougher than he looks." At his side, Agnys slipped her hand into his free one and stared at the unfamiliar woman with open distrust.

"So I gathered from the footage. He is safe then? Home…out there?" What little information she had found on Weyer indicated the cellist was a crosser, so it seemed likely Ballard was too.

"He…" Venn started again. Not wanting to admit that he had not seen Rhyd in days, not wanting her to be the one to find him when he could not imagine such a turn of events going well, worried now that the skirmish she spoke of was the cause of Rhyd's absence and that he was lying injured or dead somewhere, abandoned, Venn glanced at Agnys, forced a smile and shrugged his shoulders. "I'll tell him of your concern." Let her think Rhyd was safe. And do not worry Agnys. Such worry would not help anything.

"Such a man could be a valuable ally. Do you think he would be willing to meet with me? Dinner perhaps?"

"I don't know…maybe." He could not speak for Rhyd, although he felt sure the other man would decline an invitation from the Mam out of principle, and he did not think Rhyd had any inclination to be her ally. Venn would not promise a meeting he could not guarantee.

Something icy in its neutrality settled in place of her previously cordial demeanor and she stepped back from the obviously hostile expression on the child's face. Parah were wild, feral things. Neoma expected the little beast to attack her.

"See that you do, Mr. Weyer. His safety is my primary concern. We have a great deal to discuss…and I would hate for something unfortunate to happen before we do."

She did not bid him farewell, made no mention of the orchestra, but such words would not have gotten beyond the tangle of the threat left in her wake.

Agnys' hand in Venn's trembling one clenched; he did not dare look away from the retreating woman to see the child's expression.

He did not need to see it to understand she felt threatened too.

Was Mam threatening him, he wondered, or Rhyd? Or Agnys?

Did she know the truth about Scarecrow?

He needed to find Rhyd. Needed to warn him. Needed to find out what was going on before it was too late.

❧*❧

Skin damp with the sweat of exertion as his body fought against the continuing barrage of pain, it made the sting of the buzzer's electronic fingers more excruciating when each moment of contact came. Familiar with the way buzzers worked, in the back of his mind he knew the settings had been altered, decreased enough to cause pain instead of rendering the subject unconscious and incapacitated.

Odds were, if they had a stolen buzzer, they were brako.

Whoever they were, they knew they could not get answers from an unconscious man.

Try as he did to focus on faces in the dark, Rhyd still did not know who they were.

He doubted they were bugorra. Unless his captors were acting against orders, Grainger had outlawed the tortures practiced by generations of his predecessors and the Founders they had served. The

❧236❧

masked silhouettes he occasionally glimpsed through slitted eyes suggested brako, but he could not be sure.

If not brako, who?

And why, he struggled with the lucid question as his body shook beneath another electric assault, did they want to know his name?

❧*❧

She did not often go inside the metal bird's nest now, and never alone…at least never alone further than the door where she sometimes met Venn or Rhyd at the end of a long day.

Once had been enough.

Now she understood that it was no nest.

Now she understood that those once feared as birdmen were no more birds than she was a fish.

They were men and women, like those she knew in the village, though they were alien in their oddness, preferring the dark and wet to the warmth of the sun, preferring paths and stairs of metal to dirt and rock and trees, to fields of hemp and pastures of sheep, goats, and pigs.

She did not like it inside, but she was no longer afraid of it, unlike the majority of her elders and her peers. Now that she understood the pitfalls, now that she was no longer hunted as an unclean, dangerous, anomalous beast, she considered inside to be no more dangerous than outside. But with few reasons to enter, particularly alone, she was content to keep to the world she knew, the world where Venn and Rhyd had joined her.

Rhyd, however, was not as happy outside as Venn. She did not know why he kept going back, to work, to fight, did not understand the complexities of adult relationships and the ways trauma could forever imprint on one's psyche. She did understand Venn's worry for the blonde man, however, just as she understood that the woman from the city intended Rhyd harm.

And she understood, from things not said, that wherever Rhyd was, he was in trouble.

Venn did not know what to do, how to find Rhyd, how to help. Agnys, on the other hand, while uncertain what she could do on her own, believed there was someone who could help.

The man with the cats.

She knew her way to Rhyd's flat, had been there several times. Sometimes with Venn, sometimes with Tox or Zara or Maemi. This was the first time she had gone back alone, and she did so slowly, repeating every step, every direction others had taken, until she came to the door of Rhyd's dark home.

She knocked.

No one answered.

Nor was there an answer at the adjacent door, where the window had been replaced to keep the cats from having free reign now that the cat-man had turned the place into a more suitable living space. No longer hunted, he did not need to hide. Eight cats loitered around the doorway, perched on the rail, hunkered under the nearest stairs, balanced on the narrow window ledge that had once been their path inside. Some scattered at the girl's approach, others meowed hungrily, and though she had nothing to give them, when she sat on the step in front of the door, several scurried to her, eager for attention.

All she had to do was wait. Eventually, the cat-man would come.

Without the sun to instruct her, Agnys had no idea how much time passed. That someone might be looking for her never crossed her mind. By the time footsteps on the stairs approached, declaring the arrival of the man with the stringy blonde hair, his pinched familiar face expressing affection at the sight of her, her buttocks and thighs were numb from the cold grating. The cats rushed to greet the one who fed them as he took the child's offered hand, helping her to her feet.

"What brings you down here, Agnys?" he asked, fishing in his pocket for the passcard to open the flat door. "Is Venn here?"

"He is worried. Rhyd is in trouble."

Lash sighed and let her in. He followed, flicking the light on.

"Why do you think that?" He knew she had not likely seen the SCAM footage shown on every Echo in Hebenon, but it was possible

Venn had. Venn would not be the only one to recognize that particular face in the midst of that fight, possibly two faces if he had seen the briefest moment before Xiaodan disappeared beneath the onslaught between Talkers and streeters.

Lash had already been told the grim news about Xiaodan. He presumed the man he was expecting to meet here at any minute knew the tale as well. With other plans dependent on Ballard's participation and welfare, whatever Agnys knew, whatever Venn might know, could be important.

"There was a woman looking for Rhyd."

"What woman?" Not any from Rhyd's circle. Agnys knew their names now. Lash's first guess was a bugger, someone sent by Grainger. No one else knew who Rhyd was to be able to find him through his relationship with Venn.

"Tall…very short hair…like mine."

Agnys' hair was long, so Lash guessed she meant the same color.

The most obvious candidate, someone who might have the resources to find Venn after viewing the SCAM footage, was the woman who had tinged the footage for her own illegal prodcast.

"Crucksake," he muttered as there came a knock at his door.

Agnys jumped, instinct and surprise prompting her to look for a safe hiding place despite her overall lack of fear within the city, but when Lash held out a hand to calm her and grunted, "Okay, stay there," she settled again on the sofa full of cats where she had made herself at home. She did not know the face of the mop-headed man at the door, but he looked friendly, and since Lash welcomed him in with a grasping hold on his wrist that pulled him inside, she knew she had nothing to fear.

"Agnys, Jaron. Jaron, Agnys."

Nervous, not about the child but about the situation in which he found himself, Jaron shuffled his feet as Lash closed the door. "Friend of yours?" he asked quietly. He had no experience with children, not even younger siblings, and he was unaware of Lash having family, but from the way the girl interacted with the host of cats that Lash went

into the kitchen to feed, he thought perhaps she lived nearby and was here for the feline army.

"Friend of Ballard's…from Marbordo."

A parah child.

The parah child.

Odd, Jaron thought, how that suddenly cast an air of sacredness around the little girl who seemed like any other he passed daily on the walks throughout the city.

If not for this child, nothing in Hebenon would have changed.

"Seems Mam Kemway is looking for him, reached out to Venn."

Jaron's expression grew long and distressed. He had yet to meet Venn, but he knew the name, knew him to be someone important to Rhyd. "Think she knows?"

Staring at the stranger as she petted her lapful of cats, Agnys' eyes were wide with wonder. The dark-haired man made words, but his mouth did not move. Instead, the tiny lights at his temples flickered and the flat illuminated disk at the hollow of his throat twinkled in near-unison. She had never encountered anything like it.

"How could she?" Lash had seen the footage. Ballard had been Ballard. Not Scarecrow. The only clues might have been the way he fought, but there were others in Hebenon who trained on the mats, in the gyms, for fitness or for sport, or as part of their occupation. There was nothing specific that Lash had seen that connected Ballard to the Scarecrow, except to those in his inner circle.

"She wants dinner with him," Agnys piped, still staring to see if the stranger would speak again. "Venn does not think it's a good idea."

"Never a good idea," agreed Lash, sitting on the sofa beside her, expecting her to carry that message to Venn…and to Rhyd if he showed up Outside. "Have you seen Ballard? Either of you?"

Agnys shook her head with a pout and lay it against Lash's shoulder. With bowls of food lining the counter, the cats had vacated her lap. "Not for many days. Venn thinks he's hurt or gone."

Matching her fearful expression, Jaron shook his head.

"I'm sure he's fine…laying low…hiding but fine…" Lash hoped his words would soothe the child's concerns.

Agnys understood hiding. She knew what Rhyd did in the shadows. She knew how often he hid.

"Mam's not the only one looking for him…Senior Kal is too." Lash's sideways glance at Jaron as he stroked the girl's head prompted the dark-haired man to continue. "He requested identification from the Archives; I did not have the chance to block or deny the request."

"Might have looked bad for you…and him…if you had. Maybe that's how Mam found Venn." There had been a time when the Voices of Faith and the Founder's family were tightly bound, held together by centuries of tradition and societal rule. Despite the very public accusation of treason Neoma uttered against the Voices, against Kal, perhaps he had provided her information about Rhyd as a peace offering or some other bit of political maneuvering between them.

"He did save the Senior from those brako…so I thought maybe that was Kal's interest…but Mam?"

This time Lash snorted. "Maybe she hopes those brako would finish the job…or that Rhyd might be able to get close enough to get the Senior out of her way."

"He's still missing." Jaron's voice was a near-whisper, reluctant to speak those words in front of the girl who had closer ties to Ballard then he did. Despite the wisdom and intelligence in her eyes, she was still just a child. "Oliver's searching high and low…"

"I've got fingers out for him too…"

"But if we don't find him soon…what'll we do about Skelt? Have you seen Enoch?"

"No." Lash sighed again. What would they do? What could they do? Skelter's clock was ticking and making plans contingent on a missing man would be folly.

To make a plan that did not include that missing man seemed to be folly too. Lash did not think they could succeed without Ballard.

"I'll find Enoch," Lash promised. Knock the planning ball back into Skelter's court. Try to make a new plan. "You keep Grainger out

of the way, keep doing what you're doing…ears to the ground. When I know something, you'll know it too."

"And we find Rhyd," murmured Agnys.

Jaron offered her his hand. "We find Rhyd," he agreed.

Whatever else the child was, she had her priorities straight. Rhyd had to be found.

⁖*⁗

He was vaguely aware of the smells of sweat, of burnt skin, of urine, of jostling and being hoisted, of the bindings around his wrists loosening, but it was his arms dropping forward, the flash of pain that shot through him as his dislocated shoulder changed position and the sudden rush of blood into his hands that came with it which brought Rhyd to full consciousness. The room was still too bright and the swinging of the light fixture meant that the glare flashing off the metal walls swung with it, so he squeezed his eyes shut, against the light, against the pain, and waited for one, for both, to pass. The door was behind him, he knew that from the sound of retreating boots that passed through it, the clack of the handle latching into place.

Now that he was cut down, he did not expect to be alone, or alive, for long.

A click. A hiss ending in a pop.

The room went black.

⁖*⁗

Returning to the medical facility, this time in uniform as she expected further resistance from the woman standing watch over the injured man, Ilya found Neoma absent and the staff willing to allow her to interview the victim and his records in an official capacity. He was asleep when she entered his room, but the medi on-call swore he had regained consciousness earlier and would likely awaken again soon. Glancing up now and then at the equipment that allowed her to

assess his condition, Ilya waited as he slept, hoping he woke before Neoma returned, before she was recalled to duty.

Ginna needed her. She had promised a prompt return home but Grainger's press for details about that fight, for arrests and for the condition of the injured participants had every available officer scrambling. The intervening passerby had not yet been located, the man whose name had been provided by Captain Grainger's man, a man of no consequence to Ilya but who Joran clearly thought worth telling her about…a man Senior Kal was also interested in finding. The Senior had avoided SCAM appearances, declined interviews, refused to divulge his location, either afraid of the brako or afraid of the bugorra who were undoubtedly looking for him as well. But he was not afraid enough to stay out of the Archives in search of his missing savior.

Something did not add up, not Jaron's interest and desire to keep the stranger's name out of the Captain's ear, though Grainger was already seeking him too, not the Senior's behavior or interest in the same man, not his being there in that fight or Blayd's connection to it. None of the pieces fit, and without an image to guide her, Ilya did not know what sort of picture she was looking at.

Talkers and streeters alike had been injured, one young man and a brako killed. The bugorra crackdown afterward had led to the arrests of a number of brako associates, the calling in of several ranking Talkers in order to search out Senior Kal, and the roundup of a number of street children for interrogation. All of those efforts prevented Ilya from returning home early as promised, and Ilya, certain her sister had fled, was restless and irritable and angry with her job.

Law and order were requirements for a civilized, peaceful society but for the first time in her life, Ilya felt the need to put Ginna first yet she was not being allowed to do so.

From the footage she had seen, the brako had nearly killed Blayd, estranged though they might be. Brako she had been unable to stop, despite her ongoing efforts, criminals that always struck in times and

places where she and her officers could do little more than clean up the aftermath.

The gorra were failing. Maybe some other means was necessary.

The Scarecrow might not be the answer, but some concerted effort by the people, standing up against the brako as that stranger had done…the stranger who had saved Ginna, had saved Blayd, had saved Senior Kal…just might be.

"Looking for me, officer?"

With his head immobilized by the brace around his neck, Blayd could only turn his eyes in her direction, but now that they were open, the two looked at each other, Ilya with enough obvious relief that Blayd hoped she was not here in a purely professional capacity.

"How are you feeling?"

Pleased by her smile, he replied, "Nothing hurts, so that's good."

"You're so full of meds you're lucky you feel anything." She looked him over carefully before lightly tapping the neck brace. "Other than this, you don't look too bad. Nothing's broken. They say you should be out in a day or so now that you're awake, soon as they're satisfied there's no cranial or spinal damage."

"Did you get 'em? The brako who did this?"

"That one went over, fell to his death. Dredged him out of the nets and have him in for I.D. The other…"

"Vanderwall…yeah." He grunted. "Wasn't expecting him to be there. Thought for sure I could take him…that we were…"

Noting the way he hedged his words, Ilya leaned nearer to ask, "What happened?"

With a pursed-lip scowl, he shook his head. "Uh-uh. I know my rights. Not gonna get me to confess to anything the SCAMs…"

Looking more offended by his suspicion of her motives then she felt, she scoffed, "Only one good recording…and it shows more of the streeters and Talkers then you, the Senior, the brako. I get the Talker and streeter clash…and the brako are always looking for a tussle…but how'd you end up in the middle of that mess?"

His shrug looked halfhearted and forced, an effect of the brace or a side effect of the meds or an effort to appear nonchalant. At least it was movement, which meant he was not paralyzed. "Was hoping for a word with the Senior…saw them pass and tried to catch up with him as the streeters took their turn…and then Vanderwall and his goon were there. Seemed to be trying to get to the Senior, and I guess they made me their first target…since I was the only one armed. It's what I'd do in their place."

Actually, what he would do, if given the opportunity, was take a distance shot, but that could be difficult in the twists and angles of the Levs unless you were a very good marksman. Congested narrow walkways, handrails and grates and swirling mist and moisture made getting a clean distance line a tricky thing. Hand to hand was usually easier, quicker…but distance was cleaner if one had the chance.

Blayd would have preferred cleaner. It would have kept the brako's hands off of him.

"And the Senior? Did you see him go down?" The question was carefully worded to hide what she knew, to prompt his own version of what had happened.

"They got him?" He was confident he had been the brako target, not the Senior, an effort to keep him from getting to the Senior Talker they were working with, but he would not admit that to a gorra.

"We think he got out clean, but the SCAMs lost him. No one has seen him since." No one except Grainger's man and maybe a couple of others at the Archives. Although Ilya believed Joran's story, she would check the Archive and those on duty that day herself, to see if any footage or data requests substantiated Kal being there Maybe Jaron had mistaken the Senior's identity or a signature. Maybe it was a forgery, a decoy, to throw them off.

Jaron had nothing to gain by lying about what he saw, but she knew how unreliable witnesses could be.

"I'd ask the brako…they're the ones who wanted him."

Wanted him alive or dead was the question.

"We intend to as soon as we find someone who knows something. That other who fell? The one who took on Vanderwall? What do you know about him?"

Again Blayd's shoulder twitched in a shrug. "Never seen him before. Brako maybe, another Talker? Maybe one of Neoma's men?"

"One you don't know about?" she asked with an arched brow.

Blayd smirked. So she knew. "I don't know everyone," was the only admission he made. He had never lied about who he worked for; he had just avoided providing information. "He dropped into the party from the half-Lev above. From his timing, I'd say most likely one of the Voices men."

"They don't typically have goons." Talkers traveled in groups, safety in numbers, but none she had met were trained to fight.

Maybe the Senior considered protection warranted. Until recently, it had never been needed. Until Neoma's hacked prodcast and accusations of treason, there had never been a call to arms against the Voices.

Perhaps Mam Kemway was where Ilya needed to go next.

It was her turn to grunt. If the stranger was a Talker, why had he fought them to protect the streeters? Another path leading not to answers but only to more questions. Another delay in returning home.

She could wait here for Neoma's return, question her, but there was no guarantee she would be back, so Ilya would have to find her.

A way that did not involve Blayd. A way that did not tip the woman to gorra interest in whatever part she played in that incident.

A part beyond sending Blayd into the thick with a motive Ilya had not yet determined.

"Drink? When I get out of here?"

She paused as she stood, contemplating the question. "Only if you hurry," she decided to offer coyly. The definition of hurry was open to interpretation…for both of them…and whatever time was involved in between would, she hoped, be enough to find Kal, the unidentified participant, and Vanderwall. Enough to clean this whole mess up.

❧*❦

"You make this harder on yourself than you need to."

Certain his ears bled, that it accounted for the pain and wetness he felt on both sides of his head, Rhyd was also sure he knew that voice.

But he did not know, in the fog and depth of pain, from where.

"I apologize for the brutal handling from the others; that was not my idea. But we need to know…"

No one was touching him, but Rhyd felt a shudder of something terrible and excruciating course through his body, reaching into his fingers and toes, into the pit of his stomach and the ends of every strand of hair. His body tried to curl in response to the stimuli, as if making itself smaller would alleviate the agony, but he could not move. Paralyzed, with no real sense of his body beyond this new horror, he could not even force his eyes open to look at the speaker or move his jaw to speak.

"A man like you, a man of your talents, has uses. All we ask is your name…and that you help us restore Hebenon to its former glory."

Glory?

Rhyd might have laughed if not for the stranglehold gripping his throat. If Hebenon had ever been glorious, it had been long before any man or woman now alive was born.

"Do that…for us…and I'll make sure no harm comes to Venn."

Not Venn!

The mental reaction to the threat should have been enough to lurch Rhyd to his feet, to push him into a fighter stance with the Speaker pummeled into the floor beneath him.

Instead, all it did was create a twisting, wrenching sensation in his belly so that whatever remained within, mostly bile after so many empty hours, was expelled with such force that it took his consciousness with it.

❧Chapter 20❧

It felt like hours, maybe days, that he lay on the floor, unmoving in the dark as the metal surface absorbed some of the fire from his skin and gave it back in tiny, barely perceptible increments. The taste in his mouth was bitter, stale and coppery as though the remnants of old blood, and the damp in which he lay smelled of fusty urine. Unable to judge the passage of time, with the lights off and no sound bleeding in from beyond the walls that might have let him judge the hour by the passing of feet and the distant shrill drone of shift whistles, Rhyd only knew that time had passed because whatever had been in his body to paralyze him, make him sick, had been metabolized enough to allow him to slowly contract into a fetal position. The pain and nausea had taken away his worry for Venn, and the more shadowy worry for Skelter, but as cognizance returned, so too did his fears.

They did not know who he was. Did they? How could they, unless one of the few people in his inner circle had been forced to give up his secret. Why then use Venn against him, unless they thought they might use the combat skills of the anonymous man who had come to the aid of streeters. But use them against who? Himself?

If the effort did not hurt so much, he would have laughed.

The thing, a sound, that brought him back to the most alert he had been since stirring here, seemed to be inside the room. Metal within metal, a click, a scrape. Distinct but still muffled by the stuffiness in his head. An earlier perusal of his cell had revealed that the only item in the room with him was the light from which he had been suspended, a construct that could not have produced that noise unless it was on the verge of falling from the ceiling.

That left only one other possibility.

Despite the pins and needles sensation scraping through his neck as he turned his face to the side, he willed his eyes to focus on the only source of light in the room, realizing with a start that it had been there for some time, that the room was not as dark as he remembered. A blade-thin line of faint greenish-blue, the sort of light given off by dimming alglamps, the sort that adorned street corners and stairwells, stretched from near the ceiling to the floor, angling there to suggest that the door to his prison was ajar.

A trap.

It had to be.

Yet there were no sounds to tickle his ears with times passage.

He did not move as he stared, waiting. For someone to come to close it, someone to open it further. Anything. When the creeping minutes brought nothing, however, a trigger tripped within and prompted him to crawl.

Whether his captors intended to kill him for an attempt to escape, whether they were watching to see what he would do, whether this was some new form of torture, it made little sense to lay here subserviently and wait to die. There were things he needed to do. He either needed to leave here to meet those responsibilities, or he needed to die trying. There were no other fitting options.

No one knew where he was. Rescue was unlikely. If he wanted freedom, he needed to gain it himself. Someone's carelessness, or deliberate action, was an opportunity not to ignore.

He was too weak to push to his feet, however, and the effort to do so shot pain through fractured bones, burned and bruised skin, and the dislocated shoulder he had forgotten about. His attempt dropped him into a jumbled, trembling heap inches nearer the door with his eyes squeezed shut and his jaw clenched. Wearied by hunger and thirst and the extended physical abuses, he did not have the willpower to push through the pain to try again. Once the worst of it was past, however, he managed an awkward three-limbed crawl that brought him to the path of escape.

For several minutes, perhaps near to an hour, he lay with his face pushed to that crack, to the damp freshness of air that cleared the smells of offal and sweat, blood and singed flesh, the smells of torture, from his nose. Gradually the odors gave way to others, industrial smells, rotting fish smells intermingled with fertilized soil and the crashing of water over stone and metal. With stiff fingers, he pried the door open to be met by the blast and spray of the Four Falls' mist across his face, neck, and hands.

Not directly beneath the deluge of one of the four, but near enough to endure the constant back spray of moisture as falling water merged with the river. There had to be grating and ducting in the walls of that room that he had not noticed, for so much moisture would have made the room impossible to use otherwise.

The light he had seen shone from an alglamp that the open door blocked, painting a psychedelic world of mist and shadow through his heavy lids, a world where distance was difficult to judge. But the proximity of the falls and the river gave him an inkling of where he was. Most importantly, it told him the direction he needed to go if he was to be away before his captors returned and noted his absence.

Assuming they were not watching him from hidden places nearby.

With the fingers of his good hand, he clawed into the grating outside the door, dragged himself over the threshold…and tumbled down steps he had not realized were there.

Two of the metal supporting beams, serving to anchor the mesh lattice suspended along the walkway's edge that prevented objects and people from accidentally dropping into the fisher tract that stretched across the river a half-Lev below, stopped Rhyd's descent and the painful impact of his ribs against one of them elicited a grunt. Neither it, nor the clatter of his fall, however, attracted attention over the noise of the river and the falls, and there was no one within visual distance as far as he could tell, to witness his tumble. But his position was too exposed to both the wet and the possibilities of being discovered by either passersby or his captors. The splash of spawning fish in the tract offered further clues to his location and an explanation for the use of

that room as well as the relative absence of people. Spawning fish did not need supervision. A couple of passes were made per shift by workers to monitor the eggs, gather them, inspect the health of the breeders, but most of the time the fish managed themselves.

He had minutes, maybe an hour or two at most, to move.

Move, he told himself.

The command grew more insistent when the vibration in the grate beneath him announced someone's approach. The fog hid anyone from his view, and he from theirs. He did not know how long he had before he was discovered, did not know if the individual would be friend or foe.

But he could not risk being found.

Lying on his dislocated arm, he ignored the agony of it to lurch up, roll, and with an awkward effort disappear over the lip of the walk on the other side, near the stanchions that supported the nearest corner of his former cell. A half-Lev. That was all the drop would be. So long as he was not impaled by anything in the fall, did not land amidst people he could not detect, did not drop into the river he vaguely remembered being fished out of, he would survive.

He had to.

He chose this intersection, where the Lev 1 Voices of Faith offered their brand of hope on one corner and herpa of competing beliefs set shop at each of the other three, to counter the belief in the doctrine of the Founder's rightful dominance over Hebenon's people. Here on Lev 1, this close to the Falls, where the city was darkest and dampest, where maintenance of filts was an ongoing effort, was the first place where the Kemway cult had begun to fade, washed away by a difference in lifestyles that those in the Uppers never dreamed of.

No one lived here except streeters, outcasts, tingers rejected by the city…or those who had rejected it in turn and came to this Lev to disappear. Many worked the lowest Lev to supply the city with food and materials sent to the factories for processing and building, but calling this wasteland home came with a price.

No one here particularly cared what the Talkers had to say.

The herpa, at least, offered housing and sanctuary to those in need, provided warmth, clothing, textured wax canvases to ward off the water, food and drink and medication to the hungry, the injured and wounded, and the outcast.

Enoch had spent his share of time in this world as far back as he could remember, before he and Skelter crossed paths. Before the Coup or the Core, long enough that it was the only sort of life he recalled from his childhood. It had been the safest place for his caregivers to raise him, the best place to protect him from those who viewed his stature as a defect to be eradicated. Here he was but one outcast among many, and for the most part, outcasts protected one another.

It was why he had chosen this place to wait. Sooner or later, someone, one of those gathered around hot cans for warmth under rain awnings, eating roasted peanuts from the little sacks the herpa offered several times a day, would hear the fate of a man fished from the river. Someone would point the way to find that unfortunate soul, and Enoch would find Ballard. Alive or dead, he would take him home.

And if the Talkers had him, where better than in their lowest House where the buggers were not likely to look?

The ripping crash of something weighty dropping from above, yanking the awning away from the building, knocked over the hot can, scattering sparks as burning waste material over the grated path and into the tumbling water. Streeters and addicts scattered, shouting in dismay, fear and alarm, but Enoch and others were caught in the canvas and had to struggle to wiggle free

By the time Enoch escaped the destroyed awning, the streeters he had shared the hot can with were staring, pointing and murmuring. One poked at the man lying at the center, a man scraped and burned raw and bloody in places, wearing only trousers on a body bearing a plethora of old scars and bruises that spoke of a difficult life. Enoch happened to rise from a position that offered an unobstructed view of the man's face and only a lifetime of streeter education that taught one to never cry out and attract attention kept him from shouting Rhyd's

name. One never wanted to attract the Crows, now the bugorra, or the brako. Particularly not now.

"Inside. Let's get him inside."

It took no further words to convince others to act.

By inside, every one of those gathered knew what the dwarf meant. The Talkers never offered aid or care to an injured man. The most they would do would be summon a medi and leave the fellow in the street until help arrived. Only the herpa would offer actual help, and only within the walls of the closest herpa church would a man find sanctuary. No Talker, no bugger, could take someone from within the herpa's walls. Even the brako had, so far, obeyed that long-standing rule of sanctuary. So long as this fellow was there, he would be safe from whoever had hurt him.

Not even a medical facility could offer that sort of safety. Though Ballard looked like he could use a medi's care, for the moment, Enoch was not going to move him anywhere until he could evaluate the situation fully.

He would summon a medi here. The only doctor, in this instance, he believed they could trust.

The world spun around him, faces moving nearer and further like hallucinogenic fish in varying shades of crimson and charcoal in a pale blue pond. The awning had broken his fall. Lessened the ground's impact, but still he landed with enough force to stun him and rob him of his breath, his faculties, and most of his senses. The dazed state lasted long enough for the faces to move in again, for some of those around him to grab up the corners of the awning and use it as a stretcher to jostle him into the nearest building.

Most, however, retreated outdoors after laying him out on the hemp-board table, understanding that if some appearance of normalcy was not quickly reestablished, anyone looking for the unfortunate fellow would arrive and know something here was amiss. With the hot can quickly righted and moved into place beneath another herpa awning so that the falling water did not extinguish the flames, with the

streeters now gathered once more around its warmth, the only thing that would appear out of place would be the missing awning and the bent poles that had given way under the falling man's weight.

Most might not even notice that.

The door banged shut, making him wince in his agony haze.

"Sanctuary, Gabby," he heard a voice exclaim, a garbled voice reaching him as if he was beneath the water. "Sanctuary and an ICD connection."

Someone replied, syllables in words Rhyd's ears refused to decipher. He groaned. He could not stay here. Though the aromatic linger of incense hung in the air, speaking of the sort of haven he knew existed in Hebenon, he could not endanger these people. He had to get away, get somewhere safe.

"Hush," said the dwarf over the shaking thunder of running boots outside. "You're gonna owe me for this…but not now. For now, let me do what I do."

Rhyd was given no choice. The splitting pain behind his blurred vision flashed and forced him into blackness yet again.

❧Chapter 21❧

Neoma's outraged roar, a rare burst of verbal passion from the normally dignified woman, shook the walls of the flat she shared with her daughter, causing the girl to cower in her closet. It barely phased the large man who had brought the news, however. It came as little surprise that Kal had cut across her wishes; working in opposition to the lead Talker had been a gamble she accepted when the prodcast was made, calling out the Voices for intended treason. She had gambled that it would bring Kal to her, that they could discuss the accusations, their purposes and intentions, and make some new arrangement, face to face, without the false pretense of honesty that had previously existed.

That hope had been a long shot even then.

While it was all part of her strategy, the brako revealing their hostage to the Senior as a show of faith and loyalty to the Voices cause, a gesture of goodwill instead of simply killing the man who had caused the death of at least one of their own, Kal had no way of knowing that Neoma knew of the capture too, that she had an interest in converting the stranger to her cause…that the man's identity had been provided to her after the Senior learned it, and that she had already made contact with the cellist in the hopes of providing leverage.

Kal was playing his own moves by letting the man escape, no doubt. Show mercy, show pity, win him with sympathy and freedom. Show his caring for the man's welfare by releasing him.

Neoma wondered now if she should have abducted Weyer instead of merely warning him. Influencing the blonde through manipulation of his fears could be just as effective as kindness.

Perhaps more so.

"Do we find him?" asked the man leaning against the doorframe without yielding to her tirade. "We know where he's employed…"

"He's not in any condition to work," she snorted angrily. Not if the report of inflicted tortures was accurate. Nothing fatal, she had demanded that much, but more than enough to provide several days of lasting pain. She would have preferred the long game, letting him recover and breaking him down psychologically after nearly breaking him physically. Now she had to make a different plan.

"If Kal's let him go…Kal will know where he is." Assuming Ballard had not gotten free on his own, crawled away like a wounded animal to ball up and die in brako territory, assuming the Senior provided the suffering man enough treatment to gain his trust, some Voices safehouse was the most likely place for him to be taken. Neoma did not know where those might be, but she assumed her guest did…or could find out. "Follow him; find him."

It was not necessary. Nothing she intended in the grand scheme of things relied on this scrappy bilger. He would be useful, but he was not necessary. Still, she was not ready to let the opportunity slip by. Particularly if there was a chance he might be able to tie his abduction and torture back to her so Grainger could use it against her.

With the Senior's influence, that was a looming concern.

❧*❧

Head tipped back to study the view above, judging the angle at which a man would have to fall in order to pull down the awning that previously shielded the herpa's doorway, Grainger wiped water from his eyes then shielded them with his hands, wishing for the first time since his days as a Crow that he had worn the protective headgear of his officers that was designed to keep water off their faces and provide enhancements for clearer vision in the mists of Hebenon's lower Levs. He had served here long ago, as a young man, before coming to the Founder's attention and being swiftly promoted through the ranks to the position of Captain.

Never in those days had he supposed he would be in the position he was in now. Never, in the months since the Coup, had he supposed he would once more be in the grit of things, sifting through available evidence at the dirty-hand level.

If his instincts were accurate, however, this was too important to leave to any underling.

Not when the best underling for the task had been on duty for nearly forty-eight hours straight and had been sent home to sleep.

There was only one point, one logical position, that would lend itself to anything falling and landing here. There were other walks overhead, the veins crisscrossing the half-Lev, stairs and paths of Lev 2, positioned to distribute Hebenon's traffic and weight and reduce the accumulation of water in any one place. But there, where the stairs led up to a Y to separate two storage rooms, would be a good launching point for someone to either jump, fall, or be pushed in order to land where Grainger now stood.

Most of the evidence, the spilled hot can, the remnants of torn awning fabric, had already been removed by someone or washed away by the perpetual spray of the Four Falls. Only the report of his officers of the wary, suspicious behavior of the streeters here…not so unusual really…and the footage from one of the few working SCAMs on Lev 1 that had escaped the Coup's destruction…and the systematic vandalism that had occurred since…had spoken of that fall. And while it was impossible to tell from that misty distorted image if the person who had fallen had been Ballard, it was, quite clearly, a person.

No one had been reported at any med facility in the interim. No deaths had been logged into the system. The evidence of this person had been completely erased.

Who else, if not Ballard?

Leaving his accompanying officers to continue investigating the area, though he expected to find nothing more than the bent awning stanchions, not when the streeters and herpa would be disinclined to talk, Grainger climbed the nearby steps alone. At the top, he took in

the view beneath him, the distance of the fall from this angle and the hatchery spread across the river's awesome might.

If anyone had fallen on that side, into the river, they likely had not survived.

One of the two ordinary cold storages was empty, unlocked, the door carelessly ajar or perhaps left so intentionally. There was evidence of old blood on the floor, stains from ages past that never completely washed away, and rails across the ceiling that typically held hooks with carcasses of meat, fish, poultry, rat and goat. The blood could have come from any or all of those sources. None of it looked fresh and there was no compelling reason to think someone had been held or tortured here.

But the request for analysis was submitted and one of his officers would remain here to protect the scene until the forensics team arrived and completed the gathering of samples.

The other unit was locked, but not pass-hacked to prevent the bugorra Captain from accessing it. Grainger's passcard, as the Founder's before him, allowed access to anywhere he wanted to go. It allowed for property raids, for surprise inspections or secretive missions, and in Grainger's experience, only those with something to hide or who were fearful of their safety bothered to pass-hack a security lock. The door yielded to his card, unlocking so that the handle depressed under his hand. Cracking the rubberized seal released no smell of butchered meat, no taint of fish except for that wafting from the hatchery, no zesty, bitter tang sometimes left in the wake of carbidi disintegration as it evaporated into the air. This room, too, contained a single light source and rows of metal rails devoid of meat hooks. The floor looked no different than the other, no cleaner. No fresh stains on the floor or evidence of recent occupation. Nothing out of the ordinary.

Except for a discarded black slicker, a torn black pull-over shirt, and a pair of boots left in the corner nearest the door.

Black boots, scuffed and well-worn, with thick-gripping soles. Similar in construction and appearance to those the gorra wore, to

those Grainger wore himself, but more specifically, as he squatted to poke at them with his thumper as if anticipating a trap, the sort worn by those men and women who worked in Hebenon's shafts.

Skolpers. Denki. Heizers. Speners.

Bilgers.

Ballard.

The boots and shirt could have belonged to anyone. Strange things to leave behind instead of disposing of, the coat and boots valuable enough for their quality alone to have been picked up by a streeter, or held on to by one, if they had been here. Not the sort of things a worker would have left behind. Odd things to leave because Grainger knew that comparing the coat to the footage of the Talker-streeter skirmish would verify it to be Ballard's.

Grainger had seen him wear it before.

An intentional clue then? But why?

This was evidence he would not leave for a subordinate to collect. He would see to it himself while increasing patrols on Levs 1 and 2.

Brako be damned. If Ballard had been here, Grainger was going to find him. Before anyone else did.

❧*❦

She did not dare approach the grieving family, did not dare risk visiting to pay her respects to the one who had been her best friend for more years than many of the Spinks had been alive. Certain they would blame her for his death, when it had been her life he had sacrificed to save, Ginna remained in the shadows, watching the sporadic shift of the group who came to say goodbye to the young man whose body was soon to be released for disposal.

Not burial. Burial was impossible in Hebanthe Falls. Only recycling, repurposing, reuse and conversion into something else the city's residents could use.

In the case of organic life, fuel for energy, fuel to fertilize that provided food.

There was no grief in that end, only the grief that came with absence and regret.

She had done this to him. If she had not raised the battle cry, egging the Spinks into that confrontation, Xiaodan would still be alive.

She listened to the voices, the children's choir singing a traditional Chinese funerary song, until she could carry the weight of grief and guilt no longer, and then retreated into the shadows, intending to make at least one thing right out of the mess they had become.

When Ilya's return was not the prompt one she promised, an assurance that gouged deeper trenches into Ginna's soul though she had not taken the promise to heart when it was made, she left the flat with no intention of ever going back. No longer could she run to Xiaodan for comfort, assurance, and company, but as one of the oldest founding Spinks, she knew there were others who would depend on her to carry out the mission Xiaodan had fashioned for them. She had to behave as he would have. She had to carry on.

It was a mission made more poignant, more important, by the loss they shared and the treasure she carried in her hand.

In the aftermath of the fight, as the Spinks fled the scene and scattered through the Levs, someone had found, and taken, a tooler left at the place where the blonde man, the one who had saved her life and tried to save Xiaodan's, had jumped into the fray. Thinking it likely to be his, thinking the fellow would want it back if he had made it out alive, the three young Spinks who found it saved it from collection by the bugorra or from theft by another streeter or tinger. None were willing to open it without guidance, and so they gave it to Ginna when she returned to them much later, after everyone deemed it safe to gather again. Relieved to be led, not to be abandoned in the wake of Xiaodan's death, they were willing to abide by Ginna's decision.

The tooler was opened.

Bilger tools mostly. Odds and ends of electronic equipment and gadgets the street kids only recognized for their trade value. Nothing extraordinary except the link the tooler provided to a potential ally well-suited to fill Xiaodan's place if Ginna would not do so.

Ginna, dragged by her guilt, chose to be the one to make contact with the man to beg him to take Xiaodan's place.

She knew where the bilger Shed was. Now that she had no home to return to, she had nowhere else to be, so she took the tooler, found an adequately sheltered position from which to watch the Shed's door near the hour of shift change, and waited.

For a time, she kept the bag on her lap, thinking to approach the first person she saw arrive without a tooler in hand, believing she would recognize the face of the man who had saved her. But the protective slickers and coats, hats and hoods, kept her from seeing the faces of most who came and went when the shift klaxon chimed, and most of those she saw carried nothing save for a small array of handled boxes and pouches workers often used to transport their meals. She realized she was not going to find the tooler's owner this way and opened it again and rummaged, hoping for something, an initialed tool or kerchy, a name tagged onto one of the more expensive items, anything that would help put a name to the face, put the tooler in his hands, prompt him to listen to her out of gratitude for returning the instruments of his livelihood.

What she did find, thanks to a snagged driver's flange, was the compartment at the base of the kit, a false bottom that it had never occurred to her to seek. Using a flat blade to pry it open presented her with a mask, protected from the scratches and dings of the tools by the shielding door.

Anyone who worked the shafts wore a mask. Like the bugorra, like many who worked under the constant exposure to the mists of the falls or the potentially toxic fumes filtered from homes and businesses by the miles of ducting throughout the Levs, a bilger's life was lived behind such a mask. Finding it, finding it protected, was not a surprise.

What was a surprise was the silhouette this mask presented when held between her hands.

This was no bilger's mask.

This was the Scarecrow's.

Her heart began to thunder as questions pounded through her head and the faintest trace of a smile tried to creep across her face. The only question she had an answer to, that she was able to answer for herself, was that this was a secret she could never share with anyone. Not the Spinks. Not Xiaodan if he had been alive. Not even her sister.

Especially not Ilya.

Ginna did not have a name, but she had an identity, an identity more sacred than any Founder could be. She would sit here and wait, however long it took, for Hebenon's savior to appear.

Sooner or later, he had to.

❧*❧

In a world of eternal damp, where the permanence of anything set to paper was subject to the whims of the Four Falls, and messages and data of all sorts were more secure and more likely to survive when encoded into the electronic systems of the Hub, the little slip of hemp parchment Blayd folded with care and tucked into the breast pocket of his longcoat was a rare thing.

Maybe she had thought his ICD would not be returned to him, or that such a message might be intercepted and decoded before it reached him. Maybe the gesture was meant as a personal touch, though such thoughtfulness was not in keeping with Neoma's personality. Most likely it had been sent this way because, on paper, there was no data trail left in the Hub…where everything could be traced, stored, and hacked by anyone who knew how.

The slip of paper could be easily destroyed, eaten if the need arose, and there would be no proof it had existed, that the exchange had been made. Even if someone else read what that slip contained, once destroyed, its existence became a matter of who said what.

An order given this way was untraceable.

He should have erased the words as soon as he read them, left them only to exist in his memory. She had never failed him, had stood by him, and he would do whatever she asked. This particular mission

would have been carried out already without the order given to do so, if not for the brako's interference. But she had not been to see him in those lonely hours between waking and release from the facility, hours in which only staff and Ilya had come, and in the back of Blayd's mind, he wondered.

Why had she not been there?

If the man he was sent to eradicate like a roach or an ohrwurm was the suitor Blayd imagined him to be, so much the better. Despite Neoma's apparent distaste and dislike for the Senior Talker, Blayd had long suspected something, something that her prodcast hack had not erased from Blayd's mind. The Senior, the Talkers, held the ear of the people, after all.

Without her husband at her side, without the Senior's support or a voice of her own, how could Neoma hope to sway Hebenon to her cause? What had happened in the hours between that fight, and this message, to cause this shift?

And why had she not come back for him?

He supposed none of those questions mattered. She would tell him he thought too much and should trust that she had the best interests of Hebenon at heart.

But did she?

As he put his signature to the discharge form with the artificial quill stylus and then turned his collar up as he left the warmth of the clinic's light for the darkness of the grated city streets, he had one other request to fill, the other left at the front desk by Lieutenant Ilya, a voice recording left on his ICD, her voice anxious and strained.

Check on her sister. Find her. Keep her safe. Whatever it took.

That seemed a better use of his time than hunting the Senior. Kal would cross his path soon enough. All he had to do was wait for the Senior to come to him.

Securing Ginna's safety then was the first order of business. If Neoma wanted her request to be his priority, she should have come and made it herself.

❧*❧

Since the opening of Hebenon's outer doors, it was not unusual to see Lash in the streets and fields of Marbordo, frequently with Doctor Tamner, sometimes with Rhyd, most often alone. The short, lanky man's limping gate was recognizable over any distance, and his interest in the flora and fauna of this new world made him a constant, accepted visitor. But often he came out just to be alone, to sit on the hill overlooking the sea and the city in the falls, Rhyd's favorite spot as well since Venn had introduced him to it, especially at sunrise or sunset, as the light of the day greeted them or bid them farewell.

The view was so much like the dek image Venn had once shared with Rhyd, that it made his heart ache to remember it. This scenic overlook was no trick of digitalization, however. This was very real. And Rhyd was not here to share it.

Hearing Agnys shout his name, turning to see her trudging up that hill with Lash's hand in hers was not a peculiar sight, for Venn knew she had a fondness for the cat-man as she called him, forged in the same fires that had forged her closeness with Rhyd.

Venn knew her, knew her from the time of his expulsion from Hebanthe Falls, knew her from the months spent learning the ways of the village and shedding the last of his addiction. He knew her, but Rhyd…Rhyd she loved.

Her expression was serious, focused as she studied the first ladybug of the year crawling over her hand while she walked, trusting Lash to steer her around obstacles. Agnys did not need the escort, knowing Marbordo's surroundings better than either Lash or Venn, and so Venn knew they were looking for him.

There were no words of greeting. No questions or comments. Only six words that sent chills down Venn's spine into his belly.

"You should come. Rhyd needs you."

Venn did not ask. He only turned away from the sky's evening display and followed wherever the man and child were to lead.

❧*❧

The sound of Hebenon's firecorp putting out a cooking fire in a private kitchen in someone's nearby flat vaguely registered in Ilya's ears as her door clattered shut. Typically, as part of the city's protectors, she would have rushed to participate in making sure the fire was out, the family in the adjoining flats were safe.

But not this time.

Exhausted, she let her gaze sweep the room, noting a lifetime worth of tiny intimate details that no one else might see.

The signed dartboard her father had treasured, left to the family by their champion grandfather, the signature fading as the memory of the man dwindled too. The handful of barnacles their mother had given to Ilya when she was a little girl that the child had memorialized on a star-shaped plaque, their shells chipped and cracked with age. The ceramic plate painted with a sun, moon, and stars that none of them had ever seen, which Ginna had made as a child and that had been deemed too precious by their mother for eating on…and the tiny flecks of paint beginning to peel from it.

Small bits of a life that had been. A life forever lost.

Despite the instruction before duty called, she had not expected Ginna to wait at the window where Ilya had last seen her. That was expecting too much…and that had been hours ago.

She had hoped, however, that Ginna would heed her and stay.

After so many hours, breaking the promise of support despite her best intentions, Ilya was not surprised, only dismayed and saddened, to find Ginna gone.

This time, the feeling seeping from the old walls spoke her fears without the need of looking through the rooms or calling out Ginna's name.

Her baby sister was not coming back.

✤CHAPTER 22✤

"Jaron?"

It was late by the time Grainger pushed between sliding doors that opened too slowly for his weary liking. He had refused to give in to the possibility of sleep until he had the analytical reports from the clothes, the blood, and the SCAM footage from the skirmish and the falling man on Lev 1. The clothes belonged, it was concluded, to the same individual, the DNA match between them undeniable. And every forensic expert on his force agreed with his assessment, that the clothing matched that of the stranger on the SCAMs.

Grainger would have felt better having Tamner's assessment, but the doctor was unavailable. None of his staff knew where he was, only that he had been called away on an emergency.

Guessing it was someone Outside, as Tamner was the only doctor from Hebenon the parah trusted, thanks to his affiliation with Ballard and the child Agnys, Grainger decided to put off gaining the man's evaluation until morning. Surely he would have returned by then.

The details of that assessment were kept to himself.

For tonight, Grainger was content with his take on the situation.

If Ballard had risked entering that fight without a mask, there was a damn good reason for it, making finding him imperative.

But tonight his rooms were empty, without even a cold meal left prepared, as Jaron was prone to do when his shift took him away. Instead of a meal, there was only silence and the steadily blinking diode on the Echo that indicated a waiting message. Hoping it was from Jaron, knowing it could be from Tamner, one of the Nau wanting an update on the unsettled situation in the Levs that was, Grainger imagined, disrupting production and distribution, or else one of his

other officers, he passed his thumb over the reader and sank down on the nearest chair to hear it.

The screen came alive as he pulled off his shoes, but rather than a spoken note left, it was a typed one. That meant Jaron, as the younger man did not like the electronic interpretation of his modulated, artificial voice. It was a brief apology, remarking with regret that Grainger imagined between the lines of text though there was no voice to support the interpretation, that he could not be there tonight and did not know when he would get in. A friend had taken ill and needed someone to stay with them. Jaron would check in when he could and bid Grainger not to worry. He sighed off the message with 'affectionately', making Grainger smile.

Jaron had a big heart. It was one of the things Grainger liked about him. Of course he would offer his caretaking services to a friend in need, even if Grainger felt that someone in need was himself. He pulled off his coat and then his damp, dark blue shirt to drop both over the back of the chair, and belatedly realized one thing.

After all of the months of knowing the younger man, he had never considered that Jaron might have friends. He had come to feel that Jaron existed only for him.

He had no idea who those friends might be and had never once thought to ask.

❧*❧

In a place of disjointed memory and nightmare, things came to him in cuts and snatches. In and out of blackness, in and out of awareness, it was impossible to focus for more than a moment or two before the disorientation closed over him again.

A clattering vibration, like cart wheels over grating.

Icy slabbed planks on a makeshift wagon, whose sides blocked the world from a view he could not see through unfocusing eyes.

Suffocating heat interspersed with blasts of cool, breathable air taken away too soon.

A waxy weight chaffing against tender flesh, distributed head to toe, shifting as he felt drawn this way and that.

The stomach lurch and grinding whir of lift gears.

Darkness entwined with snatches of pale blinding light and pressure across his belly as he was hoisted and hung head down so that the blood pounded between his ears.

And hands, always hands, poking, adjusting, smoothing, pressed now and then to his forehead, his cheeks.

The clack and jangle and whoosh of doors, of metal latches and bolts in and against metal casings.

Zara's name, repeated now and again with muffled desperation and her voice in reply, providing sequenced numbers, a 'right', a 'left' a 'stop' a 'go' to whoever was moving him.

Allies then.

Perfumed incense was exchanged for the misty rush of fish-air, oily cooking residue and the sweet ozone smell of the steam that powered so much of Hebanthe Falls' infrastructure. The copper of blood tasted cold and stale upon his tongue.

And finally, hands behind his head, his shoulders, around his ankles, pulling, lifting. One jolt that made the acid burn in his empty belly churn and push up through his esophagus, spilling foul stickiness over his chin and neck as the fullness of his weight settled into downy cushions covered with the soft scratch of hemp blankets.

Then the world was still.

The slosh of water in a container, the heat of it dabbed across his skin by a cloth immersed in its contents, bathing his face, his neck, to clean away the bile as other hands freed him from the discomfort of too long damp trousers. More cleaning, more touching, the examination of injuries, the tending of cuts and abrasions, burns and tears, the pricks of long spines injecting mending plasts at the sight of every cracked and broken bone.

It was a floating place, gentle and tender, until the oxygen mask was strapped over his mouth and nose. Hands pressed down on his chest, his good shoulder, to be followed by a rending pop of bone and

ligament that elicited an involuntary cry of temporary, blinding pain into the muffled breathing apparatus.

The jolt brought back the darkness.

❧*❦

"Here."

Lash's announcement was unnecessary as they stopped before an unfamiliar door in an unfamiliar area of the city, a low Lev where Venn had spent very little time. As a musician, he had performed where the job required, but rarely was that in a private home, rarely in a row of flats where the alglamps were dark from lack of tending, where the path was lit only by the glow of inside lamps visible between wet glass and privacy blinds that protected the inhabitants from prying eyes. He could hear indications of life behind barred doors, arguments, children laughing or crying, Echos playing with their volumes up to drown out the neighbors' noises.

He walked close to Lash, the child's hand clutched in his, uncomfortable here with his clothing stuck to his skin by the moisture in the air, fearful in a way he had not been since forced out of Hebenon into the sunlight Outside.

He did not feel this fear when traveling to the flat he had shared with Rhyd, and only felt it marginally when traveling to Vapors. But the rest of Hebenon had become a frightening jungled wasteland to him and he wondered, as they waited for someone to answer to Lash's knock, how Rhyd could bare it.

Agnys appeared not to share his fear.

The crack at the edge of the door revealed Tox's face and she quickly ushered them inside. Venn's steps over the threshold were tenuous and wary.

"Hey, baby," she murmured with a quick kiss to Venn's cheek before scooping Agnys into her arms. It was unclear who she directed the endearment to.

It was a typical flat, no bigger or smaller than any other single person's flat would be, lacking a separate bedroom or a partition between the central room and kitchen, making for a large single open area with an adjoining bathroom and spacious walk-in closet. There was a made-up bed against the back wall, narrow and barely used, a small table near it that served as both dining space, desk and a bedside table, and two unmatched chairs that looked as if they'd been resurfaced, repurposed, from some other set as they did not match the table. A collection of art prints in digital frames adorned the walls, ancient masters from a time before the city had been, evoking a world that had once existed but might never be again. The spicy, salt tang of soup bubbling came from a large pot on the stove at Doctor Tamner's elbow as he washed medical tools in the washbasin.

He glanced at those who entered with a nod.

Zara sat at the table, furiously tapping on the Echo's keypad. She waved with one hand without lifting her head, intent on whatever act she was engrossed in within the Hub's central data system. Her blonde hair was drawn up with jeweled combs and clips and her filmy, gossamer gown of lavender and pale green gave her the appearance of a queen…or a woman interrupted mid-performance in Vapors by the crisis that had brought together those gathered here. A dwarf sat beside her, flipping a small blade between the fingers of one hand as if it was a knuckle roll with a coin. Venn did not know him, did not know the mob-haired man seated on a worn cushioned footstool he had dragged over to the sofa against the right side wall.

But Venn did know the battered, swollen face of the man the stranger was gently wiping with a damp cloth.

"What happened?" Venn asked, his words both an exclamation and a question as he elbowed his way to Rhyd's side and dropped to his knees there. The stranger deferred to his action by sliding the stool back along the edge of the sofa, towards Rhyd's abdomen, but he did not leave Rhyd's side.

Agnys, once put down, went to the other end of the sofa and propped her chin on Rhyd's ankles.

"We don't know…exactly," replied the dwarf.

"Torture I'd say…carefully applied for maximum pain but minimal lasting damage." Tamner's awkward tone suggested he knew something about that of which he spoke.

"By who?"

With a hand on Venn's shoulder as he took Rhyd's between his, Tox murmured, "Don't know. Possibly brako, as that's where Enoch found him, in their zone, but these days, it could have been anyone."

Anyone, Venn thought icily, with a pang of guilt, like Mam Kemway or her agents. He did not think the woman heartless enough, to carry out such torture herself. Command it, yes. Perform it, no.

"Why?"

"We won't know anything until he wakes up."

Tamner interrupted the dwarf's words, "Which he will do, in time. He's got some mending to do…and I've got him sedated so the plasts and grafts have time to set, but he'll come around soon enough."

The man nearest Venn who had not yet been introduced said, "Everyone's looking for the stranger who tried to protect the kids in that fight…Captain Grainger, Mam Kemway, Senior Kal…probably Vanderwall too after the death of one of the brako…"

Venn glanced at him, more because of the hand the man kept resting on Rhyd's belly than because of the words or the peculiarity of his modulated, artificial voice. He made note of the speech system, understanding the concept of it without having seen it before, and he briefly wondered if the speech impediment that required it was a birth defect, an accident, or the result of the same sort of Doctet and Founder ordered punishment that Lash had endured.

Given the company he kept, Lash, Tamner, Zara, the dwarf, it was easy to believe it to be the latter.

So long as he kept his hand on Rhyd, however, Venn felt no sympathy for him. What he felt was something darker.

"She came to me, looking for him," Venn muttered, pushing away that emotion to focus on Rhyd's mottled, sleeping face behind the breather. "She asked about dining with him, said things that sounded

like threats." He glanced at Tox. "Is this because of…?" His eyes finished the question that his words failed to complete. Tox knew the Scarecrow. Zara, Tamner, and Lash did too. They had all been there, at the time of the Coup, when he and Rhyd had been reunited by the efforts of that mask. But Venn did not know if the stranger beside him or the dwarf knew that truth and chose not to be the one to say it.

"I don't think so," the stranger said. "I think this is all…"

"That damned SCAM footage she pushed all over the city," spat Enoch. "Most people aren't going to know him…or care…"

"But that selflessness might make a celebrity out of him," Tox added with a sigh. He had tried to save Xiaodan's life…and for what? "It's going to complicate things."

Then perhaps, Venn thought bitterly, Rhyd would come back to him where he belonged, forced to give up this dual life long enough for the attention to dwindle, by which time maybe his self-destructive need for violence could be nurtured out of his system.

"Skelter is running out of time."

Zara's hands faltered on the keyboard, only to resume their typing at a more enthusiastic pace.

Of those in the room, Tamner seemed the only one unaware of what Enoch's reference meant. With no idea who or what Skelter was, what that word might mean to Ballard, and thinking it better he did not know, Tamner refrained from asking.

Venn, on the other hand, realized with a frustrated groan that, regardless of his wishes, Rhyd would not likely be giving up his marriage to Hebenon, to the Scarecrow, any time soon.

Not until Skelter was safe.

❧*❧

Kal stood alone within the safety of the Talker Hall walls, his hands clasped behind his back, expression thoughtful and pensive. His efforts had paid off in that his captive had escaped as he hoped, and from the security of this room behind the modified SCAM system, Kal

had watched the chaos that ensued. The captive's ingenuity and strengths, the faces of those who had helped him.

He did not care about the streeters. They were nobodies, inconsequential to any plan unless he could manipulate them into becoming supportive followers of the Voices. And two who arrived later were obscured from view by rain cloaks. He never saw them leave, although an eventual clatter of wagon wheels over the grated metal surface that echoed beyond the reach of the SCAM's watchful eye told Kal that his quarry had been moved out of the herpa's sanctuary to somewhere his companions deemed safer.

Or at least somewhere closer to home.

There was the dwarf, however, a dwarf whose face seemed familiar when Kal froze it on the Echo screen during playback. It was enough he was a dwarf, as there were few who survived in Hebenon, few who were not killed during early childhood or put to work as some manner of oddity entertainment.

Nothing in Hebanthe Falls was built to accommodate such a person. Very few wanted to risk persecution by the Founder and Doctet if they allowed such a child to reach adulthood…at least without the necessary preventative precautions taken that would disallow such a person to reproduce and pollute the narrow scope of mankind's available gene pool.

Kal must have seen the man before. This fellow certainly made no effort to hide what he was, to disguise himself as a child. His bearded face marked him as an adult and made him all the more familiar. Oddly, for all his uniqueness of feature, Kal could not say where or when they might have crossed paths. It should, however, make the dwarf easy to find, and finding him ought to lead to the fellow Ballard.

Confident of his communication and conversion skills, even if he had not been able to get through to the man under the duress of torture, Kal intended to win the man's trust. He had not been the kidnapper, after all, and he had set Ballard free.

Abduction and torture were Neoma's path. Freedom and persuasion were Kal's.

⮞Chapter 23⮜

The squeal of grinding stoppers on the trucks of the delivery cart he had been following, using the fishmonger's shadow to mask his movements as he picked up nessies for his guests, was the first indicator Jaron received that there was something wrong.

Over the past several days, since the revelation that the Founder was still alive, Talkers now traveled only in groups of three or more, finding increased safety in the company of others. It was no surprise that Mam Kemway's accusations of treason against the Voices, against Senior Kal in particular, would make the Talkers defensive, and after the fight between some of their members and the streeter children, small groups of Talkers no longer felt safe.

Jaron had seen this band of three sharing tea and biscuits at the vindi across the street from his last stop, but had done his best to ignore and avoid them. He had no business with them, nor they with him.

He also refused to make eye contact with the four bugorra talking quietly beneath the cool glow of blue neon that lit a collection of vindis clustered at the corner of this lane. They seemed to be watching something, possibly the Talkers or the group of streeters laughing on a nearby stairwell in an effort to avoid a repeat of the last skirmish. These streeters were young, between seven and nine years old, and the likelihood that they would consider assaulting the adult Talkers in the tea vindi seemed small to Jaron.

But he kept his head down and avoided all of them, being nothing to them so long as he did not attract attention, just as the majority of others in the vicinity were trying to do. It was unlikely that any of them knew of his connection to Oliver Grainger.

His distracting thoughts were still on the captain as he left the vindi, following the cart as it began moving again. He should reach out to Oliver, give him some inkling when he would return, let him know everything was okay. But when Lash's summons had come, a request for a safehouse where no one was likely to look for Rhyd, Jaron impulsively offered his own flat. Then he saw the blonde's condition, a result of his efforts to help a group of youngsters, and Jaron felt compelled to stay with Rhyd as well, for as long as the man needed to recover.

It was his flat. He had a right to be there. He believed Rhyd needed him, if only for this respite of shelter and the support of their joint agenda. Before the arrival of the man called Venn, Jaron had nearly convinced himself he would never go back to Oliver's suite, to Oliver.

How could he, when Rhyd Ballard made him feel alive in a way he had never expected or imagined he was able to feel?

When the squeal of stoppers came, with his thoughts tangling and untangling around Oliver and Rhyd, Jaron's steps were brought up short…as voices shouting in tandem charged from the street up ahead. One of the men swung and struck the fishmonger across the shoulder, knocking him to his knees.

Maybe the fishmonger was the target. But the assailants kept running and Jaron narrowly dodged out of the way when the same thumper lashed out at him.

Brako.

There was no mistaking their stolen Crow masks.

From behind, from their street corner gathering, the buggers shouted and charged, meeting the brako in the intersection as shoppers and vindi owners, streeters and the Talkers in the tea vindi, scurried in search of shelter. Where Jaron stood, there was nowhere to hide except behind the now tipped fish cart. Others had already claimed refuge there, however, leaving no room for him.

Jaron did the only thing he could.

Clutching his bags, he ran.

❧*❧

He thought he was alone when his senses began to return. Near his head, the hiss of oxygen melded with the sound of his breathing, but beyond that, there were only the expected sounds of a living flat. The metallic sucking whirr of filt and heating systems, pulling moisture from the air, forcing warmth into the room. Those sounds, to most, were normal, invisible, only noticed when no longer there.

To Rhyd, who spent his life in the channels through which those systems operated, the subtle variance in properly working units and faulty ones meant he always noticed the sounds or the lack of them.

Beneath that endless noise was a steady, sporadic drip of a faucet needing repair, the pinging of water against metal, striking in time with the throbbing in his shoulder, undercutting the drone of systems.

He should hurt more than he did. With the memories of torture, of falling through an awning, of the clash that had precipitated all of it slowly filling his head as his nerves and limbs began to connect to his waking brain, he knew how much damage his body had sustained.

From the bitter taste in his mouth and the nervous rattle coursing through his veins, he also knew how long it had been since he had a good, strong drink.

Getting one, however, required rising, and the stiffness in his muscles and the comfort of the cushioned surface on which he lay made him ill-inclined to contemplate unnecessary movement.

"Whiskey?"

He forced his eyes open. Little in the room looked familiar, not the multitude of digital paintings he could see as he shifted his eyes without moving his head, not the circular blue glassy surface of the fixture above him with its light currently dark, not the taupe of the hemp fabric sofa, not the smoky beige of the ceilings and walls. Not his flat. His own walls were pale grey, the ceiling not quite white.

He wondered where he was.

"You're awake."

Realizing he had not imagined the voice, that he was not alone, he turned his head from the sofa back as he achingly drew one arm up to pull the oxygen mask from his face. He did not need to see the speaker to know who was there.

Fingers brushed through the hair on his forehead, not a womanly touched but a masculine one though tender and gentle, the way it used to be. Before. He did not blame Venn, not anymore. Whether it had been boredom in their relationship, frustration with a slow rise to musical prominence, or the sense of overall disillusionment with life inside of Hebanthe Falls that so many other residents felt, that had driven Venn to seek an escape in Hebbies, it was little different than Rhyd's escape into Zaolei.

Except that Venn's addiction, and some misplaced words, had gotten him arrested.

They might well do the same for Rhyd one day, when the alcohol and Grainger's forces caught up with him.

Or the brako did.

"Where am I?" He caught the other man's hand and held it there, pressed against his cheek and temple, and after a momentary perusal of Venn's face, closed his eyes and released him.

Venn looked haggard, older than when Rhyd had seen him last, only a matter of days it seemed, the appearance of sleep deprivation that Rhyd had seen on his face before, in the time when Venn's Heb addiction had kept him awake, rehearsing, for days at a time.

The dark-haired man shrugged, masking the disappointment over the moment of lost intimacy before turning on the stool on which he sat to make a better visual appraisal of Rhyd's condition. "Couldn't say. The dwarf's place maybe…or the other guy's…your friend." His reply was distant, vague in tone, but it was a tone Rhyd recognized. The tone of talking about something he would rather not.

Not Lash's home, they had knocked before entering. Not Zara's home or Tox's for Venn knew those places well. Not Tamner's for the doctor still lived in his family's flat of rooms in the Uppers where they had resided for generations. It left only two possibilities from the

group of people that had been previously assembled here, vague as they were in his memory, but maybe it did not belong to either one.

It could have been recently abandoned or owned by someone else neither of them had met.

"Jaron." Rhyd made the determination based on what little he knew of the younger man, and the fact that, to his knowledge, Enoch was a drifter, a loner, possibly even a streeter. Just because Jaron spent many off-shift hours with Grainger, it did not mean he did not have a home of his own.

He had lived somewhere before that relationship had begun. And this art, tasteful, ancient, elegant, seemed the sort that a man who enjoyed the streets of Old Pairs would favor.

One could tell a lot about a person by the art they enjoyed and the way they decorated and maintained their home.

Venn snorted at the way Rhyd said the other man's name, but other than a twitch of his brow, Rhyd ignored the reaction. He had nothing to apologize for, at least where Jaron was concerned. He had done nothing to warrant the jealousy he detected.

"Where are…?"

The cellist shrugged. "Zar went with the dwarf and Lash, something about hacking an ICD system…"

Rhyd nodded, wincing at the stiffness in his neck. He hoped it meant moving ahead with establishing reliable communication with Skelter. "Good," he mumbled, as Venn spoke again.

"Is it?" He did not allow Rhyd to reply. "Tamner went Up…duty and all that. Tox went…" His voice broke and he did not speak again until Rhyd's hand closed around his. He stared for several moments at the point of contact between them, an intimate gesture of trust Rhyd did not often make with anyone and then whispered, "to be with Maemi…for the incin…"

"Incin?" Maemi's mother-in-law, perhaps, for the ancient woman had been in decline for some time.

Then his eyes squeezed shut with the reflex of the tightening grip of Venn's hand, a grip that sent ribbons of pain up his arm to his healing shoulder.

Xiaodan.

He had failed…but he had known that as soon as he saw the boy go down beneath the Talkers' onslaught. Xiaodan's fall was what had pulled him into the fight unprotected.

"I'm sorry…I should…"

He tried to sit, but the movement jarred his shoulder and put pressure on bruised organs and muscles in a way that made Rhyd dizzy and nauseous. Venn pushed with one hand against his chest to urge him to lie back.

"Too late for that…it should be done by now…and you need to heal." After a brief hesitation, with a nervous quaver in his voice, Venn added, "And you need to come home. To Marbordo. To me." He intentionally left out where the other man had gone. He did not want to talk about the man Rhyd called Jaron.

"Venn…"

"You're going to get yourself killed."

Given the pain he was currently in, what had happened during and after the fight, it was difficult to argue that point, but Rhyd would not concede. What was his death in the grand scheme? Better him then Xiaodan, than Skelter, than Venn. "I was not protected; next time…"

"You can't wear that damn thing all the time. It won't keep you alive. Hebenon's running amok, Rhyd; once they figure out who you are, next time it'll be Mam Kemway, or a brako, or one of Grainger's…next time they will…"

"There won't be a next time…not like this." Even as he spoke the words, however, Rhyd knew he could not guarantee he would not throw himself into a fight to save someone important to him. To help an innocent victim. His priorities had shifted from self-preservation to something else. Something he realized would keep him inside Hebenon for the rest of his life.

However long that was.

Marbordo would never be his home.

"For crucksake…if you won't…if you insist on…at least let Captain Grainger have your back!"

Rhyd's eyes narrowed. "You want me to join the bugorra?"

"Would it be so bad? You're already doing what they…it would mean they, at least, aren't hunting you too. You'd have someone on your side. You're doing the same work. Would it really be so bad?"

"I will not take orders from him…from anyone…"

"You'd rather put me at risk then…"

"At risk?"

Venn's breath caught and held before slowly releasing in a frustrated hiss. "Mam Kemway wants to meet with you…and I don't think she'll take no for an answer."

"Me? Or…him?" There was a difference, and if Mam Kemway had made a connection between Rhyd, Scarecrow, and Venn, that was a warning in itself.

Despite what he wanted to say, knowing that bringing Rhyd's dual identity into questions was more unlikely to prompt him to rethink his life's direction, Venn reluctantly replied, "You."

There had been enough dishonesty between them. He wanted Rhyd to come back to him, to give up his folly, but he was not going to manipulate him into it with a lie.

"Then don't worry; I'm not doing it…"

"That is what I worry about," Venn put emphasis on the second word with a squeeze of his hand. "Someone already did this to you, and for what? If she thinks you can help her…"

Knowing it would be counterproductive to reveal that whoever had held him had wanted the same thing, Rhyd's help against the other sides in whatever political war for power was being waged, Rhyd left the why unspoken. Better Venn think he did not know why he had been taken, held, tortured. "I'm not helping her any more than I'm gonna help Grainger…or Kal…or the brako. Only side I'm taking is the people's."

"Even if it means she comes after me…or Agnys…to force…"

"She can't force anything…on anyone. She has no teeth." Neoma had a single bodyguard, as far as he knew, the man who had been with Senior Kal and was attacked by the brako that day. There was little one man could do to Rhyd. Perhaps she could manipulate the Talkers into backing her, but to kidnap or assault an innocent man or child?

Rhyd did not think either she or Kal would go that far.

"I know what this is; I've seen it. I've lived it, Whiskey. You're addicted to the adrenaline…the power…"

"If you're worried she'll…" He shook his head. "Stay in Marbordo. She won't go there." He ignored the accusation, refusing to consider if it was true. He did not crave danger or the rush that came with the hunt, the fight.

But he was not going to run from it either. He believed that if he did not stand up for, did not fight for, the people of Hebanthe Falls, no one else would.

Grainger and the bugorra were too caught up in rules to do what had to be done.

It had to be Scarecrow.

"Not without you. Not unless you stay…"

"I won't do it. I don't belong there…"

"You belong with me."

"Not…"

Whatever he was about to say was aborted by the opening of the door and the young, tousled man who came through it, his face flushed with exertion and adrenalin, his clothes askew and knees wet as if he had fallen. His arms were laden with torn bags of nessies that he nearly dropped as he stared at the two staring back at him, one with heated annoyance and the other with a mix of emotions Jaron was not keen to pick apart.

"I'll…sorry…I'll put these away and…"

"We're not kicking you out of your home," Rhyd grunted, looking quickly away from the interruption to give Venn no further reason to be angry, relieved that Jaron's arrival had kept him from saying what he had nearly said.

Something had happened to Jaron, or had nearly happened. Rhyd had not been there to prevent it. The blush of worry colored his cheeks and he bit his tongue to resist asking what had occurred.

It was too late, however, Venn had seen enough. He got to his feet with a huff and narrowly missed elbowing the stranger to whom he had not yet been introduced as he squeezed by. "I'm going. I've got fields to tend." What Jaron was to Rhyd, he could not say, but it had been a long time since Rhyd had looked at Venn that way.

Venn had no one to blame but himself. The Heb use had been his choice. Everything after that he had given away. It did not, however, reduce his feelings, the anger or betrayal towards the man he had once pledged his life to.

He had broken the pledge, but he was trying to make things right now that they had been given a second chance. Rhyd had fought hard for that second chance, but it had steered him down a path that Venn could not draw him back from.

"Venn…" They were not done talking. There was still too much to settle. If they did not finish now, there would be no finishing later.

After yanking his coat from the hook by the door, ignoring Jaron as if he was not there, Venn glowered. "When you're able, when you can stand, when you're well enough, come to Marbordo. For good."

Rhyd had never been one for ultimatums. Not with his parents, not with his teachers, not with Venn. It kept him from taking sides in a political fight that was not his, kept him from accepting Grainger's offer. He was his own man and not even Venn was going to dictate the terms of his life. And there was still something he needed to do before he could consider packing in the Scarecrow's gear for good.

"I'm going after Skelter."

Swallowing hard, Venn hesitated. He liked Skelter. He did not want the man to die. But he did not want to lose Rhyd in some ill-conceived rescue attempt into a place no one had yet proven to be real.

"When you're well enough," Venn repeated, his coat now closed for protection against the elements, "or not at all."

Rhyd's fists balled at his side and he used the pain of it to further fuel his frustrated outrage.

No one would tell him what to do.

In the kitchen, Jaron put away his purchases without a word. Maybe he had not caused this fight, but his ill-timed return had not helped.

He could not deny the warm flutter in his belly when Rhyd elected to stay.

❧Chapter 24❧

With the pain meds and healing sedatives still moving through his blood, sleep returned easily, despite Rhyd's stubborn decision to get back on his feet, to return to the streets in search of an easier way to get Skelter out of the Core than via Enoch's too narrow tunnel. Time was shorter now, and they surely had not enough of it to try to widen the passage. Being pulled back into sleep on Jaron's sofa was a blessing, however, as it kept Rhyd from thinking about Venn, subverted the need to talk about emotional matters he felt ill-equipped to deal with, with anyone else. His reaction to Jaron, Jaron's reaction to their fight, Venn's reaction in return, told Rhyd more than he wanted to know about each of them, but particularly about himself.

Sleep, and then the pressing need to get to Skelter, would keep his mind off of matters he did not want to think about. Be alive for the mission. Complicated personal relationships were not needed.

When he stirred later, it was to the sound of the evening news prodcast, the Ximenezes offering commentary on the brako-bugorra clash from earlier in the day and the similarities it bore to the streeter-Talker clash of several days past. With two more Talkers having been caught in the crossfire, as well as a handful of bystanders, of which Jaron had almost been one, there was discussion between the husband and wife and their guests, one of the Talker patriarchs and Captain Grainger, about the degree to which each of these events might be related to the accusations of treason leveled against the bugorra and Voices of Faith by Mam Kemway.

Enoch was in the flat, picking through a plate of whatever meal Jaron had prepared, and Jaron lingered at the kitchen counter. No one else appeared to be present.

Rhyd had not expected Venn to be there. He had not even allowed himself to hope for it as he opened his eyes and watched the barely audible prodcast.

"Accused him…accused both…of treason," Enoch muttered.

"It's not worse then what she's done…"

"Nothing worse than what any of them have done."

Rhyd did not ask what they were discussing. It was enough to imagine that everyone on all sides wanted the Founder as their bargaining chip, what most of them might do to get the man out of Grainger's control.

He already knew what Grainger had done to put Kemway where he was. Neither of those with him, however, knew that truth. Rhyd had been there. He had seen it. Rhyd saw no reason for them to know.

"Them fighting each other might work for us…but we still don't have a way into the Core," he rasped, his throat swollen and sticky.

Jaron smiled to see him awake and brought a cup of water, which he set on the lamp table at the end of the sofa before gingerly helping Rhyd to sit. By now the plasts had set, which would keep the fractured bones from breaking further, and though the spotty bruises were still dark and tender, the cuts, abrasions, and burns still raw beneath the salved bandages, it was the ache from his shoulder that troubled him the most. They were the sort of pains Rhyd was accustomed to, however, and though he grimaced, he sat without difficulty.

A few good, strong drinks and he could face whatever came next.

"It's only water," Jaron murmured apologetically, refusing to look Rhyd in the eye. "No Zaolei on hand, I'm afraid…lost what I got when I was out in all of…that…" he pointed at the Echo screen.

Grunting, Rhyd took the offering and drained it in long, quick gulps. He might need the whiskey, but his body needed the water too and was grateful when Jaron went to the sink for more.

The young man's proximity, the sound of his breathing, and the musky perfume of the soap he had recently bathed with, were more distracting than Rhyd liked.

"Someone in Factory East should be able to get us there…should be able to find it…" The back of Enoch's boot struck the chair leg with a repeated rhythmic motion as he spoke.

"But they haven't, or if they have, they're not talking, and Zar hasn't gotten factory floorplans yet." If she had, Rhyd did not know.

Enoch nodded in confirmation. "If it was there, it was lost in the Hub crash…or is obstructed beneath code she hasn't cracked yet."

"Or someone erased it." Jaron knew how easy that could have been for a man like Haythem, for any of the Kemways, or for certain members of the Doctet who had served on the Founder's behalf.

"We can't waste more time. We need a plan…or this won't work."

"I've got all the locations, the inventories, of freezes," Jaron offered as a second glass of water and a bowl of boiled meat, carrots and potatoes was set at Rhyd's elbow, without making eye contact.

"Freezes aren't going to get him out. Going out the door might…" It was going to be one hell of a battle going out through factory workers and bugorra, with the innocent getting caught in the crossfire. Blowing that door would not be a quiet affair. It would bring buggers and more chaos would ensue as the inhabitants of the Core, whoever they were, however many there were, fought towards freedom.

They might get out of the Core, into the Factory, but they might not make it out of the Factory as free men.

There was no guarantee in such a plan that Skelter could survive.

And Hebenon could not endure sustained damage to Factory East.

The dwarf set his spoon down with an uncomfortable expression. "I could…show you something…that might help…but it's not exactly practical either." He shrugged at Rhyd's perplexed expression and muttered, "Down on Lev 1."

Rhyd had just come from there, had intended to search there before the streeter-Talker conflict. Undoubtedly, people there were looking for him.

The Scarecrow might not be much safer.

But it was a risk he might have to take.

"I'll come with you."

"No," both Rhyd and Enoch said simultaneously.

"It's too dangerous," the dwarf continued.

"I can't protect you there…not right now." Rhyd was not in peak condition, and even if he had been, he would not put Jaron in harm's way by bringing him into the unknown any more than he would do with Venn. "Besides…I need you to do something for me."

"What?" Jaron asked with a sulky pout, the option of helping Rhyd in some other way barely undermining his regret at being unable to work at Rhyd's side. If Rhyd suffered further injury, Jaron did not think Enoch would be capable of getting him to safety.

"You're an archivist. Your pass can get you anywhere."

Jaron nodded. "Except into private residences…and forbidden or restricted areas." Some of the medical labs in the Uppers were off-limits to archivists, prisoner holding areas, and at one time the doors which led to the Outside. As passcard swipes were recorded in the Hub, theft by an archivist from warehouses and storage units, businesses or other areas, was a difficult, and recordable, thing.

He guessed Rhyd was going to ask him to start stealing freezes. He had never stolen anything in his life. Moving numbers in the Archives was one thing. Physically accessing a store and removing inventory was another.

"Go to Grainger. Get into Factory East. Find that door."

Blinking, Jaron stared, meeting Rhyd's gaze. It was not the first time that doing so had crossed his mind, but he had, thus far, talked himself out of such a risk. Now he was being asked to do just that.

He was surprised, however, that his head bobbed in agreement while his brain wrestled with the arguments about why doing this was a very bad idea.

None of this, in truth, was a good idea. Skelter being in the Core, dying because of some foolish suicide club pact was not a good idea. Jaron briefly considered simply asking Grainger to open the Core, let Rhyd go in to find Skelter, let him extract the red-head who had somehow found himself inside. But even that was a bad idea because it would introduce too many questions and too many different sorts of

new ways that things could go very wrong for Rhyd and Scarecrow, for all of them.

An archivist inspection of the Factories, however, was innocent enough. He ought to be able to do that…as long as he avoided asking obviously suspicious questions.

"I will…as long as you be careful. But I'm not going back to…"

"You have to."

Enoch slid from his seat, took his bowl to the sink counter, depositing it at Jaron's elbow, and muttered, "I'll get your things." Rhyd was going to need clothing, preferably something that would afford him protection, and nothing in Jaron's flat would do. He could get into Rhyd's flat easily enough and doing so would give the two men adequate time to talk.

It seemed they needed to.

Rhyd bobbed his head once without looking at Enoch. "Go to Tox…she'll get what we need."

Nodding again, Enoch disappeared out the door, happy to escape the awkward tension that had settled in the flat. What they intended to do was too bloody complicated as it was.

Now that Enoch was gone, Rhyd pushed to his feet and stood, swaying as the imbalance in his inner ears shifted. Then he staggered on shaky legs to where Jaron busied himself with the dishes in the sink. He was going to need to eat, to drink…cazzo he needed a shower…but those things would wait. He stopped behind Jaron, silently watching his movements, fighting the impulse to touch him, turn him around so they could face each other, speak face to face

It was better they did not do that. Better he not look into the man's blue eyes.

When had this become so complicated?

"You have to go back. He's expecting you."

"Let him expect…" Jaron mumbled.

"Not yet…not now. We need him to think nothing's changed…not attract attention. We need that access."

"Why me? He'll listen to you."

"Not the way he'll listen to you." He did not know what use there might be for Grainger in any plan to breach the Core, but keeping Jaron in play so close to the Captain could gain them access to things, information in particular, they might not otherwise be able to easily gain. Using Founder Kemway's condition was already a piece on the game board that Rhyd thought he could use, but doing so would mean Grainger, and Tamner, and thus Jaron.

No one else in their circle of compatriots had the same access to the Uppers as Jaron and Tamner. They could not lose that access now.

"When this is over…"

"When this is over…what?" Jaron's breath caught as he waited for a reply, some confirmation that he was not alone in feeling this unexpected, weighty pull between them.

Rhyd did not speak. He tried to think of words that did not sound glib or callous, words that would not commit him to feelings he was doing his best to ignore, to pretend were not real. Just attraction, surely. An overpowering admiration for those sky blue eyes, the curve of his cheek and chin, the shape of his mouth, the way his hands moved. When Rhyd's gaze dropped to those hands that now held tight to the lip of the sink like an anchor holding Jaron down in a sea of emotion, Rhyd squeezed his eyes shut with a sharp intake of air.

"When this is over what?" Jaron repeated, the awareness of how close Rhyd was behind him stretching his voice thin. "Rhyd?"

Rhyd's head came up in the same moment that Jaron gave in to the temptation to turn, his eyes opening and then widening when Jaron caught his face between his hands and their mouths met.

The taste of curry and berry wine, sweet and hot and ripe with the power to compel Rhyd to take more, devouring in its hunger and heavy need. He too caught the other man's face between his hands, allowing his fingers to stretch up into the dark waves of hair that hung like lures against the sides of his face. A familiar, but long-buried, all-encompassing need settled into his belly and sank lower, filling him with pounding blood and a degree of desire for another person he had forgotten how to feel.

Jaron's whimper, a sound from his throat, from his heart, not emitted by the digitally enhanced speech unit, severed the tie between them as it sank into Rhyd's chest with a jarring, sharp, bittersweet sort of pain. He pulled back abruptly, croaked, "I'm gonna shower," and retreated so that the bathroom door could close between them.

Jaron going back to Grainger was the best thing. For Jaron, for Skelter, for Rhyd. For all of them.

He did not deserve to be caught in the tangle of Scarecrow's life.

No one did.

They would end up like Xiaodan.

By the time he emerged from the scalding shower that stung the external injuries while easing muscles too tight from combat and torture, the flat door had opened and closed twice.

And Jaron was gone.

Better he hurt the young man like this than risk his life some other way. He was being sent into the Factory, yes, being sent back into Grainger's orbit, but neither place was likely to get him killed as an association with Rhyd would. It was better this way.

That did not make the pain of that moment between them any less.

Enoch, the only one in the main room now, thrust the duffle he carried into Rhyd's hand, not asking where Jaron was or what the result of their conversation had been. He assumed, as did Rhyd, that Jaron had gone to the Uppers as requested. If he did not, if he backed out of their plan now or chose some other action of his own, they would have to deal with that later.

As Rhyd dressed, Enoch picked up the now cold bowl of curry stew and began to eat. He exchanged a look with the blonde but did not put the bowl down. "Didn't think you'd want it, hate to waste it."

Though Rhyd's stomach growled its discontent, Enoch was right. Cold stew would not satisfy him, not while there was work to do.

They chose Rhyd's routes this time, the miles of ducts and tunnels that connected every room and every Lev with the systems that purged moisture from the air and delivered heat to otherwise inhospitable homes and vindis, rather than the labyrinth of exposed stairs and

walkways where they might be seen and recognized. The bilger's passcard moved them unchecked between Levs, the only need for caution and pause coming when a lone skolper passed on his rounds. There would be no gorra here, no brako, no Talkers, and the only streeters they saw were a horde of Heb addicts lying in their high at the mouth of the duct Rhyd chose as their Lev 1 exit…and three small children of seven or eight who stared at their idol in awe before scuttling away to tell their friends that Scarecrow had come to Lev 1.

It was a complication too late to avoid. The one thing Rhyd was confident of was that, whoever the children told, they would not be the sort of people who would come wielding weapons.

Enoch did not know the ducts the way Rhyd did. He could not direct Rhyd to their destination from inside, and Rhyd, not knowing their final destination, could not get them any closer.

They had to make the rest of the journey in the streets.

❧*❧

Wishing the archivist library would hold the answers Rhyd needed so he did not need to go into the Factory himself, Jaron pushed his nervous energy into converting the burn in his blood into the false confidence of squared shoulders and the uppity sort of smile he had seen on the faces of so many archivists when wielding the power of their office. It, and the portable Echo he carried, with the official datasheet open for others to see, gained him entrance through the door at the end of the metal tunnel connecting Hebenon's Uppers to the east Factory. Each Factory had its own tunnel, would be landlocked without them, and this one, he knew, was the one he wanted.

It was the only working Factory on the east of the city. The other had long sat unused, inaccessible, abandoned.

The mine carts that once provided Hebanthe Falls with salt, with a smattering of other minerals, ores, and an occasional find of coal, came through this tunnel. That was one fact that even Core-deniers

could not refute. There were no mines connected to the west Factories. Not as far as the Archives recorded.

It had to be here.

Jaron had never been in the Factories, had never been outside of Hebenon. He had only seen them through the windows of Oliver's office, and though he knew they were large, he had not realized how vast they were until he passed the reception desk and followed the curvy blonde through the maze of machines and workers processing raw materials and churning out the goods on which the city depended.

She pointed out things of interest, machines and pallets and particular individuals she believed an archivist would want to see and she answered all of his questions, as boring and repetitive and silly as they seemed. When she did not know answers, she called in one of the workers or floormen and Jaron dutifully recorded every fact and detail she reported, to keep his visit as official-looking as possible.

It would also give him data to dump into the Archives later, should his pretext for being here be discovered and questioned. They went up to the other factory layers, the tops of extensive conveyors and catwalks between machines and chimneys that belched steam into the air outside being similar in some ways to the Levs.

But it was below the factory ground level that Jaron most wanted to see, though he did his utmost to stave off questions about his interest in those things until they had seen nearly everything else.

Below the ground, in the single level that spread out in every direction, stretched beneath the rivers and merged with the area below the west Factories, where workers lived out their lives, where the men and women who served as bilgers and the like for the factory complexes worked on systems that kept the conditions there livable.

Some of those worked in the shafts of the Uppers too. It had been the Founders' way of keeping separate the desirables of their class above the Falls and the undesirables of everyone else.

Some had been born here, had lived their whole lives in this place, educated not with books and numbers but with the running of machines and the manufacturing of goods. Some were taken from the

Levs now and then to fill the ranks, a better use for troublemakers Vanished from Hebenon than housing them behind bars of steel. Prisoners still, but prisoners with a purpose, prisoners with better conditions and longer life expectancies, Jaron imagined, then those subjected to medical experimentation or sentenced to the Core.

Unlike the rest in Hebanthe Falls, these people had yet to glimpse the Outside and had little hope or chance of ever being allowed out in it. Not when Hebenon needed them here. Not when Grainger had no way, yet, to guarantee they would continue to work.

Jaron doubted they even knew the Outside was open.

What a regrettable, painful choice that had to be for a man like Oliver. How else to do so but to believe these people were criminals and thus here serving a sentence, not deserving the chance of freedom.

How else to view those cut off in the Core except as the very worst of society deserving the death they were undoubtedly suffering now that supplies from the city had ceased to go inside?

If Skelter did not die by the hands of the Club's fate, he would otherwise succumb to the slow gnawing of starvation.

"And that?" Jaron asked when their path took them past wide chain-link and metal frame doors held closed with a thick ring and bolt chain. The corridor through which they had walked was wider than many, growing wider still ahead to where another doorway and another lift awaited. The stone flooring looked newer here, or at least less worn, than he had noticed elsewhere throughout the living level, and benches, chairs, and small tables were in place at random intervals along the corridor, outside of rooms which served as dining and recreation facilities, a clinic, and a nursery for children too young to work the machinery.

A tarnished metal door, similar to other lift doors he had seen, was welded closed. Across from it, across the wide-open thoroughfare, behind chain fencing, was a floor strewn with rubble, dirt and debris and broad sheets of pressed hemp wood. Thick beams of hemp wood and steel, and cross braces of the same materials, extended up each wall behind that fencing, extending the length of the corridor and

across the ceiling, and a number of doors into side rooms there were similarly sealed with welded beams or thick wood. The overhead light directly behind the fence flickered and popped as if badly maintained but from the first cross brace onward, the path was unlit.

The corridor was not long enough, however, or dark enough to hide the double doors at the end bolted shut with a metal crossbar across their width.

"We had a collapse…structural integrity failure," she said off-handedly, as if it was common knowledge and something she had not witnessed herself. That failure of knowing, however, when she knew so many other details about the factories workings, did not add up, and unlike other matters, she seemed disinclined to ask those who lived here for further details or information. "We haven't had the materials or the manpower to shore it up."

If he was a betting man, Jaron would say that beneath those planks layered across the floor were mining rails that extended across the thoroughfare to the welded lift doors, and beyond that end door, the Core. He could not prove it, as he did not think his guide was inclined to take him down what she believed to be a dangerous corridor.

With the fence door held closed by an old-fashioned chain and lock, to which he doubted she had a key, she probably could not take him if he asked and she wanted to.

These were details worth mentioning to Rhyd and Enoch if he ever saw either of them again.

Absently running the tip of his tongue across his lips in remembrance of that kiss, he bid farewell to his guide at the end of his tour, thanked her for her time and information, and promised that if he had any further questions, he would be in touch. Until he reached Rhyd to share this material, or heard from him with instructions, there was only one place left for Jaron to go.

The one place right then he did not want to be.

❧*❧

They stood together in shadow on the metal precipice overlooking the churning river's tongue. It was particularly rough here, where the last of the Four Falls joined in, beyond the final straining net, where additional support pillars were drilled into the bedrock and grating was installed beyond Hebenon's exterior wall with the intent of one day extending Lev 1 further towards the sea. As old as the pillars appeared, cared for and protected against rust and erosion though they were, Rhyd had no idea how long ago they had been installed…or why the city had never spread beyond the narrow maintenance path onto this twenty-foot-wide stretch of real estate. Bait bins were affixed to the rails at the city's edge, suggesting some came here to fish for the creatures who made it through the nets on their seaward journey, daring to risk the 'outside', believing that the river's mist that billowed here would be enough to protect them.

Undoubtedly some had circumvented those rails to use these wider platforms, unprotected though they were, and undoubtedly many had fallen in, or jumped, never to be seen again. Jagged rocks jutted up from the river, from the tall cliff walls, like cactus spines, catching some of what the city lost or else battering it mercilessly.

"There."

Enoch pointed and Rhyd squatted beside him to see what the dwarf saw from the same angle.

An opening in the rock, fifty feet or so away by Rhyd's judgment, where the river crashed against those jetty stones and forced the backwash into an opening in the rock face.

"A cave?"

The dwarf shrugged. "Natural drainage maybe…I can't say. Some of the Core's waste flows downhill…what isn't channeled for repurposing that is…into there. I think it may have been intended as a freshwater source, but erosion altered it…most have forgotten it's there. From what Colyx and Otta describe, that was where they found Skelter, where they fished him up.

Rhyd doubted, many had attempted this path to escape, or had survived the crushing flow of the river if they had tried. Any who

trained to swim in Hebenon learned to do so in a stationary pool. No one would find maneuvering the water's speed and the rocks to be an easy feat…and most, believing the outside world to be poisoned and unlivable, would never have taken the risk.

"How far?"

"Inside? I'm not sure…twenty? Thirty? Straight up."

"Is it wide enough?"

"He got in that way…should fit to go out the same way. But getting here from there…against the current? Not even a swimmer can make that. I think the undertow in there is pretty strong…and it's deep. If Skelt hadn't been hung up on the rock…if they hadn't seen him when they did…he'd've been pulled under and drowned."

Enoch had considered the same point of escape, just as he knew Skelter must have, but the logistics, from the inside, were too difficult to judge. Blowing the tunnel that Enoch used to come and go seemed more feasible, safer, even if it was a long shot.

"A cable…a wench reel…good sturdy chain…some pitons and eyes…" Rhyd studied the mountainside again, using the sensors in his hood to gauge aspects of the rock he could not see with his naked eyes. "I could do it."

Enoch grunted. "That's you. Maybe you could get out of there that way…but he's not you. Otta and Colyx aren't you…" He shrugged with the side turn of Rhyd's masked face. "He's not going without them. At least not without her. Even if they had all of those things in there…could cobble it together from the mining equipment…"

"They don't need all of it, just cable or chain…if they've got it." Such must have existed in the Core for use in mining, though whether it remained after so long, whether it had been repurposed, Rhyd could not say. "Or you get it in; leave the rest to me."

For a moment, neither spoke, as Enoch tried to fathom what Rhyd had in mind. Then his face lit with an expression of disbelief.

"You're gonna go in."

On the inside, Rhyd might be able to help with blowing the doors, might be able to help the Core residents fight to freedom. There was

little surety, however, that he could get Skelter out alive through the door. But through the door was not what he had in mind. "Don't have to get in all the way…just enough to rig a safety line, as long as they've got something to drop down from the top. No one needs to swim. They only need to hang on as someone cranks the reel."

"You're insane, you know that?" Anyone willing to go into the river against that current had to be.

Rhyd shrugged and retreated back beneath the bent up corner of the metal shell that brought them back within Hebenon's protective shelter. "You got a better idea?"

Scowling before dragging the inner sheet of grating into place in front of the torn metal gap, Enoch replied, "No. But if anyone sees us here…hears us…or the others get an inkling…"

"Then we give them distractions, inside and out. Up…and down." Whatever they did was going to be a risk, but this was the first wisp of a working plan he had come up with. Though a dangerous one, it was at least a plan with a higher possibility of success than anything else they had discussed. Rhyd believed he could make it work.

Positioning the others to make it work in his favor, however, was going to be a more difficult task then braving the current would be.

❮*❯

The tablet was clicked off, to be tucked into the pocket of his longcoat as he left the tunnel to stand in the area where hemp from Outside was exchanged with the parah for whatever the city deemed fit to offer. It was the place where one parah child had dropped into the bowels of Hebanthe Falls and forever changed history.

"Jaron? What are you doing here?"

He raised his head, snuffing out the panic behind a smile he did not feel and said with surprise he did not have to feign, "Oliver."

❧Chapter 25❧

I didn't expect to see you here."

"To be honest," Jaron said in a more even tone then he expected from himself as he fell into step beside the taller man, "I didn't expect to be here." He was thankful Oliver was not one for open displays, that the other was prone to defer to public perception. The arm around his shoulder in friendly greeting was enough. Anything more would have been awkward and uncomfortable.

It had nothing to do with their relationship itself, but rather Oliver's desire to be seen as strong, unattached, focused on his work and dedicated to the city. There were rumors, of course, talk by those who knew them both that had filtered through the ranks, but so long as they remained relatively detached to the public eye, the talk remained unsubstantiated.

"We got to talking…about Outside…"

"We?" Oliver walked with his hands behind his back now, the business he had come to conduct either complete or momentarily displaced by his relief in Jaron's company.

"My friend and I."

"Ah, yes. How is he?" He assumed this friend was another man, and was aware of the little flash of disappointment that followed when Jaron nodded in confirmation.

"Better, thank you." He did not elaborate, not wanting to falsify any more details between them of an illness, an excuse, that never was. "Our discussion made me curious to see it…but once I got here…" He shrugged. If Oliver had seen him emerge from the wrong tunnel, he did not want to plant any doubts. "I could not follow through."

"You should not go out there; it is dangerous." No more dangerous than anything in Hebanthe Falls, perhaps less dangerous given the growing unrest in recent weeks, but the thought of losing Jaron to the rural splendor of Marbordo that Grainger viewed through the office windows every day but had yet to go out to see for himself, was more unsettling than losing him to another lover.

Then, because he could imagine how those words must sound, he tried to cushion them by adding, "At least, you should not go out alone. No one should."

Endeavoring to keep a straight, neutral expression, Jaron nodded. "That's what I was thinking…once I got here. Besides," he forced another smile he did not feel, "When the day comes to go out there…I'd like the first time to be with someone special."

When that first time came, he wanted to see the outside world at Rhyd's side. It was an admission he would never make out loud.

Corners of his mouth twitching, the only expression of the giddy twisting in his stomach allowed in response to what he presumed were words that referred to him, Oliver said, "Will I see you for dinner?"

"I have to check in, see if I'm on shift, but I'll be there if I can be." He had missed two days, days he had put in to have off with a claim of illness, and as he knew there would be more days to come if Rhyd needed him for whatever he had planned, Jaron knew he should try to squeeze in shifts where he could.

Giving Grainger hope, even if false, was a necessary evil.

"Good." They paused at the lift so that Oliver could look at him with a curious, perplexed expression, brushing strands of hair from his face. Jaron said all the right things, smiled to see him, and brushed his lips over Oliver's cheek before entering the lift alone. All seemed right and well. But somehow it did not feel that way, and Grainger wondered, as the door closed between them, why that was.

❮*❯

At the first junction they reached, Rhyd and Enoch went their separate ways, Enoch to reach out to Skelter in the hopes of presenting Rhyd's plan, in the hopes of convincing him that what Rhyd had in mind, as crazy as it sounded, might be their best chance for success.

Scarecrow, meanwhile, had a mission of his own. He could scurry about Hebenon in search of the equipment he needed, rushing to acquire it as quickly as possible, or he could go to the one person likely to have some of it on hand already…and who could get her hands on the rest more quickly than Scarecrow ever could.

Once upon a time, he would have gone to Skelter for those things. Now Skelter was relying on him.

"Scarecrow."

For a moment, as he prepared to slither into the shaft through which he and Enoch had first emerged onto Lev 1, he did not realize the voice was speaking to him. When he did, it took another moment, after turning to face one of the few people to ever speak to him when he was thus disguised, as he preferred to remain in the shadows with as little personal interaction as possible, to recognize the woman who stood amidst the cluster of young streeters he and Enoch had encountered before.

She was too well dressed to be a streeter. Her trousers, her coat, the gloves and hooded jacket she wore that left only her face exposed were too new, not yet scuffed and worn enough to have endured life on the street. Perhaps she was new to the struggle.

What Rhyd did know was that she was the young woman Xiaodan had tried to protect when he was killed. He also recognized the tooler she held out in offering and was grateful his mask hid the flush of panic he experienced.

"Can you take this?" she asked, the nervous quaver in her voice not one of fear but rather of nervous awe. "We saved it before, after…" After Xiaodan had left her, she thought with a teeny sniff and blinking back of tears. "If anyone can get this where it belongs…I couldn't find him…but I think you can."

They stared at one another. Rhyd could not tell if she knew who he was or if she merely believed that Scarecrow knew everyone, everything, and could find the tooler's owner where she and the others with her had failed. The younger streeters, however, clearly believed the latter and so he hesitantly accepted the tooler with a nod.

"You know…don't you? About Xiaodan's death?"

His gloved fingers closed around the tooler handle and he nodded.

"We want you to know…all of us Spinks…" She looked at the children around her and swept her gaze up into the shadows of the Levs above them, "We will do whatever it takes to save Hebenon. Xiaodan deserved better…and would want us to keep fighting."

Trusting his voice for the first time, he nodded again. "He did…but fighting isn't…"

"Just tell us," said one of the others, a tall boy with splotchy rough skin and several missing teeth. A Heb user, or former Heb user, Rhyd guessed, angry now that one so young had fallen into that life. "We're everywhere…we'll do anything…whenever you need us."

The young girl beside him, her dark hair tied back in a long dirty braid added, "What else do we got…if not making Hebenon better for the rest of the Spinks?"

The woman who had given him the tooler offered her hand. "If you need us, ask anyone. Ask for Ginna; they'll find me. We'll help."

He was loath to involve children in his fight. Pitting children against Talkers, brako, against anyone, was condoning their deaths. But the streeter life already fated many to early deaths, from Heb, from disease, from a lack of food and warmth. What the other girl said was true. What other purpose did any of them have, streeter or others alike, if not for making the city better for those who came after? Would it really be so wrong to give them the opportunity to better their lot, particularly when he was going to need every distraction he could devise when it came time to extract Skelter from the Core?

"If I need you," he promised. He had no intention of putting them in harm's way. Who in the city would willingly harm a child?

❧*❧

It was not the first time Kal had seen the big man; he had his own dealings with the fellow after all. On the day Vanderwall had first come to him, striding into the primary Talker Hall without the usual contrition or humility most exhibited when entering there, and offered his support to the Talkers to restore orders to the Levs, Kal had seen an opportunity too good to pass up, while not entirely trusting the offer made. The brako had already been on the rise, making a name for themselves in the lowest Levs. Kal did not have to approve of their methods so long as they supported his efforts to gain a semblance of normalcy and control in Hebenon's streets. He did not have to approve of their methods so long as the goods and ticks they ciphered for themselves were offered in part to the Talkers…for redistribution as bribes to those he could sway to boost power for the Voices of Faith.

This was the first time, however, in this awning-covered square, where diners gathered in the intersection between four corner food vindis, that he had seen Vanderwall sipping a tall, frothy drink at a table shared with Neoma Kemway.

But the familiarity the two shared, the way her hand covered Vanderwall's, intimate and friendly, suggested a more personal connection and knowledge of the other than Kal cared to see.

He could not explain the uneasy prickle in his belly. It might mean nothing more than Neoma trying to wheedle her way into someone's favor to manipulate them into giving her what she wanted, aid, information, a new bed partner. None of those things might work in Kal's favor. But it might also serve to be a wedged tool that Kal could drive into place between Neoma and the bugorra. A weapon to be wielded that might work in the Voices' favor…if he could convince Captain Grainger that his suspicions were the truth.

An image captured with his ICD ought to do the trick. One image taken at a good angle that would protect Vanderwall's identity but clearly show Neoma ought to be enough.

Besides, there was something else Grainger needed to know, if he did not already. Something Kal was not certain of himself. If he was right, that detail, combined with the evidence he could offer against Neoma, might be all it took to convince the Captain they were on the same side.

❧*❦

No one gave Enoch a second glance as he passed through their midst, a small man that, while not a constant figure among the Core's residents, was seen often enough to be considered one of their own. He brought hemp cigs and Hebbies, sweets and dried fruit, and sometimes physical goods to be bartered and traded, shared between them. Things from the outside, and as no one else could pass in and out, and no one knew precisely how he acquired the treasures he offered, his contributions were important ones.

That did not, however, prevent him from being the brunt of derision and insults or prevent the occasional attempts at bribing or bullying. For all the affronts they hurled however, they knew that without him, their lives would be a bit more dismal.

Colyx and Otta did their best to protect him as theirs was the room he passed through, granting them the alpha share of whatever he brought in. Colyx's size and strength and Otta's combat prowess guaranteed that few challenged their rights to those shares. And once Skelter had come into their lives, his ability to manage resources and coerce cooperation from others meant an additional level of protection that Enoch was quick to take advantage of.

It was not that he was scared. He was simply too smart to pass up a good thing.

It helped that he had known Skelter from before.

From the city.

That foreknowledge and the support of Colyx and Otta had aided in Skelter's quick rise to prominence.

If they did not get him out of this place, the Spades would see to it that most of Enoch's influence was stripped away.

He found Skelter, conversing with several others, standing over a spread of crude weapons on a low table, the mining picks and shovels sharpened into a manner of medieval polearms that Enoch decided he would do well to stay away from when they came in to use. There were short blades fashioned from anything the residents had been able to find, an array of bludgeoning hammers and tools that could break bone, crush skulls, and, it was hoped by some of those clustered around Skelter and his silent pair of guards, break through the sealed doors through which mined goods once passed into Hebenon.

"A word," muttered Enoch, tugging on Skelter's sleeve as he reached the man's side. He received several sour, apathetic, or expectant looks from the others but he ignored them. He was interrupting but did not care. This was important.

Skelter looked down, nodded, then said to the gathering, "This isn't gonna be enough. We need more if we're going to get through…"

"What about the explosives you promised?" someone growled.

"You said you'd get explosives…"

Before Skelter could reply, Enoch grunted, "Working on it. We've got a line…should be soon."

If explosives were to enter the Core, they had to come in via Enoch. Everyone knew it. So far, the too much absent of late dwarf had failed to deliver anything of value they wanted.

"We don't need freezes," argued someone else. "We've got what we need right here."

"You gonna beat through the door with your chuj?" another sneered, shoving at the previous speaker.

"Least I have one," he growled, shoving back.

Otta snarled at the pair, keeping blows from being exchanged, but the argument continued a bit more good-naturedly as Skelter followed Enoch to the most distant corner of the commons where they could not easily be overheard.

"Ballard's got a plan."

"He's alright then? After what Zar…" There had been tremendous nostalgic relief when Skelter heard Zara's voice for the first time in more than two years, but the news that someone had tortured Rhyd, not for being Scarecrow but for some other, unrelated and unexplained cause, had made Skelter worry that Rhyd would not be, either physically or mentally, up to helping him get out of this hellhole.

It was good to have his fears proven wrong, that his moment of misjudging his friend's tenacity and resolve had been unnecessary.

"Tough bastard, I'll give him that. I think he's zonked…" he tapped the side of his head, "but if anyone can pull off what he's got in mind, I think it'll be him."

Skelter leaned against the wall of chipped, dirty white tile and adjusted his eye patch before crossing his arms, holding his walking stick between his knees. "What's he got? Is he getting freezes?"

"Will take too long to widen my tunnel…you know that…but yeah. Jaron's got the list; Ballard's working on that. No, this is something else…but he's gonna need some things from us in here if we can swing it."

"What?"

A crash across the room, the upending of the table that sent the weapons scattering across the floor as the friendly ribbing turned to blows between the other two men. Though Enoch and Skelter tensed, expecting the row to develop into a full-scale fight, others nearer the dispute pulled the men apart with curses and admonitions.

"Save it," a woman snapped, waving a short hammer under one man's nose. "Save it for the Crows."

"They're gonna be surprised when it's not Crows they meet out there," Enoch muttered.

"Anyone on the other side of that door is gonna be an enemy," Otta snorted. "They're ripe for a fight…no matter who they find."

"Once out of here, gonna be no stopping them," agreed Colyx.

"Might be best if they never get out…not most of them at least. They're like rabid, uncontrollable dogs." Skelter shrugged at the looks the others gave him. It was a conversation they had shared before. In

his opinion, the majority of those in the Core were fated to die. It would be best for all of humanity outside in Hebenon if they did.

Enoch was inclined to agree, imagining an upsurge in brako membership if those brutes made it out of the Core alive. "So we turn them to the door…maybe the smaller ones to the tunnel…and the three of you go out the way you came in."

"The door?" asked Colyx. He was the only one to have come in through the door, a prisoner sentenced here for his repeated anti-social tendencies and a physical bulk that made him ideal for mining. Otta had been born here, her mother the one sentenced to the Core. She was the one who made the connection Enoch was alluding to.

"The way he came in," she murmured with a glance at Skelter. "You want us to swim."

"Not me; Ballard," the dwarf corrected with a hasty shaking of his head. "Not exactly swimming. Told him it was insane, but he intends to rig a line…platform, cave, up the channel…no swimming required."

"No swimming he hopes," muttered Skelter with a thoughtful expression. He had considered that passage as an escape route, but with the strength of the current, and his lack of ability in the water, he had come up with no feasible way to make that work. If Rhyd had an idea, he was willing to reconsider the option. "What's he need?"

"Chain or cable…long enough to get to the bottom…strong enough to hold you anchored in. Pitons, bolt eyes if you can find 'em."

"We can make them if we have to," Colyx grunted. There was mining material enough with which to create most of those things. It was doing so in secret that would be the difficulty.

"We take the links from the mining pails…from the carts…weld them together."

Despite Skelter's blossoming enthusiasm, Otta did not look convinced. "They're going to ask questions…"

"We say they're for the little shaft…to pull freezes in or…for pulling the door…if blasting it doesn't work," Skelter replied with a

shrug. "Always good to go in with a backup plan." Or at least with the appearance of one. Sometimes, one plan was all you got.

"Won't be enough if we're makin' two," Colyx reminded him.

"It'll have to do; we make binding links to join 'em…at the last minute."

"We'll get what we can from outside…I'll get it to you best I can. Don't think Ballard'll have to search very hard to find what he needs…and if its distractions you want on the outside, I think he's covering that too. Dunno how yet…but he's working on it."

Nodding towards the now righted table, where rougher than necessary mock combat was underway as the scattered weaponry was retrieved, Skelter snorted, "What we'll need is some containment for their madness should they actually get through the door."

"I'll get him on that too," the dwarf promised. Maybe it was something he and Lash could arrange. They could not put everything on Ballard's shoulders after all.

"We'll get on things," agreed Skelter. "Let us know the plan…"

They heard the buzz, and then the clatter of metal against stone inches above Skelter's head. Otta picked up the small silver blade that clattered to the floor, unable to embed in the stone and tile, and marched across the room with it clutched in her hand, her expression daring whoever had thrown it to challenge her.

The men and women gathered around the table scattered and fled.

Skelter sighed. "Better be soon…running out of time."

If not for this Spades business, he would have all the time in the world. With the rules of the Club nipping at his ass, however, time was not his friend.

❧*❧

The images that scrolled up his screen meant little to Tamner, faces of men past dead, census records from a time before he had been alive, or at least before he was old enough to care about things like the lineage of the families in the Uppers, the Kemways, the Doctet, the

old blood upon which Hebanthe Falls was founded and built. Most of those alive now, who had survived the purging plague, were men and women he had known all of his life, his contemporaries, a few his elders, some their children. Haythem himself Tamner had always been part of his life, the Founder his elder by three years.

It was why he had no specific memory of the scandal, the unfortunate death that had occurred when Tamner had been barely schoolable age. He, like everyone else, had grown up only with hushed rumors uttered behind closed doors. Until that meeting but a day before, there had never been a reason for Tamner to think about it, even in passing.

If it was true, either version of the rumor, then surely, as his parents and elders had agreed, it had been for the best.

Hebanthe Falls had depended on such unfortunate choices.

Not anymore, of course. Things had changed with the opening of the city to the Outside. But it had been a different world forty-odd years ago.

The images stopped moving. Tamner stared at the photo he had paused on, at the miniature of a face he had grown up knowing, a man whose passing he had mourned as had every other resident in the Uppers.

Those in the Levs had too…but it had not been the same. Detached as they were, such a passing was little more than an allowance for a day of leisure.

He was younger in this photo, a family portrait taken with his newly born heir, Haythem Kemway.

It was Markus Kemway whose face Tamner studied. There were some of his features…his dark hair and wide face…that he shared with his son, but to Tamner, Haythem more closely resembled his mother.

But the rest…the likenesses were undeniable. He wondered how anyone could not know, how no one else had seen the truth before.

The pneumatic lab door whooshed open and Tamner clicked off the Echo casually as if he had finished some boring report as one of the younger lab techs came in with a tray of test tubes and instruments,

the most recent samples from the beleaguered Founder who was, quite certainly, out of his mind. Tamner watched the girl drop the metal tongs, the syringe, and the pressure cuff into the tank of sterilization solution, and then he bent over a written report as if his interest was entirely casual and not at all distracted.

Should he tell Grainger, he wondered?

Did he dare tell anyone?

And would anyone, even the one in question, believe him?

Tamner was not certain he believed it himself.

∮*∾

"What can I do for you, Senior?"

Grainger had never met with the Talker alone, had never met with any Talker alone except in a few instances of interrogation, and to his knowledge, this was the first time Senior Kal had come to the Uppers. At least, it was the first time he had done so since Haythem had ceased serving as Hebenon's final voice of power.

It was the first time, to Grainger's knowledge that the Senior had been seen since the attempt on his life.

It was easy enough to presume that the man had come regarding the skirmish with the streeters, in which one of his subordinates, one young streeter, and a brako had lost their lives.

"I have come to offer a trade." The Senior sat without invitation, but at least when he sat he did not presume to take Grainger's chair as Neoma had done. Grainger, having risen in greeting when the older man entered, sat as well.

"A trade."

"Information for cooperation."

"Information from me in exchange for your cooperation, or vice versa?"

"It will be in Hebenon's best interest, I think, if your team and mine work in tandem, don't you agree? A joint effort to make Hebanthe Falls the safe haven for everyone it used to be?"

Grainger huffed. "You and I have different recollections of safety, Senior." Before the Coup, the Talkers had not been targets, and violence against the Voices had been rare. A return to that sense of security was to be welcome, but not at the expense of the oppression Grainger had seen daily at the Founder's hand.

He admitted he had been part of that oppression, believing that it had been right and good and fair even in his moments of doubt. That view, however, had changed.

The sort of agreement Senior Kal alluded to was not the life the people of the city needed if they were to survive, if mankind was to flourish and thrive.

"I support the Founder, the families, it is true," Kal said. "Leaders must be supported, else they cannot lead. And people need structure, leaders they can respect and follow…"

"Kemway isn't that anymore." Grainger was no longer sure Haythem had ever been that.

"So I saw…sadly. That is regrettable, as is his only living air being just a child, not even old enough to know her mind. If a Kemway is to rule again, it needs to be one who can speak for the people."

"If you're suggesting Neoma…"

The Senior laughed. "Heavens no. She could never speak for the people. Someone in league with the brako to undermine Hebanthe Falls is hardly…"

"In league with the brako?" Grainger leaned forward, chin on his steepled hands. "What do you mean?"

But Kal continued his sentence, ignoring the interruption, ignoring the fact that the Captain had taken his bait. "She has no concern for the Founder beyond her own gain, and I will not condone…"

"I'm sure your own gain is what you want with him as well."

"I want what is best for Hebenon, as do you. Times are changing," his sweeping hand gesture indicated the view of the world outside of the office's circle of windows. "I can see that now. As can you. You were always loyal, Captain. Loyal to Hebanthe Falls, loyal to the Founder. With my backing, with the Voices behind you, we can

convince the people that you speak for the Founder. It takes only the right words…"

"And you can provide those?" Grainger asked snidely.

"Of course I can," Kal chuckled. "I am Senior. It is what I do, talk, so that people listen. I didn't get where I am by ineptitude."

"You want me to support the Voices?" There were worse notions. The Voices of Faith had been a respected, established, institution since the building of the city. Time had morphed the Voices away from the worship of an abstract deity to the deification of the city's Founder. They had directed public policy in the Levs according to the whims and needs of those Founders. They could not be entirely blamed if the Founders, over time, had come to manipulate that support for their personal gains, but they could be blamed for allowing the organization to become something no longer innocent or anti-political.

That was not the sort of support, however, that Grainger wanted. He wanted support for his own merits, because he was doing what was right, what was just, what was best for the citizens of Hebenon…not because the Talkers proclaimed him fit to lead.

"I want," Kal paused for emphasis, "you to stop whatever Neoma is planning with the brako. I want her stopped before she destroys us."

"What proof do you have that she's…?"

"I've seen them…she and one of their…"

"Vanderwall?"

Kal shrugged. He had the image but had not sent it. He was not certain yet that playing that card was in the best interest of his game.

Eyes narrowed, wondering if the Senior had known Vanderwall's identity all along and was hiding it from the authorities, Oliver said, "I've had agents who've seen you with brako as well…and before you tell me it's some sort of privileged Faith thing, know that I do not hold with the confidential confessions of the Faith. Particularly," he snorted, "when those meetings occur in public venues."

Nothing in Kal's expression changed. If he was surprised to learn he was watched, that he was a suspect in anything, if he was surprised by anything Grainger said, it did not show.

Grainger suspected he might have known all along.

"Her charges of treason hurt, I'm sure. They will keep on hurting unless you show people that is not who you, who the Voices, are. I won't help you do that, Senior. I have more important things to do."

He stood again, clearing his throat and came around the desk to stand beside Kal. The Senior stood as well, appearing to find it discomfiting to look up at the Captain from an inferior position. "I won't be manipulated, Senior, and I won't cater to you for support with special favors. Do what is right for the people, tell me what you know…all of it…and we'll let it go at that."

"I've told you what I know, Captain," Kal began, his tone expressing insult.

"All of it," Grainger repeated. "Or peddle your blackmail material elsewhere…with Neoma if you think she'll listen. Haythem might have played your games. I won't."

In one final effort to shorten this distasteful meeting the Captain offered his hand. "I appreciate you coming, but now I must meet a friend for dinner."

Even if Jaron could not make it, the excuse of a dinner engagement was better than no excuse.

Kal swallowed enough of his pride to accept the offered hand. "You'll regret this decision, Captain…and when you do…I cannot promise the offer will be repeated."

Not expecting to regret anything, Grainger said, "Good day, Senior," unruffled by the words that were, if not a promised threat, at least a suggestion of one.

"Good day, Captain."

❧*❦

Midway through the crawling hour, places like Vapors were quiet, slow, with the usual slog of customers either on shift or at home asleep. Rhyd's hopes of finding Tox in her hidden workshop were thwarted, and she was not at her kesfek vindi when he passed hidden

in the vent system. There might have been further business involving Xiaodan's death, or perhaps she had gone in search of another apprentice, so Rhyd retreated into the safety of Vapors' empty shadows for a drink with the hopes of clearing his head.

There was a lot to think about. A lot to plan. And a lot of supplies he would need if he was going to make this rescue happen. There was a young fellow behind the bar when he arrived, unfamiliar to Rhyd, but as this was not his typical hour here, he did not know if the stranger with the frizzy white hair was a regular fixture since before the Coup or if he was new. He brought Rhyd the requested bottle of Zaolei, however, and the order of curlers the chef readied without Rhyd's request, and also brought him the asked for hemp napkin and pen.

If he could not give Tox the list verbally, he would leave it for her in writing and hope she got it. This was a list he did not feel he could send via ICD or Echo, wanting no trace of the request to be out there for anyone else to find. He was a nobody to either the swiver or the half dozen patrons seated throughout Vapors. With messages often left to pass on to Tox in her adjoining vindi, and Tox being known to fulfill some of the oddest requests for goods and materials, he did not think his order list would raise suspicions if the swiver read it.

Still, it was a relief when a familiar comforting arm slipped around his shoulders and a familiar mouth pressed gently to his cheek. It meant a trusted individual to deliver his message.

"Good to see you up, Whiskey," Zara purred. The purr did not put him off; it was who Zara was. She wore a long, gossamer slicker over the stage costume she had chosen for the next show, but Rhyd did not notice the details. Zara was his friend. He was not there to ogle her.

"Take more than thumpers and zappers to put me down," he snorted, preferring not to discuss the tortures he was doing his best not to think about. "Know where Tox is?"

"Picking up nessies for Maemi I think. Mama's not been well since…" Her voice faltered and she glanced to the side when the beaded curtain parted and newcomers pushed inside. "Pietro's been picking up the slack here…and Tox is keeping her stocked."

Rhyd nodded, his expression sad and troubled. Xiaodan had been the old woman's only remaining blood relative, her only living grandchild. His death had undoubtedly hit her hard.

"I'm sorry…I talked to him…I tried…"

"His girl was in trouble…he did what any of us would have done."

Any of us, Rhyd knew, in his circle of acquaintances and friends.

He had not known that the streeter girl had been anything more to Xiaodan than an acquaintance.

"Was hoping…you can do a few things for me…for Skelter." He added the last in case she was disinclined to help. She might claim to be willing to risk her life, and she had done so before, following him all the way to the Founder's suite, but she had not been herself for several weeks after that, and Rhyd was not certain how much of her lost soul look had been due to the loss of Skelter and how much had been due to the risks she had taken with her own life.

"Anything," she agreed eagerly. For Skelter, for Rhyd. Often times, for her, they were the same thing.

He slid the napkin towards her. When she began to pick it up, he covered her hand with his and held it there, pressed against the bar, until Pietro moved further down the counter to help other customers who approached the bar for drinks.

"Get this to Tox. Tell her I need it…soon as possible. Five days. Four would be better. Two or three would be ideal. I need time to get everything in place."

Pushing a stray tendril of white-blonde behind her ear, she gaped at the list. Five days seemed like so little, but she realized that, by her count, that might be the only days Skelter had left. Five days to find freedom or five days to die.

"I will," she whispered.

"I don't have the timetable worked out yet…but I'll need Lash, Tox, Enoch if you can reach them. I'm on shift for the next five days…but we need to talk."

"And Venn?" Rhyd bristled. "He deserves to know what's up."

"He knows I'm not leaving Skelter in there."

"Five days is the debut."

Rhyd frowned. He had forgotten. So much time had passed, with Rhyd caught in Hebenon's tangles, that he had not realized that performance was fast approaching too. There would be many guests in attendance that night, and Venn would expect him to be one of them. Would Rhyd put them in danger, so many in one place, with what he had in mind? With the timing of it?

He did not know where the performance was to be. If Venn had told him, he had forgotten that too. He needed to learn that, the place, the time, before he proceeded with his planning. He knew where the most likely performance halls were, and none of those were anywhere near the three possible passages into the Core.

"I'll talk to him."

He did not know what he would say, how he could avoid a fight, but he owed Venn that much.

"There is something else; I need you to plant something."

Zara cocked her head. "In the Hub?"

"Where Grainger can get it. Where he will get it. I want to let him know there'll be an attempt on the Founder…"

"Is there? Will there be?" she asked with mild alarm. Like most of the city's residents, she had no specific devotion to the Founder. He was there, a figurehead, an unmovable permanent part of their lives, but not someone with whom she had familiarity beyond his face on the Echosys screens.

"Not if it plays out the way it should. Not if he's moved out of harm's way." Rhyd did not know where Kemway was kept, but if Grainger's officers were intent on moving him, it would occupy at least some of the gorra. "Soon as I have a timetable, I also need you to make sure he knows there's going to be a bust out from the Core…in Factory East. He'll know where."

That, Zara quickly guessed, was not a ruse but rather a diversion. She assumed Rhyd had found some other path towards Skelter's freedom and wanted the bugorra as far away from it as possible. "Just tell me when…and he'll know whatever you need him to know."

She stared at the napkin in her hand as Rhyd pulled his away. There was no doubt this would be dangerous, for Rhyd at least and most likely for Skelter. Maybe Enoch too. But she did not expect anyone else she cared about to be near to the epicenter of events. Only one other, and when she looked into Rhyd's eyes again, she asked, "He'll be safe, won't he? When those in the Core try to…?"

"I don't know, Zar." It was not that he wanted to put any bugorra in danger. But they were trained for such things and the risk of the Core criminals breeching Hebenon during this process was too great to take lightly. The bugorra had to be there to do their job. And keeping the buggers' interference away from Lev 1 was imperative. Where Grainger fell in all of that was not Rhyd's concern. "He knows what he's doing. He's smart. He'll be okay."

Accepting his assurance as the only truth he could give, thankful he did not make promises he could not keep, she folded the napkin and made a show of stuffing it into the cleavage of her sequined bra top. "I gotta get ready. You gonna stay?"

He shook his head. "Too much to do." Especially, he mused, as he had no idea when Tox would get his list. Rhyd needed to start on his plan now…and get a few hours of sleep before his shift if he was to function the next day.

Too much to do, and so little time to do it.

❧*❧

There was a storm brewing. Venn could not smell it in the air from the hilltop on the coast as Agnys could, but he could see the distant dark clouds on the sea horizon as the sky began to grow black with night. Inside Hebenon, only those on Lev 1 who witnessed the rise and fall of the river's level, or those in the exposed Uppers who might hear the crackle of thunder or the pelting of rain and hail against the city's dome, might notice such an event. Unlike the parah village of Marbordo, the city bordering the sea, the only storms Hebenon knew

were the sort rained upon them by men such as the Founder, the Talkers, the Captain of the bugorra…

The Scarecrow.

That was a storm Venn knew was coming too, but he would not be there to witness it as he would this one. He was staying here, where he was safe from that sort of tumult, as Rhyd suggested.

With the closing of Hebenon's doors against the bluster of the rising tempest's wind, Venn knew something else.

Rhyd had made his choice. He was staying inside to face that storm. A storm, Venn believed, of Rhyd's creation, no matter how much the bilger denied it or claimed otherwise.

Venn wondered if he should speak of it to Grainger…and then realized there was nothing he could say.

❧Chapter 26❧

"Who would be stupid enough to try to get to him here?"

Tamner had his doubts about Grainger's words as they watched the slumbering man on the other side of the glass slouched in the corner of his padded room. There was one door in, one door out, and miles of Upper corridors to pass through to get here. There were medis and buggers constantly on call, on watch, chiefly to prevent the Founder from hurting himself when he drifted into one of his manic fits. Those guards and attendants had been carefully selected, sworn to secrecy about Kemway's location and condition. No one else knew the man was here.

Except for Mam Kemway.

Tamner suspected the woman's visit to her husband had less to do with seeing him than it had with some political agenda.

Did she intend to kill him? Or was she planning to take him out of this place to utilize him for some personal gain regardless of his health? Was one of those currently tending the Founder in the woman's pocket…and if so, which one?

"Whoever it is, we cannot risk it. We have to keep him safe." Neoma was a primary suspect, but after the earlier visit from Senior Kal and the reminder of the man's persuasive speech, Grainger was not ruling out the possibility that the Voices of Faith were suspect too.

There was also the possibility that any one of those carefully selected attendants might believe, right or wrong, that the city would be better off if Kemway was dead…without any prompting by the Talkers or Neoma. Fanatics were always a risk.

"We move him somewhere else until we're sure."

"This has to be the safest place…where else could we…?" Tamner shook his head. "There isn't anywhere else suitable." It had taken special preparation to pad the walls and floors of this room for the man's well-being. There were no other such rooms in the Uppers, and to Tamner's knowledge, nothing similar on the Levs.

Moving Kemway into the Levs would be the foolhardiest thing they could do.

"Then we make something suitable. If what I've heard is accurate, we can't take chances." Kemway's death would remove a significant number of headaches, but Grainger had only been prepared to kill the man once. When that effort fell short, leaving the Founder as he was now, Grainger had not had the heart to consider trying again. Nor was he prepared to give anyone else the opportunity.

Before, Haythem had been a fit, wily man, a menace. Now he was nothing but a shell.

"I'll see what I can do…find and prepare a room," Tamner reluctantly agreed, his expression dour and skeptical.

"Good. I will see to the rest.

Right after, Grainger thought, he got back to Jaron and made sure the young man was not waiting with dinner prepared.

∾*∾

Remaining for the night was not Jaron's intention, but after Rhyd's kiss, and the instruction given not to rouse Oliver's suspicions, to remain in the man's affections in order to provide a link to the Captain, Jaron had found he could not break away from either the meal or from Oliver's bed when they later tumbled into it. For many hours afterward, physically sated but emotionally drained from the effort to feel things he did not, and an abject restlessness, Jaron stared at the ceiling while Oliver slept, considering his options, considering what he had learned while in the Factory, pondering how he should get that information into Rhyd's hands and what Rhyd would do with it.

He could write it out and send written messages through Tamner or Lash perhaps, but that would leave a trail that could be traced back if letters fell into the wrong hands. He could send ICD messages, but those could be hacked. If the information failed to reach Rhyd for any reason, Skelter's rescue might fail.

He could send a video message or simply an audio one via an Echo, but they too would leave a trace, however small, on the Hub that could be followed, to him, to Rhyd, a foolish and unnecessary risk, particularly in the glow of what Jaron wanted most to do.

See Rhyd again.

He needed to deliver this information himself. Doing so in person was, he argued, the best way. The best, safest option arose from that desire and the necessity of fulfilling his Archive shift. Claiming a brief visit to his recovering friend would make delivery possible. Neither excuse for leaving, he doubted, would raise suspicion from Oliver should the man wake to find him gone. He had done his duty by being here as long as he had. What more could Oliver, or Rhyd, ask of him?

By the time the Captain woke and went about his daily routine, believing Jaron asleep beside him, the decision was made. Jaron dressed quickly when he was sure an uninterrupted escape was possible, and took the lift to the Archive Lev where he forced himself to dutifully put in his hours, inputting the Factory data he had gathered in case anyone questioned his reason for being there. The data had not been updated in some time, since its reopening after the Coup when the conditions of factory and workers alike were assessed and upgraded where needed. Jaron suspected the sealing of the Core, the covering of the cart rails, the barricading of the doors and corridor, had been done at that time. It was the only possibility that made sense.

While inspecting the Factories and recording the data about their condition was not his responsibility, Jaron did not believe anyone would look too closely at the dates or the filing agent. Figures and statistics. That was all it was. So long as the information was accurate, it was all anyone was likely to care about. It was an archivist's world.

How they came by the details they recorded was rarely questioned so long as it was current and correct.

Now Jaron stood alone, beneath the glow of the flickering alglights outside the Shed, awaiting the shift's end. He knew Rhyd's shift. The Archives revealed that much, the weekly schedule cataloged for the assignment of ticks. He knew Rhyd should be there, so long as his health allowed. The Shed's daily schedule did not place Rhyd so close to home that he would go there rather than return here first. Not knowing that, all Jaron could do was wait.

And greet the blonde with a nervous, tentative smile when Rhyd emerged from the Shed, the expression on his still-bruised face weary but eyes bright as if he was looking forward to whatever aftershift plans he had made.

Jaron wanted to believe that brightness was because of him.

Rhyd's heart leaped into his throat at the vision the slim man made beneath the shadow and glow of the lamps. Mysterious, alluring, achingly beautiful in a way Rhyd found overpowering and unwanted all at once. It was too big a risk for them to be seen together, however, a risk to Skelter, a risk for Rhyd, and after the torture at still unknown hands, certainly a risk for Jaron.

"You shouldn't be here."

When the younger man's warm excitement faltered beneath those withering words, Rhyd immediately regretted them, even though their meaning was still accurate and relevant.

"I need to talk to you…about what I found."

Glancing about, gauging the reactions of the other bilgers going in and out of the Shed, realizing they were ignoring him and that no one else was lurking nearby to see them, Rhyd nodded once and inclined his head in a direction away from the flashing red light of the Shed SCAM's eye.

How wise, he decided as they walked, that Jaron had stood out of range of that all-seeing eye. Whatever else Jaron was, he was no fool.

They pushed through the crowd of shift changers, down several flights of stairs, through vindi shoppers and down again, in the

direction of home, despite the nagging voice that told Rhyd Jaron should not know where he lived. But the man was an archivist; if he wanted the location of Rhyd's flat, he could have it without Rhyd showing him. That was the excuse Rhyd used when their seeming casual journey, taken with enough space and bodies between them to make their direction seem coincidental to anyone monitoring the SCAMs, brought them to Rhyd's flat. The cats collected around Lash's door scattered but did not go far, waiting for their daily feeding from the man Rhyd assumed had not yet returned home.

He still did not know where Lash spent his days. He had never bothered to ask.

With the door closed behind them and Rhyd stalking into the kitchen, an effort Jaron easily interpreted as keeping distance between them, he examined the viewable area of the flat without moving from the door, respecting Rhyd's unvoiced desire for that space. Unlike his own flat, there was little adornment here and the hemp green blankets and pillows on the sofa, as well as the oxygen beside it, indicated that Rhyd most often slept here instead of in the rooms beyond the closed doors Jaron could see to his right. A folded mound of clean clothes, mostly blacks and greys, filled the cushioned chair on the wall beneath the Echosys, and an empty bottle of Zaolei with work-greasy prints on the recycled glass sat in the middle of the otherwise barren table. The sink, the strainer, were empty as well, and the growing boxes on the window sills were devoid of the edible or decorative plants most households kept, and when Rhyd opened the cold storage unit, there was little to be seen within it either.

It seemed a place where Rhyd slept and little more, impersonal and most often avoided.

"Can't offer much…" Rhyd took out a block of cheese and brought it, a length of smoked sausage, and the breadbox to the table, along with another bottle of Zaolei and two glasses, deferring to a level of polite sharing rather than drink directly from the bottle with the man whose mouth he was now intimately familiar with.

"Not really hungry…" Any feelings of hunger were besieged by rampaging butterfly nerves, but still he sat in the chair Rhyd motioned to and accepted the offered plate. It was the glass of whiskey he took first, coughing at the burn he was not prepared for as it sank into the pit of his stomach where it temporarily scattered the butterflies and numbed his nervousness.

When Rhyd did not speak, Jaron cleared his throat and did so.

"I've seen the way in. To the Core. At least, I believe it's the way in. Nothing else in Factory East makes sense to be what you need." He toyed with a morsel of sausage, waiting, but Rhyd remained quiet.

"There's one underground level, a vast spread beneath the Factories, beneath the rivers where the workers live, eat, sleep, with system sheds and education and recreation facilities."

He pulled a folded sheet of paper from the breast pocket of the coat he had not removed, an added shield between them. Unfolding it, he spread it on the table and slid it over for Rhyd to study. "Not to scale I fear, but this is the basic layout. There's a fence with a door here…chained shut…and though most of this floor looks recently tiled, all of this behind here," he pointed, "is planked with hemp boards littered with dust, rock, debris. Wall and ceiling braces go all the way down this unlit corridor, and all the doors here are blocked with crossbars…just like this one. The attendant said there's structural issues, a collapse…so it's sealed. But with the level of the floors, the planking, I'd bet there are cart rails here…or there were, right to the center of these doors. Seems likely that behind it is…"

"The Core." It made sense, seeing it on paper, and was further visible proof of the area so many claimed did not exist. Three ways inside, and this one was the most obvious, the most direct…and the most easily accessible if the door could be reached and opened. "Where was the passlock panel?"

Jaron scowled. "I didn't see one." It had been dark at that end of the corridor, so maybe he had missed it, but it had not been so dark that he missed the beam secured across both doors.

Yet it had to be there, or else anyone could have gained access whenever they wished, not just the Founder as Rhyd had been told.

"How wide's the crossbeam?"

"Maybe ten inches…I was too far away to measure."

So the passlock was behind it, Rhyd thought, leaning back in his chair and picking up the drawing with one hand. Most passlocks were built into the wall so that the electronics could manipulate the doors they controlled. The door to the Core would be older, back to the original construction of Hebanthe Falls, perhaps with no original lock. A lock might have been added later, after the Core became a mine and penal colony. The easiest place to put a lock was as near to whatever mechanism had been used.

Freezes could fracture the hinges, but they might not be enough force to weaken that crossbeam from the inside. If the Founder had been the only one with the Passcode for that door, it was likely a system isolated from the Hub…which would make it difficult, maybe even impossible, for Zara or anyone else to hack, even if she could get directly to the barricaded passlock.

"I'll get this to Skelter…so he knows what he's up against." Rhyd would not be there at that door. If Grainger took the soon to be planted bait seriously, his bugorra would be the only ones there. What came when the Core residents took down the door, if they did, was not Rhyd's concern. That part of the planning was in Skelter's hands.

"Four more days; they're gonna have to blow that door, or try to."

Jaron looked mortified. "But all of those people!" The Factories, like every business in Hebenon, ran continuously, in shifts. At least a third of the workers would be on the factory floor, another third and their families sleeping, the rest enjoying whatever downtime they were allowed. That was going to put roughly two-thirds of East Factory's staff at risk in that basement level. West Factories staff would be on the other side of the distant door Jaron had not approached.

Rhyd shrugged. "Gonna be up to Grainger to keep them safe. They'll be warned; he'll have time to move them." How that was done was also not up to Rhyd. If the warning was ignored and Grainger

allowed innocent lives to be lost, he would later have to contend with Scarecrow's wrath.

Concerned both for those innocent people and for Oliver's welfare and action, Jaron grudgingly nodded with a grim expression. "You?"

"I've got a way in."

"In?"

Again Rhyd shrugged. He had to go in, at least far enough to get Skelter out. He did not want to give details to a man whose loyalties he did not entirely trust. He did not believe Jaron would betray him, but not knowing how much of that belief hinged on the overwhelming impulse to kiss him again made Rhyd reluctant to say more.

"Trust me."

There was no reassurance that everything would be alright, that he would be safe, that he would succeed. But Jaron chose to do as Rhyd asked because he wanted to trust him. Wanted to believe him.

"What should I do?"

"There's nothing…"

"Don't shut me out of this. I want to help. Skelter asked for my assistance too…not just yours…and I won't be left out just because it's gonna get messy."

Rhyd grunted and lay the drawing on the table so that he could stare at Jaron with an unobstructed view. Judging physical strengths was impossible by looking at him, although to Rhyd's eye Jaron did not bear any markers of great prowess. He looked fit enough, however, so there could be some skill there. His true strengths, however, were his mind, his determination, his connection to Grainger, and whatever bull-headedness had brought him to crossing swords with the Founder and Doctet that had cost him his voice.

He was daring and determined enough to do the right thing, Rhyd decided. And he was right; Skelter had asked for his help too.

"You'll do whatever it takes to get Grainger to help those factory workers," Rhyd started, "and tonight…"

"Tonight?"

The squeak in Jaron's digitized voice set a very specific cluster of nerves burning low in Rhyd's belly. He shook his head, hoping to dispel the image of Jaron's body beneath his on his too-long empty bed, hoping to disavow Jaron of those undoubtedly shared thoughts.

"We've got freezes to collect if we're going to get them to Skelter in time to be of any use."

Jaron's loud swallow around the anxious lump in his throat sounded as painful to Rhyd as was the effort to tamp down on the fire in his groin. Working together tonight was going to be a test of endurance and focus, but it had to be done. Jaron knew where the best scores were to be found.

Rhyd had the skill to get them, the pain in his body be damned.

At least, Rhyd decided, they would not have to work side by side to make this happen.

Jaron's voice in the ear of his helmet ICD was going to be temptation enough.

❧*❧

He should have killed the Senior when he had the opportunity, when he had seen the annoying bastard of a man leaving the Uppers, leaving Grainger's office, on what had to be some manner of official Voices business with the Captain. The Senior had been alone and it would have been so easy to incapacitate him with a single blow and drop him over one of the guard rails. How many people slipped and fell thus each year? How many were killed by the multiple concussive, bone-breaking impacts endured on the way down between rails, grated walks, and the rooftops of dwellings, vindis, and other public venues?

So long as he was careful, so long as no one saw him, Blayd would never be blamed.

Neoma, in turn, would be clean of the troublesome man's death.

Finding what he was up to seemed a more pressing course of action, however, more directly important to Neoma's success, then killing the man outright, and so Blayd followed him, the quest to locate

Ilya's sister temporarily suspended. He eavesdropped, innocently questioned a number of Talkers, roughed up a bugorra whom Kal stopped to talk to, and hospitalized two brako who did so as well.

None could tell him anything about the purpose of Kal's visit with Grainger. What he did learn was nothing more than a whisper, a spark that he could not substantiate, but on the off chance it was true, he waited impatiently as the Mam's single servant fetched the woman from the other room.

How Neoma afforded the woman's upkeep, how she arranged payment for Blayd's services, he could not say. He did not especially care, so long as he was paid. But the addition of this new woman, slight and plain as she was, suggested a change in conditions Blayd made note of. If success of any sort had been gained in her position, he thought he should know.

"It's late," Neoma groused, tightening the drawstrings of her gown around her waist before raking one hand through her tousled hair to tidy it. It was earlier than she typically retired and from one of the bedrooms, he could hear Ulynda playfully singing to herself.

"I did not mean to wake you," he began. If she was unwell, he did not want to be the instrument of further decline in her health.

"Yes…you did." Hoping for her bed again, she was sure, as she had not seen him since his release from the medical facility a few days before. "Where have you been?"

"Keeping tabs on Senior Kal, as you asked."

"I asked to be rid of him." Her expression, as she draped herself over her favorite divan, was disgusted and disappointed, dripping with a level of scorn he had seen her direct at others but never at him.

The corners of his mouth twitched but he otherwise kept his face blank. "I thought it was more important, in the short term, to find out the purpose of his meeting with Captain Grainger."

That was information that peaked her interest and she leaned forward just enough to show it, exposing the valley between her breasts to his steady eyes. "And?"

After no more than another noticing glance at the distraction he knew she intended, he replied, "I'm not certain. I've not been able to confirm anything, but I do know he made a threat against the Founder, enough of a threat to prompt the Captain to consider moving him from wherever he is to somewhere more secure."

"A threat? On Haythem? From Kal?"

Her tone was odd, thin and stretched, and Blayd wondered briefly if that rumored threat was from the Mam herself or if she knew what the Senior was up to. As she had no other capable arm to perform such an act except Blayd, he did not know how she could carry out any sort of plot against her husband…unless she was considering kidnapping or killing her husband herself. Blayd did not think that likely.

It was possible, however, that Neoma and Kal had hatched some plan together.

"Who else? The brako?" Blayd snorted. It had to be a plan including many hands. If it was to be the effort of a single, misguided individual, word would never have leaked…unless that individual was a drunkard or a Heb addict with too-loose lips. "Either that, or the Captain's paranoia is showing."

"Or he intends something himself."

"Removing the Founder from further scrutiny, after revealing he's alive?" Blayd scoffed. He did not think that likely either.

"Or killing Haythem himself and blaming it on some secret conspiracy," snorted Neoma with enough worry in her tone to suggest she cared whether Haythem lived or died. A note as false as any Blayd had ever heard from her.

"Yes…I could see him trying that." A solid political strategy, particularly if the Founder's health was improving and Grainger feared for his position…or he simply wanted to remove that playing piece from the gaming table to optimize his chance of remaining in control of Hebenon.

A cough, deep and masculine, clawed out of her bedroom and into Blayd's chest. Again his lips and jaw twisted and it took more effort to keep his expression neutral.

Swinging her legs around so that her bare feet were once more on the floor, Neoma adjusted her gown before standing, pretending she had not heard that sound, as if it meant nothing and was none of Blayd's concern. She made no effort to apologize. "Go…find out when they're moving him…to where. I want to know everything."

"At once," Blayd said with a bow of submission that allowed him to school his face into a blank expression. "I'll take care of it."

"You'd better. If something is happening to Haythem, I demand to know what it is. I expect you to stop it."

"I will." One way or another, he would prove his worth and regain the place and favor in her life, in her bed, that he appeared to have lost.

❧*❧

Rhyd had seen him safely to Zara's flat and left him there with minimal instruction. Zara was to plant the data virus, set to implement on Grainger's Echo the day of the breakout, to give him just enough time to mobilize his forces and move the vulnerable Factory workers out of danger but none of that would happen tonight. Tonight there was another plan. All that Jaron could do was sit in nervous silence, with Zara typing away at her keyboard from where she sat cross-legged on the floor, waiting with the bud in her ear for Rhyd's signal.

There had been disappointment at the nearly wordless parting, but also a strange sense of exultation, the reaffirming that Rhyd too felt the pull between them and was struggling against it. With others in the equation, Oliver and Venn, such attraction was inappropriate perhaps, but there was no denying it was there. Jaron watched Rhyd slither into the vent shaft in the flat Zara had once shared with Skelter and replaced the grate over the opening so that no unexpected visitors would notice anything amiss.

The image Rhyd cut in the Scarecrow's black body armor was powerfully alluring. As Jaron reluctantly settled on the floor at Zara's side, listening to the near-silent echoes of Scarecrow's retreat in the

shaft, destined for the first location Jaron had provided, it was difficult to get that image out of his head.

Not that he wanted to.

Ten minutes. Fifteen. Twenty-five. Silent, anxious minutes gnawed at his nerves before a static pop crackled in their ears and they heard, "I'm here."

Scarecrow emerged from the primary maintenance shaft, a wider one than those which connected to the interior of homes and vindis, into the street near his first target, one deserted at this hour as freeze manufacturers worked in the nearby carbidi shed. An alglamp glowed near the SCAM, with its unlit red eye indicating a nonworking unit, and the nearby residences were quiet with sleeping or working families. He adjusted the viewing lenses of his mask, crouching in the shadows as he waited for the signal to continue, and listened to the sounds around him in case anyone, employees, passersby or bugger patrol, happened to come along. He did not expect them to; he had investigated his targets carefully before setting out to the first of them, but as the daily lives of people were subject to change, so too might the possibility of being discovered.

He was prepared for the worst and thankful he could not hear Jaron's breathing in his ear…the way Jaron was undoubtedly listening to his. He did not need that too-powerful distraction.

Jaron tapped Zara on the arm, nervous as he pointed at the earpiece and gave a thumbs-up gesture, and the hacker tapped a few Echo keys to turn the external speakers on.

"Give me a sec." No names. Zara knew better. They both did. Jaron held his breath, straining to hear any background sounds from Scarecrow's location that might suggest danger. But he heard nothing, no hint of anything Scarecrow might be able to see or hear. "Swipe," murmured Zara.

In the silence before the instruction, Rhyd slipped nearer the door, as near to the passlock as the shadows and the glow of the alglamp

allowed. At her signal, he made a quick glance up and down the walk, noting that no one was nearby, allowing him to sidestep to his left and do as he was told. The passlock responded with the expected warning beep of an incorrect or unread card swipe, but the data the hacked card sent back through the digital system allowed Zara to remotely reprogram the lock to accept the new card.

"Again."

Swipe. Click. The storage door unlatched.

"Go."

"SCAMs?"

"Already done," Zara assured Jaron. Scarecrow trusted her enough to know she would not give the go command without covering the risk. The SCAMs' eyes inside and out being dark told him he was as safe as he could be. Zara's command confirmed it.

Door closed behind him to mask his presence, though it did not latch so that he would not be locked inside, Scarecrow scanned the labeling on the stacks of containers in the frigid room. Tube freezes for mining, for demolition, for vindi and medical refrigeration units were but a few uses for manufactured carbidi. There were blocks of it sealed in hemplastic, reusable pouches of various sizes designed to hold carbidi for use as cold compresses or for cold blanks to drape over goods in short term storage. Packs of crushed bits used in clubs, like Vapors, to create the smoky effect so many customers preferred, or in fogger units sometimes rented for use in a home or public facility for a party. There were granulated shavings to pour into pipes to flush sludge away or to be used to blast some metal or stone surface clean. There were undoubtedly other uses he knew nothing about, but the only use he was interested in now were the tube freezes he quickly collected and stuffed into the rucksack he carried.

Used correctly in mining, freezes could be wedged into fissures and blown to create cracks, to widen tunnels, to open new veins.

He knew it though he had never seen it done.

Half a case, from the partially empty box of fifty he found open.

"Twenty-five," he muttered into the mask mic.

"Twenty-five," Jaron repeated, jotting the number down next to the location from where they were taken, not expecting Scarecrow to hear him. As Scarecrow traveled to his next target, it was up to Jaron to alter the Archive records on the second Echo Zara had set up for his use. It was best the data was altered immediately rather than wait for his next shift. They could not allow any current shift worker the chance to notice a divergence in the inventory.

The electronic feedback created by his speech unit interfacing with the Echo's mic pickup squealed and Scarecrow winced. Jaron could not see it, but he heard the sharp intake of air on the other end of the comm line. He began to apologize but quickly swallowed the intended thoughts so as not to repeat that feedback loop.

The second location, in a similarly deserted stretch of the city, yielded a full case, each stash of freezes then stored in locations where Scarecrow or Enoch would be able to retrieve them, where no one else would be likely to find them. He could not carry so many. If the night's efforts went as planned, there would be too many on hand, and the potential of any one of them breaking and setting off a chain reaction while being jostled about in his pack, should he get drawn into an altercation, was a frightening risk to consider.

How Enoch was going to get all of them into the Core was a problem for the dwarf to solve. Scarecrow was doing his part by retrieving them. He presumed the dwarf had his own plan or would ask for advice or help if he did not.

The third location, however, was empty, the facility cleared of inventory sometime after Jaron's Archive assessment. Jaron frowned, and quickly found his way through the Archive database to locate where the stockpile might have been moved to. Perhaps it was moved for a recount, perhaps to prepare this storage unit for some other product, or perhaps someone else had either purchased the entire lot or had stolen them.

Fortunately, they had been moved to, combined with, the final address on Jaron's roster.

"I'll get it." Scarecrow was unconcerned about Jaron's apologetic misstep. Owners and manufacturers moved inventory all the time, and not always with the required permit or Archive notification submitted as required. Such filing of digital datasheets had grown especially lax with the absence of the Doctet demanding detailed accountings of everything. It had been many hours since Jaron had located the best, most accessible targets. The unexpected happened. It was not a setback, rather a hastening to the final storage unit.

Saving time should work in their favor.

What Scarecrow did worry about was the descent to Lev 1 and the emergence above a four-way intersection near the fisheries...an intersection, when looking at it in person instead of as an Echo-generated three-dimensional map, that made his heart hammer and his palms sweat within his gloves.

He had been here before.

The memory of where and when spiked his adrenalin so that, as he backed away from the view until the small of his back was pressed against the hatchery rail, his breathing came fast and hard. Gloved hands squeezed the rail on either side of his body as if to prevent him from falling, or, Scarecrow thought bitterly, to keep himself upright.

Not knowing what was happening as he listened to the identifiable sound of impending hyperventilation, Jaron's face bled white.

"Hey..." Zara's voice, unmodulated by Jaron's digital speech unit, did not create a squeal of interference inside Scarecrow's hood. She heard the same sound Jaron did, and as panic was an aberrant sound to hear from her friend, she, like Jaron, was concerned.

"Nothing."

"Doesn't sound like nothing." She did not press, however, knowing this was not the time for a conversation. Despite the insistent look on Jaron's face, she murmured, "If you want out..."

"No."

She nodded, though he could not see it, and said, "Let me know when you're ready."

Left with the decision to continue, to face the unknown that was swelling his apprehension to monstrous proportions, Scarecrow squeezed his eyes shut behind the protective lenses of his mask, peeled his grip from the rails and balled his fists, and forced the focus of his senses outward, away from himself, into the misty, swirling air. Sounds were muffled here, masked by the Four Falls roar and the rushing of the river, but small adjustments to his systems, automatic regulation that happened without his doing anything, tuned his hearing further until the water sounds were but an underblanket of white noise. Anything else, anything closer, anything out of place, was what he sought when he opened his eyes and faced the short set of four steps to his left that led up to an adequate-sized storage unit. An identical one was similarly raised to his right, with a catwalk and lift and pulley system beyond it used to reel in adult fish, fry nets, and buckets of worm meal used to feed hungry spawners in the river boxes.

Steps slow as though his boots were pulling against something thick and viscous, he climbed the steps and watched with disconnected fascination as he ran the passcard over the lock. Again it beeped, again Zara hacked her magic to allow the card to fool the electronic system, and again a latch clicked free.

He did not remember that sort of sound from before. It did not exist in his memory. But with the door pulled open, he remembered this place…even though it was now full to the ceiling with containers of freezes, so full that entering the room was impossible.

"This shouldn't be here…" The unit should be empty. Would have been empty of everything except Rhyd at the time Jaron had accessed the inventory records, and so it seemed the records had been altered, or not updated, in order to mask the real use, the previous use, of the room. From the rails running across the ceiling, if it contained anything at all, it should only contain the carcasses of meat beasts.

Not a previous stash of carbidi. Not relocated containers of freezes. Not this close to the river.

For a moment too long he stared, grappling with the confusion of the unexpected and the panicky weight of recollections he had

successfully repressed for the past several hours. By the time he reached to remove one case of freezes, knowing there would be no time to open one and remove just a few to suggest a small inventory miscount, he heard footsteps echoing on the walk nearby.

There was nowhere to go. Nowhere above within easy reach to leap to unless he left the case of freezes behind. Nowhere below but the river, as he could not make it the few steps required to leap into the intersection below without being seen by whoever was coming through the mist. The open door of the storage was behind him, not in a position to hide behind. His primary instinct was to fight, as a single opponent would be no obstacle for a man of his skill and training, but the instinct that undercut the primary one was one of self-preservation birthed from the remembrances of buzzers and thumpers, pain and hunger and thirst, darkness and the saltbitter of blood. It was that secondary instinct that made him crouch, waiting for the footsteps to bring the torment he anticipated.

It was impossible for those listening several Levs above not to hear the distress in his breathing. The suit's oxygen and filt unit was struggling to balance his panic and provide him with an even flow of air. With his cam system inactive, as there had been no need for them to see any of what he saw, they could not guess what was happening.

It did not sound like a fight, at least not a physical one with an external opponent. Zara gestured for Jaron to remain quiet as she hacked the city's systems first, and then punched in her own Echo's code. Nothing she could say would help. She did not think Rhyd would listen to her. But she believed she could help in other ways, by connecting him to someone whose voice mattered in a different way.

She had seen it when they parted. Jaron mattered. Maybe something Jaron could say would help Rhyd now.

The filt vents nearest Scarecrow's location belched excessive steam into the cold, already river-misty air, obscuring Scarecrow's squatted, cowed position at the storage door. A lifetime of training with the rightness of such systems registered that something was

different, something was off, but his ears also detected the pause of those approaching steps on the half-Lev stairs in the intersection.

They had not, it seemed, been coming for him but their pause in that precarious place was still troublesome and the realization did not dispel the horror-bloom in his chest.

Zara gestured again to Jaron, this time urging him to speak.

Avoiding a name as Zara had done, understanding the danger in that if anyone happened to be listening through their own hacked Echo and ICD lines, he murmured, "We're here. Tell us what we can do."

Scarecrow shivered at that voice in his ear, a voice that sounded for the first time, less digital and mechanical than before, without the wail of feedback behind it. The gentleness of tone, burdened with worry though it was, made Scarecrow's breath catch, and though his pulse still raced, the pressure of it began to ease, no longer the out of control hammering it had been moments before.

"Okay. It's okay. Should we come to you? Do you need backup?"

"No!" If the threat returned, Jaron would be in danger. Scarecrow would not allow that, no matter how distressed he was.

The continuing retreat of the footsteps drew his surging pulse and rapid breathing down further, but only a little, until he was able to assess that the steps bore the specialized grips of fisher boots and that the unbalanced whine of the filt systems around him had changed again, once more sounding normal to his ears.

Those dwindling sounds, the return to normality of the river's rumble and his own breathing's gradual return to a regular rhythm, as well as the realization that Jaron would willingly risk himself to come here, to his aid, against an unidentified threat, against a memory in his head, could no longer hurt him as the physical torture had.

Being afraid of a memory made him angry at himself, just as the dreams of Venn's Vanishing did. He had endured torture, for crucksake, had come out of the dark side of it with his life, his determination to fight for Hebenon intact. What was this foolishness that caused him to hide like a coward from his own mind?

He grunted, embarrassment and shame bleeding into the sound as he stood, pushed the case of freezes to the side with his foot and closed the storage door as quietly as he could. The mist had grown thinner. The voices of fishermen could be heard on the catwalk across the river, coming his way.

It was time to move.

"Z…you know what to do. I've got it from here. And you…go home…before he asks questions."

Jaron knew Scarecrow was talking to him, but he did not specify which destination he considered to be home. He might mean home to Oliver, but Jaron chose the answer that best suited him. The excuse of a late shift was all he would need to explain a stay in his Lev flat. Oliver would never think otherwise.

"What about…you okay?"

"Get this where it belongs…then call it a night." It would take him an hour or more to move the freezes into safekeeping for Enoch, and along the way, if he found some unfortunate roaming brako on whom he could vent his personal outrage, it might be later still. For tonight, Zara and Jaron had done enough.

Scarecrow did not want to face either of them until he no longer had the protective mask to hide behind. By then, he hoped this incident would have been shelved in favor of other business.

He did not want to talk about his ghosts.

❧Chapter 27❧

Four days.

Not much time in the scheme of a life, a life in which he wanted to do so much more. Not that he had ever made grand plans or long term goals. His upbringing on the street, amongst tingers and addicts, bouncing between caregivers and herpa until he learned to survive on his own, had made each day its own experience, its own goal.

Survive each one. That had been all that mattered.

When his persuasion skills, gained at the feet of herpa and Talkers alike, from charlatans and cons and grifters throughout Hebenon's underbelly, gave him his first taste of something better, enough ticks legitimately earned through his partnership with Zara and a rescued, repurposed andi dancer, to get a flat of their own, there had been nowhere to go but up.

Skelter had the skill to stay off the streets by then. He had the skill to make the most of living there, to appease those with needs for items and services that could not be gained through official channels. He had helped others just as he had helped himself.

He had thrived.

To end up here, in the Core, was not the end he had envisioned.

He had never considered his end, he realized as he met the passing sharp gazes of suspicion with his own cool, level, dangerous one.

Perhaps if he had not gotten involved with the Spades, things would be different. But the Club was a tool, a means to an end, to power, prestige and the manipulation of resources in this shadow world. To get ahead, to survive, it had been a crucial risk.

With any risk came rules. The Club had them too. His run had been long, carefully crafted. It had been a good one. Now he would have to pay for it.

If he did not escape the Core first.

The retreating echoing squeal of wheels on stone, as Enoch retreated once more through the passage, filled the room, bringing faces to the doorway, curious, and Skelter was certain, suspicious of his motives and actions.

Four days. He still had time. The daggerous glances were threats, warnings of what was ahead if he did not uphold the promised push to freedom. But with the collection of freezes now growing near the door, wheeled in on a tiny flat wagon in three trips thus far, freedom looked to be more of a certain reality, and so his co-prisoners continued giving him the benefit of the doubt.

"What are those for?" grunted a twisted, patchy skinned fellow with missing teeth and hair who might have been ancient or might have been younger than Skelter. Whatever the causes of his condition, it was not contagious, but it was enough that most in this place gave him a wide berth as if they too might suffer if they got too close.

"For this." With Otta hovering over his shoulder, daring any one of those who pushed into the room to cluster around Skelter's desk to make an attempt on his life, he did not fear for his welfare as he spread the drawing for the others to see. Of those squeezing in around him, many were fellow Spades, each biding their time, each willing to do what the Club demanded if Skelter failed to keep his bargain.

Four days. Freedom…or death by his own hand.

Or someone else's if he did not follow through.

"This is the door. This is the Factory underground." Skelter pointed to the specified places on the hand-drawn map Jaron had made, delivered by Enoch earlier. "This one's chained, but we can bust it with the picks and cutters. But we need the freezes in place here, at the hinges, at the center here, where the lock is…"

"Pick and drill holes…bang 'em out…shove the freezes in and…"

"We blow the fotz clean off," someone else exclaimed after the first interruption.

"Bozhe moy…we can do this?"

"Where'd you get the map?"

"You sure the freezes are good?"

Otta growled at the bombardment of questions. "Of course they're good…they're freezes." They could be fakes, but one could tell if a freeze had expired, and if Enoch trusted the outside sources, if Skelter trusted them, so did she.

"There's gonna be people out there," Skelter continued, ignoring the questions about sources and the validity of supplies. No answer he could give was going to satisfy them, as few would have heard of Scarecrow. He would be surprised if any more than two or three knew the name. "Workers, families, kids, and staff. We don't want them caught in this if we wanna live. When we bust through, hell, once we start banging on that door, it's gonna draw attention, bring the Crows."

He chose the old term because it was the word those in the Core knew, but how they could be expected to know the Crows no longer looked like Crows, who was friendly and who was not, would be a precarious thing.

If he was lucky, his and Ballard's plan would keep it from being a moot one.

"We keep aggressions on the Crows…and we force them to let us live," said Colyx from the back of the crowd near the door. "We mix in with the workers…we got a shot at real life."

Better food, better conditions, better supplies, benefits, and care. Undoubtedly some were hoping to press their advantage, fight their way back into the bowels of Hebanthe Falls and the lives they had once lived, but most, Skelter believed, would be satisfied just to escape the barrenness of the Core.

"What about this way?"

It was the first time most had seen, or become aware of, Enoch's route in and out of the Core, so the question was not a surprise. "No one fits but him," said Otta.

"The kids might," someone countered. There were few children inside, most sentenced here had been sterilized to prevent uncontrolled population growth in an area of limited resources. The eight that were here were all the results of pregnancies already in progress when their mothers had been sentenced to the Core.

The oldest was twelve.

The youngest was five.

Not one of them had a living parent any longer.

"Switz might fit…he could see to them getting out."

Appearing more thoughtful and skeptical than he felt, Skelter leaned back in his chair. He did not want to condemn the children to whatever fate the adults faced when the fight for freedom came, but he had not honestly given thought to how to ensure their survival. They had not been his priority.

Switz, while not a dwarf like Enoch, was a tiny, spidery sprite of a fellow, one of the longest surviving residents in the Core, who had survived brutes and bullies by being one of the few sentenced here with any usable medical knowledge.

He was also, Skelter knew, a man convicted of poisoning at least four wives and each of his children though he maintained his innocence to anyone who challenged him. Skelter did not trust him on the outside, but in here, the little man had been wise enough to limit his skills to those needing care…or wishing to die.

"Enoch can guide them out…and Switz can follow to keep them going, protect their backs, if he fits," Skelter finally agreed with a nod. Switz would be no use in a fight. If Skelter insisted he participate there, with everyone else, it was going to look suspicious. "We put some freezes in place…widen it a little as they go…maybe a few others will fit…"

"Or at least we seal it up to keep the Crows from gassing us." The thin-haired woman scratched her fleshy neck as others around her nodded. If the dwarf knew about the passage, someone outside might know too, and once trouble started at the door, those outside might

decide to use that passage to poison the air to knock out or kill everyone in the Core.

Her paranoid suggestion briefly made Skelter wonder why no one had considered that option before.

The squeak of metal wheels rattling on stone in the distance alerted them to Enoch's return with more freezes.

"Let's get back to work," shouted Colyx. Four days was not a lot of time to get those freezes into place. They needed to be ready if they were going to make this happen on schedule. "Jonner…you're the engineer; help us pick the best places for these things."

Jonner grinned. Older than many in the Core, he towered over the rest and had enough physical bulk to make his height intimidating.

He also had a knack for solving the mechanical problems the Core was subject to after the resources from the city outside stopped coming. His expertise made him too valuable for anyone to kill.

"Let's do this, boys!" Jonner exclaimed. He would set the men to digging stone and placing freezes while the women continued to hone the weapons they would all rely on when the fight came.

Skelter looked at Otta and nodded once. The inside distractions were in place. The others had their plan and a goal to work towards. He, Colyx and Otta had theirs, so long as Rhyd followed through.

Four days to live.

They had to make the most of it.

❧*❧

The roll of cable was added to the collection of items Tox had begun to gather into a crate near her shop door. It was thick enough, strong enough, to support the weight of several men, the sort of cable used as traveling support for each of Hebenon's lifts. The pulley unit she was working with, fabricating both a hand crank and an automatic retraction system, had come from a shed of lift parts as well. A lift box was considerably heavier than a single man, heavier than two men, used as it was to carry up to ten people at a time between Levs, or to

transport crates of goods. Tox had no doubt it would be strong enough to hold Rhyd against the river's current, so long as he had the strength to hold on to it…and as long as the locking mechanism did not fail and the cable did not snap.

She had examined the entire length and found no flaws. It was her duty to see to the structural integrity of the tools, materials, and devices Scarecrow needed. This was no different. She trusted Rhyd knew what he was doing, even if she thought him zonked. Since he had not yet laid out his plan to her, only explained what he needed to face the river, and when he needed it, she could only guess at the uses for the items she gathered…and worry about his welfare.

The river was exacting. If he failed, if her equipment did, he would drown, or be beaten to death on the river's monstrous, jagged teeth.

As she worked on collecting the pitons, and bolt-eyes, testing the filt systems in his suit and the suit itself for water and air tightness, she also aided Zara in her investigative work. Every passlock system she could find details on in the Hub, every mechanical lock they could devise, was scoured and studied in the hopes of anticipating how the Core was sealed, and how it might be unsealed. An explosion in the Core, even contained to the primary mining door, might destabilize more than the Core entrance if it was not done correctly.

And if, by a quirk of fate, they uncovered some morsel of history detailing another way in or out of the Core, another hope to save Skelter less risky then what he planned, Rhyd wanted to know.

The work would have been easier, faster, with a third pair of hands. The loss of Xiaodan was keenly felt, at home and in the work Tox did. When Maemi arrived with their middle meal, a delivery of the additional stone driver Rhyd had requested, and a bulky roll of material with which additional protective clothing could be made, the three women looked at one another with lingering sadness and renewed determination.

Scarecrow was not going into this alone, the way Xiaodan had. Each of the women was determined to help in whatever way possible, to make Xiaodan's death mean something.

Saving Skelter would not revive Xiaodan, nor avenge his death. But it was a place to start.

⤜*⤝

It was a chance worth taking.

Rafe Tamner had done as much for Rhyd as any one man could, and once, years before, Jaron had considered the man both a mentor and a friend. It had been a new relationship then, just budding into bloom as Jaron put his keen scientific mind to use in the labs, inspecting samples of soil, vegetation, and insects brought in on the hemp delivery carts or found amidst the hemp stock itself. They ran tests for toxins, for genetic abnormalities, for parasites or viruses, or changes in the genomic structure of the plants and insects that might herald either a bettering or worsening of the conditions outside.

Hebenon relied on hemp. Anything that threatened that supply, anything that might alter it, needed to be identified and understood before it became an insurmountable problem for the residents in the city. The loss of plastics, woods, oils, food, fabrics…so many products deriving from that single plant, would devastate Hebanthe Falls as surely as the river ceasing to flow would have.

The notable fact that there had been no poisons to be found in the last century or so, not in the soil, not in the moisture collected from the plant leaves, not in the plants themselves, pointed to the lie the Founder and Doctet continued to perpetuate: the outside world was uninhabitable for humankind.

The rumor persisted that those within Hebenon's protected metal borders risked certain death if they ventured beyond their walls.

Jaron's inability to accept that discrepancy, to turn a blind eye to the fallacy the city's leaders lauded over the people in the Levs, eventually led to his downfall. Despite Tamner's warnings of the pitfalls, despite repeated attempts to insist that Jaron keep his opinions, his suspicions, to himself, Jaron had acted.

Opinions, Tamner insisted. He knew better…but he had seen what had happened to his own father when such counter-claims were made too loudly.

Not opinions, countered Jaron. Scientific fact that the Founder should no longer deny.

Confrontation. Challenge. Charges of heresy, endangerment, treason. Chances offered to recant, to accept the all-knowing Founder's truth.

In the end, Jaron was robbed of the voice he used for such proclamations and was banished to the Levs with the threat of worse punishment if he ever repeated such claims.

Worse would befall him if he continued to do so.

Tamner had found him after, in the early days when his body had yet to heal from the silencing, traumatizing assault carried out not in a medical facility but in the privacy of his own home by individuals never brought to justice for it. Tamner had helped give him back his voice, of a sort, but Jaron had never been the same.

Jaron had not seen Tamner since, until chance crossed his path with Oliver's, after Hebanthe Falls was opened to the world and his work as an archivist brought him back, periodically, to the Uppers for data collection.

He and Tamner met again.

By then, however, Jaron felt he had little to say. He had been given a voice, but robbed of the will to make a difference with it. Why try if no one was willing to listen? Now the city was open, and what Jaron had tried to say was proven true, there was no need for it any longer.

The door of the lab whispered open, barely making a sound, and for a moment Jaron stared, remembering his last day in these labs, remembering the layout that had not changed, remembering the other faces who had once worked with him. Some had died of age or had been lost during the plague. Some had been promoted to other positions, other departments. Some had gone into the Levs, or Outside, in an effort to make a difference, to break down the barriers that had existed for too many generations.

But Tamner remained, his lab coat too loose around his narrow shoulders and lean frame, his hair graying at the temples but his cloth lab shoes and the steady movement of his hands as he pushed a slide into the view for inspection, were just as Jaron remembered.

He wondered, as he knocked on the wall inside the door jamb, if he would ever find the nerve, the will, to return to this place now that the Founder and Doctet no longer had a stranglehold on scientific study and advancement.

Science had been his love, his passion. Now the Archives had become a familiar, comfortable, safe home he did not know if he would ever dare to leave.

"Jaron." Surprised to see the younger man here, Tamner stood, removed the sterile gloves he wore, and crossed the room to greet him. "I'm glad you've come."

Jaron thought it sounded like he had a standing invitation to return. Maybe, with Tamner, he did. He had been uncertain of his decision to come here, to warn Tamner, as Rhyd wished him to, of trouble brewing, but now that he saw the man's friendly face, he was glad to be here. "I…nothing's changed it seems…"

"Nothing has changed…and everything," Tamner said with a chuckle. He listened to the man's augmented voice, seeking problems or imperfections that might have prompted Jaron to seek help. But the speech center sounded like it was functioning within normal parameters, with no perceptible lag between Jaron's thoughts in the conversation and the speaker's utterance of those electrical signals. Since that did not appear to be the purpose of his visit, there was only one other logical reason Tamner could think of.

"Did the Captain send you?"

"Cap…no…no, he doesn't know I'm here." There was a series of static pops and unintelligible noises emitted by the speech unit as Jaron collected his thoughts and formulated the words he wanted to say. "I'd appreciate it if he doesn't know I've been here."

"Oh?" Tamner did not know the nature of the relationship between Jaron and Grainger. It was none of his business. But he did know how

overpowering a man of Grainger's temperament could be. Even as Captain beneath Kemway's control, Grainger carried the air of a man not to be crossed.

There were many reasons why Jaron might want to keep his visit secret. But none of those were the ones he spoke.

"There's going to be…I want you to know…to keep your son safe…"

"Safe?" Scowling, Tamner sat on the stool and leaned forward, studying Jaron more closely.

"I've heard tell of…impending unrest in Factory East." He looked away, nervous and uneasy, before continuing. "I was data collecting…and heard…it might be nothing, but I think something's up…in the next few days…and I thought you might want him somewhere safe…away from there…just in case."

There was no might about it. With a potential attempt on Haythem's life being whispered about in certain circles, the timing of possible unrest could serve as an ideal cover, an ideal distraction of resources and attention, to make it easier to get access to the Founder. Tamner suspected whatever Jaron had heard was connected to that threat. He did not think Neoma or Senior Kal's influence stretched into the nearly isolated populations of the Factories, but there was still a high possibility of a connection.

Whatever Jaron had heard, if he knew anything more detailed than that, Tamner did not think the younger man would share it.

Maybe he was involved. Maybe not. But it was a warning Tamner believed should be taken seriously. For Cori's sake, if not his own.

"The Captain does not know?"

Jaron shrugged. "I dunno. I heard…but maybe he does. He hasn't talked to me about it."

Tamner took that to mean that, whatever information Jaron had, he had overheard it from one of Grainger's conversations with someone else, one of his lieutenants perhaps, as well as during a data survey. If the Captain knew of a possible threat, he had not yet seen fit to warn Tamner or anyone else. Out of the desire to reduce the sort of

panic that had led to the Uppers' evacuation into the Factories two years ago, most likely, but Tamner felt that knowledge of a threat, on his son's behalf, was better than ignorance.

He would see to the boy's welfare and then see Grainger himself.

If nothing else, they needed to get Kemway secure before whatever the cazz was on the horizon was unleashed.

❧*❧

"Didn't think you'd come," Blayd admitted when Ilya sank into the chair across from him, her uniform pristine as if she was about to go on duty. Her eyes, however, spoke of exhaustion and sadness and it made him regret the purpose for which he had asked to meet.

Not the entire purpose. After so many years of not seeing one another, crossing paths three times in a short number of days had set his mind to considering multiple possibilities with his long lost friend.

Particularly after discovering someone else in Neoma's bed.

The tea vindi's inside tables were full, off-shift workers stopping to eat on the way home or grabbing something hot to jolt them awake before their shifts began. These outside tables, however, sheltered from falling moisture and protected by mesh screening that kept out some of the mist and splattering water, were deserted. Blayd was the only one seated in the area when Ilya arrived, and it took only a glance at the crowded indoors to see why he had chosen this place.

Despite the passersby, it was private here. A better place to talk.

"I didn't think you'd be here," she admitted. A swiver came for their order and Ilya said, "Pepperhemp." The swiver looked at Blayd with his already empty cup.

"Another, same as her," Blayd said with a nod.

Ilya quirked her brow as the swiver moved away.

"I've not found a trace of her yet," he said, thinking it best to clear the business from the air and tell the bugger lieutenant what she primarily wanted to know, rather than waste time with small talk and the details of other news he wanted to share. If hearing it prompted her

to leave, better it be out in the open. "She was spotted near the bilger Shed once, and some said she'd been seen on Lev 1, but I've not been able to catch up to her or find out why she was there."

Ilya could think of a number of reasons why an aimlessly drifting girl would gravitate to Lev 1, but she did not think Ginna would be so foolish as to cozy up to the brako. Not if she held them at all responsible for Xiaodan's death or considered the mission she and the Spinks shared to be of import. But an effort to find allies against the Talkers, find some means of retaliation…that was something she could envision Ginna doing. Any alliance, for any reason, formed with the brako, however brief that alliance might be, was a dangerous thing for a young woman of Ginna's limited experience.

"I'm still looking," he swore in reply to the shadow that crossed her face. "I'll bring her back when I find her. You have my word."

"Thanks." At least knowing Ginna had been seen on Lev 1 gave Ilya a place to begin, a place to concentrate the bugorra's efforts.

Hanging around outside the bilger shed was inconsequential. Streeters often loitered around the sheds at shift change, tinging, hoping for handouts from workers with leftover meals or a few spare ticks or treasures found in the shafts.

Their tea arrived, along with the requisite tray of sweeteners, flavor additives, creams and tea cakes typically offered in vindis like this. Ilya wrapped her hands around the cup, treasuring the warmth, and dared to look at Blayd across the table when she was sure he was not looking at her.

Though the years had matured him, and his shaved, patterned hairstyle marked the nature of his employment for all to see, she could still see the boy she had grown up with. The scar above his right eye was still visible. He had always sworn he would get it tended one day, removed from the world's eyes to make his face the visible portrait of perfection the vain boy had wanted it to be.

He chuckled now when he noticed the direction of her gaze and traced his fingers over the remains of the gash gained in a childhood

fight…the first time Ilya had beaten him in a wrestling match and the last time they had fought in any sort of physical fashion.

It had all been in childish play, but evidence that he had been beaten by a girl had been a difficult thing for him to stomach as a kid.

Now he merely shrugged. "It bound us."

"Kept it to remember me by?" That seemed both silly and endearing and she laughed.

"That," he grinned, "And it reminds me I'm not immortal, reminds me to be on my guard. Adds to my mystique. I decided the reminder not to be so damn arrogant was a good thing."

"We need those reminders." She accepted the crispy tea cake he offered as a pair of boys, gym packs slung over their shoulder, strutted past, shoving and playfully punching one another the way he and Ilya had once done together. One crashed into the vindi's mesh wall and when Blayd snarled at them, the youngster sneered back and made a rude gesture. The other, however, noting Ilya's uniform, grabbed his friend by the arm and dragged him away with a rueful expression.

"Hard to believe we were like that once."

Ilya shook her head. "You were like that. I was…"

"The good girl, the studious student, the focused fitness nut," he agreed, taking no offense at her insinuations. They were true. He had been a troublemaker then, and some would argue he still was. She had kept him out of trouble as often as he had gotten her into it.

"That's what made me bring this to you…because someone has to know what I heard…and I don't know who else to tell."

Elbows on the table, teacup between her hands, she bid him continue without speaking.

"Something's up with the Founder. I keep hearing whispers of assassination…" He did not know how else to put it.

"Assassination? By who?" Such a brazen act would be extreme for anyone, but she was aware that there were people throughout the city who fostered the sort of hatred that could fuel an attempt.

Scarecrow was chief among them.

"I dunno. I've heard rumors. Guess Captain Grainger's aware of it, and Senior Kal, but they're keeping whatever they know hushed. Dunno anything beyond that…but Mam wants me in the loop, wants me to protect him…so I thought I should talk to you."

Frowning, Ilya shook her head. "No one's getting in there." Until recently, she, like the rest of Hebenon, had not known the Founder was alive. She had no idea where he was, although she was aware of a number of places throughout the city, in the Uppers and in the Levs, which were off-limits to anyone without proper clearance. Any one of those, particularly the locations in the Uppers, could serve as a secure shelter for the Founder…and for any number of other secrets.

It had never occurred to her until the news came out that the Founder lived, that Captain Grainger had secrets. She supposed anyone in power did.

"You know where he is then?"

She shook her head again. "No." But perhaps it was time for her to find out, either by confronting the Captain or through other means.

The rest of the bugorra respected her. If any one of them were guarding the deposed Founder, surely she could pry that information out of them.

At the very least she needed to prepare her officers for a worst-case scenario…another possible assault on the Uppers by people looking for the Founder.

"Will you let me know? Mam is beside herself; she just got him back. She believes Senior Kal is the threat, and I know he had a meeting with the Captain recently…but who knows? She wants him safe, wants to be sure everything is being done to protect him, and the Captain won't tell her anything."

To his knowledge, Neoma had not confronted the Captain with her concerns, but Ilya likely did not know that. Whatever future he might flirt with, with his old friend, he was not above using her to learn things that could buy him favor with Neoma.

"Let me ask around." She glanced at her ICD and finished her tea before rising. "I'll let you know." She reached for his hand across the

table and squeezed it in a friendly manner. "It's good to see you up and about, Blayd. Glad you're doing better. You take care, okay?"

"Of course," he promised with a grin, accepting her words at face value without reading anything into them or detracting from them.

She would not promise him details she might not be able to learn, nor offer information Grainger deemed too sensitive for public release. But if there was a threat to the Founder's life, she would do everything in her power to protect him.

Whether she agreed with the way the Founder and Doctet had managed Hebanthe Falls, whether she approved of the painful but necessary changes being birthed since the Coup, Kemway was still the Founder, still part of the blood-lineage that had saved humanity from certain extinction.

He deserved to be protected for that reason alone.

❧*❧

"Promise me something."

Dinner had been awkward, the silence between them thankfully filled by the splattering of rain on the thatched rooftop and Agnys' determined attempts to tell Rhyd everything that had happened in Marbordo since his last visit. It did not foster interaction between the two men who seemed unable to look at one another, but it filled the deafening, wordless void. All of the efforts Rhyd had made to find Venn, save him from a then-unknown fate, to find answers, had been eroded by time, differences, and life choices that neither could have foreseen. There was fondness still, but they were unable to get past the damage those dark years had inflicted.

Agnys could see it, though she did not understand it. She had not known who they were before.

Rhyd could see it, despite his efforts to feign blind ignorance.

And Venn, stubbornly clinging to what had been before his addiction, intent on reviving that past, could see it too. He simply chose not to believe what he saw.

The meal was over and Rhyd had things to do, streets to patrol, residual supplies to gather, people to speak to, so that everything was in place when the moment came for action. Despite the uncomfortable tension, despite Jaron's stubborn insistence on pushing into Rhyd's head when he least wanted him there, Rhyd had needed to come here, to make certain Venn was safe. To see him for what might be the last time, if the days ahead proved a failure. It would not do to rescue Skelter only to lose Venn in a possible upheaval of violence that could spill out of the factory.

Venn watched him with a bitter sheen over his eyes as the blonde stared at the clouds roiling across the sky through the open door. Such rain was typical in the spring, Rhyd had been told, although the possibility of it did not bother him. He was used to the wet. Venn and the villagers, however, were less pleased, but at least the air was warm with the promise of spring many were eager to see. Venn had endured enough of being cold and wet. He wanted the sun's return.

He wished Rhyd felt the same.

"Your recital?"

"You'll be there."

It was a demand more than a question, a demand that made Rhyd bristle, and he did not look at Venn when he spoke again. "When it's over, return to Marbordo, straight away. Don't dally in Hebenon. It won't be safe."

"Won't be…why?"

"Just promise me."

"What are you going to do?"

"Told you." Rhyd's fingers flexed and twitched, seeking a whiskey bottle he did not have. "I'm getting Skelter out of the Core."

"There's no…"

"There is."

"Why then? Why the night of…?"

"Because if not then, he'll be out of time. Spades are gonna take him down if I don't get him out. Things won't be in place to get to him any sooner."

Venn frowned. Agnys had gone home, no longer a buffer between them, and he wished she was still there. He did not believe in the Club of Spades any more than he believed in the Core, but Rhyd clearly did. An etched metal disk proved nothing. Whatever other questionable proof Rhyd was acting on, whatever he intended to do, he seemed determined to drag Hebenon into chaos again.

A man once prone to silently sitting in the background while Venn soaked up the light of publicity and popularity, Rhyd had grown into something much different. No longer quite so silent, no longer quite so hidden, no longer prone to allowing injustice to march along its cruel path around him as he went about his day to day business.

Mon dio, Venn wished it was not so.

"Skelter will get by; he always does." Venn was not sure he believed their friend was alive. How could he be after the fall Tox, Maemi, Zara and Lash had reported? He was surely two-year's dead and someone was manipulating Rhyd with false hope for some other end. "Be there, Rhyd. I mean it. Or don't come back."

He had made that ultimatum once, and still Rhyd was here. Both men had hoped that his coming here would mean a reversal of all that had gone wrong between them.

Both men now thought differently.

Coming here, coming back to Marbordo, had been a mistake.

"Promise me, Venn."

Bitter with resentment, taking those words as proof that Rhyd would ignore the demand and do whatever he believed he had to do elsewhere, not knowing for certain what danger either of them would face if he stayed in the Uppers' halls once the recital ended, Venn nodded with a single grunt. He did not have a death wish, not the way Rhyd seemed to. If there was even the smallest chance he would be in danger, Venn was not going to loiter to find out just to spite Rhyd.

Rhyd did not watch him retreat into the house and chose to believe that Venn would do as he asked. Venn longed for safety and security. Rhyd could not offer him that.

Rhyd did not belong here, in this open world that fed him an unlimited diet of anxiety. Hebenon, with its darkness, its misty moist air, its congested crowded layers of narrow metal arteries and the perpetual hum of filt systems, was his home. Whatever his future held, Hebenon was the place where he would draw his final breath.

&Chapter 28&

Is it true then? Have there been threats against Founder Kemway?" Ilya had come into the Captain's office for answers, for clarification of the threat level the city was facing, but a constant flow of interruptions left her standing in the background, invisible, as Grainger dealt with one intrusion after another. Requisition requests to the textile manager received from Doctor Tamner, the manager wanting clarification before the rush order was pushed through in lieu of the day's normal manufacturing quota. A jani's response to Grainger's inquiry regarding the whereabouts of Jaron, whom the Captain had not seen in too many hours causing concern that some ill fate had befallen the younger man since his last shift.

There was a reported theft of freezes, suspected to be at the hands of streeters known to covet the carbidi tubes to quickly cool drinks, keep stolen food fresh, or to use the misty byproduct they produced when evaporating as a screen to hide behind. Another intrusion had just left, a member of Doctor Tamner's staff who had witnessed the doctor taking his son into Marbordo in the midst of a display of lightning, rain and wind, the likes of which few in Hebenon had ever seen. When he returned without the child, the fellow was concerned that some harm had befallen the boy or that something was amiss that Tamner knew about but was not reporting if he was willing to risk his child to the unknown dangers the storm presented.

Assuming Doctor Tamner, of all the citizens in Hebenon, would be aware of the Founder's location and well-being, Ilya jumped to the same conclusion, even though she also knew that the doctor would never willingly place his only child in the path of danger.

Something was amiss. Why else would a sane man leave a child with parah barbarians in the middle of a dangerous storm?

Just a storm, Grainger said. Water, air, electricity. Inside the Marbordo houses, the boy was safe. Tamner had long ago built a solid relationship with the parah. Grainger did not know them, had not been outside of the city himself, but Tamner was no fool. If he trusted his son with the parah, Grainger saw no cause for concern. Tamner had left his son among them before. This time was no different.

And no, nothing inside of Hebanthe Falls required public concern.

The Captain's words of reassurance might have placated the lab tech, but they did not satisfy Ilya.

Grainger looked at her with a raised brow, grating at the sort of disrespectful manner and tone unbefitting his top lieutenant.

"The Founder is safe, I assure you."

"Then why move him? I've heard talk, rumors, that the Voices wish to…"

"Wish to what?" He should have bid her leave the room when the interruptions began rather than allow her to overhear the concerns of his stream of visitors.

"Abduct him. Kill him."

Attempting to dismiss her concern, he grunted, "The Kemways are gods to the Voices. That's ridiculous."

"Gods…but men…and sometimes it's better for religion when the gods die," she muttered. "Senior Kal is no fool. If he can get his hand on the Founder…manipulate him…or kill him and blame someone else…you…or us…" she corrected quickly to avoid appearing as if she held the Captain responsible for anything, "of course he'll do it."

"You don't have much faith in the Talkers, do you, Lieutenant?" Sitting behind his desk, leaning back in his chair after a brief glance at the ever-changing display of rain art forming and then running across the window glass, Grainger studied her silently. "What have you heard?" She was smart. Quick on her feet and with her thoughts. Refuting rumors she might have heard, refuting her assessment of what had been discussed in this room previously, was to devalue her

judgment and abilities. He had kept her out of the Kemway loop to control who knew about the Founder, to prevent her from needing to keep secrets from the officers she directed, officers who trusted her and her command.

He knew how he would have felt, had felt, when the Founder had treated him as incapable, untrustworthy, inconsequential. She was the one person on his staff he should, perhaps, have trusted.

"Only that there's to be an attempt. Word on the street, various sources…" She did not want to give him Blayd's name so as not to unnecessarily point fingers. "People seem to think…the Voices think Mam Kemway intends to take him…and they plan to stop her…"

Neoma's hand in any of this, in spreading rumors or otherwise, came as no surprise to Grainger. The woman who had stood silently in the background of Hebanthe Falls' leadership all of her adult life was not the sort to waste an opportunity to assert power if she saw an opening. She was too smart, too ambitious and resourceful, for that. "Let us argue, if it was true, what would you suggest?"

"Move him somewhere safe."

"You think he's not safe now?"

"I didn't…"

"How do we move him without securing a route, without marking off corridors and alerting others that something's about to happen? Announcing where he will be when, and where he's being taken?"

Ilya briefly pondered the question, wondering what she would do if she was in the Captain's position. "Implement a distraction."

"What sort of distraction?" He had ideas of his own, but had not yet settled on one and was interested to hear what she would say.

"I…don't know, sir." Her first thought was to employ her officers on some sort of Lev crackdown, picking up streeters, Heb addicts, suspected brako. Everyone's attention would be drawn to the Levs. But that was the sort of tactic the Founder had employed, and doing so would create distrust and a logistical issue of processing all of those they arrested without suitable cause.

The possibility that the action would create another riot like the Coup was high.

"Perhaps," she continued after a few moments of thought, "move him during the recital?"

Grainger nodded thoughtfully. The upcoming first orchestral recital since the Coup, comprised of musicians from the whole of Hebanthe Falls, would draw a considerable audience to one location. The music hall on the lowest tier of the Uppers would be heavily staffed with security, not to capture dissidents and criminals but to keep the peace and serve as crowd control. Keeping focus there, carefully screening anyone who intended to access any of the Uppers above that, would not be unusual.

The majority of others throughout the city would gather around Echo screens to watch what they could not see in person.

As she assumed, any movement of the Founder would be confined to the Uppers. It would mean relatively empty routes to pass through.

By limiting the knowledge of that transfer to a select few, there was little reason to anticipate interference.

"Eighteen officers. No more. I'll get you names." There were already some in the know who Grainger would trust with this duty. He trusted Ilya would know others with suitable skill and trustworthiness to round out the roster who could guard checkpoints to keep the route clear. "Take care of recital security, and I'll see to this."

It was validation of a number of points, and though Ilya felt honored to be trusted, to be included, she was also bitter that he had excluded her from something so important for so long. She might not know where the Founder was, but someone did…and that someone wanted the Founder out of the way or in their control. Waiting until the recital to move him beyond the reach of a threat seemed foolish, but moving him without a plan, without time to prepare, was too.

She would trust her Captain to make the call, however, trust he knew what the wisest course of action was.

When she knew where the Founder was, where he would be taken, she would reassure Blayd, and Mam Kemway, that he was safe.

❧*❧

"You didn't say anything about kids," Rhyd groused, his seat at the bar in Vapors warm from his extended visit since he had waited for the dwarf at the end of his shift. The message requesting a meeting had reached him mid-day, and half dreading, half anticipating, that it had come from Jaron, he made the effort to shower at the Shed, as many bilgers did at the end of their shifts, and came to the club as quickly as he was able. No one was there then, aside from the usual between-shift rabble of those come to give their ticks to the andi dancers who entertained here, to grab a quick meal so they would not have to face dining alone in empty flats, or who came to drown their troubles in liquor, hemp cigs and Hebbies sold by streeters and brako agents working the crowds inside the club and out.

Rhyd had thought opening the city to the outside would bleed the general hopelessness out of his fellow residents, ease the need for altering, numbing substances.

So far, in that respect, little had changed.

Lash and Enoch arrived together and Maemi, as if anticipating their arrival, set additional drinks and meals on the counter near Rhyd's usual place. He scowled but nodded at the woman and then at the men who joined him.

It was probably for the best that Maemi was kept in the loop. This was her vindi after all. She did not need trouble here again, and if trouble was due to follow any one of the three men at her counter, she deserved to know before it came.

Enoch shrugged as he devoured half of the mealy burger on his tray. "Hadn't given them a thought…don't think Skelt had either…but if things go the way you both plan, not really fair to punish them for being born in that posa hole. Can't send them to the door with others, in the thick of the fighting…and taking them out your way isn't…"

"Not an option," Rhyd agreed. It was already a risk bringing three adults down that line, through the river's surge. He was not going to rush the effort and try to bring terrified children down too.

"There's a guy…Switz…wouldn't trust him with my life…if I was his wife…but those kids…Skelt wants him and me to get them through my way."

"Can you?" The name Switz meant nothing to him; a possible means to an anticipated end.

Again the dwarf shrugged. "If there's time, yeah, but then what? I was supposed to be helping you, remember?"

"I'll take his place," Lash muttered over Enoch's head. Rhyd did not know if the older man knew any of the plans or not, but he wagered, from Enoch's expression, that Lash had been given the barest outline of it at least.

Enoch sucked at his drink with a scowl. "Should be both of us, two sets of hands…"

"Tox'll be there." Two people, a man and a woman, should not look suspect if anyone saw then on that catwalk extension over the river. An odd pairing, to be sure, with the age difference between them and Lash's craggy, weather-worn features next to Tox's smooth exotic ones. But they would be more likely to be judged for their choice of rendezvous locations then they were for those differences.

A hook or an andi; it would be assumed by strangers that Tox was one or the other. When it came to someone having his back, Rhyd could think of no one better. Except for Skelter.

"Think that'll be enough?"

Rhyd shrugged. As long as there was someone to manage the pulley, to reel him in if things went wrong, to draw the escapees from the river, he would make the most of whatever help was available.

"I can be there…to meet them…"

"They're not gonna trust just anyone if they make it through." Enoch pushed his empty beer glass towards Maemi, meeting her gaze as he replied to her suggestion. He trusted her, but that did not mean the kids would.

"Think I know someone." Licking his fingers of the oil remaining from the cheese curlers, Rhyd weighed the thought carefully before suggesting it. "Maemi, if you can line 'em up somewhere safe, I can get Xiao's friends in line…"

"The Spinks?" countered Lash as Maemi frowned.

"Not putting any more kids in danger," she started.

"They're out in danger every day; they know what they're doing…" Rhyd was not keen to involve children in unsafe endeavors either, but who better to gain the trust of kids than other kids?

Maemi swiped her cloth across the counter. "They're getting each other killed."

After the still stinging loss of her nephew, it was not an argument Rhyd wanted to have.

It was Enoch, assessing Rhyd's idea, who addressed the swiver's fears. "No one's risking anything. With everything else going on elsewhere, there's no reason for anyone to be here to interfere. No reason for anyone to be harmed. No one'll think twice of streeters loitering, taking shelter, and no one'll pay enough attention to more coming out then going in." The owners of the vindis near his escape passage never paid him any mind. Why should they care about streeters escaping the constantly falling water, so long as the kids did not cause trouble?

It was starting trouble that had gotten Xiaodan killed, not his living the life of a streeter.

"She'll trust you if I tell her to," Rhyd said to Enoch over his glass of Zaolei. "If I tell her you're with me." After setting the glass down, he reached for Maemi's hand across the counter. "She'll trust you because of Xiaodan."

"The one on the SCAMs? The one he…?"

Died for. The words were unsaid. Thinking them was difficult enough.

"The Spinks," he hated the term but knew of no better way to refer to the kids than by the name they had given themselves, "listen to her. If I can get to her, she'll help."

"You or…?" Enoch's twisted lips implied what he did not say.

Rhyd grunted and pushed his plate away. If Jaron was going to be here too, he was late, and Rhyd could not wait any longer. He had things to do, starting with finding Ginna.

He had few doubts the other Spinks would point the way.

*

Venn Weyer was not on the list of those Grainger expected to see in the corridors of the Uppers. Passing in the lift, on his way to or from a rehearsal, perhaps, but in this particular corridor, the cellist's presence could only mean the prelude to one thing.

An intended meeting with the Captain of Hebanthe Falls.

But Grainger did not have time to return to his office, not for what he assumed would be some sort of request for an update about Ballard or even an update on the mutual efforts to sway the Scarecrow's allegiance. Tamner had summoned him to inspect Kemway's intended new location for suitability, and with the press of time bearing down on them, Grainger did not have time for delays.

In truth, he had not heard anything since Ballard disappeared over the walkway precipice in that skirmish between street kids and Talkers, and there had been no reported sightings of Scarecrow. Grainger had been too preoccupied with other matters and he feared what that lack of news meant.

"You've got to stop him." Venn reached his side and grabbed his arm, forcing Grainger to halt.

"Stop who?" The growl in his voice prompted the cellist to release his hold, but now that he had stopped, Grainger decided he might as well spend a few moments on this exchange rather than have Venn dog him towards a destination he was not permitted to reach.

"I don't know what he's doing…but he's doing…something…he keeps going on about the Core…about a rescue…I think he's mad…"

"Who?" Grainger repeated, although it was easy enough to guess who Venn would be referring to.

"Maybe he hit his head in the fall." Rhyd had not talked to him about what had happened, but Venn had seen the multitude of injuries he had sustained. Blaming his madness on the fall, on Jaron somehow, was easier than believing that Rhyd had changed so much from the man Venn used to know.

"Ballard's alive?"

It was a relief to have confirmation, although for a moment there was a spark of question as to whether Scarecrow was the one intending to get to Kemway.

He had come for the Founder once. Perhaps, hearing the Founder was alive, Scarecrow had decided to try again. The idea was quickly dismissed, however. If Scarecrow wanted Kemway, it would not be announced as a persistent rumor scratching its fingers through the city.

Such a story could, however, be planted as a distraction from something else Scarecrow intended. Or maybe the rescue Venn alluded to was to save Kemway from the alleged threat on his life.

"Banged up pretty bad…but yeah. He's not been right since though…and I'm worried he's going to get himself killed on this imaginary nonsense about getting into the Core."

"That's not possible." Grainger started walking again, hoping to lose Venn at the lift ahead. Grainger's path would take him elsewhere, but getting Venn into that lift was his current goal.

If one dug deep enough, asked the right questions of the right people, one might prove the Core existed. But finding it would be more challenging. Generations of Kemways had seen to that, and Grainger's efforts to seal that place away while the city settled had, he hoped, put the matter to rest.

It left the city with a shortage of salt and other things, but other means of supplying those necessities were in development. That horde of criminals was one less problem Hebenon had to deal with.

Getting in or out would be impossible. Impossible enough that Grainger did not intend to think about it.

By now, most of those unfortunate souls should have starved to death. By now there was little hope of anyone surviving the sentences

that had put them there. Someday, when Hebenon's balance was restored, the mines might reopen and the truth of what filled those corridors would be revealed.

Grainger did not anticipate being alive when that day came. Whatever his legacy was twisted into when that time arrived would no longer be his concern.

Kemway's life and welfare was his priority now.

"He got up here, didn't he? When looking for me?"

Grainger's steps faltered. No one had imagined it possible for someone from the Levs to breach the Uppers defenses and safeguards, to make it all the way to the Founder's suite, to be as near to killing the Founder as Scarecrow had been. Ballard was determined, resourceful, and potentially ruthless when he needed to be.

Like Grainger himself.

If anyone could find the Core, find a way in, it would be Ballard.

But there was no logical reason for anyone to want to get in there. A man fighting on behalf of the people was unlikely to make an effort to free criminals.

To satisfy his budding curiosity, Grainger decided he would review the available records for those last sentenced there. Maybe there was a link. Maybe someone was there wrongly, someone Ballard knew. But it would have to wait until the Founder was settled.

"Tell him to talk to me."

The lift at the end of the corridor opened and a hand reached through to hold the door as others, staff and residents of this level, exited. Blue eyes caught Grainger's across the distance.

Oliver's breath released in a long, slow hiss of relief.

"He won't listen to me," Venn grumbled. "He'll deny everything." His plea, the words loudly spoken, were uttered without heed for those approaching from the lift, loud enough that Jaron could hear everything he said.

"Then what do you expect me to do?"

"Stop him."

"Stop him how?" He saw the lift try to close, but Jaron's hand remained in place as he continued to watch, to listen. Thinking Jaron was waiting for him, wanting to know where the man had been these past several hours, Grainger was in a hurry to end this conversation.

Venn's gaze faltered and his voice cracked. "By any means necessary. Hebenon has suffered enough. He's suffered enough. He needs to stop…to be stopped. You're the only one who can do that."

Not waiting for confirmation, burdened by the guilt of what he asked, knowing how his plea sounded but believing that any means necessary did not include Rhyd's death, Venn turned towards the lift where his eyes locked with the man waiting there and he scowled. He turned again, this time away from the lift, and hurried down the corridor without looking back. Grainger was an honorable man. He would never go as far as to kill Rhyd.

Venn refused to believe he would.

Jaron was not so sure that 'by any means' would keep Rhyd safe, even from Oliver. His hand dropped and the door slid closed before Oliver moved. If the Captain had any inkling of what was sparking between Jaron and Rhyd, he just might give in to the unthinkable.

Grainger shrugged, assumed Jaron had grown tired of waiting, and resumed his previous course down one of the side corridors. He had no intention of killing anyone. Like this business with Ballard and the Core, Jaron would have to wait until later.

❧*❧

Blayd perused the cluster of uniforms on the table, hoping there would be enough. Affirmation of the Founder's location was all that was needed to spark a plan that would, he believed, accomplish everything he intended. Like Neoma, he believed that no show of good faith would be accepted by Senior Kal and his staff of Talkers, and that any request of the Voices to protect the Founder on Neoma's behalf would be met with suspicion and distrust.

Rightly so. The Senior was no fool…at least not that much of one. He would know that the Mam had no people of her own to send to protect and retrieve her husband, and he would know that, after her recent accusations of treason, she would never trust Kal to keep the Founder safe, or to return her husband to her.

Logically, unless Captain Grainger intended to do away with the Founder himself, or already had, Kemway was safer where he was than in the hands of the Voices. Probably safer, Blayd assumed, then in his wife's care. The Founder had become a pawn in everyone's political gambit for power. Whether he lived or died was likely of little consequence so long as he could further someone else's aim.

Kal and his Talkers were not going to act. But with a target in hand, there was nothing to keep Blayd from doing so.

Everyone who doubted him was about to be proven wrong.

❧*❧

With the dwarf sent on an errand by the man organizing their escape efforts, it fell to Switz to be the one to place freezes into every crack and crevice in the dwarf's tunnel. The diode implanted in each would burst the thin outer shell when remotely triggered, and the sequence thereafter would cause the explosion of the contained chemicals, resulting in the fracturing of suddenly frozen brittle rock. There were enough freezes available, though most were being used at the main Core door, to widen the tunnel…or collapse it.

Closing it behind Switz, once he followed Enoch and the children to safety, seemed a wise choice. Anyone potentially trapped behind the collapse, should the effort at the main door fail, would be entombed in the Core forever.

But at least the children would live. Switz too.

Switz had to give Skelter credit for that much.

If he had known where this tunnel was before, had given any thought to how the dwarf got in and out of the Core, Switz might have taken advantage of it and left this place a long time ago. But he did not

have the nerve to take on Colyx or Otta to get into this room, not when poisoning them would have been suspect. Truth was, here in the Core, Switz meant something. He was someone. Out there in the Levs, he was nobody. He would be forced into a streeter's life and would probably not live long.

In the Core, he could survive.

He wondered what he would do when they abandoned the Core en masse…and that was why he refused to consider escaping now. He would never work again, not with his record, but maybe everyone would have forgotten his face, his name. Maybe he could find a supportive patron willing to keep him alive in exchange for his unique set of skills. It was the only chance he had.

So long as he did not blow himself up during the escape.

The drilling and pounding at the main door continued around the clock, preventing those who wanted to sleep from doing so. Sound carried far in the mines, even from the central room. This close to the concept of freedom that had not been in their reach for two or more years, many had little interest in sleep. The last of those sentenced here had come in weeks before the mythical Coup, most had been here considerably longer, some as long as thirty years. The promised taste of freedom was all they could think about, the only topic of discussion, as those capable of it prepared the stone around the door, and the short corridor between it and the primary room, for the implantation of the freezes being rigged for detonation in two phases.

Jonner took advantage of the natural fissures in the stone for the placement of freezes. He knew the weakest points, the points of stress, the places where more force would need to be applied to produce the needed results, and he set those around him to work accordingly. First, the door would blow, allowing everyone to pass into the promised reaches of the Factory Underground, and afterward, when the Core was empty, the collapse of the corridor itself.

It was their intention that, once free, they would never set foot in these mines again.

Hebenon had abandoned them, was living without what the mines offered; they would not need the mines after the workforce was free.

Those who could not dig with pick and hammer and drill continued to gather anything that could be used as a weapon, and making weapons from things not intended to be one. Molcocs were made from liquor bottles, grenners from clay pots filled with mined stones and anything that would not dissolve in the flammable liquids poured in around it. Metal plates and trays with sharpened edges were stacked for throwing, spoons and ladles likewise honed, and every bit of clothing they had was gathered to be worn in thick layers by those at the forefront of the fight for freedom. Dining plates, trays, and metal bits taken from abandoned mining carts were sewn between their layers, forming the only sort of armor and protection they would have.

The burn of buzzers would be stifled by the layers, stingers would find it difficult to penetrate to skin, the bite of popper pellets would be softened by the padding, and while the crash of thumpers would still hurt and bludgeon them down, so much thickness would weaken their effectiveness too. Smeared with salve and cooking grease they would be slippery to grab, although the risk of the buzzers, or someone's ill-placed torch, or the sparks thrown by metal against metal, metal against stone, setting someone ablaze was there. It was a risk many were willing to take, a price they were willing to pay for freedom. It might not be enough, but it was better than no protection at all.

The doors were thick. The rock thicker. Some of the factory workers, new to the creaks and groans that sometimes echoed through the underfactory, spoke of subterranean demons, of monsters clawing out of the earth, great mutations from the time centuries past when mankind had made the world outside unlivable. Others spoke of collapse, of the potential that their home, and the factory above, would fall around them and crush them…prompting many to take their families upward, to crowd into the disused corners where old equipment waited for repair, repurposing, or discard, where goods made waited for distribution into the city. Makeshift roofs and walls

were fashioned from bedding, from crates and pallets and reorganized factory equipment.

The factory floor and the catwalks surrounding each layer of the great machines quickly filled. There was little privacy to be had, and an ever-present whirr and clunk and chatter of machinery meant not a moment's peace, but it was better than the rumored looming possibility of death.

And still, people came.

Safety was their primary concern, and the reports made by supervisory staff over the linking Hub-Echosys were met with silence. None came from without to assess the day's production, the cessation of it as people scrambled and jostled in search of a safe haven, none came for a daily report or a new request for commodities.

There was no way of knowing if the messages had gone through. There was no way of knowing if help was coming, or if help was necessary. No way of knowing if they had been abandoned.

There were others who remembered before. Remembered that there had been men and women behind the sealed doors, miners, prisoners, locked away in much the same way the workers in the factory now felt they were locked away. Separated from the rest of humanity the way the Levs had been isolated from the Uppers. The Coup had opened Hebenon's doors, the doors between below and above, and the doors to the Outside that none within the Factories had ever seen. But the Coup had not opened the Factories, only enough to allow the residents of the Uppers to seek sanctuary here for a brief time before subsequently returning to the city.

The others, the workers not dead from plague, remained where they were, a workforce unable to leave.

If any still lived behind sealed doors, trapped in the black of the unlit mines, were they too seeking the opening of doors? Would the others, living or dead, take the Factory workers with them if they came through those doors?

If those doors did open, what, those who remembered wondered, would come through them? Were the spirits of the dead seeking revenge for being forgotten? Or was this something much worse?

❧*❧

With little chance of reaching Rhyd in time, no way to warn him that whatever truce he might have carried with Oliver appeared to be forfeit, Jaron, from the relatively hidden safety of the Archives eating room, sent the ICD message in the hopes that the blonde would get it in time to be protected. At this hour, Rhyd was not on shift. At this hour, Jaron imagined Scarecrow was deeply entrenched in last-minute preparations. There were only two more days, two more shifts…and one night in between…before Skelter ran out of time. Rhyd did not need the hindrance a bugorra manhunt could cause, could not risk being arrested while on shift and having his dual life exposed.

This was the only warning Jaron could give, and unable to go back, unable to face Grainger knowing the things he knew, Jaron did the only thing he could think of.

Message sent, shift over, he went to Ballard's flat and huddled, shivering like a streeter beneath a rain tarp, under the nearest set of stairs, watching anxiously for the man's return. So close to the largest of the falls, so near to the heaviest spray, it was wetter here than his own home was, colder, louder. There was nothing else to do but wait.

Expecting Oliver to look for him after that brief lift encounter, going to his own flat was not an option. Oliver did not know where he lived, had never been inside of Jaron's home, but he could easily trace him there if he wished to. Enoch had no permanent home in which Jaron could hide. Lash, too, was nowhere to be found.

Unless he hid in Vapors, there was nowhere else for Jaron to go.

❧*❧

He knew how to find her. It only took one Spink, and then another, and another, until he was directed to the young woman sheltered in an

abandoned flat in a section of the city that had been ravaged by the Coup and was yet to be repopulated. There was a cluster of squats here, small two-room affairs whose inhabitants had moved into abandoned flats previously designated for larger families. Without the Doctet to regulate the disposition of housing, and with so many casualties suffered during the violence of that uprising, those who remained took the opportunity to better their lot in any way they could, regardless of how it might impact future generations of Hebenon's residents, or those still living within the city.

Spinks and streeters, addicts and miscreants, took advantage of these empty flats when they could and no one yet seemed inclined to stop them. Why would they, when it got the unfortunates off the streets and removed them from the public eye?

"Something I need you to do."

Alone in the flat save for a scatter of younger children sleeping in huddled piles for warmth beneath ratty, stained blankets, Ginna started with surprise to see him through the gaping maw where the door had been broken off of its hinges during the Coup. She had hung a blanket there to reduce the drafts, but it did little good, and with no functioning heat or filt systems, the room was cold and damp.

She glanced at the children to make sure none had stirred, pushing down the nervousness in her belly, then ducked past the hanging blanket to join him on the catwalk outside the flat. The alglamps on the corner of the building and to the side of the doorway were broken, as were most in this cluster of abandoned flats, making this portion of path darker than most. She was more curious than afraid, excited in his presence, elated he had reached out and wanted to talk where they would not wake up the children.

He had been an acquaintance of Xiaodan. He was the Scarecrow. There was nothing for her to be afraid of.

"Anything," she promised, breathless and bright-eyed. He could even ask her to kill and she would do it, the need for action since Xiaodan's death boiling an ulcerous hole in her belly that waiting, tagging, trying to hold the Spinks together was failing to soothe.

From one of the many pockets of his long, slick coat, a plastic-coated page with a hand-drawn map on a napkin was pulled free and pressed into her hand. "Do you know where this is?"

She studied the drawing of Lev 2, pinpointing landmarks penned in there and the sheer rock wall labeled as the face of the eastern cliff before nodding her head.

"I can find that." The vindis there were unremarkable, nothing the streeters normally frequented, but any interest the Scarecrow had in them was worth noting.

"Two nights from now…I need you and the Spinks to be there. Right there." He pointed at the location he meant.

"Why?" It was not a refusal but she was curious.

Instead of answering, he continued. "There's a makeshift shelter…floor grates and canvas…you get under from this side. As early as you can. Gonna be some kids there. Eight of them…and a dwarf. Maybe another fellow. Dunno when exactly…but once they get there, take them to Vapors…to Maemi. You know her, right?"

Ginna's eyes misted as she nodded. "Yeah…" She did not know the woman directly, but she knew Vapors, and she knew the woman's relation to Xiaodan.

"If she meets you before you get to Vapors; follow her. She'll get all of you safe. You, the Spinks, the others. Don't talk to anyone; don't get detoured. They're gonna be scared, you'll have to keep calm, keep them in line…get them safe. Can you do that?"

Though she could not see the human eyes behind the black lenses of his mask, she could imagine them staring at her expectantly.

"We'll be there." She did not need to know who those kids were, where they were coming from or why. Parah maybe, though why they would come down here instead of continuing to bask in the sunlight Ginna had heard tell of, made little sense. Maybe he was getting them out of a bad home situation, out of a kids' home or a vindi that had pressed them into labor. Scarecrow wanted them welcomed, protected, and the Spinks would do precisely as he asked.

The vibrating buzz of an ICD traveled up his arm, an attempted communication he assumed from Zara or Tox or maybe even Enoch, if the dwarf had encountered some problem or change in plan he thought Rhyd needed to know about. Ginna did not hear it. Unwilling to take the time to listen in the open, he pressed a hand to Ginna's shoulder and with an added note of gravity to his artificially distorted voice, added, "Tell no one; no one can know of this. Promise me."

"I promise," she nodded solemnly.

Accepting her words, he scrambled into the shadows of the platform above them and out of sight, only the echo of his weight as he swung up and slithered away giving a hint of the direction he traveled. Ginna looked at the drawing again and began to make a plan of her own. Tomorrow, when her Spinks awoke, they would spread the word to every other Spink in Hebenon. The route between this designated location and Vapors would be littered with Spinks, guarding, keeping an eye open for trouble, assuring that she and those she chose to accompany her would not be harassed as they escorted the eight on a path to safety. Coded directions to allies would be tagged everywhere the Spinks could reach.

Scarecrow asked for their help.

The Spinks existed entirely not to let him down.

❧*⚮

Quiet in the shadows, believing himself undetectable, Jaron's heart leaped into his throat, cutting off air and the involuntary shrill squawk that accompanied the violence of being yanked from beneath the protective stairs and shoved against the exterior wall of Ballard's flat, an arm across his throat, holding him so that his toes barely touched the ground. Unable to breathe, less because of the press of that arm than the shock and terror coursing through his blood, he stared wide-eyed, uncertain for a moment who he expected to see.

Brako, perhaps. A bugorra about to accuse him of loitering or some other mischief.

But never the mask of the Scarecrow.

"What do you mean I've been betrayed?"

"I…" Not needing to breathe to form words, since the implanted speech system traveled from the electronic impulses of his brain into the speech unit modules at his temple and the hollow of his throat, the sound was muffled and distorted as it bled out around the pinning arm that covered it. "I…please…let me…"

Thankful for the mask between them, which avowed him of the demanding, angry kiss he would otherwise have forced on the terrified dark-haired man, Scarecrow listened for the span of a few thundering heartbeats for the evidence of someone near enough to see or hear them, for a rush of bugorra boots. When he heard nothing, he opened the flat door with a swipe of his hand over the passlock, pushed Jaron inside, and without turning on the lights or removing his helmet, barked "Talk," as soon as the door clattered shut behind them.

Jaron's trembling knees gave out and he sank down with his back against the door, rubbing one hand across his neck, staring at the shadow towering above him. He was not scared of Rhyd, and the rational part of his brain told him he did not need to be afraid of Scarecrow either. But the flash of adrenalin that sparked the fight or flight impulse bid him be very afraid. It was difficult to look at the Scarecrow with anything other than a fright-tinged degree of respect for the other man's anger.

"He wanted Oliver to…told him you're planning something, asked him to stop you in any way he could." His emotional state brought a flutter of crackling interference to his voice, the mirror to the shock and panic in his wide blue eyes.

"Who?"

But Rhyd already knew. Few knew of his intentions. Few knew he was planning anything. Most of those who knew were part of the plan. There was only one other person it could be.

One man who would endeavor to protect him from himself at any cost. A man whose notion of helping others was limited to donations

of clothes, a helping hand to someone in need, a home-cooked meal or the purchase of a vindi meal when the ticks could be spared.

"Venn."

When Jaron said the name at the moment Rhyd thought it, he did not even hear the other man's voice.

If he had, he might have hurled an accusation of jealousy.

"He doesn't know anything." Not the plan, not the location where Rhyd intended to work, not the nature of the effort he would make. But not knowing was not enough. Venn knew the date, and the estimated time, Rhyd intended to act. And Grainger knew Scarecrow's face. If he wanted to prevent him from some unknown, unspeakable act of vandalism, terrorism, all Grainger needed to do was come…

Here.

As if he had the same thought, or had at least considered the danger of discovery and arrest before, Jaron managed to rise to his knees and draw something from his pocket to offer to Rhyd, his arm extended as if in prayer, his expression nearly that of a man making a devout offering.

Voice tremulous with the sizzle of desire seeking an outlet, unable to look in the other man's face because he was certain Scarecrow would see that need in his eyes, Jaron whispered, "Take it. Go. No one will think to look for you there."

Rhyd did not ask where. He knew the obvious answer written in invisible bonds of something on the passcard in Jaron's hand and in the sweet quaver of his voice.

No. Grainger would not think to look for him there. In time, Venn might consider it, might inform Grainger of his suspicions if they looked and failed to find Rhyd elsewhere. By that time, however, Skelter should be free of the Core or Rhyd would have died trying. Jaron's flat was the safest place to be.

Rhyd did not want to go there, did not want to be surrounded by the sights, the memories, the smell of the man that would seep through his skin and take nest like a caterpillar in its cocoon, to be born in the spring as something else entirely. But he could not remain here either,

not tonight. Grainger might have declared Vapors off-limits to his buggers, or so Rhyd assumed since not a single on-duty bugger had been there since the Coup, but to find Rhyd, find Scarecrow, Grainger might lift that ban to look, might drag Zara into the mix, and Rhyd would not risk endangering any of the women in his life that way.

He could not take shelter with them. It was out of the question.

He could not be caught. He was not prepared to halt his plans and he would not allow anyone else to stop him.

Not just for Skelter. There were things Rhyd wanted to do still, goals he felt he had just begun to attain, scars on the world he both wanted to leave and wanted to heal. He could not do it if he remained in the light where Grainger could find him.

A day's shiftwork tomorrow would be risky enough.

Jaron understood. For this purpose, Jaron was the ally he needed.

But he did not want to be there, in the midst of the details that made up Jaron's life.

His acceptance of the passcard and a grateful exhaled breath that escaped when his gloved fingers brushed Jaron's bare ones, however, were answer enough to the choice he felt compelled to make.

"You must go back." Grinding out those words between clenched jaws created a painful stabbing in the back of his skull. He might accept the offer of shelter, but he was not staying in Jaron's company.

"I can't…he knows…"

"He knows nothing." Even if Venn harbored jealous suspicions about Rhyd's connection to Jaron, he did not know Jaron's connection to Grainger. He would have no reason to reveal anything to the Captain unless they both came here, to this flat, and failed to find Rhyd where they expected him to be…and found Jaron here instead.

Then Venn might guess.

Then Grainger might learn more about Jaron than they wanted him to know. Right now, Venn knew nothing. And neither did Grainger.

"He saw…"

"Convince him what he saw was wrong. You need to be there…to make sure those in the Factory are safe." And you need to be far away

from me if you are to stay safe too, he thought with a growl. Damn this hood. Damn the burning that pushed him to kiss the curly-haired man again. "I need you to be safe. I need…not to be distracted…if I'm to do this."

Slowly understanding, words it both hurt and thrilled him to hear, Jaron nodded and rose the rest of the way to his feet. Going back to Oliver frightened him in a different way than Rhyd did, but if going back was his way to help, Jaron would do it…until he came up with some better way to be of use.

Besides, he could not go back to the flat if Rhyd was to use it. Not if Oliver might come looking for him there. And he could not stay here in this flat. Returning to Oliver's side was the only place to go.

Returning to Oliver's bed, however, was out of the question.

❧Chapter 29❧

Scarecrow's journey through the Levs, from the flat he called home towards the haven he had been offered for the night, was punctuated by the angry poundings he doled out to one bully streeter attempting to rape another, to a man swiping an armload of nessies from a mother with two screaming children in tow, and a pair of brako trying to force a vindi owner into compliance with some illegal demand. He did not kill anyone, as it was his intention to never purposefully cause death to another, but each of those who crossed his path, and his temper, bore the brunt of the betrayal he felt.

He thought Venn knew him better than that. He thought Venn trusted him.

He thought Venn would always be supportive, or try to be.

He had, it seemed, thought wrong.

The string of those left in his wake to be hospitalized was the only testimony to the darkness he was clawing to rise above.

There were tags popping up on Hebenon's walls, fresh directives to Spinks, clues and a rally to arms that, although he did not know their color system or the codes the various symbols represented, he was assured that Ginna and the Spinks, at least, could be trusted. His ICD brought no updates from Zara, from Maemi or Tox, from Lash or Enoch, but he was not expecting any. They each had a part to play in what would soon be underway, and he assumed they were working towards that goal or else were sleeping by this late hour.

If they, too, betrayed his trust, Scarecrow was going to be forced to rethink his allegiance to the city he called home.

Thankfully, by the time he reached his destination, battered and bloodied behind the mask and body armor, his previous injuries

throbbing with overuse, the passcard he had been given opened the intended door. The emptiness of the flat proved that at least in this he could trust Jaron. It remained to be seen whether he would make it through the night without anyone finding him here.

He prayed to whatever benevolent forces existed in the universe, if there were any, that Jaron did not betray him too.

Rhyd did not think he could bear it if that happened.

Behind the security of the locked door, where he dared not turn on the lights for fear of detection by neighbors who might think he was Jaron, he dropped one piece of clothing and armor after another in a wet, weary trail from the door to the bathroom. In that room only, with no windows to give away his presence, he closed the door and turned on the light in order to inspect his reflection in the wide mirror hanging above the sink. The fresh injuries were almost unnoticeable against the evidence of his abduction beatings, a collection of wounds that had yet to heal before being joined by the new ones. He could not recall the last time he had not seen his face, his torso, without bruises, abrasions, burns, and blood.

In the Shed, no one asked questions. With a number of fight clubs and sporting venues scattered throughout Hebanthe Falls, some legal, some not, it was easy to assume that someone in his constant state of disrepair was a member of one of them, particularly since a small man like Rhyd was bound to take a beating at the hands of larger opponents.

It meant he never had to lie. It meant his secrets were safe.

At least they had been.

His future felt to be on unsteady ground thanks to Venn, but that uncertainty would not keep him from the pledge he had made. He would see his friend free if it was the last thing he ever did.

He growled and yanked open the mirror cabinet., hoping for salve and bandages.

What struck him was the wafting spicy sweetness of cologne soap, the smell of Jaron showered and fresh, and he quickly slammed the cabinet closed to instead scrub the blood from his skin with a vigor that he hoped would purge and overpower the scent. It did not, nor did

the pain of rubbing with the cloth grabbed from the rack on the wall leave him. Having nothing else to wear, not having considered the need for clothing when he had left his own flat, he pulled his trousers back on, refusing to use a towel that would, he was sure, feel and smell like wrapping Jaron around him. He stomped back into the main room, making sure to turn the light off before he opened the bathroom door. In the kitchen cabinet, he found a bottle of liquor, not Zaolei but a weaker ale with barely enough alcohol content to quicken his tongue. It would have to do for the night.

Thankfully, as he dropped onto the sofa where he had previously slept, and yanked the upper portion of his body armor across the floor towards him, the hemp fabric smelled more like him than Jaron. There was an oxygen tank and mask left by his ordeal, as few days had passed since then to allow for its return to a med facility for recycling.

Or maybe Jaron had kept it with the underlying hope that Rhyd would return.

He growled again, refusing to glance at the unused single bed, checked the oxygen contents of both tank and body armor and decided to use the freestanding tank instead of the smaller one in his suit. Scowling, he positioned the mask over his mouth and nose.

"Ain't a cazzing love song," he muttered, turning the nob so the increased flow of oxygen into his struggling lungs began to calm him.

Nothing in his life had ever been a love song. What he had believed to be so had, as of tonight, turned into a bitter lie.

He was not going to mourn that loss. Venn had made his choices, time and again, just as Rhyd had; he was not going to pine for something lost or beg fates for something better.

Rhyd would cling to his anger, to the betrayal, and use it as fuel to bring Skelter home.

He refused, as he allowed the oxygen and the mild alcohol buzz in his blood to overtake him, to think of anything beyond that.

❧*❧

Instead of returning to the Uppers, to a bed he could not face and a man he feared in a way he never had before, Jaron took an extra shift at the Archives, filling in for someone who could not fill their assigned time, agreeing to take another shift off at another time rather than put in for additional ticks. Requests for overtime ticks required paperwork that the managerial staff did not appreciate, and would be too easy for Grainger to learn about, should he be at all interested in doing so. Staff in all trades swapped shifts all the time for the same tick pay. Jaron doing so tonight would not look unusual.

Unless Grainger looked too closely at why Jaron chose a shift instead of a shared bed.

By the time the shift ended, however, there were few options open. He had checked Rhyd's schedule, a shift two slot meant he was likely sleeping still…if he had slept at all…and though it was tempting to return home, to imagine Rhyd asleep in his bed, it would be too tempting to crawl in beside him and allow the rest of his world to disappear into the oblivion of lust-dreams and shared body warmth.

Rhyd did not want him there, or could not afford to want him there. Jaron was not sure which was true, but he would not be responsible for any failure of Scarecrow's mission by taking that step.

After this was over, maybe things would be different.

He knew for certain they would never be the same.

Besides, Scarecrow had given him a duty. Here in these waking hours, when the sun shone outside of the glass dome over Grainger's office, the Captain would be busy…too busy to seek a shared bed. Jaron could sleep there, uninterrupted, and do his best afterward to complete the tasks Scarecrow had asked of him.

It did not surprise him to find Oliver hunched over the Echo, scanning the early morning SCAM reports for the night's happenings, his breakfast growing cold at his elbow. Over his shoulder, Jaron caught a brief glimpse, and heard a muted mention, of the brutal beating of a rapist on Lev 9, the beating by someone believed to be Scarecrow, before Oliver faced him, the sound of the door opening announcing someone's arrival.

No one else had free rein in these chambers.

He would know who it was without seeing him.

"You've been out late."

On the screen, the woman who had been saved spoke glowingly of her savior…without ever seeing anything more of him than a shadow that yanked her assailant away. She had run off without staying long enough to see more, in case her attacker won that fight, but she was convinced her rescuer had been Scarecrow.

Jaron noted the probing nature of the accusation at the same time as he noticed the large glass in Oliver's hand, and the familiar tang of orange, cinnamon, and vodka that hung in the air like an invisible cloud. Opening his mouth as if to speak, a reflexive, unnecessary action, left the taste of it on his tongue and he frowned.

"Bit early for a Brompton's, isn't it?" he challenged in a tone of physical exhaustion only marginally felt.

He hoped it did not also convey emotional weariness. That would lead to questions he did not want to try to lie his way through, nor answer truthfully just yet.

There was likely an empty vodka bottle in the recycles. The orange juice was probably empty as well. If Oliver was drinking so early, he had probably not slept either.

"Duty demands sacrifices," Oliver said with a shrug.

While he might have only meant the sacrifice of lost sleep, Jaron believed he meant more. He did not ask what.

"Anything I can do?"

The momentary sparkle in Oliver's eyes made Jaron regret the offer, but he was grateful that the dark-skinned man only shrugged and shook his head no instead of pursuing the perceived offer.

The Echosys screen went dark with a press of his hand to the button, the glass was drained of its pungent contents, and Oliver rose with a stretch. He might have consumed a full bottle, or most of it, of alcohol, but other than a slight swaying, he did not appear intoxicated.

Like Rhyd, the big man held his liquor well. He just did not drink as much of it as Rhyd.

"You look beat…and I've got a meeting with Tamner in twenty. You should get some rest."

Thankful there was no time for more interaction, and that Oliver was willing to let him sleep, Jaron nodded. Oliver paused to lay a lingering kiss over his ear, breathing deep of the scent of Jaron's hair as if to carry it with him…or perhaps as if he was looking for evidence of some misdeed. Jaron turned his face to kiss the man's mouth, action enough to cause the Captain to smile with a look of apologetic acceptance and gratitude, and then he was gone.

After a long, exhaling breath of relief and listening to the steps retreat from the door, Jaron took the man's abandoned chair and turned the Echo back on. He would sleep…but first, he wanted to be certain that nothing had happened to Rhyd during their long hours apart.

▷*◁

"How are things out there?"

Switz had finally taken a well-deserved break to eat and sleep, but Skelter had no concrete proof that the freezes the man had taken into the tunnel had been put into place, that the little murderer had not stashed them all in one place to bring the whole futzing tunnel down, or that he had not gone out the other end of the tunnel, into the city now that he could, to trade the freezes for Hebbies, for ticks to use later, or for a quick andi blow. That the freezes were not on Switz' person when he returned every so often for more suggested he was doing something with them, but Skelter did not trust the man any further than he could throw him.

Skelter hoped Enoch brought better news and concrete assurance of progress.

"Looks good," Enoch replied, thumbing towards the tunnel as if to address Skelter's concerns about Switz. "Ballard's got the kids covered…and he'll be ready when we're ready. Tomorrow night…"

"Cutting it close," Otta muttered from the desk, where she twisted fine wires together to rig the remaining freezes left to be placed.

Enoch shrugged, refusing to be baited. "Ain't my fault…what he wanted." He looked at Skelter, the man he referred to. The fates of the universe had conspired to cut their efforts close, but it was the timing Skelter had intended, and it was the timing Ballard was prepared to observe. It was tomorrow night…if Skelter did not fulfill his card's destiny, provide the escape, or the Spades came for Skelter the following day.

Maybe if they all got out of here, they still would. Enoch and Skelter were wagering that the demise of some and freedom for the others would release him from that pact with death. But if any Spades survived, they might not be so forgiving of the broken pact

Once outside, the chosen cards should not matter. Skelter should be free of the pact and most of the other members of the Core's club should, they hoped, be dead.

"The tunnel?"

Again the dwarf shrugged. "Looks like a drunk's been in there, but they ought to do the trick." For their purposes, the freezes did not need to be set by some mining expert's rules or with an engineer's proficiency. As long as they collapsed the opening when the ignition was set off, the effort of placement did not need to be precise or pretty.

"Come…let me show you what we've got."

Though he felt more inclined to take advantage of a good long sleep, Enoch nodded and followed Skelter through the corridor to the community room the Core residents shared.

There were tables littered with more weapons, and another stacked with what looked like every scrap of food the Core had. The air, barely recirculated by the marginally functioning filts and fans, was heavily laden with the aromas of cooking, of impending indulgence, of sweat and the unmistakable odor of metal tools chipping at stone, a smell only miners would recognize. There were few freezes left to place, and plenty of men were still congregated around the short tunnel and door to see the job completed. From the looks of the room, the residents were intending the feast to end all feasts.

Some would undoubtedly die, assuming they got the door open and the bugorra were there to meet them. They knew it. Whether they were buried alive by debris or taken down by the gorra, none of them planned to remain in this forsaken place any longer.

It was down to all in, or nothing at all. A dream within a nightmare. Freedom or oblivion.

"You should stay…eat with us," Skelter offered with a smirk, adjusting his eyepatch with one hand as he used his walking stick to gesture at the rich spread. "Never gonna be another meal like this one."

Even if they got out of the Core alive, no one, except the Founder and the Doctet families, had ever shared an abundance like this, though Enoch doubted those meals had consisted primarily of rat meat, chicken, eggs, potatoes, mushrooms, and the dregs of previous foodstuffs he had smuggled inside.

They would skip the vodka and whiskey, however, preferring to stay alert and sober, at full capacity when the moment of escape came.

Besides, most of the alcohol had contributed to the stash of prepared Molcocs.

In the meantime, what else was there to do but eat, cazz, and try to sleep?

"Unless you need to be out there…?"

Enoch studied those gathered in the common room. Unless Ballard needed him, he had nowhere he needed to be until tomorrow night. Seeing as he was the children's piper, nothing bad was going to happen here tonight. The Core's residents needed him.

Switz was a barely trusted last resort.

"I think," Enoch decided with a nod and half-grin, "I shall join you. One more time…for old time's sake."

"One more time," agreed Skelter.

⁂

Every level of Factory East, every crevice and catwalk he could see from the doorway upon entering, reminded him of the streets of

the Levs, where the marginalized dregs of humanity had once crowded into any available space they could find for shelter. It was not dark and wet here, however, lit as it was by a rarely fluctuating supply of lights driven by the electricity the Factory produced as well as used. Even without the suffocating damp, however, it felt very much the same.

Staring with disbelief, Grainger grunted at the foreman, "This is normal?" He had read the reports, the records. He knew there was housing below the Factory floor. Housing, recreation and public facilities, education and medical resources, everything to make the workers comfortable and to keep them productive. The Doctet would never have evacuated to a place like this if they had been aware of these conditions, and in truth, Grainger had never been here to see the area for himself.

At least one of those Upper residents who had survived the Plague would have complained if this was the Factory standard.

Maybe it was only Factory East.

Maybe he should have come here before today.

The woman with the shoe brown braid coiled at the back of her head and held in place with unadorned clips and pins of metal shook her head. "No, Captain…that's why I wanted you to see this…for yourself." Her stern, craggy features were tight, pulling out a few of the wrinkles around her mouth and eyes. She had not thought the Captain would heed her summons, as long as it had taken him to come, but was relieved that calling this a 'dire emergency' had been enough to spark interest and bring him into the Factory at last.

"They don't live here." She waved an outstretched arm around them to include the whole of the factory in her statement. "But there have been…noises…below. After the collapse, they're worried about structural security."

"Collapse?" He paused, cleared his throat, and then nodded. "Yes…the collapse." A collapse had made a good excuse for closing the mine at the time, sealing it from the curious, the adventurous. "What sort of noises?"

She shook her head, her expression making it clear the sounds frightened her. "It's best if you hear for yourself."

With the preparations for the Founder's new facilities underway and out of his hands, Jaron asleep in his bed, Lieutenant Young handily overseeing the security preparations for tonight's recital, and the brako unusually silent after the violent assault two of the numbers had endured during the night, Oliver had time to spare before his next appointment. He did not, however, like the idea of going underground.

Traveling into the Levs was one thing. The thought of being under the earth made him peculiarly uncomfortable.

He trailed behind her, trying to smile and make eye contact with the workers they passed who either stared agape at someone most only knew by rumor and reputation, or else shied away from as if he was there to bring them harm, make threats, to force them to confront what was going on below.

Stepping off the lift, however, into the long wide corridors, empty now with the residents having relocated into the Factory, brought only silence. Only the sound of their shoes on the stone tiled floor and the foreman's rapid, heaving, anxious breathing echoed back to them. When they eventually stopped at the chained double gates to gaze into the dim chasm beyond, even the sound of footsteps stopped. The door at the far end of the corridor that connected Underground East to Underground West was closed.

They listened.

There was nothing.

"It was constant before, like something trying to break through."

"Nonsense." It was unlikely that anyone possibly still alive behind that door of thick metal plating, anyone who managed to stave off starvation this long, would have the strength or tools necessary to break through. If the miners had possessed the means necessary to tunnel through the rock on either side of the door and affect an escape, they would have done so a long time ago.

A desperate act by a handful, perhaps, as their food, their water, their air, ran out. An act unlikely to succeed.

He had taken great pains when sealing the mine, to assure the Factory workers that the miners had been extracted. And he did not believe in monsters…except those with human faces.

"Tell them they're safe. Tell them to clear the factory floors…and get back to work."

The foreman scowled. They're not going to believe me, Captain. I've tried."

"Fine," Grainger muttered with exasperation. "I'll do it." He would see to it that anyone who did as instructed received a bonus of some sort, extra food, time off without penalty, perhaps even a chance to visit Outside if they desired. But Factory East would continue normal operations.

Hebanthe Falls relied on them doing so.

❦*❧

"Here, this way; stand there." Tox got her crew, disheveled sorts with dirty, weary faces, into place on the street corner. In her earbud, she could hear Maemi and Zara exchange instructions as the owner of Vapors placed a placard in her window for the purpose they intended.

At the end of the street where Tox waited, a trio of streeters was hastily tagging the biggest flat surface they could find.

"We're live," Tox muttered into her ICD.

"Gotcha," replied Zara through the static pop in her earpiece.

Tox gestured to her team. Shouts of "poq Gai!" and "pushi kuratz!" and "We demand our worth in salt," echoed across the Lev.

The SCAMs and ICDs were recording. Elsewhere, safely away from the chaos, Zara processed every bit of footage and data received.

Interrupted by the shouts of approaching gorra, Tox barked, "Three!"

The group scattered, intent on eluding arrest, intent on reassembling elsewhere as they had already done twice.

Footage in Vapors collected, Maemi moved her placard to another location as well.

❦*❧

"Where've you been?" snapped Neoma before Blayd had the flat door closed behind him. She was dressed with her usual aristocratic grace, her short hair gelled back away from her noble features, her nails polished, her makeup flawless, giving Blayd the impression she was preparing for some other urgent business, a public appearance of some sort, or waiting to see her new lover perhaps. The last possibility spawned a growl at the back of his throat, and though for a moment he regretted the sound, he quickly realized, as a flash of darkness peaked in her eyes then bled out of them, that there was nothing the Mam could do to him.

She could not arrest him. She did not have the resources to hunt him. She had no evidence, to his knowledge, that she could present to the bugorra against him.

No one, not Senior Kal, not Captain Grainger, not even Scarecrow was a match for him. Without his might behind her, Neoma was Mam in name only. She had only as much power over people as they allowed her to have.

Today, with events spinning in his favor, Blayd was tired of kowtowing to someone unwilling to show him respect.

"Taking care of the Senior, as you asked."

"He was just here," she bitterly retorted, dropping into the nearest chair and crossing her legs languidly. Her movement, her fashion, always lent to her long-legged appearance. Normally he found that alluring. Today, he barely noticed. "You aren't doing…"

"I'm not taking the risk of dropping him in the street, if that's what you mean," was his icy retort. "I got your message. I'm here. What do you want?" He had things to do before tomorrow, contacts to make, plans to put into play. As much as part of him itched for the rough sexual play she preferred, the next time he met her here it would be with an achievement under his belt she would be unable to ignore.

He would deserve a place beside her. And he would make her beg.

Ignoring his question, refusing to allow him to change the subject, she countered, "Then what are you doing?"

"I told you, taking care of the Senior…"

"How?"

Believing he heard something there, wanting to believe it was not merely his imagination, he grunted, "You'll see."

The Senior's visit had unsettled her. Alarmed her. Made her anxious. But he knew she would not tell him what the Senior had said or done if he asked, nor would she admit to being afraid. Believing that how a man or woman handled their problems defined who they were as a person, defined their deepest desires, Blayd relished the thought that her turning to him, summoning him, in her moment of weakness and fear, made him truly the one in her heart, the invaluable person she most relied on. He forced a small, enigmatic smile.

"Tell me."

"You'll see. Tomorrow evening."

That was the most he was going to give her.

Choosing not to continue to beg in the role of weak submissive, she brushed him off with a dismissive wave. "Tomorrow evening you are coming to the recital with me and Ulynda."

He was surprised to hear it. Not surprised that she would attend the recital that had been the buzz on every corner, in every vindi, on ongoing rotation of prodcasts every hour of the past several days. He was surprised she wanted him there. Surprised that she took for granted that he would attend at her side without a spoken invitation.

Maybe she wanted his company. Maybe she wanted protection.

He was flattered. But still he shook his head. "I have plans."

With narrowed eyes she leaned forward, looking like a cat contemplating its prey, but he did not flinch, even when she hissed, "Cancel them."

After a moment of wondering if Kal's visit had prompted a fear for her safety that she dared not show, some threat against her if she risked showing her face at this immensely public event, an event

where she was guaranteed exposure that would display her face, her daughter's, on every Echo in Hebanthe Falls, Blayd shook his head.

"You gave me a duty. Duty requires…"

"That you be here when I need you."

Her tone prompted him to square his shoulders and lower his voice instead of raising it to match the tone of hers. "You don't own me, Mam. You don't pay me enough. I swore an oath…and I'll keep that promise…but that doesn't mean I'm your performing lap dog…"

"He's going to kill us!"

Blayd faltered, wondering at the sincerity of her assertion or if her words were a calculating ploy to get what she wanted. Finally, he answered, "Not if I get him first."

With a smug, triumphant smile, she relaxed back into her chair and said, "Then you are going to kill him. You think so highly of yourself, don't you?"

Scowling at her manipulation, wondering again if anything she said was real, if her words held any meaning, he took a step back and opened the door. "I'm taking care of it. That's all you need to know."

That did not necessarily mean killing the Senior, but let Neoma think what she would. Blayd was doing this his way, or not at all.

❧CHAPTER 30❦

After a day and night's effort, with each corridor and duct around the recital venue scoured for safety and security, the hall itself inspected, cleaned, and verified to be in peak order for its first public use since the Coup, Lieutenant Young was satisfied there were no physical threats to either the potential audience or to the orchestra. Each of her officers knew the post they were assigned to, each knew what their duties would be, and each was sworn to uphold that duty regardless of anything else occurring around them.

Only an unforeseen threat or crisis would sway them. The repeated prodcasts of SCAM footage and ICD images from the Levs, renewed tags on walls of 'komeada Kemway' with the familiar but long-unseen donkey stick figures and 'kistama' revealed a more pervasive knowledge of the threat against the Founder, or else a burst of dissatisfaction with the man's continued existence, then Ilya, her team, or her Captain had been aware of. There were groups of protestors with signs, some hand-painted on sheets of hemp board or thin metal plates, sandwich boards or signs created from neon tubing, expressing the same sentiments as the tags, suggesting a pre-arranged intent to these protests instead of a spur of the moment, pan-flash inspiration.

She doubted that the timing of the protests, occurring the same day as the recital, was a coincidence.

There were similar signs displayed in vindi windows or propped on vindi counters. Demands for salt, demands for other minerals in short supply since the closing of the mines, demands for the Founder to be tried for crimes against the people of the Levs, of the city.

It was all the more distressing and disturbing when she confronted the Ximenezes about the contents of those prodcasts. It was the

captain's request that the protestors not be permitted cast time in order to strangle the spread of their message, to inhibit the likelihood of others joining in, of the protests growing into something bigger, worse. But the Ximenezes claimed that, not only were the prodcasts not originating from the Hub, they were having no luck in their efforts to shut the casts down. Each time reporters were sent to a location to confirm the pictured events, they arrived to find nothing, not even working SCAMs that could capture and transmit the images.

Someone was going to a substantial amount of trouble to create what was either a distraction or a hoax, and the reflection cast on the Captain and the Nau was one of an inability to control the city.

Ilya's first thought was that it was the work of Mam Kemway. She had hacked the prods before. But it made little sense for her to slander her husband, no matter how distant their relationship might be.

Not with the Founder's heir in her care.

So her suspicion shifted to the only other man in Hebanthe Falls who she believed could rally so many people to a cause and possessed the reach and resources to make this sort of prodcast happen.

Senior Kal.

The troubles below worried her. She should go home. She should find Ginna and be sure she was safe. She should sleep before the night's work. But she could not rest while the possibility of trouble burned fever blisters in her mind. Leaving her officers to their duties, trusting them to carry on preparations until her return and believing the Captain would summon her should he need her before the recital, Ilya stepped into the lift intent on a single location, a single man.

Of course, he might not be there. But it was the best place to start.

❧*❦

Jaron gave up on the effort to sleep within two hours of Oliver's departure. He tossed, he rolled from one side to the other, he pulled the bedding up around his neck only to kick it off again when the sense of strangulation grew unbearable. This bed, everything in this room,

reminded him of Oliver, and clashed with memories of Rhyd that were too fresh and vivid.

Maybe there was no future with Rhyd. Jaron suspected, despite any attraction Ballard felt, the man was the type to push others away from inner-circle closeness. Those already there were those he had known for a long time. Perhaps all of his life. Jaron knew Skelter, knew Zara. He knew Lash and Enoch. He fleetingly knew Tox and Maemi. But not well enough to say how well any of them knew Rhyd. Not well enough to know how close any of them were.

Rhyd's association with Jaron was too new for trust. Jaron had to prove himself, without having any idea how he was meant to do that.

Without knowing if he could.

He gave up on elusive sleep, escaping the bed and the reminders of something, someone, he would have to put behind him when this was over…regardless of the outcome. Jaron opted for puttering around the suite, cleaning, reorganizing, setting things back to the way they had been the first time he had visited here, the first time Oliver brought him to the rooms he called home. The changes had come gradually, a product of oft-shared living space, but whether Oliver noticed the rollback when he returned for the night, after Jaron left, he would not be there to see.

If Oliver noticed and thought it meant what it meant, the extraction of Jaron from his life, Jaron did not expect to have a convenient opportunity to talk about it for several hours. If at all.

Resting on the sofa between reorganizing spurts, with the mind-numbing background noise of laughies, product pitches, and news prods that made up a typical day's fare on the Echosys filling the air, he tried not to think about what he was doing and why. It was a compulsion he had to obey. In between, he stared at the screen without thinking, listen without hearing, until his shift was scheduled to begin. After that, there were only the hours of waiting for whatever the night would bring.

He was one of the first to view the SCAM footage of the protests. Protests were common enough since the Coup, particularly with the

ever-present salt shortage and the ongoing threat presented by the brako. It was no surprise that the news of the Founder being alive had sparked its own spate of protests, both in favor of the Founder, demanding his release, and in favor of his trial and execution. The widespread nature of this protests, however, was of interest, and after the fourth snippet of street-corner rallies, Joran wondered if he was the only one who caught onto the one telltale detail running through each.

The demonstrators' placement in the groups changed at each location. The placement of the signs and placards alternated, along with the colors of the neon-lit protest signs. The voices varied, the language and tone, male-prominent or female-prominent depending on who was in the front line of the protestors.

But the members of each group remained the same.

This was no city-wide protest, but a staged ploy to make it look like one. Though the tagger evidence was undoubtedly real, each location different from the last, and the ICD evidence of protest signs in vindi windows or on vindi counters changed, it was the sort of plan or prank only an organized group could pull off.

There. There it was.

Vapors.

A distraction. A diversion from Scarecrow's plan. The protests limited to four Levs, away from where the children, and Scarecrow, would be.

Away from Factory East and the performance hall.

Aimed, Jaron mused, at keeping gorra activity confined to a small number of locations. If the bugorra responded to the protests, it would keep them away from everything Scarecrow intended.

"Thought you'd be asleep."

Jaron did not look up when Oliver entered the room, afraid to look into his face, afraid of what his own would reveal. He had not planned to be here long enough for their paths to cross, had planned to escape the Captain's dominating presence to avoid the possibility of being talked out of what he was about to do, the possibility of an unpleasant

confrontation. Acting more surprised and pleased to see him then he felt, Jaron forced a smile.

"I did for a bit…then…" He shrugged. His gaze circled the room as if to indicate the cleaning and reorganizing he had done, but Oliver appeared not to notice either the direction of his gaze or the changes.

"Something on your mind? Haven't seen you in a while."

There seemed to be something on Oliver's, Jaron judged by the weight of the other's tone, and when he sat on the sofa at Jaron's side, Jaron distanced himself by glancing at his chrono and swearing softly.

"No, just busy. Too many…crucksake…I didn't realize the time."

Though Oliver frowned, disappointed, he did not, verbally at least, jump to any negative conclusions about Jaron's sudden bending over for boots and the effort he took to put them on, which kept Oliver from sliding nearer.

"Shift?"

"Yeah. Filling in for someone else doesn't mean I get out of my rotation." Not without prior authorization. It explained his too frequent absences over the last several days, without sounding like the lame, implausible excuses Jaron feared.

"Call in."

He shook his head. "Can't…not on such short notice." The chuckle that accompanied his words sounded as forced as it felt, but it could not be helped. He had just called in recently to stay in Oliver's bed and the Captain knew it. His request was hopeful but unrealistic.

"Will you be back in time for the recital? We can attend together."

It was the first request Oliver had ever made of him that involved a public outing together. It was the first time Oliver had ever attempted to include him in his public life in a way that everyone in Hebenon would see and talk about for days and weeks to come.

Once, not so long ago, it had been what Jaron believed he wanted.

Now, the possibility of such exposure, of the commitment a public appearance portrayed, brought cold sweat to the surface of his skin.

"I…maybe…I'll try to swing early release." If he worked fast, if he told his foreman that an early departure was at the request of Captain Grainger, it might be easy enough to accomplish.

Others would be working for early release too, to attend this anticipated event, and Jaron had no intention of trying. Not only was he unprepared to be publically seen with Oliver, he was unwilling to be near the Uppers when the Scarecrow's plans were put into action.

Oliver nodded, tossed him his coat from where it hung over the arm of the sofa, and went to the desk as Jaron pulled it on. "Fair enough," he agreed, assuming, as Jaron did, that the weight of the Captain's name on such a request would guarantee permission. The Echo beeped as it powered on again, and with the tightening of Jaron's coat belt, another sound, a series of dual-tone beeping, like a siren's warning, spewed out of the speakers.

Only Oliver turning off the sound canceled the racket.

"What is…?"

A message in bold font began to scroll up the screen, repeating itself as the letters moved off the top.

"It's not possible…"

"What isn't possible?" Jaron approached to read the screen, although he could see the words from where he stood without effort.

"Those people in there are long dead!"

"In where?" Sounding confused, Jaron scowled. He knew Zara had planned a hack, a warning, regarding the Core but he could not say the word lest Oliver decide he knew more about that secret place than he should. He had not known when that hack would come, if it had already come, and despite Rhyd's admonition to be here to make sure Grainger did the right thing, Jaron had not expected to be here when the warning came.

"This isn't possible," Oliver repeated, though his earlier excursion into the East Factory's underbelly, the reports of noises behind a sealed, fortified, and locked door…and Venn's insistence that the Scarecrow intended to get inside that barred zone, suggested that people still living inside was not only possible…but highly likely.

It had been easy to pretend they had died long ago, however that end had come. It had held feelings of guilt at bay, sealing them behind that mine door with any unfortunates left inside. Could he live with himself if he continued to allow them to crawl towards an inevitable suffering death…thieves, murderers, and dissidents though they were?

On their own, he did not think they could ever escape that door. If Scarecrow intended to be there, however, to see to it that they did, was it not Oliver's responsibility to be there too, to stop Scarecrow if he could, to help any inside who might be suffering, to keep any intent on resuming their lives of crime and mayhem from escaping into the Factory, into Hebenon, into the Outside?

Jaron's hand on his shoulder bid him look up into the younger man's face. Jaron, who stared at the screen and could not possibly know the details bursting and jumping inside of Oliver's head. Jaron whose skin reflected the green-white burn of the glowing text in the otherwise unlit, early morning room.

"You should help them."

Jaron realized as he spoke that he could not specify who he meant, that he could not urge aid to the Factory workers without revealing that he not only knew what the Core was but where the entrance was as well. He could not encourage Oliver to aid whoever might be inside without hinting that he knew what kind of people were there.

Nor could he remain here to encourage Oliver to act when doing so would endanger himself and possibly Rhyd's mission. Remaining here was not going to accomplish anything beyond fueling his worry and possibly giving away secrets to Oliver.

There was nothing he could do in the Uppers. He had to escape to the Levs. He had to get to Rhyd, do whatever it took to help Scarecrow.

Not knowing how he could help or who Jaron meant to include in those words, Grainger nodded once. His fist slammed into the Echo's keypad and he barked, "Get me Lieutenant Ilya. Now," to whoever was on the receiving end of that message. Without getting to his feet, he swiveled on his chair to stop Jaron at the door long enough to say, "Be careful down there. I'll see you tonight."

The Archives were well away from the Core. Well away from the protests. Well away from Founder Kemway and the efforts soon to be made to move him to a safer, once more secret, locale. Grainger told himself there was no need to worry about Jaron's safety.

As Jaron disappeared behind the closing door, however, worry was the only feeling on Oliver's mind.

❧*❧

Beyond the door of his Marbordo home, Venn watched the torrents of mud wash past his feet as the heavy rain continued, flooding the unplanted fields, filling the furrows dug for seeding, carrying the fertile soil into the swollen rivers. A child had been lost yesterday, playing too near the rough water's edge, and the parah community mourned the loss as one, families keeping their children closer as the torrent continued. Many of the parah had relocated to higher ground, though they had not crossed the rivers to find shelter in the forest or on the mountains out of fear that the rains would wash the mountain down or take down trees, and bury or trap them there. Most did not dare risk the river.

The rest had lifted everything of value off the damp earthen floors to wait for the water to recede. The damp was familiar to Venn, so he knew how to keep things dry, but in Hebenon there was little risk of water filling rooms inch by inch or sweeping houses away.

Not unless the filt systems failed. Not so long as men like Rhyd, and those who purged the nets of debris, did their jobs.

The fleeting thought of Rhyd brought tears to Venn's eyes and he kicked angrily into the muddy stream at his door, splashing the contents but accomplishing little.

He did not expect immediate results from Captain Grainger or the bugorra. Venn knew Rhyd was not an easy man to find. Locating him at the Shed would be the easiest guarantee, but there was a general reluctance in the city to pull bilgers, skolpers, heizers, or other system workers from their jobs. Hebenon's infrastructure failed without them.

And with no inkling of what Rhyd intended, finding him was probably not the Captain's priority as it was Venn's. The Captain had other things to do, tedious day to day business, seeing to the Founder's welfare, pursuing the brako, arranging security for the recital. So long as no one but criminals were being hurt by Scarecrow's efforts, the vigi was not the Captain's enemy.

Scarecrow was, in Venn's opinion, his own enemy. Venn guiltily believed he should be looking for Rhyd too, but he resisted doing so. He argued the rain, argued rehearsals he had been wrapped up in for so many hours of late. He argued fatigue, he argued tonight's recital. He argued that he was not Rhyd's caretaker and that the man should stop on his own.

Tomorrow. Tomorrow he would look he kept telling himself.

Tomorrow might be too late.

But it would not be Venn's fault. Whatever happened, it was not his responsibility.

Still his heart ached with worry.

A small hand slipped into his. Agnys watched the rain with a child's fascination and curiosity, and very little of the worry of the adults around her. She had lost a friend, yes, as all Marbordo children were her friends. But the rivers were unforgiving, sometimes demanded sacrifices, and what more could she do but cry now and then for the friend she had lost?

Besides, she had another friend behind her, the Tamner boy Cori, who taught her new games, how to read, how to do numbers the way the children in Hebenon did them. She liked those new things and they occupied the hours not spent in the fields or learning the ways of her people, where he joined her to learn too. He had quickly become her favorite friend and the center of attention among the parah children.

She was glad he preferred her company to any of the others.

Cori was drawing now, a bit of charcoal from the fire pit serving as his instrument, and so she felt no guilt for leaving him to his diversion to comfort one of the men she felt kinship for.

"Will he be there? Will he come?"

Without seeking clarification he did not need, without looking at her, Venn frowned and replied, "I don't know." He hoped so, but he had little belief that Rhyd would set aside his plans for Venn's sake. Not if what Rhyd said about Skelter, and the Club of Spades, was true.

He had set aside several years of his life for Venn, before Venn Vanished. It had turned Rhyd into what he was now. Venn felt guilty asking for more, even if this asking was, he believed, in Rhyd's best interest.

"I want to hear."

"You will." Whatever Rhyd intended, he would surely not put Venn at risk. If Agnys remained near Venn, in the recital hall, she would be safe too. He had already promised her and Cori that they could attend. There would be other children there. It would be good for them, particularly the Marbordo children, to be exposed to something new. Agnys only had one living relative, a cousin who trusted both Venn and Rhyd enough, after they had saved the child's life, to allow her to go into the city with them. Other children had asked to join them, but after the river death of one, few families were willing to risk their young ones in the strange metal nest they had feared for so long.

Fear of the unknown, it seemed, worked both ways. The parah were friendlier, more accepting, then those in the dismal cold and dark of Hebenon, but that did not make them foolish.

If only Rhyd would spend more time here, among the parah too, the walls he had erected around himself might come down and he would be himself again.

Venn had, however, given up on that happening. Not even Agnys would change Rhyd's mind.

∾*∾

"I'm not afraid of you," Ginna snarled, turning her back on the Senior Talker to complete the tag she had been engaged in when he found her. Tagging a Talker Hall was risky and could bring down both

the Voices and the bugorra, particularly since the Senior had caught her in the act and knew her face. But she had leverage of her own that she would not hesitate to use, no matter how flimsy it might be. And if it was true, what Mam Kemway said…that the Voices and Talkers were traitors to the Founder and to Hebanthe Falls, then this puffed-up man bloated on his own power was nothing to fear.

"You should be."

It was happenstance, and her all-night tenacity in a search for Senior Kal, that brought Ilya to this particular Hall, happenstance that led her to find her prey, and her long-absent sister, in the same place at the same time. She scowled at the tag her sister had left, the donkey tag with kistama hastily, but cleanly, written in crimson beneath it and a Scarecrow tag a little further away on the same wall in yellow. Ilya imagined that her sister might be key to learning about the riots, the SCAM hack and the prodcast jacking of riot footage that had played repeatedly until the Ximenezes shut down the prod system.

For now, Echo screens all over the city were dark.

But grilling Ginna for information could wait.

Particularly since the Lieutenant's primary suspect and Ginna stood side by side.

That could not be coincidence.

Ginna looked well, weary from a lack of sleep perhaps, a little thinner due to an inconsistency of meals that was part of a streeter's life, rumpled as if she had slept in her clothing, likely in a pile with other streeters as most often was the case for people seeking warmth to replace Hebenon's chill. But she did not look unhealthy, did not look as if she had fallen victim to the Hebbies scourge so many streeters fell prey to. That was reassuring.

It would be better if Ginna gave up this foolish crusade and came home, but that was not going to happen just because Ilya had found her. Trying again to convince her would have to wait.

She turned a hard eye on the Senior and cleared her throat. "Senior, might we have a word?"

"I'm busy." There was no hostility in his words or tone, no guilt, only a note of boredom she imagined he used more often than he realized. He was that sort of man, the sort who thought everyone and everything was beneath him, and who found little interest in the world and life around him unless it could be manipulated to his benefit.

She was sure he had become a Talker purely to influence and control others, purely for the powered entitlement it afforded him.

"So am I," growled Ginna, scooping up the tag cans at her feet and shoving them into the canvas drawstring sack she carried.

"Oh no you…" Ilya caught her sister's arm before the younger woman escaped, but in doing so, her attention was taken off of the Senior, who sauntered towards the Hall door as though he was done with whatever matter he had been engaged in with the two women.

"Senior, I must speak to you about the Founder." Ilya turned to say more, to demand he come back and talk to her, tell her what he knew about the prodcasts and the rumored assault on the Founder.

He only paused long enough to look at her and say, "What if I told you, Lieutenant, that there exists a viable alternative to Haythem Kemway?" as her ICD buzzed on her wrist.

The Hall door clattered closed behind him.

Words were a Talker's tool. In a Talker's mouth, language was there to be mangled, reassembled, twisted and manipulated just like people. He might mean anything or nothing by that question. This was not the time to ponder it more deeply.

A glance at the ICD indicated an emergency priority message from the Captain, one Ilya could not ignore. With a growl, she released Ginna's arm and snapped, "I want you home, inside, tonight. Off the streets. Don't get caught up in any of…" she pointed at the fresh tags, "this. It isn't going to be safe tonight."

Ilya did not know for certain that their intent to move Founder Kemway would be the catalyst for violence. There was no reason it should be, since only a small number of people knew where he was, that he was to be moved. And a smaller number still knew where this new location was to be. But a threat had been made against the

Founder, and Ilya took the danger seriously. With so many bugorra scheduled as security around the recital hall, and now the Captain's urgent summons, the sense that something else was brewing raked against her skin like nails on a chalkboard.

"Promise me."

"You ask for a lot of promises," challenged Ginna as she slung her bag strap over her shoulder, "and you suck at keeping them. Save the city. I'll be fine."

She did not expect what she would be involved in, what she had been asked to do, to involve anything dangerous. Move some kids through the Levs to a secure shelter.

How dangerous could that be?

The ICD buzzed again. Three words on the screen demanded obedience. Captain's office. Now. Ilya messaged back, OMW, looked up, and Ginna was gone.

❧*❦

Haythem had been still since last night. Not the mumbling quiet of a man bumping his head against the padded wall to a rhythm song only he could hear. Not the drooling, glass-eyed silence of oblivion that most often was the precursor to violent, uncontrolled outbursts.

This was something that, before today, Tamner had never seen.

Maybe it had been there all along. He did not stand at this window twenty-four hours a day, and there was no time to view all of the footage himself. The techs assigned to monitor the Founder here or behind the Echosys, might not have detected this difference if they were not specifically studying the man's normally slack face.

But Tamner noticed.

He went with the kit, took blood and fluid samples, and sent them to the lab for analysis. If something was different, if something had changed, he wanted to know what it was.

Holding a handful of the man's thick hair as gently as he could, he tipped Haythem's head back and flashed the ophthialight across the

Founder's eyes. Pupil dilation, iris color, the whites of his eyes, all looked good, normal. The same. But for a moment, just for a moment, Tamner swore that Haythem not only met his gaze but recognized him.

Though he covered his shock, limiting his expression to his usual doctor-patient smile, it pounded like a spike between his eyes.

The man's brain and body were adapting. Changing. Perhaps recovering. Or else Tamner was operating on too much stress, too much caffeine, and too little sleep.

After tonight, Kemway would be secure again. And tomorrow, Tamner would devise a new regimen of tests to determine what, if anything, he had just seen.

❧*❦

"Haven't found a hack for the lock," Zara muttered, shifting her bare feet on the sofa so Rhyd could sit. She sat on the floor, her back against a cushioned chair, with an Echo on her lap, two more on her left, one to her right, and two perched on the chair behind her head. Each screen flashed different sequences of characters, numbers, letters, the symbols forming a code Rhyd did not comprehend.

He grunted as he sank down and tipped his head to rest it on the fluffy sofa cushion back behind him.

"You look tired. Sleeping?"

He grunted again. There had not been much time for sleep, with his focus on making tonight's efforts pay off. Surrounded by Jaron's scent in that man's home, imagining him in every corner though Rhyd had never shared that living space with him, meant that what little sleep he had gotten the night before had been plagued with dreams of a sort he had not had in years. In a lifetime, he mused, unable to recall such erotic dreams with Venn at their center.

The only dreams he could remember with Venn were the nightmares that had plagued him after Venn's arrest.

Too much time, too much pain, too much darkness had passed in the long months between, erasing so much of what had been before.

He regretted the loss, but regret got him nothing. He could not allow the past to be a distraction. Not today. Today was all he had.

"Up for tonight?"

"Nothing's changed." He would be where he planned to be, do what he intended, regardless of weariness. He lifted his head to watch her fingers flit over the Echo keys for several minutes and then went to the kitchen for whatever alcohol Zara had on hand.

"Want breakfast with that?"

She had been up most of the night hacking, just as he had been up most of the night getting his pieces into place on the playing board. The footsteps of shift change could be heard clattering up and down the nearest stairs, across the passing walkways, now that the shift whistle had called an end to third shift and summoned workers to first.

Rhyd's was to be second. What he needed instead, Zara thought after a glance at the fading bruises still marking his pale, unshaven face, was a hot meal and a solid eight.

She had little food on hand as she ate most of her meals in vindis or as takeaways so she did not have to cook, and she was not a drinker. Her cupboards, since Skelter's disappearance, were nearly as barren as Rhyd's. Any alcohol left there had probably belonged to Skelter, or else, he mused as he dragged the bottle of Zaolei from the cupboard, had been stocked there for his benefit.

When he sat again, uncorking the bottle with his teeth and taking one, long burning drink with his free hand resting innocently on Zara's ankle, he muttered, "Information gathering?"

"Between hacking…yes…and no. Monitoring ICD chatter after yesterday's prod blitz, watching what Grainger's done after the…"

"So he knows now? About the breech?" Rhyd wiped his mouth on his sleeve after his second swallow of whiskey.

"He got it. He's called his lieutenant in. Probably strategizing."

"If he doesn't get people in there, the workers are gonna get slaughtered." Assuming, of course, Skelter's work on the inside was adequate to blow the door as intended. If that effort failed, Skelter and

his companions might not have the chance to get free before angry miners and convicts jumped them. No one needed that complication.

"You let me and Jaron worry about it. You worry about you." She chuckled and ignored his half-hearted attempt at a rude gesture as he set the bottle on the table to his left. Rhyd did not delegate well. He was used to playing Scarecrow's business by solitary rules. Scarecrow was not a team player. Being forced to function as one was not an easy thing. "But I may have found something that can help."

"Mmm?"

It was a question, but a glance at the man on her sofa revealed he was moments from dropping into a desperately needed sleep. Better he had that then heard what she had begun to say. What happened in Factory East, what happened at the Core door, was for Zara to focus on. Keeping Grainger out of Rhyd's way was her business. She might tell Rhyd her idea later, if there was a chance. Otherwise, she knew he would be reluctantly satisfied to trust her to do what she did best…and leave him to what he did.

❧*❧

The girl half-heartedly allowed her mother to turn her this way and that, tucking stray wispy curls into the intricate wrap of the hairstyle chosen for tonight. There had been a time, a few short years ago, when Ulynda was finally deemed old enough to attend her father's public functions, allowed to socialize with the Doctet and their families and others of import, in preparation for the day when she would become more fully one with them. Her sister had been presented as entertainment, her musical talent on display to support and promote the superiority of the Kemway bloodline, and her brother had been paraded through as the heir to the position of Founder he was intended to take. Lacking musical talent, but possessing budding beauty and grace as well as a sharp mind, Ulynda's destiny would have been different, a marriage pawn in a game of strengthening ties and power between the families in Hebanthe Falls' Uppers.

The Coup that followed soon after upended all of that, bringing an end to parties, to the exclusive rights of the Founder's family, to the privileges enjoyed by those in the Uppers. It had brought an end to the 'marriage market' and Ulynda's marriage prospects. It had exposed her, at least marginally, to the life the majority in Hebenon lived.

She was not encouraged to formulate her own opinions about such things. Her mother endeavored to forbid it, changing the subject or chastising her every time Ulynda brought up sensitive topics. Lacking the strict guidelines her father's position and title had placed on her was a blessing of sorts, but she was reminded again, as her mother tightened the ribbon sash around her middle and plucked at the fabric above and below to give her a more defined waist than most girls her age possessed, that her mother still had hopes and plans for her outside any Ulynda secretly harbored for herself.

"Do I have to do this?" It was not attending the recital that she was resistant to. She liked music, understood the importance of the first orchestral performance in Hebenon in more than two years, and was eager to hear a live concert that she had never had the opportunity to attend before. But after being kept in seclusion since their evacuation into the Factory, when life in the rest of Hebanthe Falls had fallen apart, Ulynda was smart enough to know that every eye in the hall would be on her.

Not on her mother, despite the woman's desire to be the center of attention. They would be on Ulynda, the last living member of the Kemway bloodline.

There was her father still, but with what little Ulynda knew, her father no longer counted. He was in no physical or mental state to carry the role of Founder. While not yet old enough for the part, Ulynda, the last Kemway, carried all of the potential on her shoulders and everyone would watch her. Judge her. Lay their hopes at her feet.

She did not want to be part of that.

"Of course you do, darling. We both do. It is expected of us."

"By who? No one will care…"

"Of course they will care."

Ulynda smoothed the front of her dress, pulling away some of the accentuated waist her mother had given her. "We could both die and they wouldn't care. They might even be happier…"

"Nonsense. You fail to understand…." Neoma snapped, slapping away Ulynda's hands and making adjustments to her waistline again.

"No, you," the girl emphasized the second word, "fail to understand. They don't want a Founder any more. They don't want…"

"They're all fools, not realizing what is best for them. We kept this city successful, surviving, from the start. Without us…well, you see the mess things have become."

Ulynda shook her head. Actually, she had seen very little on which to comprehend her mother's beliefs. All she saw was a prodcast here and there that suggested that not much in the Levs had gotten better, or worse, since the Coup. The only differences now were who was in charge…how much control they wielded…the abundance of the ones called brako, and the newly won chance to go Outside."

"I would like to go Outside," the girl murmured, changing the subject so as not to fight. Her mother was all she had and Ulynda was not yet ready to stand up to her. As much as they might butt heads, Neoma was family.

"It is poison out there. Never forget that. We will get our rights, our place back, and everything will be as it was before. You'll see."

Ulynda sighed. "Yes, mother."

There would come a day when her mother was no longer in control of every aspect of her life. Ulynda intended to step into the sun on that day and prove her mother wrong. Until then, she was forced to endure and obey.

"Come…we will dine with our friends and then be on our way."

Their friends. Remnants of the Doctet who still supported Neoma, the Kemways, out of a generational, ingrained habit of loyalty.

Ulynda could not help but believe that, if not for the history that bound them, these people would not be their friends.

⮞*⮜

The world went on, life made its demands, and Zara still had to dance to earn ticks to feed herself and purchase the never-ending supply of Echosys, ICD, and comm parts needed for hacking and creating specialized bits of tech for clients willing to reward her work accordingly. Fortunately, she loved to dance as much as she loved her side business, and as she had given up sex work in favor of managing the andis she inherited with Skelter's absence, she was not required to put in the sometimes-overlong hours in Vapors she once had.

Tonight there were plans, plans that Maemi willingly accepted because she was part of them too. With her ailing mother-in-law as an excuse, the family still trapped in the grief of recent loss, Maemi would hand the reins of her club to Pietro when the hour came to act and he would not think twice about covering for her. Instead of sitting with the bedridden woman, Maemi would leave that duty to Zara. Her dance shift complete, her andis protected by Vapors management and staff, it did not matter where Zara set up her Echos to work.

One array of tables, chairs, and floor space was as good as any other, so long as there were no interruptions. The ailing woman, sleeping a lot as she did these days, was not likely to be one of those.

She left Rhyd asleep on her sofa to begin the transfer of equipment to Maemi's flat and he did not stir throughout her comings and goings. Sleep deprivation was a bad thing, destroying memory, fueling depression, impairing judgment and skills. Rhyd could afford none of those things tonight, suffered enough depression and deprivation as it was, and so after taking the time to hack the Hub and change Rhyd's Shed schedule so he would not be required to take a shift today or the following two, she let him sleep.

He would not even need to call in to use precious wellness days.

He was still healing, beaten down by physical attacks and inner demons he would not discuss. He needed to sleep if he was to be at his best tonight.

They all needed Scarecrow at his peak.

She felt bad that none of them would be at the recital to offer Venn their support on this important night. It could not be helped. Maybe in time, he would forgive them for it. Maybe he would forgive Rhyd too.

❧*❧

The nagging sense that this could be a hoax continued to plague Grainger as he gave orders to the three dozen officers selected to face this warned-about threat beneath Factory East. With so many assigned to the area around the recital hall for later this evening, all of his officers required to report to duty, it meant the bugorra resources were stretched thinner than usual throughout the Levs. But if the rumor was true, he could not risk the lives of the Factory workers.

Hebanthe Falls needed them. If production came to a halt in any of the three Factories, the city could fail.

What if this was a ploy meant to give the Lev protestors freedom to run amok, Lieutenant Young had challenged?

What if this was a distraction to draw the bugorra away to allow the attempt on Founder Kemway to come to pass?

What if, Grainger secretly argued with himself, this was part of whatever plan Scarecrow was hatching?

There were a lot of 'what-ifs' and very few answers. Only guesses. He had confidence in the officers posted around the recital hall, confidence in those the Lieutenant selected to aid in the relocation of the Founder. And if the space behind metal doors at the far end of this barely lit corridor remained quiet, if Scarecrow failed to show and no attempted breach of the Core came to pass, Grainger's embarrassment would be the worst of it.

If the warning was accurate, however, to do nothing meant death and destruction and an impact on the city that, on top of the losses suffered in the Coup, might forever cripple Hebanthe Falls.

Weapons at the ready, poppers and buzzers in hand, most of the officers shuffled with anxious anticipation while a man with a welding torch cut away the metal loops holding the chain-link double doors

closed. There had been very few people to evacuate from this underground level, as few had taken his earlier admonition to return to their homes as an order to be obeyed. Rightfully so, it appeared, when they watched Grainger arrive mid-day with so many armed and armored officers in tow. All it took was a glance at the bug masks for the few who had come down to hasten back to the ground level.

But the corridor was quiet. Nothing stirred behind the door at the end. And when the length of chain slid free of the links they bound, to clatter and jangle onto the hemp-wood planking on the back side, one man's muffled voice dared to ask what the others were thinking.

"Someone's trying to get in there? Why? What's there that…?"

"Salt," muttered someone else.

They were young. They did not know. From the attentiveness of the others, nor did they.

Grainger had no answers, none that were not part of the lies, and correcting the assumption that they were here to keep someone from breaking into the mines would be a mistake.

Who would believe they were here to keep someone, or something, from getting out instead?

If the assumptions were true, and it was the Scarecrow daring to worm his way past to reach those doors, that was a conjecture Grainger preferred to leave unvoiced.

A lot of these officers were afraid of the Scarecrow. Their morale did not need to take that hit.

"Quiet," he growled instead. "Listen…stay alert…be ready."

"Yes, sir."

Cautiously they moved ahead. Five steps. Ten. Then Grainger held their position. Not too close, lest something burst out on them without warning and killed them with exploding rock and debris. Not too far, lest the door open and the effectiveness of their range weapons be useless and Scarecrow, or whoever might come from behind, would not have too much room to maneuver.

Grainger did not know how long they might be here, how long they might have to wait, before whatever was to happen, happened. The warning he had received had not said.

If he had to keep men here in shifts indefinitely, he would find a way, a rationale, to do that.

ॐ*ॐ

They were in place, the six he had chosen, anonymous faces unlikely to be missed or recognized by those they encountered over the course of the night.

Talkers were aplenty. Becoming a Talker afforded one a degree of comfort that many other life posts did not. All it took was a willingness to listen to the problems of others, the ability to dispense advice and ask for donations, the willingness to put on a face of pious, zealous faith in the Founder whether one believed it or not.

With so many Talkers milling about as the largest audience in Hebenon's history, comprised of guests from both the Levs and the Uppers, began to fill the recital hall, six more would not be suspect.

To reach their ultimate destination, however, would require something other than the attire, the insignia, of the Voices of Faith. The heightened security around the recital hall needed to be taken into consideration if they were to pass higher into the Uppers.

He had planned for that as well. Beneath the robes, something else that would allow free movement without suspicions.

Either way, no one would care if they were there.

No one would care when they were not.

They would not care, until it was too late.

ॐ*ॐ

His shift had been hell. Busy, with the barrage of hacked SCAM footage to be viewed, tagged for accuracy or tagged as false, faces identified if they could be for the brusque bugorra who came in demanding evidence they could use to arrest the troublemakers.

Fortunately, those particular duties had fallen to other archivists.

Jaron did not recognize the faces but he did not want to have a hand in getting any of them arrested. Since, to his knowledge, no one else had realized the 'protestors' in those clips were all the same, he did not want to be the one to point that detail out to the gorra.

He just wanted to go home.

He did slip away earlier than expected when the foreman announced that the Archives would close for the duration of the orchestral recital and for an hour before and two hours afterward, allowing everyone to attend if they desired, allowing all workers time to break away from what promised to be a significant crowd and make it back to the Archive office. Of course, not everyone would attend; the whole of Hebenon would never fit in the hall and some had no interest in that sort of music. But the performance would be broadcast over the Echosys, now running again after their long period of darkness to discourage the hackers from continuing the riot footage. Vindis all over the Levs, street corner Echos, and those in every home would show the momentous event and many who could not be in the hall, who dared not brave that crowd, would be viewing elsewhere.

Jaron wanted to.

He would not.

His Echo was on when he opened the door of his flat, and for a moment his heart soared with the hope that Rhyd was still there. There was a blanket haphazardly flung over the back of the sofa, an empty liquor bottle on its side on the coffee table, and a used but nearly dry cloth hung over the edge of the bathroom sink, leaving the puddle on the floor as evidence. The oxygen mask lay on the sofa cushions and the tank that was there, a different one then Jaron recalled, was empty when he picked it up.

He pressed the blanket to his nose and breathed, smiling behind its folds.

Rhyd had come here after all. But he was not here now.

He had a shift today, as Jaron recalled, so he might be coming off shift soon. There was no evidence, however, to suggest he would

return. Rhyd would go where his equipment was, would engage in whatever pre-battle rituals he needed before the night's work began, leaving Jaron to wonder what he was supposed to do. How he could help instead of being left alone in his flat.

How could he best benefit Scarecrow, Skelter, and his friends?

Staring at the walls, at the silent figures milling in the pre-recital space displayed on the Echo, hardly seemed right or fair, when others would be risking their lives this night. There had to be more Jaron could do.

❧Chapter 31❧

He did not remember being in that great chasm. From here, within the Core, there was no seeing the bottom without a light, the swirl of icy water that churned there, but on quiet days, in this room used for storing equipment awaiting repair, replacement, or repurposing, one could listen and hear it, the sloshing, rumbling, and gurgling like the stomach of a great beast at the pit of its great black throat. Some fate had led Otta and Colyx to be here that day, to hear the sounds of a man at the bottom of the maw over the typical water sounds. It had permitted them, and Enoch, to work together to pull the barely conscious, badly injured man into the purgatory that was the Core.

His fate had been life in the Core or certain death.

As the heavy chain, the sort used for binding mining carts together, now fused to create a long, limp arm, clattered against the stone sides of the chasm, Skelter did not know how the trio had fished him out. But he did know that his fate still might be a watery death if for some reason Rhyd failed.

He had every faith in his friend. The only way Skelter was dying was if Rhyd died too, either before he could arrive to help or in the process of getting Skelter, Otta, and Colyx out of here.

In the main room of their exile, some were picking over the remnants of their last supper while others bid tentative farewells to friends and lovers. Colyx could be heard urging everyone into their places, while Enoch waited at the opening of one corridor for the children to gather so he could escort them out. They too were bidding whatever families they had or knew farewell. The children would likely survive this night.

The adults might not be so lucky.

Enoch, and Skelter if he survived, would see to the reunification of any families that made it through, or would find families for the children whose caregivers did not. It had already been decided.

There were still dissenting voices heard over the rattle of the chain. However this night played out, it would not pass easily.

"You're gonna go down first." It was a repeat of an earlier sentiment, but again, Otta shook her head.

"The chain doesn't reach…I can't swim." She had never faced a body of water larger than a washbasin. It suggested that she had not been the one to descend into the hole to pull him out, but Skelter had never bothered to ask for details of his rescue.

He was simply grateful to be alive.

"He'll be there. He'll make sure you get through."

"And if he doesn't?"

Skelter tested the chain to be sure it was secure, the weight of the hook anchored into the stone wall suitably strong, he believed, to hold the weight of each of them long enough to descend. Satisfied though nervous, sharing no fondness for water after nearly dying in it, he took her face between his hands and kissed her mouth. He understood her fears, for though he did not remember being there, the horrors of the water still clutched at his belly in his nightmares from the shadows of things not recalled. But he had to remain strong for her, as she had been strong for him since the day she helped save his life.

"Then we go out together.

If the Club required his death, she had already vowed to follow. If the river demanded hers, Skelter was going to be right behind her.

⟡*⟡

"Don't look like much."

Ginna had to agree with the boy beside her as she lifted the canvas flap of the lean-to shelter they had been directed to. The space behind the canvas and floor grates was empty, big enough for maybe four children at the same time, so not all of the dozen clustered around her

were going to fit, not if they were to greet others coming out of the opening in the stone that made up one wall of Hebanthe Falls.

She backed out and looked at her Spinks and the dead-ended street they were in. Other Spinks had been stationed in alleys, under stairwells, beneath awnings and in abandoned structures from here to the doorway of Vapors, where she had been instructed to lead the dwarf and his kids to for safety. If any danger approached, any trouble reared its head along the way, the Spinks knew their signals. One bird whistle for buggers, another for brako, another for Talkers. She could hear the echoes of those things as the Spinks on every level reported the movements of potential interference from one Lev to another, the whistles falling silent in one place when the threats moved off in an unimportant direction. The system worked well, and Ginna was contemplating other uses for the signal system that might benefit Scarecrow later.

Tonight, they had a mission. Later would be time for planning.

"Bils, take Wio and Trix there. Gully, you take over there." She directed all of the Spinks except three, an older boy who went by the moniker of Cyro and the two smallest children, into secure, relatively unobtrusive and unsuspicious places in the street around them. If she needed muscle to help the kids out of the tunnel, Cyro was the best she had. He was strong, but his heavy-set soft features and freckled nose made him appear friendly and harmless…not intimidating, she hoped, to the arriving kids who were already going to be scared.

She had no idea where kids coming out of that opening would come from. Maybe she would find out later, but it did not matter now.

"Cyro…wait here…guard the flap…I'm going in."

"Sure." He crouched in the open-flapped doorway with the two smaller kids once she was inside and kept his gaze focused back down the street and the catwalk above.

If anyone came, he would move them off.

In the meantime, all they could do was wait.

❧*❧

"Is Captain Grainger here?"

Venn had not seen the Captain since his arrival earlier in the afternoon, not during rehearsal, not while the orchestra members shared an early light meal, not as the curtain dropped and the flutter of the audience began to fill the hall. But he had seen the Lieutenant giving orders to the host of bugorra serving as sentries and ushers, speaking in hushed tones to the Ximenezes and their prodcast director where they were positioned for the best recording of the concert in its entirety. He had seen her giving directions to random individuals who picked her out as someone who might know where the restrooms were, where the refreshments were served, and who might be able to answer nearly any question they had.

Venn hoped the Lieutenant being in charge of the bugorra tonight meant that the Captain was engaged in the process of finding, and stopping, whatever madness Rhyd intended.

"Good evening, Mr. Weyer." Ilya knew his name as the organizer of this event, the man, more than the conductor, who was making this recital happen. The individual who had rebuilt the orchestra after the Coup and who would be given credit for this event once it was over…so long as everything went according to plan. She hated to think what might happen if it did not. She forced a smile, distracted though it was, noting with annoyance a group of her officers clustered not far from the nearest lift. But after one pointed one way, and another, somewhere else, and the group split up, she relaxed.

Her officers were supposed to be in place already. If there was a problem, or some question of assignment, she trusted her officers to come to her or work it out for themselves. It appeared they had.

So many together had been briefly troublesome.

"The Captain is attending another matter and will be here later." There was still a considerable amount of time before the recital began, no reason for the cellist to think the Captain's absence meant anything was amiss. To know there was, or could be, something brewing beneath Factory East, was more troublesome than that brief cluster of

officers, but there was no reason for Venn to know any of that. She did not know he had made a request of the Captain himself.

"Good." It seemed he had expected some other reply as he did not seem satisfied, but he reluctantly accepted her statement.

"Shall I send him to you when I see him?" Thinking he might not trust her leadership, a lieutenant in charge rather than the Captain, it seemed the offer to make, even though it rankled her to be doubted. She hoped she would see Grainger before the recital began, hoped his business beneath the Factory proved to be nothing and he would be here where the public expected him to be. She hoped that making the offer would put the cellist at ease.

Venn shook his head. "That's not necessary. I'm sure he'll…I'll see him after if I don't before. Thank you, Lieutenant."

"Good luck tonight."

He nodded and moved off, tension visible in his slightly slouched shoulders, and Ilya decided to make one more pass around the recital hall perimeter. Maybe he was worried about a flawless concert, or maybe something else. Ruling 'something else' out was her duty before she saw to other, more urgent priorities tonight. The recital security would be left with her instructions, left to do their duties without her, as soon as she was satisfied that everything was in place.

❧*❧

No amount of effort to pry information out of Zara provided Jaron with the location where Rhyd intended to be tonight. While he understood her reasons, her argument that Rhyd did not need distractions from duty, especially not the sort of distraction Jaron would provide, the need to act, to help, eroded Jaron's resolve to remain trapped inside the walls of his flat until the night was over. Hoping that satisfying his curiosity would settle his nerves, he used every one of his archivist skills, privileges, and passwords to dig through Hub records with the hopes of pinpointing the likeliest places to extract Skelter from the Core.

Not Factory East. Oliver was there. Rhyd would not take that risk.

Distracting Grainger and the bugorra away from where he intended to be, however, using the fake protests to pull buggers to a few Levs, knowing where Enoch found passage and that Skelter would never be able to fit there, limited the locations Scarecrow might use.

The logic of any place built into the mountainside, a need for water and waste disposal, suggested access to the river, and the only way to utilize the river was to have access to Lev 1.

Lev 1, somewhere near the city's edge. Somewhere near the stone and earth surface that served as Hebenon's eastern wall. That still left a significant portion of real estate, but it was a start.

Knowing his assessment could be wrong, as Jaron moved about his flat looking for something to clean, something to put away or reorganize to stay busy while the Echosys played the ongoing arrival of recital guests, he forced himself to find a small measure of contentment in the possibility of exactly where Rhyd could be…and what he might be doing.

The not knowing, and the whisper-worry that haunted him with questions…how safe would Rhyd be in brako territory, what if he panicked and froze up as he had the other night, what if he fell into the river…eventually forced Jaron to accept that he would find no peace here. Wherever Rhyd was, he would need Jaron's help.

If Jaron did not find him where he expected, at least he would be doing something in looking instead of fretting alone in the dark.

Boots. Gloves. Coat. Hood up as protection from the water and the cold. Anonymous and plain enough not to attract attention.

He was not afraid of the brako. He had nothing they would want. But he was afraid for Rhyd and fear drove him to lock his flat door and start deeper into the Levs.

∾*∾

So many faces.

For all of her life, the populace of Hebanthe Falls had been statistics on a page, numbers without faces, invisible with no concept of how many those figures truly represented. The recital hall grew fuller each time the doors opened, and though it was far from full, there were more faces here already then Neoma had ever fathomed existing in the city the Kemways and Doctet had lauded over.

This was, she knew intellectually, but a fraction of those calling Hebenon home. But how, she mused, could there be so many faces?

"Neoma…so good to see you…" Philippa Underwood, whose family had been connected to the creation and upkeep of Hebenon's solar array since the city's inception, was much thinner than when Neoma had last seen her. Not sickly, but the loss of her family and her Doctet position had not been kind on the brown-skinned woman. Arm in arm with Leslie Isaac, another survivor of the Coup and plague, whose family had been linked to both the recycling industry and the factory processing of hemp products, Philippa offered a one-armed embrace to the Founder's wife, one of the friendliest greetings Neoma had experienced since reemerging into the Uppers after the plague.

These two had not been at the dinner Neoma and Ulynda had just come from. In truth, very few had been there. Legitimate excuses or spite, it had been awkward and hurtful all the same. This greeting, in part, made up for it.

But Leslie's smile masked her scorn. Neoma knew it without having to look deeper. Leslie had at one time hoped to marry Haythem, had been one of his more ardent passions. Neoma, thanks to her father's influence and her own persistent efforts, wheedled her way into Haythem's life, then into his bed.

Leslie had never forgiven her, despite Neoma's belief that the other woman had remained Haythem's lover regardless of their marriages to different people. Once, Neoma had believed Leslie's children were Haythem's.

Because the woman had yet to tout her son as the rightful heir to Hebanthe Falls, Neoma had reluctantly shelved that belief.

Still it lingered.

"Did you see Ogden? You should; he'll be elated you're here"

"And Zeb and Rabia…you know they're married now, don't you? They have a new son! I heard about your children; I'm so sorry…"

If Ogden, or any others, would be thrilled to see her, they would have made it to the dinner, Neoma thought bitterly.

"Ulynda is…" she began, resenting the reminder of the children she had lost, resenting the assumption that all of the Kemway children had perished.

Philippa continued without heeding the disruption or noting the slight she caused. She had always been erratic and sometimes blind to the feelings of others, but Neoma had no chance to speak. "The news about Haythem is just the best. When will we get to see him?"

"Yes," piped Leslie, the peculiar note in her voice hinting at the continuing unrequited torch she bore for the man. "We must see him. Hebanthe Falls deserves to know he is alive and well…not those silly still shots. It will be the best thing for everyone…to see him again…"

Philippa nodded in agreement. "Get things back to the way they were; the children shouldn't mix this way. It isn't healthy being in the damp. Vittorio is already laying the foundation with Senior Kal to…"

The mention of the Senior made Neoma bristle, as did the chittering small talk Philippa tried to engage her in. Even before the Coup, Neoma had felt little in common with the frivolous women society forced her to mingle with. Their concerns for the children's trivial endeavors, for fashion and banal entertainments seemed so petty, so unimportant, to her.

Now, in the grand scheme of what she had planned, Philippa's words and cheery voice struck Neoma as even more unimportant.

Hearing names of survivors whom she had not yet reconnected with, however, meant people who might help reassert her authority over Hebanthe Falls, for her daughter, the way it should be.

But not tonight.

And not if it meant aligning herself with the Voices any more than she already had. She had thought the Voices could benefit her. She was no longer convinced that it was true.

"I must find Ulynda…if you will excuse me." Noting the look on Philippa's face, a mixture of embarrassment that she might have called a child dead who was not, and surprised to hear it…as well as the understanding of the urgency to see to that child's welfare, Neoma gave her very best diplomatic smile and offered her hand to each of the women. "We will share lunch soon…all of us. We must make a plan if we are to reclaim and rebuild Hebanthe Falls."

Relieved that she had caused no lasting offense, Philippa smiled and fervently clasped the offered hand.

"Yes, we must. We will. I will speak to the others and let you know. We'll have a grand time."

"Please, do that…and enjoy the recital."

Leslie, her voice cooler than Philippa's overeager one, nodded and replied, "You as well, Mam."

Each expected they would lunch together soon. Each, Neoma was certain, had vastly different expectations about what that lunch would accomplish.

❧*❧

This suit had been altered for the likelihood of time in the river, making his movements feel stiff and sluggish as he worked through the shadows of Hebenon, alert for confrontations he did not want to have tonight. He could not afford to get sidetracked or to have his plans derailed by an unexpected injury. The initial details had been timed to coincide with as much precision as possible, which meant Rhyd had to reach his destination in time or else miss Zara's cue.

He began his descent early, knowing he needed time to adapt to the changes in this version of his suit, knowing that his nerves needed time to settle if he was to make it through the evening successfully.

He was ahead of schedule, his passage through the Levs quickened by the absence of patrolling buggers and the fact that so many people were either at the recital or were watching the event in their homes, in

tea vindis and clubs and other public places, some on street corners watching on external Echos.

When he heard the cries, the clangs and shudder-thumps of a skirmish, he estimated there was time to investigate at least, to judge if it was a matter he needed to address or one he could ignore. He argued with himself as he swung down a half-Lev and crabbed along a rooftop for a view of what was happening, reminding himself that he could not afford injury, that tonight the Scarecrow's time was spoken for, reserved to help a man who had gone missing during their efforts to locate a mutual friend.

He owed Skelter. Whether Venn believed it or not.

But Scarecrow also believed he owed the people of Hebanthe Falls, particularly since it was the distractions he had helped put in place…in addition to the one provided by the recital…that created a shortage of buggers in the Levs tonight.

He counted nine men, four armed and attired in the stolen Crow uniforms that marked them as brako, five who, while also wielding buzzers and thumpers, wore normal street attire. With the broken window of a vindi nearby, the not-yet soaked strips of rolled fabric that fluttered through the opening suggesting a window newly broken, he guessed that the fight had begun inside and spilled into the street or else had begun here and someone had been pushed through the window…and through the door broken off its hinges lying half in and half out of the vindi.

The brako were outnumbered, the weapons evenly matched. Only the lack of armor on the combatants of one faction set them apart, made them vulnerable. Logic suggested he should leave the vindi owners, if that's who these men were, to finish the job of putting the brako down as they had started to do. But the impulse to act, to bleed off some of the nervous pressurized energy that made Rhyd feel tense and high-strung, was impossible to resist.

It was an easy in, would be an easy out. With one gloved fist around the lip of the catwalk, Scarecrow swung down and caught the nearest Crow-beaked brako in the face with his boots, snapping him

backward, rendering him unconscious when his head struck a recycle bin. Two unmasked men lay groaning, bleeding, conscious but incapacitated, while another wrestled a brako to the ground, snapping a shoulder and busting a leg bone in the process, knocking his weapon away so that it skittered and slid over the edge of the street to clatter to rest somewhere below.

Scarecrow's leap landed in a crouch, allowing him just enough time to scan those still standing to determine who was the biggest, imminent threat. One brako turned his buzzer on the intruder, only to have one of the vindi owners charge him like a bull and knock him back against the door frame. The blue-white buzzer light went black. The man's back made a sickening crack as he struck the corner of the doorway. But it was one of the unmasked fellows, a handsome man with a faded white scar running from temple to chin, and a crooked nose gained in some previous fight, who leaped at Scarecrow with swinging fists aimed for the newcomer's head.

"Piss off," he roared, enraged that Scarecrow eluded his fists and came up with his head in the unmasked fellow's gut. There was enough force behind the head-butt to wind him but not before he squawked, "This is brako business! You're not wanted here!" and dropped to the catwalk on his hands and knees, gasping for breath.

There was not enough time to contemplate the words as the last of the unmasked fighters standing also made the effort to remove Scarecrow from the fight. A roundhouse kick knocked the bully down, and with all nine either unconscious or otherwise immobilized, Scarecrow grabbed the man he had just kicked by the lapels and shoved him against the side rail, holding him at a precarious angle where one false move, or one wrong word, might result in a nasty tumble to the roof of the building below.

"Vanderwall's gonna have your head for interfering…"

Vanderwall was brako. Everyone knew it. The brako wore gear stolen from the Crows, everyone knew that too. It was an effort to make themselves intimidating and an effort that hid their identities.

Maybe this was just Vanderwall sending in muscle to give a warning to members not playing by his rules.

Scarecrow did not know. At the moment he did not care.

"Just…please…" The distorted growling voice through the Scarecrow's mask was more menacing then the men he had been fighting were, and though he had made that initial threat, he quickly realized his life was held only by the hands at his lapels. He had no interest in dying. "I won't say anything…he'll never know you were here…just let me go…and stay out of our business."

"Don't get in my way," Scarecrow growled again, "don't mess with people, and we won't have a problem." He turned enough that the stranger hung safely back over the wet grated catwalk. "And don't," he added, "ever come at me again."

One fist. One fist to the side of the man's head and the fellow dropped silently to the ground. He would live, they all would…except for the man one of the others had thrown against the edge of the doorframe whose spine was undoubtedly broken…but none of them would come after Scarecrow tonight. Just to be certain, he kicked the fellow, still on his hands and knees, gasping for breath, in the ribs hard enough to topple him and leave him moaning in pain.

Then Scarecrow was off about his business. The puzzle of internal brako politics was for solving some other night.

❧*❧

Tamner handed the syringe to one of his assistants and removed his sterile gloves to toss them into the cleaning solution for later use. The results of the tests he had run came back inconclusive, although a few were still in process, creating an unsettled rolling in his stomach as they prepared the Founder for relocation. There was no obvious reason, no obvious change in the man's bloodwork, to account for what Tamner thought he had seen that morning, causing the doctor to second guess himself as he watched the tech administer the concoction that would keep Kemway calm and submissive as they moved him.

Tamner did not want to drug him into unconsciousness and be forced to carry him. It would be much simpler to move him if he could walk, and given his fragile health, Tamner did not want to induce a sleep state he might not be able to reverse.

Calm and submissive were good enough.

He would rather be at the recital with his son; it had been a long time since he had enjoyed a good turn of live music.

Tonight he would have to settle for viewing the prodcast later. This was, he agreed with Grainger, the best time to move Kemway.

When no one was paying attention.

He received the message before reaching the lab. Lieutenant Young was on her way. He would rather it be Grainger helping with this move, would rather not be introducing someone else to either where Kemway had been, or would be, but Grainger assured him that his business was of the highest priority and Lieutenant Ilya could be trusted with this duty as if she was Grainger herself.

The assurance was barely enough to soothe Tamner's nerves.

He heard the whoosh of the lift door. He stuck his head out of the room long enough to see that no one stepped out of the lift as it passed between floors, knowing that it sometimes stopped and opened its doors to other levels as well.

That knowledge should calm him. A glance at Kemway, however, who stared ahead as impassive as ever, did not.

He would not be at ease until Kemway was secure where Neoma, and anyone else who might come for him, could not reach him.

❧*❦

Watching her mother walk away, off to mingle with the familiar faces of the defunct Doctet and the new faces of the Nau, was no surprise to Ulynda. It was what her parents had always done, political maneuvering and posturing at similar events always knowing their children would be safe amongst members of their own Uppers class.

Things were different now, a host of strangers swirling about, Lev faces that offered no reassurance of friendliness.

She should have been more thoughtful of her daughter's welfare, but old habits were hard to give up.

Forgetting her child was there, might have need of her in this unfamiliar setting with people they did not know, was an unfortunate fact Ulynda expected as she felt the burn of resentment creeping across the back of her neck. For several minutes, the girl did not move, waiting instead for her mother to remember her, for someone familiar to find her just inside one set of recital hall double doors and take her under their wing.

But no one came, no one paid her heed, and when she felt confident that no one either recognized her as a Kemway or cared that she was alone, she instead sought somewhere to sit, somewhere that did not look to be reserved for dignitaries. She doubted seats had been reserved for her and her mother.

"Ulynda!"

A voice she knew, an unexpected voice, made her smile. "Cori!" She and Cori Tamner had never been close; their parents' positions moving them in separate directions even at such young ages, but the Tamners had been ever-present fixtures at Upper events, and Cori and Ulynda had started to attend social functions the same year.

She did not, however, recognize the younger blonde girl at Cori's side, a girl whose warm skin tone suggested considerable time in the sun. A prosser's kid who now spent time Outside when her parents were there, perhaps. There would never be parah here, at a recital like this. Parah were heathens, barbarians, surely with little interest in cultural refinement.

Seeing Ulynda's interest in his companion, Cori said with a smile, "This is Agnys."

"Hello, Agnys."

"Hello." Agnys offered her hand the way she had seen the adults in the city do and was pleased when Ulynda accepted the handshake. It might not mean they were friends, but it meant that the girl with the

brown hair done up in an elegant coif and a dress cut of a style Agnys had never seen, was not afraid of her. "Do you want to sit with us?"

Unaware that such engagements had rules, that Ulynda might be here with her family and obligated to sit with them, the offer seemed the polite thing to do. And Ulynda, comfortable in Cori's familiar company, happy to have found someone she knew to talk to, saw no harm in accepting.

"Yes," she replied. She took no more than six steps with them, however, laughing politely when Cori made a mock formal bow and gestured in the direction of the chairs Venn had assigned to him and Agnys, when a hand hooked around her arm.

"Come along, Ulynda." Neoma's haughty sniff was not lost on any of the children. Cori gave an apologetic shrug as he lowered his gaze, a gesture of respect ingrained in the children of Upper families when in the company of the Founder and the Mam. Ulynda looked embarrassingly horrified at her mother's rudeness and tried to think of something to say to excuse or correct it. It was understandable that she would not recognize Agnys, whose family was likely part of the Nau or else had come up from the Levs to attend the recital. But surely she recognized Doctor Tamner's son.

Ulynda wanted to protest, to insist on staying with Cori and her new friend. She wanted to address Cori's identity to the woman dragging her away. With her mother's seemingly foul mood, however, and the increasing distance between them, Cori, and Agnys, all Ulynda could do was look back and wave with her own apologetic gesture.

❧*❧

The brako were taking advantage of the buggers being stretched thin, as Lash and Tox, his arm tight and steering around her shoulder as if protecting a prize, or else preventing her from escaping, passed their third group of brako Crows on their way to Lev 1. One group had been emptying a warehouse, taking crates from inside and stacking them outside, either for movement elsewhere or for the purpose of

inventory. Maybe they were stealing it. Lash and Tox could not tell. A second group was passed escorting a collection of dog-pulled wagons over the catwalk, the rattling announcing them though no one in the surrounding vindis seemed to care. The third group emerged from one of the lifts as they passed; they gave the couple a suspicious once over, looking them up and down, but allowed them to continue without interfering, focused instead on their own business.

The cord wrapped around Lash's arm was a common adornment for addicts, tied tight to keep a vein exposed for injections. Tox's overdone makeup and too much exposed skin beneath the transparent slicker borrowed from Zara left little doubt as to her occupation. Whether andi or human, no one dressed like that unless they did only one thing for a living. Nothing demeaning about it, a job like any other, and not one of the brako they passed did more than look.

Lash, knowing the way, led Tox to the southeast corner of Lev 1, where the earthen wall met the man-made barrier designed to protect everyone in Hebanthe Falls from the poisons in the world outside. Though the belief in that poisonous atmosphere persisted, it had not stopped some from finding ways around that barrier, or through it, onto the catwalk meant for maintenance and eventual city expansion if the city had ever needed it.

It had not.

With the paneling peeled back to provide an opening big enough for a man to wiggle through to access the unencumbered fishing location, or a place untroubled by law enforcement for the pursuit of illegal activities, the possibility of poisonous air was moot. The Outside was open. There was nothing to keep anyone in the city any longer, to keep them from removing this southern wall altogether.

Nothing except the undercurrent of lingering fear.

The river was high and full, the water sloshing over the Lev 1 catwalk, creating a symphony of its own as debris washed over the falls bumped and scratched and crashed against the grating. It sounded as if the river nets had failed, with the clatter the debris made, as Lash held back the bent panel enough for Tox to squeeze through without

catching on any sharp edges. The netters would be working overtime tonight. From the exterior catwalk, in the mist and spray thrown up by the turbulent water, they could see where some of that debris was being hurled against the jagged, exposed rocks. With the water shooting up between the crisscrossed coated metal of the runway, it made the surface more slippery than usual and presented, at a glance, an unexpected obstacle that Tox wagered Rhyd had not planned for.

Or maybe he had. Maybe that was why he requested the extra waterproofing changes to his body armor. But even though there was heavy cable coiled around the winch, secured tightly to the handrail which stretched from the eastern rock wall across the whole length of the catwalk to the western rock wall on the opposite side of the river, there appeared to be no obvious or direct path of entry or extraction.

She looked up. Maybe it was above them. Maybe he was going to climb, and that was the reason he had requested bolt eyes.

She was worried, but Lash seemed as nonplussed as ever, his slack skinned posture and expression revealing none of his thoughts.

"Should be here soon." Lash looked over the rail, testing the stability with one hand while testing the winch welded to a sturdy stanchion with the other.

"Long as the brako don't hold him up."

"They won't." Lash sounded certain, and Tox suspiciously side-eyed him. He shrugged again. "He knows what's at stake. I trust him."

So did Tox…just not to leave the brako alone if they crossed him.

"Scarecrow's here."

The burly man with the trencher pulled up around his neck and the brim of his hat pulled low to ward off the dripping moisture faced the speaker, a smaller, plain dressed fellow limping in pain, clutching the side of his ribs as if the effort to breathe and speak was agonizing.

"Where?"

"Going down." He had not seen where Scarecrow had gone, once he disappeared into the shadows and steam of the city, but he had judged his trajectory and down was the only logical option from where the fight had occurred.

If Scarecrow had wanted to go up, he would have gone back the way he came. And if he was staying on Lev 2, there was very little of 2 left on that section of the street.

But down still meant a lot of city to cover, miles of street, hundreds vindis, fisheries, and wares.

Especially wares.

"Trenton tried to warn him off our business."

Vanderwall scowled.

"And we saw…"

"What?"

His prattling irritated the big man, but he felt it was his duty to report what he knew, regardless of the irritation it caused. To say nothing was to get a worse beating than the one Scarecrow had given. It would mean more than cracked ribs and a bruised diaphragm.

"A couple…a streeter and an andi…heading towards the soaper."

Nothing so unusual about a streeter taking a shot at a soaper. It happened frequently enough. It was the best place to pick up pure product, if one had the ticks to score with or something of value to trade. And if one had the ticks to pick up an andi…or had something else to offer her…like the prospect of the strongest Hebbies on the streets, then a run at a soaper, the source, was always worth the risk one faced of being beaten down at the worst or being run off with a handful of Hebbies at the best.

Maybe he intended to trade the andi for a score.

Still, tonight of all nights, with the reshuffling of brako inventory around the Levs to keep ahead of the distracted buggers, it would not do to have a confrontation at the soaper.

"Check it out…make sure they're not causing trouble. And turn over one and two. Find Scarecrow and bring him to me. Alive."

There were people interested in the meddlesome specimen. Picking him up, or at least fingering his identity, would be worth a lot of ticks, a lot of favors, to someone.

Who the highest bidder would be, who Vanderwall passed the vigi over to, would depend on how the rest of this night played out.

❧Chapter 32❧

Thanks to the chirps and whistles, Ginna and Cyro knew about the approaching pair of buggers before the two reached the end of the street where Cyro sat half in, half out, of the lean-to shelter, playing bones with the two younger kids kept close to give him company. Streeter kids rarely traveled alone, finding safety in numbers, and the older ones protected the younger ones, so it made Cyro look less suspicious to have other small bodies, covered head to foot in nondescript rags that kept their identities hidden, nearby. A face peeped out from an adjacent vindi, a nervous face that appeared concerned about unfamiliar children loitering in the area.

"Hello," called Cyro, his friendly voice matching the merry look on his dirty, round, cherubic face. "Spare a few ticks maybe?" He held out one hand beseechingly, smiling still.

The front-most bugger looked the boy over, noted the foldable metal game board the children were rolling bones on, frowning as he assessed the level of danger the children represented. The other bugger was sweeping her gaze up and down the dead-end path, evaluating where threats might be hiding, whether there was a valid reason for the vindi to be concerned about this group of streeters or if the call had only come because the woman did not know the children's faces.

Maybe streeters did not often come to this particular place.

"You shouldn't be here."

"Shouldn't?" With the profusion of streeters in Hebenon, there were few actual regulations as to where they could and could not be. So long as they were not loitering in vindi doorways, harassing vindis or customers, were not violent or committing some other crimes, they were typically left alone, ignored. Chasing the children away from this

location would mean they took root somewhere else, and as far as the gorra could see, they three were not causing trouble.

"What's in there?"

"Here?" Cyro indicated the interior of the lean-to with a tilt of his head while Ginna scurried to block the opening in the stone from anyone looking in. "Just my sister."

The bugger leaned to look inside, flashing a light to better see by. The girl beneath the canvas, obviously older than Cyro or the other two, lifted her arm to shield her eyes, not wanting anyone to recognize her as Lieutenant Young's sister. Her raised arm hid the opening with the flap of blanket that hung over her head and arms to the ground. She was as much the boy's sister as night was the day, but streeters, especially the kids, were known to create makeshift families with the kids collected around them.

Ginna forced a cough, a sound too dry, too harsh, but one that prompted the bugger to withdraw without question. If the girl was contagious, had taken shelter to rest, the buggers did not want to catch whatever she had.

With the opening of the city to the Outside, the paranoia about unknown contagions was particularly high.

"Get her to a medi; she needs care," the gorra grunted, shutting off his light and tucking it back into the loop on his belt.

"Once she's had a good sleep," Cyro agreed with a nod. "That's all we're doin'…lettin' her sleep a bit."

"And don't be troubling these nice folks. No tinging…stay out of trouble. Brako are out in force tonight; stay clear of them, okay?"

"We will," agreed one of the smaller children.

"Just a few hours," Cyro reiterated with a smile. "We'll move on."

The bugorra grunted, decided no harm was being done here, and ambled back down the street. With reports of brako movement all over the Levs tonight, streeter children were the least of their worries.

Cyro looked at Ginna when the buggers were out of sight, listening to the Spink calls that followed the route the two took until they were no longer on the path the Spinks had marked as theirs.

So far, so good. But they might not be lucky enough to ward off the next buggers to find them. Or the brako.

❧*❧

Not hearing anything unusual beyond the rushing of the swollen river and the pair of voices uttering occasional tense, anxious comments, Scarecrow ducked through the bent-back panel and joined the two on the exposed catwalk. The elevation of the river, higher than it had been when he had positioned the winch and secured it in place, concerned him. Its flow was stronger, meaning getting in and out of that chasm was going to be a greater challenge and he could barely see the mountain opening past the surge. There was maybe two hands' width of an unsubmerged gap behind the slosh and churn of the high water. He was grateful he was mentally prepared for the likelihood of submersion, that the suit and his oxygen equipment were prepared for that prospect. It was no longer just a possibility. It was a certainty.

How he would get Skelter and the others out without similar equipment for them was a question of great concern.

"Brako are moving," Lash said in a low voice.

"I know." Scarecrow shrugged his pack off his shoulders, dropped it at Tox's feet, and tested the handrail and winch as both Lash and Tox had done. They were secure, but would the welds be strong enough to hold against the rapid pull of the river?

Tox stepped sideways to let Scarecrow pass, scooting the pack out of his way. "Think they'll trouble us?"

"Wouldn't surprise me." The roar of the river was louder, thanks to the increased water volume and the banging created by the debris clattering against the metal catwalk. Without Scarecrow's enhanced hearing, there was little reason anyone should hear them here, as long as they weren't shouting and screaming, and he was confident no one had followed him. But after his earlier altercation, and whatever the brako appeared to be up to, there was no guarantee that they would be

left alone. Someone might come looking for him…or come here for some purpose of their own. "Want these?"

He did not use buzzers, injectors, or poppers, could not use them in the river, but he drew his thumpers from his belt and offered them to his allies. "Not gonna need them over there." He had debated bringing them at all, but the possibility of needing them, before or after the rescue, prompted him to prepare as he usually did. He preferred his fists, but sometimes a thumper was a better alternative.

"You bet I do." Lash took them both when Tox hesitated to do so. She would change her mind, once things got underway, and if she did not, Lash could work just as well with a thumper in each hand.

❧*❧

"Enough," Colyx barked. The children had been separated from the adults, sent with Enoch and Switz, and he was confident Skelter had their escape route secure and was ready to proceed when the signal came. They were waiting for it now, the cue to blow the door, but his efforts to settle the rest of the Core population felt as though he was herding rabid rats. There was bickering as they anxiously jockeyed into position, grousing and shoving and a few thrown punches, with no one willing to listen to his previously softer, sterner efforts to restore order.

His roar, however, a sound the others respected from years of experience with the violence that would follow if they did not respond, brought an uneasy hush.

"It's almost time…get in there…let's make this count!"

"Where's Skelt?" someone shouted back in challenge.

"He should be here too," called someone else.

"Having a final cazz," sneered another, someone near enough to Colyx to earn an elbow in the side that hurt enough to silence him…and possibly fracture a few ribs.

Colyx did not care if the injury took the fellow out of the fight or contributed to his death. He knew the plan. If everything went the way

Skelter intended, most of these people would not survive to trouble Hebenon as they once had, and Colyx would never see them again.

Their crimes had sentenced them to hard labor and death. Death it would be for most.

He would not warn them again. They would listen and obey or he would start breaking skulls.

They were not his friends. He did not care about their fates. He doubted most in the Core could call any others friends, as most cared only about themselves. At best, they were alliances made to ensure personal survival, shifting day to day, week to week, sometimes hour to hour as necessity dictated. The only people who mattered to Colyx were the ones Skelter was making sure had a way out.

Everyone else could rot.

❧*❧

Tamner scowled as the woman clicked the wrist restraints into place. "Those aren't necessary," he repeated. Haythem did not react to having his arms pulled in front of him, to the cold metal locked electronically that made it impossible for him to strike out at anyone. Haythem was beyond that sort of rational action, unless he dropped into one of his manic modes. But sedated, calm and compliant, there was about as much of a chance of that happening as there was of the man sprouting feathers. The sedative would last until the Founder was secure in his new home, closer to Tamner's personal rooms where he could keep a more vigilant eye on the man's welfare and condition.

But Lieutenant Young had orders and she would follow them, regardless of the doctor's admonitions.

"The Captain wants him there in one piece. Without incident."

"Where is the Captain?" Grainger had reached out to Tamner earlier that morning with the news that something had come up, a matter he could entrust to no one else, so that the movement of Kemway to his new, more secure location, was entrusted to Lieutenant Young's capable hands. Tamner had known the Lieutenant as long as

she had been on the force, as a young Crow, as Grainger's top subordinate, and then as the head of the bugorra once Grainger was thrust into the position of leader of Hebanthe Falls after the Coup.

It was not that he did not trust her. Tamner would only have felt better about this move if Grainger was here seeing to it himself.

Ilya rechecked the bindings to be sure they were secure. They did not pull loose and when she tugged at them, nearly pulling the Founder off balance, his only reaction was to stumble. Satisfied that he would not be a problem, she replied, "Occupied."

Tamner snorted. That was no answer.

ICD to her mouth, Ilya pressed the side button and said, "Check one…copy?"

"Check one secure."

"Check two…copy?"

"Check two secure."

She repeated the call with each checkpoint and each answer came back the same. Secure. Prepared for the transfer to begin.

"We ready to do this?" She glanced at Tamner as she drew her popper from its holster.

"Soon as the techs are back." He was not moving Kemway anywhere with just Ilya and her two bugorra for escort. If he had to put himself, and the Founder, in someone else's hands, he was going to do so with other medical personnel along for assistance.

❧*❧

Straddling the rail, heart hammering as he faced immersion in Hebenon's life-saving river, Scarecrow did not expect anyone to squeeze through the folded opening. A hand, then a leg, and he was certain the intruder was brako…or some hapless individual intending some fishing from this dangerous point.

He was not expecting Jaron Rei.

Nor, it was obvious, were Tox and Lash expecting the dark-haired fellow to join them.

"You shouldn't be here," Scarecrow snarled, the beating of his heart faster now for reasons much different than the river's threat.

The menace of Scarecrow's mechanically altered voice sank directly to the one place Jaron wished it would not go and he swallowed, uneasy and discomfited by the high-pitched whine in the tone of his digitized words when he responded, "I need to help."

He was surprised his hunch had been correct, that he found Scarecrow on his first try. But he could see nothing from where he stood with his back against Hebenon's metal-skinned southern wall that suggested how Scarecrow intended to access the Core or bring anyone out of it. All Jaron could see was Scarecrow…and the river, the river he had never viewed before, the river that seemed too full, too treacherous…and yet was clearly where Scarecrow intended to go.

"You're supposed to be with…" started Lash.

Voice shaky, now with fear as he continued to assess the location and calculate Scarecrow's plan, Jaron countered, "Oliver's in the Factory, at the Core door." At least, that was where Jaron assumed Oliver had gone. He had not seen the Captain since much earlier, but he knew that Oliver had taken the Core threat seriously and had not seen him on the prodcast footage of the pre-recital arrivals. "I can't do anything there…but I can…"

"I don't need you in the way…in danger…"

"Not the one about to be in danger."

"I know what I'm doing…and you're in the way."

It was not true, as Jaron still hugged the wall and was in no position to interfere with Rhyd's next action. But this was no time for arguing. Time was against them, and Tox could see that Jaron was unwilling to back down…and Scarecrow was just as unwilling to leave Jaron in harm's way.

"We could use his help," she said evenly, doing her best not to take sides in this disagreement. "One of us should keep watch…and it may take two to turn that thing against the current."

Behind the mask, Rhyd scowled. Under normal circumstances, he trusted Tox was strong enough to winch one or two people at a time

out of the river with the cable line he had rigged. But with the storm swell he had not expected, one person's strength indeed might not be enough. With the brako active tonight, setting someone as a lookout while the others took post here made sense.

He should have considered this sooner, but even if he had, asking Jaron to help would not have been his first choice. He did not know who he would have turned to, but it would have been anyone but Jaron. If Jaron was harmed, Rhyd would never forgive himself.

Lash reluctantly agreed. "He's stronger. He should stay. I'll keep watch." Besides, he looked the most like a streeter, a harmless relic, so taking a place on the inside of the city wall, slouching there smoking hemp smokies, would attract less attention than Tox and her sex-toy attire, or handsome, young Jaron. He also had the thumpers, should he need them, and Rhyd believed he could take care of himself.

The man with the stringy blonde hair had been taking care of himself far longer than any of them.

He also knew Jaron better than either Rhyd or Tox.

Without looking directly at them, knowing he was defeated in his effort to send Jaron away and knowing that continued argument would waste several more precious minutes, Scarecrow grunted, dropped his coat on the catwalk at Jaron's feet in a gesture of surrender, and secured the line through the loop hook on his utility belt. He muttered, "Stay out of the way…don't interfere."

The words were meant more for Jaron then they were for anyone else. The other two knew the plan. He trusted them. He was not, however, entirely prepared to trust his life in Jaron's hands.

They were not the words that came to mind as he lowered into the current, holding tight to the line while Tox kept the cable from uncoiling as the river tried to pull Scarecrow with it. The rolling rapids and his sharply inhaled breath swallowed the words he wanted to say.

❮*❯

The delay in getting the children into the room, into the tunnel, could not be helped. Farewells between children and the only families they had ever known were not ideal, but after several false starts and stops, the time had come to move, to get the children safely away before armageddon erupted in the Core.

"Just follow me; it'll be alright," Enoch assured them as he crept forward into the darkness just far enough that whoever came next could see him. The flare he carried in one hand popped and sizzled, and though he worried about the heat of it somehow setting off the freezes, there was no other choice. There was no other light source he could bring, and without one, the children were not likely to follow.

"Go on," urged Otta. "Just like follow the leader."

Only her urging and the fact that they knew both her and the dwarf…and trusted the two as much as any child brought up in such a place could trust anyone…allowed the first child, the youngest, to start his journey. And the next. And another. One by one, the oldest child coming at the end, with Switz bringing up the rear with another flare sparkling in his hand.

"You got this." There was a warning in Otta's tone as Switz started in. If any harm came to the children because of the spidery man, she intended to be there on the outside to make sure he paid for it.

"We'll get 'em out," Switz promised, ignoring the threat in favor of his own reassurances and intentions. Getting the children out of the Core was his ticket to freedom, might procure him benefits on the outside with the Core's survivors, and he had no intention of messing up his chances for a good life.

Otta's ICD, supplied in one of the deliveries of smokeys, tools, flares, and other goods Enoch had brought in popped in her ear. "Otta. Time."

She nodded at the nearly dark tunnel, only barely able to hear the scurrying of hands, knees, and feet through the narrow space. With the children on their way to safety, she could begin to consider her own.

❧*❧

The swift-moving water took the effort out of Scarecrow's reaching the craggy stone surface of the eastern cliff. The river pulled and tugged, trying to take the movement of his limbs out of his control, but Scarecrow was stronger than that. So long as he had something to grasp, so long as the systems and the seals in his suit did not fail, he was confident he could beat his battle with the river. Catching a secure hold with gloved fingers on the rocks when he reached the wall, however, holding himself there against the pull that wanted to drag him to the sea or beat him to death on the multitude of boulders jutting up from the bottom in the process, took more effort. The barely visible mouth of his target was beyond his reach, and getting to it without overshooting was the next challenge.

The bolter, protected from moisture as best as Tox had been able to design, was shaken out and prepped for the first bolt-eye piton to be inserted. Fighting to hang onto the stone with one hand, ignoring Jaron's nervous gasp, Scarecrow focused on his work. Lash had left the platform, and both Tox and Jaron held a strong grasp on the winch handle. If everything else was in place elsewhere throughout Hebenon, Scarecrow was as ready as he was ever going to be.

If he was forced to wait much longer in the icy water, despite the insulation inside his body armor and the steady oxygen supply from the built-in tanks, he risked hypothermia and running out of air.

He tapped the side of his hood.

Tox nodded.

"Hold this," she instructed Jaron. She released the handle with one hand in order to tap her ICD and raise it to her lips, causing Jaron to throw more effort into keeping the cable taut.

Letting go might send Scarecrow to a watery, bloody beaten death.

Tox nodded twice. Once to Jaron. Once to Scarecrow. She judged the situation as best she could and murmured, "Zar…we're ready."

❧*❧

The recital hall was full, the final arriving guests forced to make do with either sitting separated as the gaps in the rows were filled in, standing, or accepting less comfortable benches along the edges of the room. Filling the room had been expected. Providing additional seating created a potential hazard in case of an emergency, but no one seemed concerned about that possibility. Captain Grainger was elsewhere, Zara knew, and she had not seen Lieutenant Young moving about since sometime earlier. Perhaps Oliver had summoned her for backup. Perhaps there was some other pressing matter afoot, in addition to the rumored threat at the Core door.

So long as the bugorra stayed well away from Scarecrow and the Lev 2 Spinks, where the Lieutenant might be was not Zara's concern.

Her absence, however, was undoubtedly the reason someone thought that overfilling the recital hall was an acceptable risk.

A row of Echos lined the sofa table, each one set with different tasks, different hacks, different functions, interlinked so that the night's events were synced with one another. Zara was confident of her work, confident of success, but because so many lives depended on her, she remained there, on her knees, watching each screen and the events on the prodcast carefully.

The seating lights in the recital hall dimmed and the curtain lifted. Welcoming applause thundered across the prodcast speakers.

Unaware that Enoch and the children were in motion, knowing only that Skelter was in place by the message her rigged communication line offered, and that Rhyd was ready and trusting others were as well, Zara uttered a silent plea to the deities of the universe for Oliver's safety, for the safety of all involved, and said, "Go," as she pressed the first Echo key.

"Go," shouted Colyx.

As the first notes of a sweet cello were lifted by the supporting swell of violins, the lights on the stage went dark.

Scarecrow's bolter discharged, driving the first bolt-eye piton into stone.

There was a single, piercing blip from the barred door of the Core before them. East Factory's underground was swallowed in pitch at the same moment as the door erupted outward, in their direction, the concussive force throwing every bugorra off their feet.

❧CHAPTER 33❧

The explosion shuddered through the floors as Tamner led Kemway out of seclusion into the corridor behind Lieutenant Young and her two bugorra. Glaring white corridors turned black, and for a few moments remained that way until the red flash of emergency lighting kicked in. The backup circuits kept the filt systems running, kept the air moving through the Levs and Uppers, kept the city livable in the event of a disruption to the primary systems. It was a rare occurrence for both systems to be down at the same time. Thankfully, they were not both down now.

Tamner remembered the last time.

The last time had been precipitated by one small parah child.

Everyone in the group froze, having no idea what they had just felt, but a quick look at each face and their cessation of movement was enough to know he was not the only one to feel the tremor.

Only Kemway, in his sedated stupor, did not react, although he stopped moving when the hands on his arms forced him to.

Ilya nodded. She had no explanation for that unexpected concussive vibration; there was no sound with it beyond the shaking, and no immediate eruption of chatter over the ICD. If there was an emergency, she expected to be summoned soon enough.

"We have to move."

Tamner agreed.

❧*❧

With the clapping of hands and the stomping of excited feet, the tremors through the city were lost to both audience and orchestra. Only

the loss of the stage lights marked a difference, and Venn swallowed the first angry thought that pushed through his head.

Rhyd, if you did this, I will never forgive you.

He knew tonight's numbers by heart, however. He had rehearsed them over and over, played them in his dreams, so that his fingers continued over the cello strings without faltering, without the need of seeing the sheet music on the Echostand in front of him. As he continued to play, the rest of the orchestra followed suit, their minimal faltering barely noticeable to the audience.

As the orchestra continued in the dark, most in the room assumed the lack of lighting was an intentional part of the night's experience. They settled in their seats to listen after the first moment of unease, eagerly content to enjoy the music even if they could not see.

Only the bugorra around the perimeter, protecting each of the now-closed doors, worried that something was amiss. On the outside of the hall, someone tried to reach the Lieutenant.

But the ICD system was dead.

Not one of those buggers noted the peeling off of six others who converged upon the nearest stairwell and began to climb. If they did, they presumed the six were seeking the Lieutenant or the Captain.

The red backup lights came on. The suction of the doors, which had sealed in the moment of power failure, unstuck again. The recital continued. There was no reason for panic.

৯০*৩৬

"Hold."

Enoch's command was unnecessary, as the violent shaking through the stone baptized them with falling dirt and instigated frightened cries and whimpers from the children. He did not think the distant explosion was powerful enough to collapse the tunnel and there was no blowback of debris in his face to suggest a collapse ahead of them. It was a possibility he and Skelter had discussed, the possibility being the primary reason they had intended to send the children

through much earlier, the primary reason the delay in starting through the tunnel worried the dwarf although it had not seemed to trouble most of the other adults in the Core.

They were miners, for crucksake. They knew what explosives underground did. If the tunnel had come down once the children were outside, the explosion would have been inconsequential, but it seemed few had thought of that.

"Sound off."

One by one, the children began to call back their names.

Assuming the way ahead to be clear, knowing it was inconsequential if the tunnel collapsed behind Switz so long as they could keep moving forward, Enoch carefully counted the names. If the tunnel had collapsed in the middle of their queue, he would have heard and felt it. But all of the children were accounted for, scared but alive, and with Switz the last to report, it was a relief that no one was hurt, no one was lost.

For now, they were safe.

"Let's go."

It was not so much further. If they hurried, they could be out before anything worse happened or the shaking came again.

&ous;*&ous;

Engineering and planning by the Core's residents and Zara's hack of the Factory power grid that shut off the power flow through the electronic lock she had been unable to decode, hurled the Core door outward. The force of the explosion blew backward, throwing those inside who were closest to the door into the people behind them so that many were knocked off their feet. Through the dust and debris and rock that fell in the now-empty archway from the hewn roofing above and in the corridor around the Core's captives, they could not yet see anything beyond it. They could hear coughing, choking, moaning, and with the flash of red illumination that burned through the haze when the emergency systems kicked in, they could begin to make out the

masked, silhouetted shadows picking themselves up from the ground, steadying themselves against the shuddering walls.

A few had been pinned down by the expelled doors.

Not the Crows they had expected, but shadows equally ominous, equally menacing.

The threat of the unknown did not thwart the aim of someone inside the Core; an edge-sharpened plate soared out of the dust and caught a shadow with enough force to sink into his unprotected bicep.

The Core erupted in a triumphant roar. Footsteps thundered forward…

…and Oliver Grainger rushed in, leading his officers, to meet the charging threat head-on without a thought to what he would find in the middle of the falling dust.

The gorra tried to avoid trampling those caught beneath the blown doors. Those rushing from the inside did not.

❧*❧

He worked as quickly, as steadily as he could, hand over hand, one bolt-eye piton shot into place after another, the cable that secured him to Hebenon's rail threaded through each and attached to its secure loop each time, and with each extension, a tug on the line that prompted Tox and Jaron to coil out another length of cable. With his hands full and occupied, he could not pause to turn on the helmet ICD he had intentionally left silent so as not to have to talk his way through every action with those on the catwalk, particularly Jaron who he imagined would be uttering a stream of nervous chatter if he believed Rhyd could hear him.

As it was, in the one moment Scarecrow glanced back, he was surprised to see Jaron focused on the winch, not hovering like a nervous fool.

He might have misjudged the man. But he preferred to think he was protecting himself, limiting distractions to concentrate on the task at hand.

One more tug on the line and a gesture back, like a wave or a salute, and then he swallowed an unnecessary lungful of air before ducking his head beneath the surface of the water.

"Tox!" Having seen the gesture but having no idea what it meant, what the plan was, it was frightening to see Scarecrow disappear from sight, swallowed by the river he had struggled against for the last several minutes.

Before she could speak, a solid rapping sounded on the metal wall behind them, a signal they could not ignore although for a few moments she thought perhaps she should do so. If Rhyd's vanishing meant trouble, if it meant he was in distress and needed extraction, she did not know if Jaron could do it alone.

But the warning about approaching trouble from inside the city was not to be dismissed either.

The cable was tight. Not overly so, not pulling towards the main flow of the river as it might if Rhyd was floating helplessly. From the direction of the line, the way it now angled around a previously unnoticed lip of rock, she guessed Rhyd had found some way inside, a cave or tunnel, that had been his destination all along.

"Long as the line's tight, he's okay," she muttered. "Hold this…don't let him go. I'll be back."

"Tox," Jaron started, body jerking as her stepping away left the full force of the winch and line in his control. She ripped off the ear ICD she wore, shoved it into his ear none too gently, and was already ducking out to where Lash waited.

Jaron swallowed and looked at the river, to the place where the line disappeared from view. Determined not to fail Scarecrow, not to fail Rhyd, not to fail Skelter, determined to help as he had come to do rather than give in to the panic that made him want to throw up, he planted his feet more securely on the slippery grated floor, tightened his hold on the winch, and whispered, "I'm here. I've got you."

Scarecrow would not hear him, but he felt better uttering that promise out loud.

❧*❦

The recital hall lights flashed back on. The orchestra still played.

The audience relaxed more and smiled at one another.

The buggers on the perimeter relaxed too.

Behind closed lids, Venn took back the threat he had silently made against Rhyd. A power glitch. Nothing more. Known to happen in the city at random intervals as systems were modified, repaired, rebooted, it was no emergency, no precursor of worse to come. Bad timing on the part of the work crews, nothing more.

❧*❦

Haythem blinked and cringed as the corridor lights flashed back on. Not an unusual reaction, given that those around him did likewise, but still Tamner noticed. He made a mental note to check those test results again, and to run more, to continue studying Kemway's changing condition, as soon as they got the man settled and secure.

❧*❦

Blinded by the flash of the returning main power and the glaring white light, Grainger's team was at a temporary disadvantage. So too, he noticed, were the Core fighters, at least those who had made it clear of the blown door and the still settling dust. Probably not used to bright lights, he thought smugly, dropping two assailants with his buzzer before it was knocked from his hand.

He reached for the injector. Less effective, as it took a few moments for the Hebbie sedative to take effect, but it would take some of the attackers out of play without killing them outright.

Grainger resolutely accepted the compromise as his team pushed into the fight.

❧*❦

Beyond the folded flap, the pair of brako squared their shoulders in an attempt to intimidate the stringy-haired streeter and the woman who had joined him. Lash stared at them dispassionately, sucking on a hemp smokey as if he had nothing to fear, as if he was, perhaps, already under the influence of something that impaired his judgment. Not having heard any exchange of comments, Tox did not know if questions had been asked or threats made, so she wrapped one arm around Lash's neck and tucked the other hand down the front of his trousers. He wore a long coat but no shirt, so the direction and location of her hand were obvious to the brako who she imagined were either frowning or smirking behind stolen Crow masks.

"What? Can't a girl take a piss?"

The beaked heads turned slightly towards one another. Not an andi then. Andis did not piss. But still a hook, and this was not, in anyone's view, a good place for a cazzing rendezvous. Too cold, and with the river surge beneath them sloshing over their boots, too wet.

"Take it somewhere else," said one, his muffled voice high pitched as though he had barely entered puberty.

The other, deeper voiced but smaller in stature added, "Inside."

"Inside where?" asked Lash, trying not to express surprise at Tox's boldness, trying to play along with the ruse without giving it away as a sham. With the appearance of being a streeter, it was likely he had no home to go to, and there was likely, he knew, nowhere nearby they could send him. He knew where the soaper was, knew the contents of most of the buildings nearest them as they were all part of the fishing and growing industries. Nowhere suitable for sex except here, in the shadows, where no one else was likely to be.

Paying a hook by the half hour meant moving anywhere would eat up what little coin he had spent to get this beauty to have him.

With the pair showing no immediate inclination to move off, Tox drew her hand from Lash's pants and held it open-palmed to them. "If you're gonna watch, you're gonna pay," she growled sweetly.

Again the brako looked at one another. They had been charged to make sure the strangers were not interfering with the soaper, and they

obviously were not. They were not even here to score a hit. Just a desperate man looking for action, and a down-on-her-luck gal desperate enough for ticks that she would take a man like this.

"Hurry it up…and move along,' the deeper voiced brako grunted before steering his companion back down the street towards the door of the soaper. They went inside, where they could not watch what the unlikely couple did, but where they would, most likely, watch for the pair to pass when their transaction was complete.

If they were lucky, the brako would think they had climbed up to a half-Lev or gone their way the moment they were out of sight. Or maybe that the strung-out streeter was harder to satisfy with too many drugs in his body. Or they would believe they passed when the brako's backs were turned.

If they were unlucky, Scarecrow's business would be cut short, or his assistants would have to abandon him to fend for himself.

The brako would be back. One way or another. The night had barely begun and already Scarecrow was running out of time.

❧*❧

Grainger had been barely involved in the carnage of the Coup, his role in it having been limited to the Uppers, to the confrontation with Scarecrow and the Founder, and afterward, to orchestrating the end, the mop-up, the chaos of the aftermath.

He had, however, participated in his share of street skirmishes in the Levs with hooligans and disgruntled citizens, and since then with the brako and the followers of the Voices. He was no stranger to combat and was confident that his outnumbered forces could handle the stream of barely washed, almost animalistic bodies that pushed out of the Core into the inevitable confrontation.

Had he done this to them, he wondered, as he swung his thumper and knocked down a feral woman who lunged at him, all teeth and dirty nails and pocky skin that made her age impossible to guess. Had

shutting them in, abandoning them, turned these souls into monsters, or had they been monsters all along?

The woman dropped, unmoving, when he struck her. He did not know if she was alive or dead. There was no time to check as the hoard continued its push towards freedom.

Colyx had swiped the igniter, determined to take this matter out of Skelter's hands. Otta was not going down that shaft without Skelter to encourage her, and there was no more time to lose. He had endured enough at the hands of those in the Core, before gaining their respect, endured the death of Otta's mother, endured the abuses that Otta had endured. Those abuses had made the woman tough, made her someone to be feared here in their outcast community, but they had also made Colyx bitter and resentful.

Once he had vowed to see that every one of those who had caused Otta to suffer would suffer in kind. Skelter's arrival, this plan, was the means to exact that promised retribution. Watching those he had shared the bunker with for more than twenty years, those he had worked the mines beside, suffered with, fight and kill and struggle to survive as they swarmed into the narrow space between the Core and the world beyond their door, pushing and shoving to engage in a battle they were fools to think they could win, Colyx did not feel a morsel of regret for what he was about to do.

He heard someone scream. Blood and tissue sprayed across faces and chests of several others as someone's head was fractured by the force of a popper the likes of which Colyx had never encountered. Or maybe it was something else. Shocked, some of the Core horde attempted to retreat.

Colyx depressed the igniter fuse.

A second detonation of freezes was set off, bringing down the remainder of the entranceway too soon.

He should have waited until every one of them was outside the Core, until every one of them had a chance for survival. Many were

trapped outside, between a wall of collapsed earth and stone and their bug-masked opponents. Some were buried beneath the crushing rock.

Those left on the inside screamed and scattered, bumbling in panic or racing towards the only other exit they were aware of.

Enoch's tunnel.

Colyx dropped the igniter and ran with them, allowing the unit to be trampled beneath pounding feet as if he too was part of their search for another way out of the Core.

No one would ever know what he had done.

He hoped he had given the others time enough to get free. If he died here, it would be a good death, with Skelter, Otta, Enoch and the children safe and away.

Switz was a loose end for the fates to tie up.

Off-balance again, startled by the second explosion, it took Grainger moments to realize that, whatever the source, the explosion had worked in his favor. The Core escapees were trapped though not yet outnumbered. His forces still had the upper hand. Forcing them to submit was the only chance those from the Core had for survival.

Whoever fired that deadly shot would be dealt with later.

From the way they fought, however, with the ferocity of caged, desperate beasts, he realized survival was not necessarily their intent.

There would be no punishment for them. Freedom or death were the only options they sought.

❧*❧

The doors behind them clicked shut as the world returned to blackness one more time. The sucking sound that followed indicated a sealed system; they would not be getting out of the stairwell until the doors opened again.

"Crucksake!" swore Ilya as she slammed the side of her ICD. "Check three…report!"

Without emergency lighting, they were immobilized on the stairs in the dark. The techs tightened their grip on the Founder's arms and Tamner toed down the steps to reduce the space between himself and Kemway, intending to grab him should he stumble on the stairs and knock the Lieutenant and her buggers down before him.

The shaking produced tremors in the Founder as well. Tamner could feel it through his hand on Kemway's shoulder. If the man was aware enough of his environs to feel that tremor, to react in fear to the dark, then perhaps he was not as sedated as Tamner hoped.

"Easy," Tamner murmured against Haythem's ear, not expecting the man to heed his words. "It's okay."

The Founder's almost immediate calming was further proof that Kemway possessed more awareness then he had in the last two years. Tamner worried now about what would happen if the transfer continued to be delayed.

"We need to get him secure…"

Ilya nodded, though Tamner could not see it, just as she could not see the Founder's reactions or behaviors. Kemway was strapped, was not getting away from them, but she agreed with the Doctor's assessment. This business was taking much longer than it should.

"Check three…report."

Again, there was no response, but she did not expect one. The ICD system relied on the Hub for connection, and if the power had gone down throughout the city, or at least through the levels directly above and below them, there would be no way to contact anyone outside of the stairwell, no way to summon assistance or to ascertain what was happening elsewhere. The rattle and shudder that had pulsed through the metal stairs and handrails suggested another disturbance similar to the first, an explosion perhaps or an earth tremor that sometimes occurred in the ground outside of Hebenon's borders. There had been no reports of fire or damage or any other sort of incident after the first shaking, and so an earth tremor seemed likely, particularly as they typically happened in swarms.

With no word from Captain Grainger either, where the possibility of some attempt to get into or out of the Core might include explosions, Ilya worried.

And where, she fretted, was Ginna?

"Stay there…gonna check the door." It was likely locked, sealed and inaccessible to the electronic passkey so long as the power was out. But keeping the others safe where they were while she investigated was wise. Safety was a priority, as was finding a way out. With any luck, they would not be trapped in the dark stairwell for long.

❦Chapter 34❦

The sounds of scrambling somewhere behind him, heavy breathing, frustrated swearing, scraping and clawing in the earthen passage, were unsettling things, particularly after the second tremor that showered him and the children in yet another flurry of dust and dirt and small stones. Switz could tell others were trying to push into the tunnel, hoping to make it their escape route when he imagined the front door had been blown, that egress no longer an option.

"Hurry up," he hissed impatiently, trying to push the boy in front of him along faster. Being the last in the queue, if any of them was going to be trapped in here, Switz felt sure it would be him and he had no intention of dying today. If he could accomplish it, he would have scrambled over every one of the urchins to get safely away.

Getting past Enoch would be more difficult, but Switz had a plan for that eventuality, if it became necessary. He was not above stabbing anyone, child or dwarf, to get what he wanted.

"Nearly there." Enoch could hear the distant voices too, new voices echoed and distorted by the narrow tube surrounding them. He guessed the secondary blast had brought down the main exit, as intended, although it had, in his opinion, come too soon.

More than likely it was the delay in getting the kids into the tunnel in the first place that made it seem that way. Everyone else's world was running on schedule.

Only Enoch's was out of sync.

"Blow the damn thing," growled Switz. If others pushed through, he and the children might be trampled in a rabid attempt at escape. He would rather the tunnel be sealed now, the others kept far away.

"Eblan," Enoch muttered, crawling faster. Detonating the freezes in the tunnel was going to kill all of them, Switz included.

He was of a mind to create some delay that would keep the murderous medi inside and do exactly as he asked the moment the last child was pulled from the tunnel.

Unfortunately, if he knew Switz at all, the man was following so close to the last kid he was practically shoving him along.

"It'll be okay," he reminded everyone. "Keep coming; we'll be there soon." Those far behind them were not going to be a problem. None of them would ever make it this far. None of them would fit.

᠊ * ᠊

Breaking the river's surface inside the chasm made Scarecrow blink to clear the water from his eyes, but it took swiping the lenses of his mask with his gloved fingers to brush away most of the moisture. There was light far above him, and a silhouette looking down that he could only make out the shadowed edges of. He took a moment to catch his breath, the exertion of fighting the typhoon swirl of current in this narrow tube wearing on his limbs, but there was no time for rest. Each delay meant the reduced likelihood of getting all three targets to safety.

He waved, aimed the bolter driver again, and with another bolt-eye piton in place, then another, started to hoist himself out of the water towards the swaying chain he could see hanging above.

He did not talk. The effort would take oxygen he needed to conserve for each subsequent round in the river. Words needed to be saved for the assurances he imagined would be required for those he was extracting to freedom.

"Down ya go."

Otta opened her mouth to protest, the thing coming up the shaft seeming like a frightening sea creature. But Skelter was not afraid of it, seemed relieved to see the shadow firing one metal spike after another into the stone and pulling higher with each one.

What sort of man was this, with the strength, the nerve, for such actions? Otta considered herself strong and brave, Colyx and Skelter too, each in their own way. But what she witnessed emerging from the river below was like nothing she had ever seen.

"I'll be down soon…you know I will," Skelter promised, cupping her face in his hands to kiss her one more time. The blast and sway of the second explosion and the subsequent rumble had died away, bringing Colyx into the room followed by the footsteps of other survivors that echoed as they thundered past the barely lit storage room in the direction of Enoch's tunnel.

Colyx, panting, nodded at Skelter before repeating to Otta, "Go."

Someone was bound to backtrack here when they realized the tunnel was not a viable escape, seeking the obvious absence of Colyx, Otta, and Skelter. Too long of a delay would mean a fight they could not afford. Colyx would fend off anyone he needed to so the others could get away, but Skelter did not plan on leaving the man behind.

Otta carried nothing, no weapons, no material goods. There was nothing of value in the Core besides food and survival supplies. Out there, she would get those things when she needed them. Goods and extra clothing would weigh her down, hinder the escape, and as strong as this Scarecrow seemed to be, he did not need the dragging weight of indulgences slowing them down. With Skelter's assistance and a good grip on the links of the heavy chain, she wiggled over the edge of the shaft and began her clumsy descent towards the river.

"That's it…I've got you."

The mechanical voice was further distorted by the hollow echo and rumble of the water, but the words were understandable. Otta did not realize when it happened, as she refused to look at the frightening throat of water rising to swallow her, but in time she had Scarecrow's arm around her. The transition was made from the chain to the cable now attached to it, secured in the wall where the pitons served as steps and handholds.

Until the moment her feet touched the water, the cold of it shocking as it soaked through her poorly constructed boots and light

rat-hide and hemp fabric clothing, she felt no panic only nagging apprehension. Skelter was a shadow above her, and from where she waited, held in place by Scarecrow's grasp, she saw no way out.

"Hold the line; hold tight," he instructed. "Gonna count to three; on two take a breath and hold it. On three, we go in. Don't let go of the cable. Hand over hand; follow me. I'll get you back to the air."

She nodded in spite of her fear. Overhead, Colyx was already stepping over the lip of the chasm to begin his descent. She could not hesitate. If Skelter was coming last, she had to be sure he had time to make it out alive.

One. Two. Three.

Under the water, in frigid, murky darkness, where she could not see beyond lids squeezed tight in fear, she allowed the gloved hands to guide her, Scarecrow's body bumping against hers as the river jostled them, as he directed her hands along the cable in the direction he wanted to move. How many seconds past, she could not say. It felt eternal, her lungs straining for air. Scarecrow could feel her growing more tense, closer to panic state, with every second that passed.

Soon enough, just before her fear bloomed full flower into terror, he had her head lifted out of the water, her face in the air where her lungs could seek oxygen again. The river splashed against their skin like slapping hands with icy fingers, but the cable held her high enough that, as long as she did not let go, she was not going to drown. He urged her along, drawing the cable with them until she was able to grasp hold of the lip of the grated catwalk.

Trusting Tox to pull the woman to safety, Scarecrow passed the now looped end of the cable into Jaron's hand. He could not feel the man's skin through his gloves, but there was a lingering moment where the contact held, a thank you, an assurance, a grounding. Resolve steeled, Scarecrow muttered, "Keep hold. I'll be back."

No drama. No tears or hysterics. No mumbled apprehension. Jaron nodded once and said, "I'll be here."

It was what Scarecrow needed to hear as he dropped back into the water for his second run, as Tox wrestled Otta from the river and

wrapped her shoulders in Scarecrow's discarded coat. It was not warm, but it was better than the river's chill.

❧*❧

Again the flash of the power returning, the blinding white of the light reflecting off pristine walls made everyone, including Kemway, flinch and shield their eyes. Having expected no more than bleary-eyed blinking from the sedated Founder, Ilya, at the bottom of the stairwell, waved the others to follow her down.

"Give him more," she muttered, noting Tamner's concern as he watched the Founder stumble on the stairs. He had not been so sedated as to make taking the stairs impossible, but Ilya knew she was not the only one to think the man's behavior was unusual. Sedated men, drugged men, were not so steady on their feet, did not act like this.

Or maybe they did. She did not know what Tamner had given him, did not know the Founder's baseline condition or mental state.

What she did know was that Doctor Tamner looked uneasy.

"Can't. Any more will kill him." Perhaps not kill him, but it would be damned unhealthy and likely send him relapsing into the state he was in when Tamner first saw him after the Coup. He was not going to risk it, not risk being the one responsible for the Founder's death.

If a manic episode was in the offing, as he feared, Tamner did not want to be responsible for that happening here either.

"Let's get him moving."

"Check three…report." No response. The same with Check four. Ilya frowned. Maybe the electrical wiring in the stairwell was interfering with transmission, or not all of the grid was back online.

Being unable to raise either checkpoint after the relatively smooth passage thus far was troublesome.

"Sure we shouldn't go back?" asked one of the tech's, voice reedy.

The on and off power, the earth tremors, and Kemway's peculiar behavior were grating on everyone's nerves. Tamner could not fault his anxiety.

"No point," Tamner sighed after a shared look with Ilya. "Unless you think we should?" They were at least halfway there. Without knowing why the Check teams did not respond, they could only guess what was ahead. The route had been secured ahead of time, the checkpoint teams only a precaution. There was no reason, beyond nagging suspicion and the ragged nerves caused by the shaking and power dips, to think that there would be trouble.

Putting Kemway back where he had come from, as vulnerable and compromised as that position was now that Mam Kemway knew of it, was not a good option.

"Carlo…go ahead…we'll follow. Signal back if there's anything to report, or if it's all clear."

"Yes, Lieutenant."

The stairwell door opened. Ilya looked left, looked right, and into the corridor ahead. All ways were clear and Carlo raced forward to sweep their path.

"Move."

The Founder's feet started again, though this time with reluctance. Only Tamner pushing him gently prompted him to increase his pace.

No, Tamner thought as his attention split between Ilya, the path ahead, and the man directly in front of him. This was not right at all.

❧*☙

The muted light filtering between the grates and canvas covering that masked the shaft filled Enoch with a much-anticipated sensation of relief. Whatever lay behind them, the fighting and struggling he could still hear from the distant end of the tunnel and whatever awaited them on the outside, they had made it safely this far. He expected the Spinks to be in place, waiting for them, but if they were not, he would find a way to get the kids into safekeeping before worrying about whatever came next, about what might or might not be happening elsewhere in the Core, in Hebenon.

He whistled once, the pre-arranged signal, and a young woman's head popped into view.

"Enoch?" She shuffled aside and offered a hand to help him emerge from the passage.

"That's me." He did not mean to seem rude, but he had been in and out of this tunnel so many times he did not need anyone's help to be free of it. He slid out without taking her hand, nodding his appreciation for her offer all the same.

"We feared you'd be trapped…after the shakes…"

He nodded, brushed off his knees, and said, "We thought so too,' as the first small child's face peered into the world outside of the Core for the first time in his short life.

"I'm Ginna," she said brightly, offering her hand instead to the little boy. From behind her, Cyro peeped around her side, his boyish grin adding a further friendly air to the frightening situation.

"Let's get you outta there and into something clean, warm and dry. We got sugar tea and crisp biscuits waiting for us."

The little face blinked at this new world, wide-eyed as he huddled against the wall with his arms wrapped around himself. Slowly, he accepted Cyro's offered hand.

Ginna gave Cyro a scolding glance; they did not know what Maemi might have for them at Vapors. But as the children, one after another, did not seem likely to know what sugar tea and crisp biscuits were, she decided the bribe did not matter nearly so much as Cyro's friendly nature and the promise of warmth and dryness.

If they had lived their whole lives inside of a mountain, as Ginna was beginning to suspect, the damp into which they emerged was probably as scary as anything else they had just endured.

Two children at a time were escorted out and dispersed among the other clusters of Spinks up and down the street, a pause made between each movement so as not to attract too much attention from the nearby vindis. It made their progress slow, but it was better than someone summoning the buggers back down on them.

∽*∜

There were six bugorra clustered in front of Carlo by the time Ilya and the group she led reached the intersection they were expected to pass, the intersection where Check Three should have been stationed. There should have been at most three officers here, Carlo and the checkpoint agents, so seeing six was unexpected and brought the Lieutenant to an abrupt halt. Her hand signal stopped those behind her, but none of them could see around the corner to gauge the cause of their stop. The techs and Tamner tightened their grips on Kemway who, while not tense or uneasy, did not seem as relaxed as Tamner thought he should be, given the level of sedative in his blood.

Thinking that perhaps the six were a gathering of officers from the last checkpoints, that they had come together during the outage to assess the threat level and deal with the problem as a unit rather than remain at their posts in pairs as they had been instructed to do, Ilya barked, "Everything's fine. Return to your posts."

She was not moving the others forward until her officers were at their station and she was assured the entire route was secure.

"The Captain sent us," one said.

That, to Ilya, seemed highly unlikely given the circumstances.

∽*∜

"Told you to move on…"

The return of that particular brako voice had come as Tox feared, just as she wrapped Scarecrow's coat around Otta's shoulders and Scarecrow reached the wall of earth to the east a second time. There was a shuddering thump as something, she assumed a body, hit Hebenon's southern metal wall. Expecting it to be Lash, Tox scrambled to her feet, placing herself protectively between the bird masked figure that emerged through the bent metal opening and the other two with her. He was undoubtedly surprised to see three of them there and his surprised squawk that came when Tox swung bare-fisted at him, brought another through the wall as well.

Reinforcements, she guessed, as the audible evidence of an unseen skirmish beyond the wall meant that, for the moment, Lash was still on his feet and holding his own.

How long he could do so depended on the number of supporters the two nosy brako had brought.

Jaron, unwilling to release the winch that held leash on Scarecrow's life, played with the tension to get the man's attention. He could not help in the fight, and Otta, hunched, wet and chattering, looked disinclined to move. The man Tox struck with her left fist was thrown into the railing right next to Jaron. The extra moisture spit up by the too-high river made the grating treacherous even for the wet-boots the brako wore, and when the second arrival lost traction, it was to fall beneath a two-fisted blow at the side of his neck.

The second brako swiped with his leg as he was robbed of his balance, pulling Tox down to the catwalk with him. Jaron tried to kick the first brako, as the man attempted to regain his footing, but the man's hold on the handrail kept him from falling, only allowing him to slip and stumble.

Jaron did not think the brako had yet had time to notice the winch or determine its purpose, or to assess what the trio was doing on the catwalk. It did not seem they cared. But when a quick glance sideways revealed that Scarecrow now had hold of the stony surface, that he was no longer relying on the cable as his sole source of stability, Jaron released the winch, turned sideways, and yanked the brako's mask from his face with both hands.

Scarecrow looked back, the play in the line an unexpected signal but one he did not think accidental. He saw the brako emerge through the panel opening, saw Tox engage them both.

And over the roar of the rapids, he heard the distinctive crunch of a thumper against a man's skull.

He took no time to think about what he heard. He trusted Tox, he trusted Lash…and he trusted what he saw of Jaron in that split second

before he allowed his own weight and the slack cable to submerge him beneath the river's surface.

Otta, realizing that no amount of cold and wet were going to save them, was going to save Skelter if they did not fight back, lurched up from her crouch.

"NO!" shouted Tox, lunging for the winch, sideswiping her assailant as she tried to catch the spinning metal handle. He slid again, striking his head against the handrail and lay still, face down against the catwalk with the river's surge pushing into his mouth and nose.

Otta's lunge caught the now maskless brako across the shins so that his torso fell forward into Jaron's forearm. There was enough force to the fall that Jaron was nearly knocked off his feet as well, but the ensuing three-body skirmish resulted in Jaron clinging to the rail, his legs swept and tugged by the current, and Otta lying flat on the grated ground, clutching one edge of Scarecrow's coat as the brako, pushed into the river, strained at the other end of a sleeve to pull himself back to the safety of the platform.

Jaron made the choice for her, and though it fleetingly made his position more perilous, he yanked the coat from Otta's hand and released it so that Hebenon's source of life swept the man to the sea.

All he could hear was Tox shouting, "What have you done?"

❧*❧

"Time to move." Switz was out of the tunnel at last. Hunched over and covered with the ratty blanket Ginna had been using, he could pass as one of the streeter children, albeit a taller one like Ginna. Enoch made sure Ginna went with Switz when they exited the lean-to, not intending that Switz or any of the children should witness what he would do next. Switz knew, of course; he had already encouraged Enoch to do the unthinkable…bury people alive in that tunnel.

Possibly burying any family and friends the children had left.

But it had to be done. More than likely, if the second blast had done its work and the bugorra as well, there were very few left alive. Sealing this passage was the only way to hide the evidence of what they collectively had done.

If what he was about to do sealed Skelter in the Core too, if the redhead failed to get out as he planned, the Scarecrow help him.

No Founder, no god, was likely to do so.

He watched Ginna, Switz, Cyro and the smaller children with them start down the catwalk in the direction of safety. They collected the others as they walked, an act that was going to result in a considerably large pack of children before long.

Safety in numbers. So long as it did not draw the gorra's attention.

Enoch looked at the tunnel as he pulled the detonator from his coat.

Now or never.

Leave the dead, he reminded himself. Only the living mattered.

Enoch depressed the electronic signaling switch and the mountainside shook for the third time that night.

❧Chapter 35❧

A risk worth taking, and with the oxygen tank continuing to purr as it should, the body armor protecting him from the most dangerous debris the river could throw at him and the icy chill of its caress, it seemed barely a risk at all to Scarecrow at the moment it took him to make the decision to submerge. Whatever was transpiring on the catwalk, he could not get back in time to help, and if the brako saw him, clinging to the line, to the wall, it would raise alarms that would bring many more than the number of brako that were here now.

Better they think the group was fishing illegally, or were up to some other manner of mischief, then being involved with Scarecrow. The brako's attack seemed excessive, as if they assumed the worst without asking questions…as if they already suspected or were aware of Scarecrow's presence. But if his friends made it through that confrontation, as long as he remained out of sight, the brako could not prove anything. His friends would never betray him.

It might, however, make getting Skelter to freedom more difficult.

With the slack cable in his hand, using it and the mountain façade as his guide, and the push of the river to steer him, he continued beneath the water until rounding the corner into the cave's whirlpool meant that he would be out of visual range of anyone on the catwalk.

He listened.

He heard nothing but the pulse of the river outside and the echo of the maelstrom around him.

"Bout time you made it."

Colyx had felt no need to wait for the stranger's return to begin his descent down the chain. He could have argued about who was to go

first, who should go last, but arguing would waste time they did not have. Not anymore. Not now that a third thundering tremor blasted through the walls of their subterranean home.

The tunnel was sealed. This was the only way out.

Eventually, the others would come. Others would find it too.

He and Skelter needed to be gone from here before that happened.

So he began to climb.

Every day could be his last. Could be Skelter's last. Could be Otta's last or anyone else's. Living with that in mind, trying to outrun the inevitable was the only choice anyone had. The surprise of death would snatch them all eventually, but Colyx had no intention of that surprise finding him or those he loved on this day.

He hung onto the cable for as long as he could, his lower body submerged in the cold flow, the swirling current battering him against the wall when the chaos outside allowed the cable to go slack. The slam of it was painful, but the icy water dulled the impact. He was not in a position to see anything, he could only listen and allow the adrenalin in his blood, fueled by the remote possibility that they had been betrayed and that Otta was not safe, to warm him, until the masked head popped up from beneath the water. Colyx did not speak at first, as it was obvious the stranger was listening to the sudden quiet beyond the alcove as well. But his legs were growing numb and unless this man intended to manage Colyx's entire weight and bulk, they needed to move before he lost control of his limbs.

They looked at one another, the mask hiding Scarecrow's surprise at finding the second person already in the water. There was fear in the big man's eyes, a reluctance to take the only way out they had, but there was determination too.

"They okay? Out there?"

"Don't know," Scarecrow answered honestly, weighing his choices. The cable had tightened once more, either because it had snagged on something or because someone had regained control of the winch. He could duck back out to see, wasting valuable minutes as

this man succumbed to the cold, or he could relent to necessity and turn on the ICD. Almost afraid to hear nothing at the other end, to be met with a silence more ominous than what he currently heard, it was the best choice, the only choice, he knew he could make.

One hand came out of the water; the ICD was switched on.

"Tox…you there?"

"I'm here."

Scarecrow swallowed hard at the voice in his ear. Not her voice but Jaron's, sounding oddly distant. A voice that made his heart pound with both the timbre of it and the likelihood that it meant something had happened to Tox.

"Where's…"

"She's…"

A burst of static feedback looped through the helmet, echoing from one ear to the other and then the voice he had expected to hear snapped sharply inside his head.

"Crucksake, thought we lost you…"

"Is it clear?" If Jaron and Tox were able to communicate, then he assumed the skirmish was over, but he wanted her to say it before he made another move.

"Lash took a beating, but he's okay. We all are for now. But I'd hurry if I were you."

"Copy." His head tilted upwards, where Skelter sat on the lip of the chasm, waiting for his turn. Skelter was the reason for all of this. Scarecrow did not know what was happening elsewhere in Hebenon, but he was certain that time was pressing in on him like the surge of the current sucking around them.

To the man at his side, he asked, "You swim?"

"Once…but not anymore."

Scarecrow nodded. He did not need details. "Hold the line. On two…deep breath…under on three. Hand over hand. I'll get you out."

"You sure?"

"I'm sure." Dragging the man against the flow would not be easy, but the pull of the winched cable would help.

From the lip above, Skelter watched, listening as the words bounced off the damp stone up to his ears. One. Two. Three.

His breath caught.

Colyx and Scarecrow disappeared.

❧*❧

The last encounter the group of children, with Ginna, Enoch, and Cyro at the lead, expected to have was with a group of thirteen Talkers in the priestly garb, descending the stairs the Spinks intended to pass up. The whistles had been a warning that brako were approaching, and so Ginna had taken the chance of another route, one the Spinks had not secured. Without the warning system, she had not known the Talkers were there, and while Talkers, for the most part, paid little heed to streeters, her group was significantly larger than normal.

Not one of the Talkers' faces were visible, but the one in the lead was obviously the one in charge.

"What do we have here?" The lead Talker did not care what the streeters were doing. He saw no evidence of tagging gear, saw no trace of weapons, but with the brako afoot, with the bugorra few in number tonight, with the street crowds sparse as the orchestral recital played on, bleeding out of every open vindi door, every partially open flat window, every street building Echo, an unsupervised group of children could intend trouble.

Or they were searching for their own vantage point from which to watch and listen to the recital prodcast. He imagined such a group had been shooed from somewhere else by vindi owners or buggers already.

"Out to cause trouble?" he continued when no one replied.

"Only if you want some," Ginna spat back, her effort to lurch forward with balled fists, still eager to make that familiar voice pay for what he had done to Xiaodan, thwarted by two sets of hands on her arms. She felt confident that she knew the voice, but there were too many conflicting sounds around them…the recital prodcast playing on

Echos, the roar of the falls, sounds of cooking and chatting in a nearby vindi, her own blood hammering in her ears…for her to be certain.

Cyro, on one side, earned only a condescending glance from the leader…and Enoch, on the other, frowned.

The leader appeared to be staring at the dwarf from inside of his hood for several breathless moments…and then began to smile.

❧ * ❦

The enhancements to his goggles, while stripping away some of the natural black and white contrast from the eternal night of Hebenon's underbelly, allowed Scarecrow to see clearly the many wounds Lash had received at the hands of the brako, while he, Otta, and Tox worked together to wrangle Colyx out of the river. There was no visible head wound to suggest that Lash had been the recipient of the thumper to the skull Scarecrow had heard, and most of the bruising and abrasions he had sustained were covered by his trencher, but his chest, stomach, and face were visibly battered and bloody.

And still the thin man pushed on, continued to work towards the goal they had laid down for the night. Hopeless or not, they would only accomplish the impossible if they kept trying and Lash was determined to both try and succeed just as Scarecrow was.

Colyx's legs, despite their thick, well-muscled layers, were fighting a bitter battle against the cold and multiple lacerations sustained from both his impact with the cave wall and several of the stony daggers protruding from the river. It had been a struggle to drag his bulk against the current, and when the flow of it pinched the man's weakening left leg between two stones, it had taken longer than Rhyd liked to get him free. Now the others began to do what they could to rub the circulation back into the man's legs, to rub life and blood and warmth into the tissue while monitoring the blood flow from the cuts and gouges. Colyx would be difficult to move from this place if they did not get him on his own two feet.

Only Jaron stood at the winch, watching, alert and attentive, focused on the duty he had been given. His knuckles were bruised and bloody too, there was blood on his nose and lip, and beneath one eye the blood was beginning to pool to the surface, turning the skin to a familiar darkening purple.

And still he fought on just like the others.

He met Scarecrow's masked gaze and nodded. The others would see to Colyx. He and Scarecrow had one more job to do.

Scarecrow nodded in return and started back across the river.

❧*❧

Some of those behind her had crowded forward, curious or concerned about another delay. Lieutenant Young felt them clustered at her back, her other officer at her elbow, popper shaky in his hand but not yet raised, one of the tech's pulling Kemway along as he edged forward to see. Kemway's movement drew the second tech along, and Tamner, not wanting to be left where he could not react if necessary, or was unprotected by the presence of the other bodies around him, followed.

It left the group exposed in the T-intersection, but with the corridor's previously cleared in order to facilitate this move, there was little reason to expect trouble from ahead or behind.

Only from the left, where those they unexpectedly encountered stood in such a way that seeing beyond them, to the position where Check Four should have been, was difficult to do.

This should have been Check Three.

These officers were supposed to obey her.

"Stand down and return to your posts," Ilya repeated. If the Captain had sent reinforcements, sent others to find her when the grid had gone dark, he would have sent some sort of signal to expect them. He had not done so.

At the rear of the cluster, Carlo caught her eye, shaking his head…

…as Kemway charged into the gathering of bugorra, knocking the technicians aside, pulling free of Tamner's hands.

"Founder!"

Carlo swung at the man nearest him, catching him across the ear with his thumper. Someone fired an injector, the drug-tipped dart zinging past Ilya's ear and sinking into the second tech's shoulder. His spin sideways, as Tamner made one lurching attempt to grab Haythem's arm, knocked both he and the tech to the floor. Other hands, bugger hands, tried to close around the Founder too before he tripped over someone's booted foot and crashed to the floor.

❧*❧

The raucous bang and clatter behind him announced that all of those who remained alive in the Core, however many the series of explosions and the law officers on the outside had not managed to kill or subdue, had found their way here, to where Skelter was. He and Colyx had barred the door as best they could in the short time they were allowed, but the weight of the debris haphazardly stacked as a deterrent would not hold off the effort to get inside for long. While Skelter did not think any of them were aware of this pit, or that any would think of it as a viable route of escape, it only took panic and desperation to make even the worst risk better than no risk at all.

When it came down to the inevitability of slow death, sometimes a risk was the only choice to make.

The door pushed open a crack, enough for hands to grasp the edge in an effort to provide leverage. Feet would be next, arms and legs, and the blockage would no longer bar the way.

Skelter glanced into the maw, fingering the pouch he had sewed into his breast pocket, closest to his heart, feeling the finality of what he carried. "To be…or not to be," he muttered into the dark, the growl of water swallowing the words so there was no echoed return.

Scarecrow had not yet come back. The first elbow and knee pushed into the room, along with outraged, frightened shouts.

To be or not. He had made a pact with death, but it was one he never intended to keep. Maybe he would regret the lie of that pact. But if Otta and his child lived, it would be a lie well told.

To be or not, the only way out and through was down.

❧*☙

The Talkers behind him, rubbed raw by Mam Kemway's slander, were itching for a fight. A fight with this group of street children, however, was not one they could win. They might do so physically, but the damage such a win would do to their public face, particularly if they were viewed as the instigators, was not worth the effort to settle the score they felt they were owed after so many repeated attempts to besmirch the increasingly thin reputation of the Voices of Faith.

The streeters too, having recently suffered the loss of their leader, had their own score to settle. One word, one signal from the restrained young woman, and the lead Talker had no doubt the swarm would wash over him and his followers like hunger beetles.

But there was another possibility now, a rumored hope for a future that the Senior had only barely considered before.

All he needed was proof.

"What do you say?" he asked, smiling at the dwarf, as he lowered his hood a guarded, dangerous smile that made Ginna's hair prickle across her arms and the back of her neck. "Shall we fight or discuss this like civilized people?"

The Spinks did not reply. The dwarf did not reply.

There was only one way to test if his hypothesis was accurate and so he shrugged, not expecting a verbal answer, and ignored the glowering from both dwarf and woman beside him. Kal would get his answer another way.

"Let's not keep our hosts waiting," he said with a cool sneer to those with him. He motioned for them to go around him, down the steps and to the right so that their backs were turned to the streeters as they continued on their way. He waited until the last Talker had

passed, pleased that his gamble had paid off. The dwarf had some control of the Spinks. He had not allowed them to attack the Talkers when their backs were vulnerable.

That was good to know.

"We shall meet again…Kemway."

The Senior saw it. A twitch at the corner of the dwarf's eye, at the corner of his mouth. A slight tremor and reflexive tightening of the hand on Ginna's arm that he suspected she barely felt in her continual growling posture.

Kal was not even sure the dwarf was aware of those physical reactions to that name. But he saw them and it was proof enough.

❧*❧

Scarecrow was there to greet him with an open-armed gesture when a crash in the room above and a clattering scramble announced that the Core's survivors had broken inside. Skelter did not need to look to know they were converging on the chasm; the sway and drag on the heavy chain to which he clung told him enough.

"Good to see you, old son," Skelter drawled, trying to sound more calm and confident then he felt despite the assurance of the man's grip.

"Looks like you brought friends."

Skelter shook his head. "Bad case of parasites, I'm afraid."

Within the hood, Scarecrow scowled. The movement of the others trying to climb down the chain, those who had no idea where they were climbing to, was going to have an unpleasant effect on the remainder of the descent. They did not have far to go, fifteen feet to the water's surface, but if any of those people fell, clogged up the mouth of the cave, their way out, things were going to get messy.

"I can cut loose…solve it…but we won't be anchored."

Skelter grabbed the nearest bolt-eye piton, wedged a foot against the wall of the chasm, and looked down to the one beneath…through which the cable stretched that was serving as their lifeline out of here. "Can you get us out without it?"

Scarecrow nodded. Cutting one side of the cable would mean it was no longer secure, but it would still be looped around the winch and pulley on the catwalk. If they held on, they should not be swept downriver and Jaron and the others should be able to reel them back.

Otherwise, he would have to rely on the bolt-eye pitons to crawl to the city's edge.

Neither option was ideal, both were dangerous, potentially deadly. Despite the affirmative answer, Skelter knew it.

"If it's in the cards…" he shrugged, struggling to sound more nonchalant than he felt, and after tightening his hold on the bolt-eye, he opened his other hand. "Shall I?"

It made sense to make the cut higher up. But not yet. "A few more feet," Scarecrow instructed. The closer they got to the water's surface, the less distance they would have to fall, the better he might be able to control their trajectory.

Chain and cable swayed and strained with the added weight as they wiggled down half of the remaining distance. There were numerous bodies above them now, and Skelter felt sure they would not have to cut the cable at all. The added weight was going to pull the chain from its anchor in the Core before that happened. But when Scarecrow felt the movement of water against his ankles, his urging having enabled them to make it nearly to the bottom instead of the few feet or halfway he had suggested, he removed the one other tool he had secured to his belt and tapped Skelter's foot with it.

Skelter glanced down, noted their proximity to the water, and looked at the cutters in the man's gloved hand.

"Always prepared, eh?"

The only response was a snort and a muffled, "Do it," as Scarecrow jockeyed higher to use his body to pin Skelter against the wall, to hold him there as the cable snapped loose. "Head down."

Skelter caught the cable between the metal-bladed jaws, jammed it against the chasm wall so it could not escape his efforts, and then looked down at Scarecrow with a smirk.

"Head down. Check."

Crunch.

The cable snapped, recoiled, through the hook that secured it to the chain caught on Scarecrow's belt with enough jerking force to yank them both into the water.

❧*❧

She knew the voice…or thought she did…but her head was ringing from the thumper strike that had knocked her into the corner of the wall and off her feet. In the confusion, she saw Doctor Tamner scramble over fallen bodies in a desperate attempt to catch hold of the Founder, but she saw little else as the silhouette of one bugorra stood over her, looking down, a popper aimed at her head. There was no time to berate herself, no time for the scurry of thoughts to second guess her choices of officers, to guess who might have betrayed her.

She could see, on the periphery of her gaze, that someone was pulling the Founder out of the cluster from where he had landed, but her main focus was absorbed by what she assumed would be the instrument of her death…and the bugorra holding it.

The mask hid his face. He was anonymous, featureless, and yet familiar in his stance, his build. Those were familiarities she only noted in passing before he bent low and struck her across the side of her head with the butt of the popper, leaving her in darkness.

❧*❧

On the platform, Tox and Jaron were yanked off balance as the winch cable stretched abruptly taut…and snapped.

"Pull!" Jaron shouted. "Pull hard!"

Lash elbowed in to lend strength to that of the two struggling to retract the cable and bring the man, or men, on the other end to safety.

❧*❧

"What did he mean?" Ginna hissed, ushering the Spinks and the rescued children up the stairs as quickly as they could move. The Talkers were out of sight, but she was not going to feel safe until there were several Levs of distance between them.

The lead Talker would not know where they were going, but the faster they moved, the less chance there was of being found.

Enoch did not look at her but he knew she could read the scowl on his face. "Just move," he grunted. No time for talking.

By the time they were safe, there would be no need for it.

❧*❧

Skelter was unprepared for how icy the water was, nor for the rush of memories that slammed into his head as his body broke the surface and he slipped down beneath it, into the dark, into the cold, into black, invisible, certain death.

That was what he had believed before, when the water had robbed his battered body of oxygen and the stones in the river beat mercilessly upon him, adding to the bruises and fractures he had sustained as he had fallen through the Levs to end up here. He remembered a series of impacts, of rolling, of falling. He remembered the cold, the scramble and flail of broken, dislocated limbs that had fought to keep his head above the surface of the watery grave. He remembered the pressure of the current pinning him against stone, and some bit of washed away flotsam from the Coup that had, by pure coincidence, kept his face above the water until darkness claimed him.

There were vaguer memories after, jostling and pulling, tines of metal, looped control poles, and ropes, the tearing of muscles and ligaments, sharp broken bones ripping through his flesh.

And then waking, much later, to searing pain…and the Core.

Most were details long forgotten, details he would rather not remember as they birthed panic that made him fight in the direction of a surface he could not find. His arms and legs struck stone but found

nothing to grab, and as those memories replaced more immediate knowledge, he forgot that anyone was there to help him.

For a moment on impact, his hold around Skelter slipped and the redhead broke from his grasp. The cable held to his waist by the looped hook on his belt and the way it ran through the bolt-eye pitons secured in the mountainside yanked Scarecrow back to the surface before the river could sweep him away. Despite the oxygen tank, the impact with the water robbed him temporarily of breath, but once the surprise and shock of it passed, he could breathe again, normal but labored, as he frantically sought his friend. The recoil of the chain above made the first victim, someone Scarecrow felt rather than saw, fall with a scream, to be immediately thrown by the circular motion of the water against the stone wall.

The scream ended. The body was sucked under, joined by more screams of those struggling to hold on to the chain, to crawl back up, to make the horrifying choice to let go and fall to an unknown fate.

Without light, without Scarecrow's visual enhancements, they could not know for certain what awaited them. And not one, in their panic, had thought to procure a light source before trying to escape the certain death that waited in the now sealed Core.

Maybe there were no light sources available.

The maelstrom pulled everything in the cave towards the center, including the individual who had fallen, and it was there, in a brief instant between the sloshing of the current, that he saw a hand break the surface. Believing it to be Skelter, staking his safety on it, Scarecrow kicked off from the wall, angling his movement in sync with the current so that his trajectory brought him to his target.

His gloved hand closed around the man's wrist. He pulled hard, using the swirl to pull the body against him, feeling the strain in his previously dislocated shoulder, and then used a shove off of the opposite wall, and his continuing grip on the cable he could feel tugging at him, to aim for the opening they needed to be free.

A thud, his head grazing the top of the stone opening, slamming his body into the mouth of the passage as a surge in the river lifted him higher than expected, leaving him momentarily stunned, sending lightning bolts of pain through his back and limbs. It did not cause him to release either the cable or the man he held tight. For a moment his vision swam to crimson, then black, as unconsciousness threatened, but the moment of rest he took there brought it, and his labored breathing, back under control.

"Hold your breath; let's do this."

He had not looked to see if it was Skelter in his one-armed grasp.

He knew it was by the sound of the man's labored breathing.

❧*❧

"Enoch. Over here."

He had not expected anyone to call his name, and none of those with him expected the woman to meet them anywhere other than in the security of Vapors. Scarecrow had asked her too, but they had not expected her to take the risk.

It made sense, however, that she would not want to expose her establishment to a bugger raid or brako incursion. Vapors had been, for reasons none verbally questioned, off-limits to bugorra since the Coup, but if any of tonight's events were traced to Scarecrow, or if they came to Vanderwall's attention, there was no reason to believe that sense of security and protection would last.

Better to take the mountain mites somewhere they would not likely be found, or bothered, at least for the next handful of days.

Maemi crouched a half-Lev above them, dressed in black instead of her usual bright business colors, and lowered the hood of her rain slicker when she spoke so that they could see her. Neither Ginna nor Cyro questioned her being there, having been told to meet her, deliver the children to her, and whether it was here or Vapors did not matter. Their mission was fulfilled.

Though Ginna ushered the evacuees up the stairs to where the woman was, Enoch and Spitz going with them so that they would know they were not being arbitrarily deposited in some stranger's care, she was not ready to turn the night's work over to someone else's hands. A quick spate of orders scattered the Spinks into the city, into alleys and side streets, into positions where they could watch from a distance, follow if needed, provide whistled alerts if danger approached, and then Ginna and Cyro followed up the stairs as well.

At the top, Ginna stopped, coming face to face with Maemi, with a member of Xiaodan's family for the first time. The two women stared at one another for several moments until Maemi nodded once. She took the group down a largely desolate stretch of street, either abandoned or with of its residents gathered elsewhere to watch the recital prodcast, without a word.

Xiaodan would want Ginna to help.

Maemi wanted it too.

And, Enoch thought with a touch of worry as he turned to discover that Spitz was nowhere to be seen, Scarecrow would want it as well.

❧*❧

Jaron, struggling against the barely useful winch, was the first to spot the two heads bobbing in the river's ebb, pulled towards the sea by the current but moving gradually nearer to the catwalk as the trio did their best to retract the cable. The sight was enough to prompt Jaron to release the winch, leaving Lash and Tox to struggle with it as he leaned out over the edge of the catwalk, beyond the safety railing, one arm outstretched in the hopes of adding a further safe anchor. He scrambled left, then right, as the flow altered their position, until at last, he was able to wrap around Scarecrow's arm with both hands.

The man in the water jerked at the tugging of the arm that threatened dislocation again, but no one could see the wince and expression of pain behind the mask.

Colyx's weight on his legs kept Jaron from sliding into the river.

With Tox and Lash securing the cable so it would be unable to uncoil and release their catch to sea, Otta reached out next to Jaron, to grab Skelter and pull him free of Scarecrow's hold. She was strong enough, braced against a stanchion, to lift the redhead from the water. Jaron's grip on his arm pulled Scarecrow nearer so that, with his other hand free and the need to rely on the cable gone, he caught the lip of the catwalk with both hands, clearly favoring one arm over the other.

He had the strength, but barely the energy, to haul himself one-armed out of the merciless river. Only Jaron's assistance allowed the effort to look easier than it was, and he lay on the grate, next to the younger man's bent knee, sucking heavily on the last of the oxygen in his tank and trying to will the pain away.

Jaron could not see it, assumed Scarecrow's eyes were closed behind the protections of the mask, as he lay one hand on the man's heaving, armored chest.

He could not see the eyes looking up at him in a weak moment of respect and wonder behind the overwhelming weariness and pain.

❧*❧

He groaned, clawing out from beneath the mound of bodies who had rushed at him as soon as those in the Core determined that he was the one giving orders. Take out the mountain of a black man and the masked horde would surely scatter.

That, Grainger was smugly satisfied to see, had not happened.

They smelled bad, like animals kept in confined spaces without anyone to clean up after them, felt dirty and greasy to his touch as he shoved them aside, so he tried not to breathe, tried to keep his mouth closed to keep the stench out and tried to push against their clothing so as not to touch their skin.

With the calf muscles of one leg shredded, one arm twisted in its socket so that it hung limp and useless at his side and dragged behind him he moved. Something jagged protruded from his side from an injury that bled profusely and he was sure it would kill him if it was

removed without a medi's immediate care. He was lucky to be alive. So too were the less than a dozen men and women his bugorra had pinned to the nearby wall as others dug through the debris and the field of bodies looking for the living among the dead. Many of his officers, it appeared, were still standing. Who the others were, those moaning and groaning across the room, he could not distinguish through his cotton stuffed ears.

How many victims, miners, criminals, the monsters of his own making, had died in this assault? How many were incapacitated by an injector's sting? Grainger was afraid to find out.

"Over now, sir. We got 'em. We'll get you out of here, Captain," said a nearby voice, someone who grabbed hold of the bloody hand at the end of his good arm and pulled him the rest of the way free of the collection of flesh and bone and blood which had nearly buried him. Whatever was imbedded in his side ripped, tore, blasting a burst of white-hot pain that erupted behind his eyes and deposited him into merciful oblivion.

❧*☙

"Lieutenant. Ilya. Please. Open your eyes."

From somewhere in the brain fog left by the blow that knocked her out, she expected to see the bugger who had loomed over her urging her awake, urging her back to the reality she now had to face. Seeing that bugger's face might have offered a trace of assurance that the world she had so meticulously crafted was not about to crumble.

Doctor Tamner's harried features, blood dripping down the side of his face, confirmed what some part of her already knew.

"Good…you're okay…"

It was only good in the farthest reaches of that word, as around them bodies littered the corridor. Two dead lab techs, six dead bugorra, including Carlo and the other officer who had accompanied the Founder during this relocation effort. The others were gone.

So was Founder Kemway.

As Tamner helped her to sit, Ilya smashed the ICD and groaned, "Check four… anyone there?"

She did not expect a response. If these four were those she had stationed, they had already left their posts. If these four were others, rogue officers acting under some other authority, those she had stationed at the remaining checks were likely dead as well.

Crawling to the nearest unknown bugorra officer, she yanked off the mask to expose the person's face. Ilya had a good memory for faces, for names, she knew her officers, down to the newest recruits…and she knew this was not one of them. She was filled with disgust and dismay as she yanked open the front of the man's body armor, seeking clues when his face revealed none, to find what she had never imagined seeing.

Talkers…disguised as bugorra.

Talkers had taken Founder Kemway.

On the off chance that they had not, that the Founder had crawled into some nearby doorway or room while his escorts were incapacitated, on the off chance that the fake bugorra had not killed him further down the corridor, Ilya scrambled to her feet, with Tamner's help, and began to stagger in the direction of Check Four.

Two more dead officers and not a trace of the Founder. But at least she knew the guilty had come this way.

But it made little difference. This had happened on her watch, under her command, and no matter what excuses she offered, it boiled down to a single painful truth.

Founder Kemway was gone.

❧*❧

The dizziness of the head injury combined with the pain in his shoulder did not hit Scarecrow until he attempted to rise; the suddenness of nausea made him yank away his mask so that he could vomit into the river below their feet. If not for Jaron on one side and Tox on the other, he would have dropped to his knees on the catwalk

and knelt or laid there retching in a struggle against unconsciousness. The effort to stand contributed to an unexpected seizing of muscles so that his limbs felt tight and no longer under his control. Somehow, Skelter managed to fight to his feet, and though his steps and effort to support Colyx, whose legs still cramped and spasmed from the cold, were slow and unsteady, he remained upright.

Lash had guided the others through the folded metal flap, carrying the bag Scarecrow had dropped earlier, but Scarecrow did not follow.

He believed his presence would slow them down. And the vigi, with or without his mask, would expose those who helped him to certain danger if he was in their company.

"Go. Get them safe."

His own thin voice, the weakness of his body, troubled him, but he hoped that a few more minutes of rest would allow him to move, to strike out on his own…or give him the fortitude to fight the brako if they found him here. One nearly useless arm was going to make for a difficult, possibly futile fight, but what other choice did he have?

Jaron shook his head with a stubborn frown. Rhyd was trying to hide it, but Jaron could see he was in pain, could hear it in his voice, and it worried and frightened him to see the man so vulnerable. "I'm not leaving you here…not like this."

As much as part of him appreciated that sentiment, it also irritated Rhyd that his advice was not being heeded. "I'll be fine."

"Like hell…"

"Not when the brako come back," Tox scolded, also seeing what Rhyd was resolutely trying to hide. The cataleptic brako on the other side of the wall had been dragged into the shadows, out of immediate sight of passersby, but sooner or later someone would come looking for their comrades, or the unconscious brako would wake up.

"Won't be here that long. Just long enough to…"

"Put that damn thing back on and come on," she warned, nodding at Jaron to follow her lead as she pulled Rhyd to his feet.

Rhyd growled, but she ignored him, and though this time the world continued to sway and his muscles complained about doing his

bidding, there was no accompanying impulse to lose anything remaining in his stomach as he was pulled up, thankfully by his good arm. After a few gulps of air and a sour look at Tox, one of the few whom he ever permitted to tell him what to do, he reluctantly put the mask back into place and turned up the oxygen flow from the reserve tank Tox had already replaced. He was glad now he had thought to put the extra in his bag.

Breathing easier helped. He felt better, stronger after a few deep breaths, but the pain in his head and shoulder did not subside and his legs continued to shake and seize. With Tox on his good side and Jaron on the other, he was maneuvered through the bent metal gap back into Hebenon's interior. Jaron knew he was in pain. Rhyd could tell by the way he worked to avoid jarring his shoulder, to support his weight around his ribs rather than below his arm or around his shoulders.

Though he did not acknowledge the effort, Rhyd appreciated it more than he was willing to admit.

A slight shift in his head, and the roar of the water beneath his feet, reminded him of where he was, and how far he was going to have to go to reach anywhere safe.

"Not gonna make that…" he began, head tilted to look up into the crisscrossing lattice maze of walkways and structures above them.

He hated feeling weak, feeling dependent, feeling like he was failing those he had come to help.

He had gotten these three, hopefully the children, and possibly others out of the sealed certain-death of the Core, but he had not yet gotten anyone to safety.

"I know a place," murmured Skelter as he aimed the group for the nearest stairs. "At least…I knew a place…"

A lot would have changed in the two years he had been gone. In a world that relied on favors and in-kind gestures, friends and allies might be that no more.

But it was the best choice they had, since no one else seemed to have an immediate solution to their need for shelter and rest.

Stairs would not be easy to maneuver, but thankfully they would not have far to go. The risk of using a lift, with the increase in brako activity and Scarecrow's company, was too great. Stairs would have to do.

Lash clutched the buzzer, lifted from one of the brako, wishing it was a popper instead so that he could avoid close contact combat. It would have to be enough. "Follow me." He did not know the way, but he was the only one not supporting anyone else who could lead and protect their front.

They had to hope that, should it be necessary, Scarecrow would regain his strength in time to protect their rear.

Lash went first, up the half-Lev steps, securing the way for Otta and Skelter, who struggled with Colyx between them. At least all three were mobile, if unsteady, slow, and on the verge of collapse. At the platform, Skelter pointed to another half-Lev passage, towards a row of what looked to be flops, a place Lash recognized now that he saw it. He had stayed here a time or two in the years after being expelled from the Uppers, in his years without a tongue, voiceless, jobless, struggling to get by.

Skelter had found him here and he had never looked back.

He should have considered the flops before.

Barely reaching the mid-Lev catwalk, with the others already starting up the second set of half-Lev steps ahead, they were bombarded by the trembling rumble of boots on the metal grated roadway. Scarecrow whipped his head around, instinctively expecting to meet any threat that came for them, but the too-swift movement sent a crippling spasm up his dislocated shoulder, into his neck, into his skull, drowning his consciousness and seizing every other muscle in his body. Tox, on the side his body fell, stumbled with his weight as the man's leg cracked against a stanchion and twisted awkwardly to the side. Their fall left Jaron alone to react, to spin and strike out with a kick that caught the stranger, a lone, hulking man, square in the center of his chest.

Caught off-guard by the unexpected kick that met his roar and outstretched talon hands aimed to snatch the back of Scarecrow's armored neck, the stranger sprawled backward and landed twisted awkwardly at the foot of the stairs.

There was no witness to his fall, except those who did their best to scramble back and up to get Scarecrow to safety.

Not realizing what he had done, Jaron's only thought was protecting Rhyd.

❧EPILOGUE☙

She had not seen him since before the Coup, since his discovery of the part she had played in Scarecrow's push into the Uppers and insurgent efforts made against the Founder. She had thought, after the look of disappointment and heartbroken betrayal on his face that night, that he would hate her for how she had used him.

That he had prevented the bugorra from troubling her, her friends, her place of employment, could have been read as either a 'leave her alone, I never want to see her again' gesture, or as an effort to protect her out of some deeper connection between them.

She hoped for the latter, but was inclined to believe the former.

Maybe he felt, when all was said and done, that he had used and betrayed her too.

The part she had played this time, however, had taken a greater physical toll on the man, and she felt she owed this to him. Not an apology, perhaps, for that would be admitting to involvement in events she would never expose. But she believed, as the door to the medi fac room where he lay, wrapped in hemp gauze bandages and plasters with a contraption that kept his shoulder from moving as the healing set, that seeing him again was a necessity.

He looked up, groggy beneath his body's bombardment by medication prescribed to keep the worst of the pain at bay. His eyes lit as they met hers.

Zara swallowed hard and found it in her to smile softly as she murmured, "Hello, Oliver."

❧*☙

He sat on the stool in Vapors, watching Maemi and Ginna behind the bar as the older woman instructed the younger in the initial stages of swivving. He had not been privy to the conversation that had lured Ginna into a place like this, but he suspected it had something to do with Xiaodan. It gave the younger woman a purpose, an income, and it provided her with a sense of family that it appeared she was desperately seeking.

He doubted her sister would be very happy about this, but at least the Lieutenant might appreciate the illusion that Ginna was no longer bunking with the Spinks.

Zaolei bottle empty, a drink that tonight had been in honor of the men and women who should be with him but were not yet, he set it down heavily on the counter to signal his desire for another, when the shadow cast by someone occupying the stool next to him made him frown.

Enoch's expression deepened into a scowl and a desire to be left alone when the uncomfortably familiar voice of Senior Kal said, "I have a proposition for you.

❧*❦

The legs of the fire pot had settled into the mud, but Skelter barely noticed. Here, on this spit of land that extended towards the sea, beneath a clear, cloudless sky of stars he had never imagined he would see, breathing the fragrant salt air unfiltered by year after year of mechanical systems, Skelter felt overwhelmed by the simple joy of being alive to witness this, of having endured so much to be given a blessing so few in Hebanthe Falls had yet ventured forth to see.

This was the reason, the black sky, the muddy earth sprouting new vermillion shoots, the shadows of still snowcapped mountains in the distance far to his left, across the Four Rivers whose plunging water he had somehow twice survived. This was the reason, the village of the miracles of humanity who had survived all of those generations

against the odds touted by every Founder since the day Hebanthe Falls had closed its doors.

This was the reason he lived again.

He hurt all over, and there was work to be done, but Skelter would not change a single thing he had endured for this single moment of precious opportunity.

Well, he thought grimly, casting a side glance at the solitary figure who stood in the doorway of one of the huts, he might have changed one thing. Venn had greeted his old friend with joy and relief and a shadow of guilt, asking dozens of questions about the Core as he had aided in building the firepot in use now. But Rhyd's arrival in the open door of the city had sent Venn back to the hut where he had remained ever since, despite the fact that Rhyd had come no closer.

Still unsteady on his feet, the grav-chair Rhyd was forced to endure would not make it through the mud and, it seemed, when Skelter looked back at him, that he was content to stay where he was.

Skelter did not yet know what had happened between the two men to create this divide, had been surprised, in fact, to learn that Venn was alive despite Rhyd's stubborn previous insistence that he must be which had led to the opening of the Outside world. Skelter did not think that any of what was wrong in that struggling relationship was his doing.

Still, he would have changed it if he could.

Leaning on the walking stick he clutched in one hand, the tip of it kept from sinking into the mud by a large stone Otta had found, Skelter took the water-damaged deck of thirteen cards she handed to him, and fanned them out between his fingers until he saw the card he wanted.

The Ace of Spades.

He snorted and dropped all of the cards except that one into the mixture of oil and hemp pieces that burned in the bottom layer of the pot, watching them turn to ash. Never again, he thought, would anyone fall victim to this particular deck of horrors. Those other twelve club members were likely dead, devoured by the Core. Or they would be

as soon as hunger and thirst claimed them. He felt no regret, only relief that that particular chapter of his life was closed.

The Ace, saved for last, joined the others, the edges blackening and curling as a hot sliver of wood seared through the heart of the card. In the pot above, all thirteen spade coins, collected during his final days in hell, slowly melted into a pool of liquid metal.

Otta, trembling in wary, wide-eyed amazement at this view of the Outside world, took his hand and squeezed it.

It was over.

In Hebenon's doorway, Rhyd watched the rising full moon that turned Skelter and his new family into shadows against the silver glow, welcoming Agnys' arms around his shoulders in place of the others that could have been there. Jaron was behind him, watching his first glimpse of true night in awe, refraining from words or actions, touches or gestures, that would send Rhyd into a place of uneasy silence. Jaron was here to maneuver the chair, nothing more. Or so each man would have told anyone who asked, with enough confidence and emphasis to be believed, though each knew, without admitting it, that the truth was something much more complicated.

Only two would have cared, would have questioned. One lay immobilized in a medi bed, where Jaron had not yet gone. The other stood too far away from Rhyd to see, but he knew Venn was there, watching across the unfathomable distance for something he hoped he would see. Watching for something he did not want to see.

Instead, Rhyd revealed nothing. He did not know for certain if either Venn or Jaron knew the other was there.

The hoot of an owl accompanied the vibration of his ICD. Absently, he glanced at the tiny screen, expecting it to be Tamner's reminder of the exam and therapy treatments Rhyd was expected to begin in the morning.

The message was Tamner's.